BEDTIME STORIES FOR GROWN-UPS

BEDTIME STORIES FOR GROWN-UPS

EDITED BY BEN HOLDEN

**SIMON &
SCHUSTER**

London · New York · Sydney · Toronto · New Delhi

A CBS COMPANY

First published in Great Britain by Simon & Schuster UK Ltd, 2016
A CBS COMPANY

3 5 7 9 10 8 6 4 2

Simon & Schuster UK Ltd
1st Floor
222 Gray's Inn Road
London WC1X 8HB

www.simonandschuster.co.uk

Simon & Schuster Australia, Sydney
Simon & Schuster India, New Delhi

The author and publishers have made all reasonable efforts
to contact copyright-holders for permission, and apologise
for any omissions or errors in the form of credits given.
Corrections may be made to future printings.

A CIP catalogue record for this book
is available from the British Library

Hardback ISBN: 978-1-4711-5375-4
Ebook ISBN: 978-1-4711-5378-5

Typeset in Perpetua by M Rules
Printed and bound by CPI Group (UK) Ltd, Croydon, CR0 4YY

Simon & Schuster UK Ltd are committed to sourcing paper
that is made from wood grown in sustainable forests and support the Forest
Stewardship Council, the leading international forest certification organisation.
Our books displaying the FSC logo are printed on FSC certified paper.

For Salome, George and Ione –
my dreams-come-true.

Contents

Introduction

Seize the Night

The house was quiet and the world was calm.
The reader became the book; and summer night

Was like the conscious being of the book.
The house was quiet and the world was calm.

Wallace Stevens

While I sleep I have no fear, nor hope, nor trouble, nor
glory. God bless the inventor of sleep, the cloak that covers
all man's thoughts, the food that cures all hunger, the water
that quenches all thirst, the fire that warms the cold, the
cold that cools the heart; the common coin, in short, that
can purchase all things, the balancing weight that levels the
shepherd with the king, and the simple with the wise.

Don Quixote by Miguel de Cervantes

Each evening, before the lights are turned out but after the
blind is drawn, I read my young children a story. The long
day done, they quieten down and listen to me. They some-
times hang on my every word, if it is an especially good tale,

interrupting me only to ask valid and wide-eyed questions, such as, 'In real life, what does that mean?'

Little do they know that the true joy of our routine is mine. I love curling the words out for them, my inner troubadour piping up, as I too – the writer's mouthpiece – grow absorbed in the stories. Sometimes I have been known to make one up myself for them, my brain rushing to and fro to find the right twists and turns.

More often than not, though, we will read a classic. Many of them I recall from my own childhood. Old favourites that I have dusted off – Lear, Wilde, Barrie, Dahl and the like – remember themselves to me, unheard from since I was a boy. Characters will jump out from behind corners of the page, smilingly, exclaiming shared memories. Nostalgia ain't what it used to be, sure, but this is something altogether more precious. I commune with my own childhood and parts of myself long forgotten.

I am reminded of how my own mother or father would read to me. They would make sure that Micky, my favourite bear, to whom my daughter is now guardian, was by my side. Having tucked me in and bid me good night, they would leave the night light on at my request, its soft glow a further blanket, the sepia shadows it cast on my walls benign, and – like Peter Pan – still lingering in my mind today.

Wafts of adult activity would then slip up the banister to my bedroom. The routine complete, bedtime story told and mind taken off things, the hum of the grown-up world would lull me into innocent sleep.

Similarly, my twin son and daughter now are lolled into a true sense of security by my reading them a story. Nocturnes complete, the light goes out and the glow-in-the-dark solar system on their ceiling – astrological stickers bought from the Science Museum and positioned by me while precariously atop a ladder – twinkles their very own night sky of little stars and planets. On their cupboard doors, fluorescent sheep – one black – vault over one other.

Before they fall asleep, the adult activity that my own children might hear this evening is likely to be the television. A faint white noise of Mum and Dad's viewing entertainment will seep past the ajar door and serve as a last subliminal, distorted lullaby.

They won't see me eat ravenously and then slump, the work-day done, in front of something good on TV, often a film. I'll check my social media, digits fidgeting over the bright touch-screen of my smartphone, while the show unfolds on our big television screen. I might then attend to some final work-bound emails on my laptop.

My wife and I will retire to bed, teeth brushed, and both reach if not for each other, then for a book, magazine or – increasingly – our phone or tablet, yet again, before turning off our bedside lamps.

I will try to read something in print form: a chapter of a novel, say, a short story, or a long-form article. Sometimes, though, a glowing device of some sort will be the last thing I see. When my eyes weaken, I know the time has come to succumb to night and sleep.

I go out, mostly, as fast as the light itself.

I have long valued sleep. It takes up a third of my life. Should I reach sixty, approximately six years will have been spent dreaming vividly.

3

It is true that people do need different amounts of sleep. We each have our own *slumber number*, just as we have different *chronotypes* (which refers to the fact that some of us are night owls, while others are morning larks), yet it is also widely acknowledged that we adults generally need seven to nine hours a night. Humans are somewhere in the middle of the spectrum for animals' sleep requirements, which, apparently, more or less comes down to size: the bigger the creature, the less shut-eye needed. We certainly sleep more than horses, who average two hours, but less than the two-toed sloth (twenty hours). Grown-ups need to sleep at different times from teenagers, whose body clocks slip later during adolescence. I think back to my outrage at my mother drawing open my curtains early on a weekend morning and realize now that my indignation was utterly justified.

I know from those teenage years of staying out all night what pain the following day can bring. Similarly, I look back on the not-so-distant years when my twins were babies and acknowledge now that I was spending my working hours in something of a foggy fug. I know from night shoots on film productions what shift workers go through and, from long-haul travel, the hazards of jet lag.

Yet my experiences, however compelling as validation of my long-held instinctive arguments about the importance of sleep, are trivial compared to the cold facts.

The advent of electric light, a mere hundred or so years ago, allowed us to unhook our body clocks in a dangerous way. Today's computer technology means we live in a whirr of twenty-four-hour connectivity – rolling news, constant consumerism, ceaseless social media and communications. We can be reached anytime anywhere. Every day, we create some 2.5 trillion bytes of data. Increasingly, in this fast world of bite-size, digital interactions and electronic content, whenever and wherever – circadian rhythms be damned – a way of 'resetting' the brain in anticipation of a good night's sleep seems as important for an adult as a child.

Don't take it from me. Ask the scientists. Professor Russell Foster, CBE, of the University of Oxford, a current champion of the value of sleep, says: 'We are the supremely arrogant species; we feel we can abandon four billion years of evolution and ignore the fact that we have evolved under a light/dark cycle. What we do as a species, perhaps uniquely, is override the clock. And long-term acting against the clock can lead to serious health problems.'

This body clock is innate. Insects, plants, even bacteria have circadian rhythms. What makes us so special to think that we can ignore them and still thrive? We humans have a built-in clock: it is as tick-tock present as Hook's crocodile's, only ours is the size of a pinhead and located not in our belly but deep in the centre of our brain, just north of the pituitary gland within the hypothalamus. It is called the suprachiasmatic nucleus.

Once we override that tiny pendulum, which sets itself primarily by light and darkness (clocked, in turn, by our eyeballs' melanopsin receptors), we lay ourselves open to all manner of diseases. Sleep is the great leveller and straddles horizontally whole columns of illness: cancer (particularly breast cancer), diabetes, strokes and cardiovascular disease, to name but a few.

It is well documented that most major industrial accidents or man-made disasters occur at times when we shouldn't be awake, let alone at work (from Chernobyl to *Exxon Valdez* to *Challenger*). These catastrophes are as alarming as the

5

statistical studies of the proportion of more everyday medical and surgical errors that occur during long shifts for our doctors.

Of course, is it no accident that sleep deprivation is the first tool in the torturer's arsenal nor, conversely, should it surprise anybody that problems with sleep are also found to accompany (and contribute to or exacerbate) many psychiatric disorders, from mania, schizophrenia and bipolar disorder to post-traumatic stress disorder.

US studies recently showed that adults are sleeping on average a whole hour and a half less during weeknights than fifty years ago. So why are we blasé about the fact that we are sleeping less and less? Indeed why do we grown-ups fight sleep? Especially when – as, for instance, Japanese culture markedly celebrates – it is such an innate joy for our species.

Still not convinced? If the medical statistics won't persuade you, just listen to your own body. Many of our genes, the very building blocks of life, have a twenty-four-hour pattern of activity that influences so much of who we are and what we do.

So why do I – as so many grown-ups do – disregard the very balanced, easy and sensible bedtime routine of our childhoods, one that we now, if parents, insist upon repeating for our own offspring?

I would never dream (not even in a nightmare) of letting my kids play with my phone or tablet before turning the light out; not least because I know that artificial light is a terrible idea for anyone wanting to get a good night's sleep (especially someone who is still growing). Moreover, the short wave-length bright blue-green light emitted by such devices is the *last thing* we should be gawping at last thing before sleep, as it has been shown to diminish the amount of melatonin that the body produces, the hormone that is crucial to regulating our sleep cycles.

The night is time to switch off – devices but also ourselves. Today, there is a delicious rebellion in turning the mobile phone off. Logging off allows for a Cartesian splendour, in which we can lose ourselves, in the knowledge that others will fail to get hold of us. This is not about 'hell being other people' but about reconnecting with ourselves rather than Facebook or Twitter: 'heaven is ourselves', you might proclaim instead.

Such rebellions against the digital apparatus of the modern age have led many adults to reconnect by disconnecting. More 'analogue' pursuits have recently taken wing: mindfulness and meditation. Many men and women have rediscovered the ways of childhood: in publishing, notably, the bestseller lists have been dominated by adult colouring books and in the UK, as I write, ironic grown-up Ladybird picture-books.

Let us all grow up then, together, and take our minds off things. Forget the ignorant protestations of people, including prime ministers or presidents, who blag and brag that they 'get by on little sleep' or need only a few hours a night. People have variable slumber numbers, sure, but there are also simple, baseline minimums required for good health. Listen to your body when the alarm goes off.

Let's instead find a simpler path through this forest to sleep, so that we can see the wood for the trees again come the morning. We might even climb a beanstalk or two on the way! I want to help you restore and consolidate your memory and illuminate a neurological path for your brain to process yesterday's events and information – so that you can more ably deal with the challenges of the waking, squawking day with a refreshed constitution.

I suggest we overtly hark back to our childhood routine: bed-time reading of (preferably) a printed book. Let's tell ourselves a story.

Storytelling, after all, is the engine that motors our daily existence, as we construct narratives for our lives or, more simply, stop to have a gossip with a mate. The oral tradition, of which the bedtime routine is arguably the most powerful mainstay, has been venerated since the Ancient Greeks. Recent research has proven that various fairy tales, which still dominate a child's bedtime routine and feature regularly on our grown-up big screens, have their origins in times before even the English, Italian or French languages existed – some harking as far back as the Bronze Age.

While our minds might drink more deeply words written on a page – and often literary works demand we see the written rhythms rather than hear them – at least one recent medical study shows that people to whom stories are read are more absorbed in the details, and subsequently retain more information about the tales, than if they had read silently to themselves.

Indeed, those children who benefit from a regular bedtime-story routine are proven to perform better academically.

Yet this routine represents far more than a means to sharpen the mind or, more simply, to get the little ones to sleep with minimal resistance.

Bedtime storytelling verges on a primal need.

In making this claim, I am not only thinking of Carl Honoré, distinguished author of *In Praise of Slow*, who decided to change radically his entire life upon the cataclysmic realization that he was so pressed for time by workaday concerns that he was scheduling 'one-minute bedtime stories' for his young children; or of the mother who lost her daughter and now heartbreakingly craves, above all else, to be able to read her child 'just one more bedtime story'; or the other mum whose life was cut short by cancer but, before she died, insisted on recording a ghostly bank of bedtime stories for her toddler children; or, finally, of the thousands of imprisoned dads who have managed to develop a loving relationship with their young children despite being absent behind bars, by reading stories to camera (thanks to the brilliant organization, Storybook Dads).

No, I am also making the point that storytelling doesn't stop once the lights are turned off. After all, when we dream, and vital neurological faculties are restored and repaired during REM, our brain *tells itself a story*!

In these ways, the volume you now hold in your hands is designed to be the perfect bedside book. We have to relinquish control when we get into bed. It's no accident that we *fall* asleep, just as we *fall* in love. This anthology should provide a safety net beneath your brain, like the pillow under your skull, gently cushioning that drop downward.

(The most important part of any journey is the point of departure. You have made it this far without nodding off, evidently. I'll keep going then . . .)

It is an anthology of pieces designed to set your adult mind at ease. The selections – which are eclectic in that they include poetry and prose, fiction and non-fiction, short stories and extracts from longer works – are not intended to stimulate anything more than contemplation or meditation. Perhaps they will ignite a sense of delight or wonder at our human faculties through the beauty of poetry or prose, before the light goes out. Some are funny, others rather elegiac and sad. Many of the pieces themselves began life as bedtime stories or are by wildly successful authors who have acknowledged a debt to the oral tradition of storytelling. They are not all about night, sleep or dreams. Yet, of course, just as the day's events will inform a night's dreams, they are *nocturnes* at heart and so many touch upon moonlit states of mind.

My choosing of pieces may have led to some personal emphases in tone and literary milieu, not always by design. I ask forgiveness if any reader should detect any narrowness in my choices and outlook. To temper this inherent subjectivity, some truly great storytellers and writers – several of whom have written tales for younger and older readers alike or are master practitioners of the short-story form – have generously lent me a hand. These kindly experts have themselves chosen a personal favourite, something that they would recommend to you as the perfect bedtime story or happily have read to them as a last tale before the light goes out.

We have offered introductions to the poems and short stories and passages herein, to explain the selections. I have tried to explain many of my own selections, but not all. It is not wise to write over the top of everything. Some things simply can't be explained and others, like the punchline to a good joke, just shouldn't be.

As an anthology, this book is intended to be dipped into. You can open it almost anywhere, I hope, and find something to enjoy. There is nothing here that should make you feel on edge or stressed. The gothic imagination is explored: it would be remiss for us not to have anything that at least skims over those darker welled waters of the soul. Honestly, though, the last thing I want to provoke is a nightmare. Indeed, I have spent many of my working hours exploring the gothic recesses of our imaginations, via the development and production of supernatural feature films for Hammer Films, and this anthology is intended as a personal departure from those old haunts.

Some of the pieces, though brief, will stretch out time (just as we lose such elasticity when we sleep). A drop of great poetry can fill an entire ravine of imagination. Such concentrated, pure depth of thought or emotion elongates time: much as you plonk the book onto the bedside table, turn off the light and, then, as if in the blink of an eye, awaken in the morning, refreshed for a brave new day!

All that aside, should you choose to read *Bedtime Stories for Grown-Ups* beginning to end, let alone in one sitting, you will discover that I have sought to replicate in these pages the patterns of a night's sleep. Just as we like to analyse our dreams, I want to try to graft a logical structure onto this diffuse whole. I have attempted, in some instances more wilfully than others, to order my selections as well as those pieces chosen by contributors, in mimicry of the course of a night's sleep (albeit a single, rather potted cycle of sleep, whereas in fact our brains run several such circuits during the course of a night).

The first pieces echo evening and the close of day.

Then, we will tell ourselves a story, and explore bedtime as a routine. A number of more traditional bedtime-story archetypes are showcased. I urge you to read some of them (and anything else in the book that takes your fancy) aloud to your bedfellow, if you have one.

These tales will prime you for those initial *hypnagogic* throes of sleep, which will be replicated to a degree by the subsequent section of pieces. There, after your brain fidgets its last throes, the body flips involuntarily into slumbers. This book will hold your hand as you paddle into the shallows of your consciousness.

The next section of the book will be weighted to pull you down with the tides – hook, line and sinker – as your brain-waves deepen and you dive downward.

Increasingly, the pieces then slipstream in rhythm with those more immersive stages of sleep, when mobility and muscle tone seeps away, just as body temperature drops. Such later selections at times run longer and may perhaps, occasionally, tip into sur-reality, just as your brain vividly dreams during this stratum of sleep. A sense of circularity within the pieces themselves will at times arise, almost as if they are sleepwalking in one another's footsteps, or rather like those curious somnial echoes of daily life.

Then the final pages should surge you up again. You will bob back to the surface. These last pieces might promise an awakening. It was all a dream, after all! You can close the book with a sense of renewal, as befits a new dawn.

As you might have deduced, I have come to think of these stages of sleep, in many respects and like some other writers who have explored them in detail, as akin to the phases of a deep-sea dive. In turn, there is perhaps a fluidity or aqueous quality to some of the pieces and introductions. I have never scuba-dived, except in my dreams, yet I agree with Kafka that a good book should be an 'axe to break the frozen sea inside us'.

This one certainly intends to uncover a reflective, silvery surface for you. It might even at times – through the powerful pieces magpied here – provide a ripple-effect that reaches the outer edges of your mind, the furthest-flung frontiers of your ever-whirring brain.

Such lofty aims aside, I hope primarily that this collection simply helps you get to sleep.

My children laugh at its title. My daughter, when I first told her it, exclaimed, 'But, Daddy, grown-ups don't need bedtime stories!' Oh, no, my angel? Perhaps one day, when you're all grown-up and reading those same beloved tales to your own children, you might then enjoy curling up with the stories herein and change your mind. You can imagine me reading them to you. Or maybe, instead, read one aloud to your decrepit, fond old dad, while he toddles into second infancy.

Similarly, reader, I hope that the pieces gathered here fire your imagination. I would like this book to ignite the trillion neurons and all their countless little dendrites, so that you can then dive down, deeper and deeper, over and over again.

The firework display inside our brains, the light-fantastic that is aflame throughout sleep even while the body is glacial, is as wondrous and mysterious as the galaxy of stars that flares the night sky – or, more humbly, the glow-in-the-dark firmament sprayed above my sleeping children on their bedroom ceiling.

Have a great night.

Sleep well.

1

EVENTIDE

'Evening' softens and sings. It rolls, homeward, off the tongue – flattening out, from its yawning *'ee'* – veering back upward – and into a round, definitive *'ng'* finish. It heralds a levelling.

In the words of Mick Jagger, 'It is the evening of the day'.

As the day dwindles, mellifluous milestones fleetingly pass us by: elusive *magic hour* or *golden hour* and the spellbinding *witching hour*; through to the downright beguiling *gloaming* (a Scandinavian word), *twilight* and, more bluntly, *dusk*. These are our cues, being diurnal creatures, to get in step with our circadian rhythms. Hesperus, the evening star, twinkles and heralds the transition to night and, soon enough, sleep. The day is done.

In the early twentieth century, after the First World War, 'Eventide Homes' sprang up, retirement homes for the elderly that were maintained by the Salvation Army. These were final destinations for those who neared the end of their pilgrimage. 'Eventide' evoked a comforting vanishing-point and last resort. No wonder, as evening itself ushers daily returns from workaday cares: the revenant's melancholic homecoming, the child holding her mother's hand on the half-lit walk home from school, the lamps twinkling alight in windows, and sundown's mauve blush.

As the day is evened, and we return home, so journeys in time and space are embarked upon. Evening is the crepuscular creatures' cue to come out and play: *it's vespertine time!* These animals thrive on the transformative and furtive: the skunks prance; deer gambol; ocelots oscillate, their night vision sparking up; velveteen chinchillas leap out of their burrows; Strepsirrhini prod their wet noses into the air; while jaguars stalk onto the twilit turf, ready to hunt.

Eventually even evening itself drifts off and flattens out.

Night falls. As do we—

Asleep.

Time begins to pass at another, altogether different pace.

Consider the poetry of twilight.

One of contemporary poetry's masters, Billy Collins, sets the scene (for this book, as a whole) — both in his poem I have chosen here, 'In the Evening', and with a selection of his own.

Evening's poetics (and, yes, all these poems are themselves bedtime stories) here themselves drift off, diffused by nightshade.

Moonlit musings follow, in prose too, the shift reflecting that gradual but inexorable turn in time and space, onward into the darkness of night.

In the Evening
by Billy Collins

The heads of roses begin to droop.
The bee who has been hauling her gold
all day finds a hexagon in which to rest.

In the sky, traces of clouds,
the last few darting birds,
watercolors on the horizon.

The white cat sits facing a wall.
The horse in the field is asleep on its feet.

I light a candle on the wood table.
I take another sip of wine.
I pick up an onion and a knife.

And the past and the future?
Nothing but an only child with two different masks.

(2005)

BILLY COLLINS

A strong poem should awaken its readers by dramatizing in vivid language some crucial truth about being alive. Jane Kenyon's poem 'Let Evening Come' does that. But its calm tone of resignation to the daily passing of time, which will inevitably end in the 'evening' of death, also relaxes us with its gently repeated advice ('Let . . .') and leads us finally to an affirmation of a caring God. Notice how the poem guides our attention from one delicately chosen image to the next (sunlight, barn, cricket, hoe, stars, moon, fox, bottle, scoop), each locked in its own rural, unpeopled scene, until in the last stanza, the poem dissolves into prayer. For all its wise maturity, the poem delivers a reassurance similar to that of the bedtime classic 'Now I lay me down to sleep . . .' Yes, go gentle into that good night, is Kenyon's quieting advice as well as the poem's blessing.

Let Evening Come
by Jane Kenyon

Let the light of late afternoon
shine through chinks in the barn, moving
up the bales as the sun moves down.

Let the cricket take up chafing
as a woman takes up her needles
and her yarn. Let evening come.

Let dew collect on the hoe abandoned
in long grass. Let the stars appear
and the moon disclose her silver horn.

Let the fox go back to its sandy den.
Let the wind die down. Let the shed
go black inside. Let evening come.

To the bottle in the ditch, to the scoop
in the oats, to air in the lung
let evening come.

Let it come, as it will, and don't
be afraid. God does not leave us
comfortless, so let evening come.

(1990)

Billy Collins has served two terms as US Poet Laureate and also was selected as the New York State Poet 2004–2006. He has published fourteen collections of poetry, including *Aimless Love: New and Selected Poems 2003–13*. He is currently a Distinguished Professor at Lehman College of the City University of New York.

Evening Walk
by Charles Simic

You give the appearance of listening
To my thoughts, O trees,
Bent over the road I am walking
On a late summer evening
When every one of you is a steep staircase
The night is slowly descending.

The high leaves like my mother's lips
Forever trembling, unable to decide,
For there's a bit of wind,
And it's like hearing voices,
Or a mouth full of muffled laughter,
A huge dark mouth we can all fit in
Suddenly covered by a hand.

Everything quiet. Light
Of some other evening strolling ahead,
Long-ago evening of silk dresses,
Bare feet, hair unpinned and falling.
Happy heart, what heavy steps you take
As you follow after them in the shadows.

The sky at the road's end cloudless and blue.
The night birds like children
Who won't come to dinner.
Lost children in the darkening woods.

(1990)

Born in Calcutta in 1861, Rabindranath Tagore led an extraordinary life. A painter as well as a writer of plays, novels, short stories and songs, Tagore was the first non-European to win the Nobel Prize for Literature. A political progressive, he was also a close friend but critic of Gandhi, and played a key role in India's independence. The national anthems of both India and Bangladesh are Tagore compositions and his poetry also directly inspired that of Sri Lanka.

Tagore's grander designs of social morality and nationhood

permeate 'A Single Night'. Much of the story is taken up by a man's matter-of-fact, great expectations of his future. Yet for all his big schemes, in this old-fashioned patriarchy, pride seems bound to come before a fall. Life is happening to other people while he makes plans. By the time our protagonist notices this, a more poignant cautionary tale has emerged, complete with careful-what-you-wish-for wistfulness. Before he or we realize, life has crested onto its downward slope, and the story slides into retrospection.

'Twas ever thus! Priorities and perspectives change over time, as our emotional axes shift. It seems ironic that we humans sleep and dream less as we age, just as we have so many more experiences and regrets to dream on, and time to rest. Nevertheless, we all still find space, between the now and then, to realize in dreams, tantalizingly, our what-might-have-beens.

Sure enough, this narrator's pining and solitude, amid the fragrant moonlight – the dreamer's anguish – is eventually washed away by a cosmic deluge . . . during one single, extraordinary night.

A Single Night
by Rabindranath Tagore

I went to school with Surabala, and we played 'getting married' games together. Surabala's mother was very affectionate towards me whenever I went to their house. Seeing us as a pair, she would murmur to herself, 'They're meant for each other!' I was young, but I understood her drift fairly well. The feeling that I had a greater than normal claim to Surabala fixed itself in my mind. I became so puffed up with this feeling that I tended to boss her about. She meekly obeyed all my orders and endured my punishments. She was praised in the neighbourhood for her beauty, but beauty meant nothing to my barbarous young eyes: I merely knew that Surabala had been born to acknowledge my lordship over her – hence my inconsiderate behaviour.

My father was the chief rent-collector on the Chaudhuris' estate. His hope was that he would train me in estate-management when I was grown up, and find me a job as a land-agent somewhere. But I didn't like that idea at all. My ambitions were as high as our neighbour's son Nilratan's, who ran away to Calcutta to study and had become chief clerk to a Collector. Even if I didn't become that, I was determined to be at least Head Clerk in a magistrate's court. I had always noticed how respectful my father was towards legal officers of that kind. I had known since childhood that it was necessary, on various occasions, to make offerings to them of fish, vegetables and money; so I gave a specially privileged position in my heart to court employees, even to the peons. They were the most venerated of Bengal's deities, new miniature editions of her millions of gods. In pursuing prosperity, people placed greater trust in them than in bountiful Ganesh himself – so all the tribute that Ganesh formerly received now went to them.

Inspired by Nilratan's example, I also took my chance to run away to Calcutta. First I stayed with an acquaintance from my home village; later my father began to give me some help towards my education. My studies proceeded along conventional lines.

In addition, I attended meetings and assemblies. I had no doubt that it would soon become necessary for me to lay down my life for my country. But I had no idea how to accomplish so momentous an act, and no one to look to for an example. I was not, however, short of enthusiasm. We were village-boys, and had not learnt to ridicule everything like the smart boys of Calcutta; so our zeal was unshakeable. The leaders at our meetings gave speeches, but we used to wander about from house to house in the heat of the day, without lunch, begging for subscriptions; or we stood by the roadside giving out handbills; or we arranged benches and chairs before meetings. We were ready to roll up our sleeves and fight at the slightest word against our leaders. But to the smart boys of Calcutta, all this merely demonstrated our rural naïvety.

I had come to qualify myself to be a Head Clerk or Superintendent; but I was actually preparing to become Mazzini or Garibaldi. Meanwhile my father and Surabala's father agreed that I should be married to her. I had run away to Calcutta at the age of fifteen, when Surabala was eight; now I was eighteen. In my father's opinion my marriageable age was elapsing. But I vowed I would never marry: I would die for my country instead. I told my father I would not marry until my studies were completely finished.

Two or three months later I heard that Surabala had been married to the lawyer Ramlochan Babu. I was busy collecting subscriptions for down-trodden India, so I attached no importance to the news.

I passed into college, and was about to take my second-year exams when news came of my father's death. I was not the only one in the family – I had my mother and two sisters. So I had to leave college and search for work. With great difficulty I managed to get a post as assistant master in a secondary school in a small town in Naukhali District. I told myself I had found the right sort of work. My guidance and encouragement would raise each pupil to be a leader of the new India.

I started work. I found that the coming exam was much more demanding than the new India. The headmaster objected if I breathed a single word to the pupils outside Grammar and Algebra. In a couple of months my enthusiasm had faded away. I became one of those dull individuals who sits and broods when he is at home; who, when working, shoulders his plough with his head bowed, whipped from behind, meekly breaking up earth; content at night to stuff his belly with cattle-fodder; no energy or enterprise in him at all.

For fear of fire, one of the teachers had to live on the school premises. I was unmarried, so this duty fell upon me. I lived in a hut adjoining the large, thatched school-building. The school was rather isolated; it stood next to a big pond. There were betel nut, coconut and coral trees all around; a pair of huge old *nim* trees – adjacent to each other and to the schoolhouse itself – gave shade.

There is something which I haven't mentioned so far and which for a long time I didn't think worthy of mention. The government lawyer here, Ramlochan Ray, lived quite near our schoolhouse. And I knew that his wife – my childhood companion Surabala – was there with him.

I became acquainted with Ramlochan Babu. I'm not sure if he was aware that as a child I had known Surabala, and when we met I did not think it appropriate to mention this. I did not particularly think about the fact that Surabala had at one time been involved with my life.

One day, during a school holiday, I went along to

Ramlochan's house for a chat. I can't remember what we talked about – probably India's present plight. Not that he was very well-informed or concerned about the subject, but it was a way of passing an hour-and-a-half or so, smoking, and indulging in pleasurable gloom. As we talked I heard in the next room the soft tinkling of bangles, the rustle of garments, the sound of footsteps; it wasn't hard to deduce that inquisitive eyes were observing me through the half-open window. Suddenly I remembered those eyes – large eyes full of trust, simplicity and childish devotion: black pupils, dark eyelashes, an ever-calm gaze. Something seemed to clench my heart, and an anguish throbbed within me.

I returned to my hut, but the pain remained. Writing and reading were no distraction from it; it oppressed me like a huge weight in my chest, thudding in my veins. In the evening I calmed down a little and asked myself why I should be in such a state. The inner answer came, 'You are wondering why you lost your Surabala.'

I replied, 'But I gave her up willingly. I couldn't let her wait for me for ever.'

Someone within me said, 'You could have got her if you had wanted then, but now nothing whatsoever you can do will give you the right even to see her. However close the Surabala of your childhood lives to you now, however often you hear the tinkle of her bangles or feel the scent of her hair brushing past you, there will always be a wall keeping you apart.'

'No matter,' I said, 'who is Surabala to me?'

The reply came: 'Surabala is not yours today, but think what she could have been to you!'

That was true. Surabala could have been mine. She could have been my closest, most intimate companion; she could have shared all my sorrows and joys; but now she was so far away, so much someone else's, seeing her now was forbidden, it was a fault to speak to her, a sin to think about her. And a certain Ramlochan Babu, who was nobody before, was suddenly in the way. By mouthing a few mantras, he had whisked Surabala away from everyone else in the world.

I am not about to propose a new social morality; I do not wish to break convention or tear away restrictions. I am merely expressing my real feelings. Are all the feelings that arise in one's mind reasonable? I could not drive from my mind the conviction that the Surabala who reigned behind Ramlochan's portals was more mine than his. I admit this feeling was highly illogical and improper, but it was not unnatural.

I was now unable to concentrate on my work. At midday, as pupils burbled over their books, and everything outside shimmered, and a soft breeze brought the scent of the flowers of the *nim* trees, I yearned – what I yearned for I don't know – but this much I can say: I did not want to spend the rest of my life correcting the grammar of India's future hopefuls. I hated sitting alone in my large room after school hours, yet I couldn't bear anyone coming to see me. At dusk I listened to the meaningless rustle of the betel-nut and coconut trees by the pond, and reflected on life. What a baffling tangle! No one thinks of doing the right thing at the right time; instead, wrong and unsettling desires come at the wrong time. You, worthless though you are, could have been Surabala's husband and lived out your days in contentment. You wanted to be Garibaldi, but look what you became – an assistant master in a village school! And the lawyer Ramlochan Rey, why did *he* need to be Surabala's husband? She was nothing to him, right up to the wedding:

he married her without giving her a thought, became a government lawyer and was earning nicely, thank you! He ticked her off if the milk smelled of smoke, and when he was in a good mood he ordered some jewellery for her. He was plump, wore a long coat, was perfectly pleased with life, never spent his evenings sitting by the pond staring at the stars and regretting the past.

Ramlochan had to go away for a few days on a big court-case. Surabala must have been as lonely in her house as I was in mine.

It was Monday, I remember. The sky had been cloudy since dawn. At ten, rain began to patter down gently. Seeing the look of the sky, the headmaster closed the school early. Large chunks of black clouds rolled across the sky all day, as if grandly preparing from something. The next day torrential rain started in the afternoon, and a storm blew up. It rained harder and harder through the night and the wind blew more and more fiercely. At first it had blown from the east, but it gradually swung round to the north and north-east.

It was pointless trying to sleep that night. I remembered that Surabala was alone in her house. The schoolhouse was much sturdier than hers. I several times thought of fetching her over to the school – I could spend the night on the raised bank of the pond. But I could not bring myself to do this.

At about one or one-thirty in the morning the roar of floodwaters became audible – a tidal wave was approaching from the sea. I left my room and went outside. I made my way to Surabala's house. The bank of the pond was on my way – I managed to wade as far as that, up to my knees in water. I scrambled up on to the bank, but a second wave dashed against it. Part of the bank was about six or seven feet high. As I climbed up on to it, someone else was climbing from the other side. I knew with every fibre of my being who that person was; and I had no doubt that she knew who *I* was.

We stood alone on an island nine feet long, everything around us submerged in water. It was like the end of the world – no stars in the sky, all earthly lamps extinguished. There would have been no harm in saying something, but no word was spoken. I didn't even ask if she was all right, nor did she ask me. We just stood, staring into the darkness. At our feet, deep, black, deadly waters roared and surged.

Surabala had abandoned the world to be with me now. She had no one but me. The Surabala of my childhood had floated into my life from some previous existence, from some ancient mysterious darkness; she had entered the sunlight and moonlight of this crowded world to join me at my side. Now, years later, she had left the light and the crowds to be with me alone in this terrifying, deserted, apocalyptic darkness. As a young budding flower, she had been thrown near me on to the stream of life; now, as a full-bloomed flower, she had again been thrown near me, on the stream of death. If but one more wave had come, we would have been shed from our slender, separate stems of existence and become one. But better that the wave did not come. Better that Surabala should live in happiness with her husband, home and children. Enough that I stood for a single night on the shore of the apocalypse, and tasted eternal joy.

The night was nearly over. The wind died down; the waters receded. Surabala, without saying a word, returned home, and I also went silently to my room. I reflected: I did not become a Collector's chief clerk; I did not become Court Clerk; I did not become Garibaldi; I became an assistant master in a run-down school. In my entire life, only once – for a brief single night – did I touch Eternity. Only on that one night, out of all my days and nights, was my trivial existence fulfilled.

(1892)

Translated by William Radice

After Apple Picking
by Robert Frost

My long two-pointed ladder's sticking through a tree
Toward heaven still,
And there's a barrel that I didn't fill
Beside it, and there may be two or three
Apples I didn't pick upon some bough.
But I am done with apple-picking now.
Essence of winter sleep is on the night,
The scent of apples: I am drowsing off.
I cannot shake the shimmer from my sight
I got from looking through a pane of glass
I skimmed this morning from the drinking trough,
And held against the world of hoary grass.
It melted, and I let it fall and break.
But I was well
Upon my way to sleep before it fell,
And I could tell
What form my dreaming was about to take.
Magnified apples appear and reappear,
Stem end and blossom end,

31

And every fleck of russet showing clear.
My instep arch not only keeps the ache,
It keeps the pressure of a ladder-round.
And I keep hearing from the cellar bin
That rumbling sound
Of load on load of apples coming in.
For I have had too much
Of apple-picking; I am overtired
Of the great harvest I myself desired.
There were ten thousand thousand fruit to touch,
Cherish in hand, lift down, and not let fall.
For all
That struck the earth,
No matter if not bruised or spiked with stubble,
Went surely to the cider-apple heap
As of no worth.
One can see what will trouble
This sleep of mine, whatever sleep it is.
Were he not gone,
The woodchuck could say whether it's like his
Long sleep, as I describe its coming on,
Or just some human sleep.

(1915)

On the Beach at Night
by Walt Whitman

On the beach, at night,
Stands a child, with her father,
Watching the east, the autumn sky.

Up through the darkness,
While ravening clouds, the burial clouds, in black
    masses spreading,
Lower, sullen and fast, athwart and down the sky,
Amid a transparent clear belt of ether yet left in the
    east,
Ascends, large and calm, the lord-star Jupiter;
And nigh at hand, only a very little above,
Swim the delicate sisters the Pleiades.

From the beach, the child, holding the hand of her
    father,
Those burial-clouds that lower, victorious, soon to
    devour all,
Watching, silently weeps.

Weep not, child,
Weep not, my darling,
With these kisses let me remove your tears;
The ravening clouds shall not long be victorious,
They shall not long possess the sky – shall devour the
    stars only in apparition:
Jupiter shall emerge – be patient – watch again another
    night – the Pleiades shall emerge,
They are immortal – all those stars, both silvery and
    golden, shall shine out again,
The great stars and the little ones shall shine out
    again – they endure;
The vast immortal suns, and the long-enduring pensive
    moons, shall again shine.

Then, dearest child, mournest thou only for Jupiter?
Considerest thou alone the burial of the stars?

Something there is,
(With my lips soothing thee, adding, I whisper,
I give thee the first suggestion, the problem and
        indirection,)
Something there is more immortal even than the
        stars,
(Many the burials, many the days and nights, passing
        away,)
Something that shall endure longer even than lustrous
        Jupiter,
Longer than sun, or any revolving satellite,
Or the radiant sisters the Pleiades.

(1871)

The latency of evening – its hovering and lingering – is dis-
pelled by an infantile utterance in this next poem: and, in that
instant, the wonder of our earliest reaching-out towards lan-
guage is captured – in moonlight – for ever (apparently 'moon'
was one of the first words uttered by Frieda Hughes, daughter
of Ted Hughes and Sylvia Plath).

The moon itself serves as a mirror, an awed orb, reflecting
the child like her poetic father, as the evening is cowed . . . by
a new imagination springing to life.

Full Moon and Little Frieda
by Ted Hughes

A cool small evening shrunk to a dog bark and the
    clank of a bucket—
And you listening.
A spider's web, tense for the dew's touch.
A pail lifted, still and brimming – mirror
To tempt a first star to a tremor.

Cows are going home in the lane there, looping the
    hedges with their
warm wreaths of breath—
A dark river of blood, many boulders,
Balancing unspilled milk.

'Moon!' you cry suddenly, 'Moon! Moon!'

The moon has stepped back like an artist gazing amazed
    at a work

That points at him amazed.

(1967)

★

When John Dickens, a clerk who had fallen on hard times, was
arrested for debt in 1824, he was sent to the Marshalsea Prison
with his family . . . that is, with all but young son Charles,
aged twelve, who was instead dispatched to work in a factory
at London's Hungerford Market, making pots of blacking for
boots. Little Charles (he was small for his age) would work long

hours in the half-ruined Thames-side factory, above a basement of rats and alongside an orphan called Bob Fagin. At the end of the working day, Charles would walk in his child's pale suit a full four miles by night to his dirt-cheap Camden lodgings. If he ever had any time to himself, he would wander the city, waiting for London Bridge's gates to open, making up stories about the wharfs and the Tower of London. On Sundays, he would visit his family in the prison.

These hardships infused Dickens' subsequent fiction, of course, notably the early chapters of *David Copperfield* and the character of Little Dorrit. Indeed, the grown-up Dickens frequently revisited the blacking factory in his mind, its shadow forever inked over his inner life. 'I often forget in my dreams that I have a dear wife and children; even that I am a man,' he wrote, 'and wander desolately back to that time of my life.' It should be no surprise then that this adult Dickens, when struck down by a bout of his chronic insomnia, would take to the streets of London, striding for hours by gaslamp.

From *Night Walks*
by Charles Dickens

I chose next to wander by Bethlehem Hospital; partly, because it lay on my road round to Westminster; partly, because I had a night fancy in my head which could be best pursued within sight of its walls and dome. And the fancy was this: Are not the sane and the insane equal at night as the sane lie adreaming? Are not all of us outside this hospital, who dream, more or less in the condition of those inside it, every night of our lives? Are we not highly persuaded, as they daily are, that we associate preposterously with kings and queens, emperors and empresses, and notabilities of all sorts? Do we not nightly jumble events and personages and times and places, as these do daily? Are we not sometimes troubled by our own sleeping inconsistencies, and do we not vexedly try to account for them or excuse them, just as these do sometimes in respect of their waking delusions? Said an afflicted man to me, when I was last in a hospital like this, 'Sir, I can frequently fly.' I was half ashamed to reflect that so could I – by night. Said a woman to me on the same occasion, 'Queen Victoria frequently comes to dine with me, and her Majesty and I dine off peaches and macaroni in our nightgowns, and his Royal Highness the Prince Consort does us the honour to make a third on horseback in a Field Marshal's uniform.' Could I refrain from reddening with consciousness when I remembered the amazing royal parties I myself had given (at night), the unaccountable viands I had put on the table, and my extraordinary manner of conducting myself on those distinguished occasions? I wonder that the great master who knew everything, when he called Sleep the death of each day's life, did not call Dreams the insanity of each day's sanity.

(1860)

Dickens' likening of dreams to madness can, of course, now partly be explained away by science. J. Allan Hobson, Professor of Psychiatry at Harvard Medical School, has done just that, stating that during REM sleep and dream states we experience 'frequent visual hallucinations (in the perceptual domain), instability of orientation and recent memory loss (in the cognitive domain) . . . the mental state that dreaming simulates best is delirium.'

★

Old Bud
by James Wright

Old Bud Romick weighed three hundred pounds if he weighed an ounce, and he weighed an ounce. He used to sit on his front porch swing, enraged and helpless, while his two tiny grandchildren, hilarious and hellish little boys, scampered just out of his reach and yelled hideously, 'Hell on you, Grandpa.' His unbelievable Adam's apple purpled and shone like the burl of the root of a white oka, and he sang his God Damns in despair.

Old Bud Romick has fallen asleep as the twilight comes down Pearl Street in Martins Ferry, Ohio. The window shutters close here and there, and the flowing streetcars glow past into silence, their wicker seats empty, for the factory whistles have all blown down, and the widows all gone home. Empty, too, are the cinder alleys, smelling of warm summer asphalt. The streetlight columns, faintly golden, fill with the cracked mirrors of June bugs' wings. Old Bud Romick sags still on the porch swing. The rusty chains do their best for his body in the dark.

The dark turns around him, a stain like the bruise on a plum somebody somehow missed and left under a leaf. His two hellions have long since giggled their way upstairs. Old Bud Romick is talking lightly in his sleep, and an evening shower brings him a sticky new sycamore leaf in his sleep.

Whether or not he is aware of leave, I don't know. I don't know whether or not he is aware of anything touching his face. Whether or not he dreams of how slender sycamores are, how slender young women are when they walk beneath

the trees without caring how green they are, how lucky a
plum might be if it dies without being eaten, I don't know.

(1982)

★

They Sit Together on the Porch
by Wendell Berry

They sit together on the porch, the dark
Almost fallen, the house behind them dark.
Their supper done with, they have washed and dried
The dishes – only two plates now, two glasses,
Two knives, two forks, two spoons – small work for
      two.
She sits with her hands folded in her lap,
At rest. He smokes his pipe. They do not speak,
And when they speak at last it is to say
What each one knows the other knows. They have
One mind between them, now, that finally
For all its knowing will not exactly know
Which one goes first through the dark doorway, bidding
Goodnight, and which sits on a while alone.

(1998)

ANNE ALVAREZ

I wouldn't mind rereading the following excerpt about night-
fall in the Italian countryside, even if it wasn't written by my
husband and therefore very familiar to me. I am still astounded
by the way he lives with, breathes in and somehow inhabits the

39

slowness and gradualness of the night's arrival. I myself always got the beauty of it in patches and snatches, but he is totally with it, helping us to savour every second's change. He is, after all, a poet, and, by the way, a gourmet. The great art critic Robert Hughes called this kind of art and sensibility 'Slow Art'.

It is not only children who need to be read to, or later, to read to themselves at bedtime, it is also we adults. Our reads don't necessarily have to have positive content but nor should they be too disturbing. What they do have to do, I suspect, is have meaning. In my experience, it is the undigested shards of the day, the worries, the disappointments, guilts and fears which are as yet not fully thought about and through and therefore remain unprocessed, that become those sharper shards that cut into our peace of mind at night. Psychoanalysis teaches that the undigested or semi-digested stuff gets into our dreams or even produces nightmares. The most those dreams may do is allow us to remain asleep, but it is now known that they can also do real processing work for us, and even produce highly creative solutions to problems.

Note, however, that although Alvarez ends the passage with the predatory cries of the screech owl who haunts his mountain retreat and of his relief at never having seen its face – or that of the death that he reminds us awaits us all – the underlying rhythm of the piece and the dying fall of that closing passage is beautiful, brave, and strangely right.

Extract from *Night*
by A. Alvarez

Once I had grown out of my childhood fear of the dark, night not only lost its power over me, it lost its separateness, its distinction, and I forgot all about it. At most, it was a minor inconvenience, but only irregularly. I rediscovered it, however, twenty years ago, in an old farmhouse in Italy. The house is in Tuscany, though not in Chiantishire, the expensive rolling countryside south of Florence, with its vineyards and cypresses and swimming pools. It is up in the mountains, on the edge of the wild Garfagnana, Tuscany's northernmost boundary, on a steep hillside covered with chestnut trees beside a stone mule-track that was once a Roman road. The Apennines rise up behind it, slowly at first and thickly wooded, then bare rock and turf. In front is the valley of the River Serchio, with Barga, a little Renaissance town crowned by a diminutive Romanesque cathedral, poised on its hill just beyond the flank of the next mountain. Across the valley are the Apuan Alps – the Marble Mountains above Carrara, where the stone was quarried for Michelangelo's statues – fold upon fold of them, rising to the bleak cone of the Pania delle Croce. It is a place full of history, yet history has left it behind because it is too rough and remote to smooth down and assimilate.

In summer, life at the farmhouse goes on outside, on the cramped little terrace; people eat there, sunbathe, read, or potter in the terraced garden beyond. But most of the time they simply stare out at the Apuan Alps, hypnotised by the shifting light, by the mist rising from the Serchio in the morning, by the clouds drifting across the peaks in the afternoon.

This being Italy, it is not quite as peaceful as it sounds. The Italians are addicted to noise and they have a genius for making it. They like their motorbikes unsilenced and their car engines rorty, and the road in the valley below is the kind of temptation they can't resist: a sporting series of sharp curves which gives them an excuse to play arias on their car horns and make their car tyres squeal. The sound bounces off the hillsides and rises, mingling with the hiss of the wind in the chestnuts and the dry clatter of the leaves of the walnut tree at the edge of the terrace. The din is just far enough away to be comforting, rather than irritating, a reminder that life goes on, despite indolence and isolation.

Twenty years ago, the house had no electricity and a cable had to be strung up from the valley below to connect it to the grid. Not all the other houses were electrified at that time. There were still *contadini* on the mountain who got by with oil lamps and candles, and regulated their days by the sun: they got up at sunrise, worked until sunset, ate by lamplight, then went to bed. The *contadini* are dying off now, their children have gone up in the world and have mostly emigrated to the big towns – Lucca, Viareggio, Pisa, Florence – and the mountain is gradually emptying. But that primitive diurnal rhythm seems to be part of the place, and when I am there I fall into it without even trying.

In northern cities, night is something you shut out. You switch on the lights, close the doors, draw the curtains and forget about it. But out in the country night is a presence to be reckoned with and its slow approach is a subtle pleasure. Twilight – particularly summer twilight – is always the best time of the day in Italy. In town, people come out on to the streets to enjoy the cool air and watch the *passeggiata*. Up on the mountain, there is no *passeggiata*, so the only thing to do is go out on to the terrace and watch the night fall.

The weather begins to break in late August. The days remain hot and sticky, with a haze over the mountains and, every so often, a faint roll of thunder somewhere off to the north. But at sunset, the sky usually clears in the hills and the heat relents. The mountains are layers of blue, each layer shading imperceptibly into the next, and the air is full of feeding swifts, dipping and arching. Far above them, a single hawk glides lazily towards the Apuans, riding a thermal, not bothering to stir its wings. Traffic rasps in the valley. The last rays of the sun pick out the white façades and pink roofs of the houses in Barga and the honey-coloured cathedral floating above them. As the light thickens, the nearby trees seem to gather weight and greenness, and extra dimension.

Every evening I wait for the critical moment when the swifts and the bats change guard: a brief stir and confusion, always expected yet always astonishing, a muted flurry of wings and small, high-pitched cries. Then the swifts regroup and vanish towards the Apennines with a rush of wingbeats. With their narrow heads and curved wings, swifts are perfect creatures, taut and precise and aerody-namically flawless, and they fly like acrobats on the trapeze, a sequence of graceful miracles. Compared with them, the flight of the bats is pure anarchy. They erupt from the darkening trees into what is left of the sunset, flickering, stuttering, impossible to predict. They seem to stop dead and go into reverse, dipping towards the house, then off somewhere else entirely. This is a chaos theory of flight, bewildering fractals instead of direction and purpose. Bats seem less like creatures of flesh and blood than emanations of the night, blobs of darkness, soft-edged; if you touched one, your hand might go right through it.

By eight o'clock, the light is rosy mauve, deepening to purple. The moon swings up above the ridge opposite the farmhouse, pink-faced at first, as if vaguely embarrassed to be visible this early. It storms up the sky so fast that the earth seems to be tilting under your feet – five minutes from the first curved sliver of light to the full glowing disk. When it touches the outermost branches of the walnut, the tree seems to grow; its outlines become sharper and deeper; it acquires a new, commanding, nocturnal presence.

Slowly, the lights come on across the valley: a line of four along the houses bordering the road at the foot of the mountain, a rising tangle marking the place where Barga climbs its hill, two strings of pearls slung across the villages on a distant Apuan foothill. Cars are points of light on the road below, white or red, coming or going. Night spreads its black skirts and settles slowly, almost formally.

The stars come out, first one by one, then suddenly in their thousands. The Milky Way is a thick smudge of light, trailing back towards the Apennines, so bright that it seems artificial. Every so often, somebody cries, 'Look, a shooting star!' but no two people ever see the same star together. Instead, they watch the satellites, tiny points of light moving unnaturally fast from one horizon to another, and the winking red and green lights of the planes flying south to Rome. Occasionally, an intercontinental flight goes over high up, dragging behind it a grey-white, moon-lit con trail.

By nine o'clock, the valley is studded with scattered lights, Barga Cathedral is floodlit a ghostly green, and even the local village church is illuminated by a yellowish spotlight. Twenty years ago, when not everyone was hooked up to the grid, people around here thought of electricity as an expensive luxury and used it sparingly. The nights were darker then and the valley was a great lake of blackness, its surface broken intermittently by pinpricks of light that seemed too inconsequential to survive. Year by year, the lake has begun to fill. But there are still broad stretches of darkness out there, night as it has always been in these parts, and blackest of all is the ridge opposite the farmhouse. It sweeps straight down from the high Apennines and has only two buildings on it, shepherds' houses, both of them far back into the mountains, high up and out of sight. The rest is untouched forest – chestnut, scrub oak and fir – too steep and tangled for anyone to bother with, even in this part of the country, where every foot of usable earth is terraced and cultivated and has someone's name on it. By day, the ridge is silent and forbidding; by night, it is a great slab of darkness, a night within the night, the real, true thing. It makes all attempts at illumination seem intrusive as well as pathetic, so in deference to the ridge and the night and the mosquitoes, when the household has dinner outside they keep the house lights off and eat by candlelight.

People go to bed early in the Garfagnana and when the lights go out the night creatures emerge. One evening someone left scraps of food on the terrace table; in the morning they were gone and the white plastic tabletop was smudged by the paw marks of a fox. All this happened without a sound and there has been no trace of fox before or since. Yet the night is full of small noises, faint scrapings and rustlings, a strange unquiet, punctuated, every quarter of an hour, by the chime of the village clock. Whenever I am in the house, I have to share the mountainside with creatures I never see.

Above all, I share it with a screech owl, an *assiolo*. It lives in the woods behind the house and every night, in the small house, it goes hunting for food. Screech owls screech and so does their prey, repeatedly and with increasing desperation, loud enough to wake me and sometimes, when the mayhem

45

seems to be taking place right outside, to send me stumbling out of bed to the window. But even when the moon is full, there is never anything to be seen: no owl, no prey, just icy light and black shadows, the looming mass of the ridge and, beyond it, the few scattered street lights that stay on in Barga after the cathedral floodlights are switched off. The screech owl might be part of my dream-life, mysterious and insubstantial, except that I am always wide awake when I hear its sinister cry.

There used to be doves at the house, plump, amiable creatures that strutted around the parking lot, made love incessantly, fussed over their chicks, and filled the days with pleasant cooing. Occasionally, they would take off all together and fly in formation over the valley, banking and gliding. With the sun on their white wings, they looked like a flight of angels. But the screech owl got them one by one, however carefully they were shut in at sunset, however often they were replaced. Finally, I gave up trying. I chopped up the dovecotes to use for kindling and left the night to the owl.

I see now that the doves were a kind of wishful thinking, a city-boy's gesture, well meant but essentially absurd, and based on the frivolous conviction that night and its creatures could be eliminated by turning on a light. And it seems right that I have never seen the screech owl. Shakespeare thought it was a bird of ill-omen, a 'shrieking harbinger, Foul precursor of the fiend'. These days, it is probably just another timid endangered species. But that is not how it sounds when it goes about its business and I am glad I have never seen it. The screech owl is secret and predatory and it belongs to the other darkness, the darkness of death, the night that gets us all in the end, the night that no amount of electric light will ever illuminate.

(1995)

Anne Alvarez is a consultant child and adolescent psycho-therapist. Her books include, most recently, *The Thinking Heart: Three Levels of Psychoanalytic Therapy with Disturbed Children*. A book in her honour, *Being Alive: Building on the Work of Anne Alvarez*, was published in 2002. Her academic positions have included Visiting Professor at the San Francisco Psychoanalytic Society. She has been working and teaching at the Tavistock Clinic, London, for over fifty years.

2

ONCE UPON A TIME

As eventide crashes its banks, our nocturnal routine commences.

We encircle ourselves – whether in a nest or a duvet (which the Americans more aptly call a 'comforter'). We find somewhere secure, be it the warren or the closed bedroom. We shut away the world, cocoon ourselves in darkness. The rabbit burrows. The sloth settles onto his arm-branch. The otter wraps herself in kelp or seaweed and floats, while the walrus digs his tusks into the ice. The seal may ready himself for sleep in the water, but will first ensure that one side of his brain (including his eye and flipper) remains fully awake, while the other retires. The dolphin, with similar ingenuity, will fall asleep while swimming, also allowing one half of its brain a break while the other keeps on the move. Reef fish dart into tiny gaps in the coral, at the same exact moment each day, their timing as precise as the speaking clock's. The giraffe, who gets by on just two hours of sleep out of every twenty-four (as opposed to the blind mole rat who simply spends most of his life asleep), languidly curls her long neck around herself, tucking her head onto the ground. Just as we assume the foetal position or curl our body into a cosy question mark beneath the blanket.

If we are smart and able, we will regulate the temperature of our nook, then luxuriate into a properly plump pillow and welcoming bed. We must first exert some self-control, so as to forego it and lapse into healthy, golden slumbers: we should ideally not have drunk coffee for a few hours, or alcohol; and, in this brightened day-glow age of tablets and such, we will not have looked at bright light sources (including the television) for an hour or more. Studies have shown that the blue light transmitted by smartphones and tablets is antithetical to what our eyes should be seeing prior to sleep.

Once our surroundings have been neutralized, our brains can begin to prepare for sleep. We tread water before diving in. To humour those who are still clinging to their brightly lit devices, despite their now better judgement, this final slumberous passage between the waking day and a sleep state can be regarded as similar to logging off a computer or shutting down its hard drive. We need to defrag our conscious brain.

To aid our children, we turn to a bedtime story. Much as our little ones cling to their cuddly bear, rabbit or lion, so might these age-old, matter-of-fact stories feature speaking animals. Using zoological effects, they can smuggle home truths into our children's minds, and talking beasts are, ironically, probably more common in such fairy tales than fairies. Transmogrification allows for appealing archetypes, however surreal or absurdist. These allegories don't merely provide quiet moral tuition, they also rehearse the brain for what dreams – with all their echoing surrealism and wonder – may imminently come.

Marina Warner, a world authority on fairy tale and folklore, not to mention a masterful storyteller in her own right, has written that 'a fairy tale keeps on the move between written and spoken versions and back again, between print and per-formance ... [it] is as fluid as a conversation taking place over centuries.' Scientists in Durham and Lisbon Universities have taken this argument further, using phylogenetic methods to show that this exchange in fact has taken place over millennia. They have claimed to trace, among others, *Jack and the Beanstalk* back to a group of tales originating more than 5,000 years ago. In this sense, these bedtime stories are in fact a wellspring of humanity itself.

Other terms for 'fairy tale' include 'magic tale' and 'wonder tale'. Perhaps these are better-fitting glass slippers for the genre, that impish world of ambiguity, enchantment and mischief that at times slinks into malice – just like the Land of Nod (as coined by Swift). This is J. R. R. Tolkien and C. S. Lewis' 'secondary world', as legitimate as our own primary universe. The 'wonder story' dreamscape is an imaginary hinterland, one that bridges our minds (and chil-dren's more impressionable ones) into real reverie. Auden, discussing the 'secondary world' of the imagination, might as well have been exploring dream state when he wrote: 'Every normal human being is interested in two kinds of world: the Primary, everyday, world which he knows through his sense, and a Secondary world or worlds which he not only can create in his imagination, but also cannot stop himself creating ...' The storyteller, if not overtly its narrator, is the voice of our imagination, coaxing us forward. Often in fairy tales it will be through the mouthpiece of a Mother Hen (just as our mums themselves related the tale to us before whispering good night, the nightlight aglow).

A small tale before lights-out snugly completes the workaday narrative. It offers a distinct end-point to the day's story and, as such, takes our mind 'off things'. Storytime rounds out the routine. Soon sleep will no longer itself be dormant. We are ready to leave our shadow – along with one more day – behind. Bedtime is almost over. We have been lulled by a bye.

Another Bedtime Story
by A. E. Stallings

One day you realize it. It doesn't need to be said—
Just as you turn the page – *the end* – and close the
      cover—
All, all of the stories are about going to bed.

Goldilocks snug upstairs, the toothy wolf instead
Of grandmother tucked in the quilts, crooning *closer,*
      closer—
One day you realize it. It hardly needs to be said:

The snow-pale princess sleeps – the pillow under her
      head
Of rose petals or crystal – and dreams of a lost lover—
All, all of the stories are about going to bed;

Even the one about witches and ovens and gingerbread
In the dark heart of Europe – can children save each
      other?—
You start to doubt it a little. It doesn't need to be said.

But I'll say it, because it's embedded in everything I've
      read,
The tales that start with *once* and end with *ever after*,
All, all of the stories are about going to bed.

About coming to terms with the night, alleviating the
      dread
Of laying the body down, of lying under the cover.

That's why our children resist it so. That's why it
    mustn't be said:
All, all of the stories are about going to bed.

(2012)

From *Peter Pan*
by J. M. Barrie

It is the nightly custom of every good mother after her chil-
dren are asleep to rummage in their minds and put things
straight for the next morning, repacking into their proper
places the many articles that have wandered during the day.
If you could keep awake (but of course you can't) you would
see your own mother doing this, and you would find it very
interesting to watch her. It is quite like tidying up draw-
ers. You would see her on her knees, I expect, lingering
humorously over some of your contents, wondering where
on earth you had picked this thing up, making discoveries
sweet and not so sweet, pressing this to her cheek as if it
were as nice as a kitten, and hurriedly stowing that out of
sight. When you wake in the morning, the naughtiness and
evil passions with which you went to bed have been folded
up small and placed at the bottom of your mind; and on the
top, beautifully aired, are spread out your prettier thoughts,
ready for you to put on.

(1911)

Lights Out
by Hugo Williams

We're allowed to talk for ten minutes
about what has happened during the day,
then we have to go to sleep.
It doesn't matter what we dream about.

(1994)

★

Lights Out
by Edward Thomas

I have come to the borders of sleep,
The unfathomable deep
Forest where all must lose
Their way, however straight,
Or winding, soon or late;
They cannot choose.

Many a road and track
That, since the dawn's first crack,
Up to the forest brink,
Deceived the travellers,
Suddenly now blurs,
And in they sink.

Here love ends,
Despair, ambition ends;
All pleasure and all trouble,
Although most sweet or bitter,

Here ends, in sleep that is sweeter
Than tasks most noble.

There is not any book
Or face of dearest look
That I would not turn from now
To go into the unknown
I must enter, and leave, alone,
I know not how.

The tall forest towers;
Its cloudy foliage lowers
Ahead, shelf above shelf;
Its silence I hear and obey
That I may lose my way
And myself.

(1916)

★

In his lecture 'On Fairytales', J. R. R. Tolkien claimed, 'The incarnate mind, the tongue, and the tale are in our world coeval'.

His own children's bedtime-story routine would prove incredibly fruitful. While many of us may try to make up a simple tale for our offspring, forgetting the details soon after each little performance, the yarns that Tolkien spun for younger sons Michael and Christopher took on a 'secondary life' of their own. These bedtime stories would burgeon into one of the world's most widely read books (and, later, most garlanded and viewed film series) ever.

Biographer Humphrey Carpenter sets the scene: Tolkien has

just left his close friend C. S. Lewis in the centre of Oxford, before bicycling home.

From *J. R. R. Tolkien: A Biography*
by Humphrey Carpenter

Edith has gone to bed and the house is in darkness when he gets home. He builds up the fire in the study stove and fills his pipe. He ought, he knows, to do some more work on his lecture notes for the next morning, but he cannot resist taking from a drawer the half-finished manuscript of a story that he is writing to amuse himself and his children. It is probably, he suspects, a waste of time; certainly if he is going to devote any attention to this sort of thing it ought to be to *The Silmarillion*. But something draws him back night after night to this amusing little tale – at least it seems to amuse the boys. He sits down at the desk, fits a new relief nib to his dip pen (which he prefers to a fountain pen), unscrews the ink bottle, takes a sheet of old examination paper (which still has a candidate's essay on the Battle of Maldon on the back of it), and begin to write: 'When Bilbo opened his eyes, he wondered if he had; for it was just as dark as with them shut. No one was anywhere near him. Just imagine his fright . . .'

We will leave him now. He will be at his desk until half past one, or two o'clock, or perhaps even later, with only the scratching of his pen to disturb the silence, while around him Northmoor Road sleeps.

(1977)

★

In 'The Word Shed', Colum McCann recounts how his father would tell him stories back when he was a kid. The innocent shimmer of the child's-eye view is evoked touchingly.

It just so happens that my dad used to arrive home from a newspaper office and that my son, to whom I now read stories, is called Georgie and adores football.

So while McCann's story – although intensely personal – is, like all great tales, recognizable to us all, this particular tale is one for my boy. Perhaps you'll like reading it when you're all grown-up, son.

The Word Shed
by Colum McCann

Every afternoon, when my father arrived home from his job as the features editor at a newspaper in Dublin, he disappeared into his writing shed. To get there, you had to squeeze your way past the coal bin, the lawnmower, cans of petrol and paint, ancient bicycle parts. The shed always smelled damp inside, as if the rain rose up out of the carpet. The bookshelves sagged. The low-slung roof had a murky skylight with a hat of gray Irish cloud.

From the house, I could hear the tattoo of two-fingered typing. The ping of the bell. The slam of the carriage return. It all sounded like a faint form of applause. My father's books – *The World of Sean O'Casey*, *The Wit of Oscar Wilde*, *All the World's Roses*, *The Fighting Irish* – sat on the coffee table in what we called the D. & D. room: reserved for the dead and the dignified. The books didn't mean much to me. I wanted to be what every other boy wanted to be: a professional soccer player.

In his youth, my father had been a semi-professional goal-keeper. Nothing very glamorous. He played second string for Charlton Athletic, in London, and got paid ten shillings and sixpence a week. What he remembered most vividly was having to polish the boots of the first-team players, and sweeping the rat shit out of the canteen in the morning. He never played for the first team, but he didn't see this as a failure so much as an adventure in limitations. He came back to Dublin, had a family, and began to write.

One winter evening, when I was nine years old, he came into my bedroom, carrying under his arm a sheaf of papers, some of them two or three feet long. (Like Kerouac, he used large rolls of industrial paper in his Olivetti.) It was a carbon copy of what he had been writing for the previous few weeks: a book for kids titled *Goals for Glory*.

'Read it for me, will you? Tell me if it's awful or not.'

I read it by flashlight. Georgie Goode was a sullen Gypsy boy, fifteen years old, with long black hair. He travelled around the fens of England in a battered caravan, with a father who was sometimes there, sometimes absent. Georgie had no money for soccer boots, so he slipped around in the muck in his plimsolls. It was the stuff of children's myth – Georgie had an eye for the back of the net and a left foot like chain lightning – but it all seemed plausible.

Years later, I would read James Joyce and mull over the idea that literature could 're-create life out of life', but back then what stunned me was that another boy could emerge from my father's ramshackle shed, as real to me as the dirt that caked on my own soccer boots. This was new territory: the imagined coming to life. My father's typewriter sounded different to me now. More and more, I disappeared into books.

When *Goals for Glory* was published, the following year, I took the hardcover to school. My teacher, Mr Kells, read a chapter aloud every Friday afternoon, that time of the school week when the world promises escape. We sat in our prefab classroom and waited for him to crack the spine.

In the last chapter, Georgie's team had to beat the rival team, Dale Rovers. Georgie had been given a new pair of soccer boots. The championship was at stake. I knew the ending already, but my classmates didn't. They were latched to their desks. Of course, Georgie started the game off badly, and of course he got rid of his new boots, and of course his father arrived late to cheer him on, and of course doom loomed, as doom so often does in a good story.

I will never forget Christopher Howlett, my red-headed desk mate, jumping around like a prayer in an air raid as Mr Kells reached the final page. Georgie scored the winning goal. The classroom erupted. The kid from my father's shed – that tangle of hair that had somehow sprung up from behind a typewriter ribbon – was carried with us outside the school gates, down Mart Lane, through the swamp, and into the field at the back of Dunnes Stores, where, with a soggy leather ball at our feet, we all became Georgie, at least for a minute or two.

Such euphoria seldom lasts, but the nostalgia for it remains. My world had changed enough for me to know that I would try to write a character into it one day – not a Georgie, necessarily, but perhaps a father, or a son.

A few years on, when I was a teen-ager, my father sat me in the shed and recited, from memory, Philip Larkin's 'This Be the Verse': 'They fuck you up, your mum and dad. / They may not mean to, but they do.' Fair enough, and I knew what he was trying to say, but I also knew that sometimes — just sometimes — the father you get is the father you want.

(2014)

★

I have always loved the word 'moonshine'.

Perhaps this is down to my mother, a musician. As a child, she adored the musical *Annie Get Your Gun*, written by Irving Berlin, and later fostered that affection for its show tunes onto her own kids.

My favourite number was always 'Moonshine Lullaby', with its clandestine, candle-lit wonder. Annie Oakley sings her young siblings to sleep, by painting a picture of their dad's night shift:

Behind the hill, there's a busy little still,
Where your Pappy's workin' in the moonlight . . .

That a 'little still' could, contrarily, be 'busy' seemed unreal and inviting to me. Annie goes on to explain that her dad's job is, by the light of the moon, to fill up a jug with 'moonshine', with which he'll be 'very happy'. In such ways, the ditty, to my innocent little ears, over-frothed with mystery and gleamed with magic. Its gentle melody added another comforting glow.

Of course, not being an expert in prohibition, I didn't realize that 'moonshine' refers not to the moon's radiance itself but to a barrel of hooch or white lightning; nor did I cotton on that the 'still' was a 'distillery', not a silvery clearing.

That Annie Oakley should sing her siblings to sleep with a ditty about their absentee pop making illicit manoeuvres by cover of night could be regarded as irresponsible! Yet, remember, this is a musical and, instead, it's a romantic irony; not to mention, a heroic rendering of the father figure – despite it all, and because of its downright loving tone.

In this next story, written by Tobias Wolff, a narrator recollects a yuletide night he spent as a boy, with his father. It is apparent that their times together were infrequent, and so doubly precious to them both, as the dad in question – estranged from the boy's mother – likes to push his luck (just like Annie's Pappy).

There is an elegiac tone in this recollection, adding to the mythical haze that swirls around this father figure. Wolff conjures filial love with a touch as deft as snowfall. He blizzards the reader. We slalom together, through a whiteout of longing and love.

Powder
by Tobias Wolff

Just before Christmas my father took me skiing at Mount Baker. He'd had to fight for the privilege of my company, because my mother was still angry with him for sneaking me into a nightclub during his last visit, to see Thelonious Monk.

He wouldn't give up. He promised, hand on heart, to take good care of me and have me home for dinner on Christmas Eve, and she relented. But as we were checking out of the lodge that morning it began to snow, and in this snow he observed some rare quality that made it necessary for us to get in one last run. We got in several last runs. He was indifferent to my fretting. Snow whirled around us in bitter, blinding squalls, hissing like sand, and still we skied. As the lift bore us to the peak yet again, my father looked at his watch and said, 'Criminy. This'll have to be a fast one.'

By now I couldn't see the trail. There was no point in

trying. I stuck close behind him and did what he did and somehow made it to the bottom without sailing off a cliff. We returned our skis and my father put chains on the Austin-Healey while I swayed from foot to foot, clapping my mittens and wishing I was home. I could see everything. The green table cloth, the plates with the holly pattern, the red candles waiting to be lit.

We passed a diner on our way out. 'You want some soup?' my father asked. I shook my head. 'Buck up,' he said. 'I'll get you there. Right, doctor?'

I was supposed to say, 'Right, doctor,' but I didn't say anything.

A state trooper waved us down outside the resort, where a pair of sawhorses blocked the road. He came up to our car and bent down to my father's window, his face bleached by the cold, snowflakes clinging to his eyebrows and to the fur trim of his jacket and cap.

'Don't tell me,' my father said.

The trooper told him. The road was closed. It might get cleared, it might not. Storm took everyone by surprise. Hard to get people moving. Christmas Eve. What can you do.

My father said, 'Look. We're talking about five, six inches. I've taken this car through worse than that.'

The trooper straightened up. His face was out of sight but I could hear him. 'The road is closed.'

My father sat with both hands on the wheel, rubbing the wood with his thumbs. He looked at the barricade for a long time. He seemed to be trying to master the idea of it. Then he thanked the trooper and with a weird, old-maidy show of caution turned the car around. 'Your mother will never forgive me for this,' he said.

'We should've left this morning,' I said. 'Doctor.'

He didn't speak to me again until we were in a booth at the diner, waiting for our burgers. 'She won't forgive me,' he said. 'Do you understand? Never.'

'I guess,' I said, though no guesswork was required. She wouldn't forgive him.

'I can't let that happen.' He bent toward me. 'I'll tell you what I want. I want us all to be together again. Is that what you want?'

'Yes, sir.'

He bumped my chin with his knuckles. 'That's all I needed to hear.'

When we finished eating he went to the pay phone in the back of the diner, then joined me in the booth again. I figured he'd called my mother, but he didn't give a report. He sipped at his coffee and stared out the window at the empty road. 'Come on, come on,' he said, though not to me. A little while later he said it again. When the trooper's car went past, lights flashing, he got up and dropped some money on the check. 'Okay. *Vámonos.*'

The wind had died. The snow was falling straight down, less of it now and lighter. We drove away from the resort, right up to the barricade. 'Move it,' my father told me. When I looked at him, he said, 'What are you waiting for?' I got out and dragged one of the sawhorses aside, then put it back after he drove through. He pushed the door open for me. 'Now you're an accomplice,' he said. 'We go down together.' He put the car into gear and gave me a look. 'Joke, son.'

Down the first long stretch I watched the road behind us, to see if the trooper was on our tail. The barricade vanished.

66

Then there was nothing but snow: snow on the road, snow kicking up from the chains, snow on the trees, snow in the sky, and our trail in the snow. Then I faced forward and had a shock. There were no tracks ahead of us. My father was breaking virgin snow between tall treelines. He was humming 'Stars Fell in Alabama'. I felt snow brush along the floorboards under my feet. To keep my hands from shaking I clamped them between my knees.

My father grunted thoughtfully and said, 'Don't ever try this yourself.'

'I won't.'

'That's what you say now, but someday you'll get your license and then you'll think you can do anything. Only you won't be able to do this. You need, I don't know – a certain instinct.'

'Maybe I have it.'

'You don't. You have your strong points, sure, just not this. I only mention it because I don't want you to get the idea this is something anybody can do. I'm a great driver. That's not a virtue, okay? It's just a fact, and one you should be aware of. There aren't many cars I'd try this with. Listen!'

I did listen. I heard the slap of the chains, the stiff, jerky rasp of the wipers, the purr of the engine. It really did purr. The old heap was almost new. My father couldn't afford it, and kept promising to sell it, but here it was.

I said, 'Where do you think that policeman went to?'

'Are you warm enough?' He reached over and cranked up the blower. Then he turned off the wipers. We didn't need them. The clouds had brightened. A few sparse, feathery flakes drifted into our slipstream and were swept away. We left the trees and entered a broad field of snow that ran level for a while and then tilted sharply downward. Orange stakes had been planted at intervals in two parallel lines and my father steered a course between them, though they were far enough apart to leave considerable doubt in my mind as to exactly where the road lay. He was humming again, doing little scat riffs around the melody.

'Okay, then. What are my strong points?'

'Don't get me started,' he said. 'It'd take all day.'

'Oh, right. Name one.'

'Easy. You always think ahead.'

True. I always thought ahead. I was a boy who kept his clothes on numbered hangers to ensure proper rotation. I bothered my teachers for homework assignments far ahead of their due dates so I could draw up schedules. I thought ahead, and that was why I knew there would be other troopers waiting for us at the end of our ride, if we even got there. What I didn't know was that my father would wheedle and plead his way past them – he didn't sing 'O Tannenbaum', but just about – and get me home for dinner, buying a little more time before my mother decided to make the split final. I knew we'd get caught; I was resigned to it. And maybe for this reason I stopped moping and began to enjoy myself.

Why not? This was one for the books. Like being in a speedboat, only better. You can't go downhill in a boat. And it was all ours. And it kept coming, the laden trees, the unbroken surface of snow, the sudden white vistas. Here and there I saw hints of the road, ditches, fences, stakes, though not so many that I could have found my own way. But then I didn't have to. My father was driving. My father in his forty-eighth year, rumpled, kind, bankrupt of honor, flushed with certainty. He was a great driver. All persuasion, no coercion. Such subtlety at the wheel, such tactful pedalwork. I actually trusted him. And the best was yet to come – switchbacks and hairpins impossible to describe. Except maybe to say this: if you haven't driven fresh powder, you haven't driven.

(1996)

Golden Slumbers
by Thomas Dekker

Golden slumbers kiss your eyes,
Smiles awake you when you rise;
Sleep, pretty wantons, do not cry,
And I will sing a lullaby,
Rock them, rock them, lullaby.
Care is heavy, therefore sleep you,
You are care, and care must keep you;
Sleep, pretty wantons, do not cry,
And I will sing a lullaby,
Rock them, rock them, lullaby.

(1603)

The late Angela Carter wrote in the introduction to her bountiful *Book of Fairy Tales* that such stories represent: 'the great mass of infinitely various narrative that was, once upon a time and still is, sometimes, passed on and disseminated through the world by word of mouth – stories without known originators that can be remade again and again by every person who tells them, the perennially refreshed entertainment of the poor.'

One holiday, I read to my young son and daughter a range of these fairy tales, all of which centred on a female protagonist, to gauge which they liked best. If we all really loved a particular tale, I told them, I might even put it into this book.

Carter deftly plucked tales from all corners of the world. Some seemed familiar yet different to my kids (for 'Rumpelstiltskin' read 'Tom Tit Tot'), like a hall of imaginary mirrors. We enjoyed all of them; however, somehow none quite fitted for this collection that you are now reading.

Then, on the last night, I fixed on reading them a Russian story. My daughter was being mischievous, though, and kept interrupting me. Tired myself, I began to grow impatient, eventually throwing my own 'toys out of the pram' by refusing to finish the story, storming out of the room with stern (but entirely faux) finality, like a performer sashaying off-stage before his encore.

It worked. They piped down.

Only then did I realize that I had fallen through the story's trapdoor – and that this was the one to incorporate into this anthology.

How a Husband Weaned His Wife from Fairy Tales

There was once an innkeeper whose wife loved fairy tales above all else and accepted as lodgers only those who could tell stories. Of course the husband suffered loss because of this, and he wondered how he could wean his wife away from fairy tales. One night in winter, at a late hour, an old man shivering with cold asked him for shelter. The husband ran out and said: 'Can you tell stories? My wife does not allow me to let in anyone who cannot tell stories.' The old man saw that he had no choice; he was almost frozen to death. He said: 'I can tell stories.' 'And will you tell them for a long time?' 'All night.'

So far, so good. They let the old man in. The husband said: 'Wife, this peasant has promised to tell stories all night long but only on condition that you do not argue with him or interrupt him.' The old man said: 'Yes, there must be no interruptions, or I will not tell any stories.' They ate supper and went to bed. Then the old man began: 'An owl flew into a garden, sat on a tree trunk, and drank some water. An owl flew into a garden, sat on a tree trunk, and drank some water.' He kept on saying again and again: 'An owl flew into a garden, sat on a tree trunk, and drank some water.' The wife listened and listened and then said: 'What kind of story is this? He keeps repeating the same thing over and over!' 'Why do you interrupt me? I told you not to argue with me! That was only the beginning; it was going to change later.' The husband, upon hearing this – and it was exactly what he wanted to hear – jumped down from his bed and began to belabour his wife: 'You were told not to argue, and now you have not let him finish his story!' And he thrashed her and thrashed her, so that she began to hate stories and from that time on forswore listening to them.

(1866)

Translated by Norbert Guterman

Carter – playing the Mother Goose of fairy-tale tradition with distinction – wrote that 'the stories women told could not in any way materially alter their conditions . . . [This tale, however,] shows just how much fairy stories could change a woman's desires, and how much a man might fear that change,

[and] would go to any lengths to keep her from pleasure, as if pleasure itself threatened his authority.'

The story was published in 1866, in a collection of fairy tales by Aleksandr Nikolayevich Afanas'ev (1826–71), the Russian counterpart of the Grimms.

In the notes to her collection, Angela Carter elaborates: 'Federal Russia was an extraordinarily rich source of oral literature at this time, owing to widespread illiteracy among the rural poor. As late as the close of the eighteenth century, Russian newspapers still carried advertisements from blind men applying for work in the homes of the gentry as tellers of tales, recalling how, two hundred years before, three blind ancients had followed one another in rotation at the bedside of Ivan the Terrible, telling the insomniac monarch fairy tales until at last he managed to sleep.'

Details of the identity (or identities) of that most famous fabulist, Aesop, are scattered among works by the likes of Aristotle, Herodotus and Plutarch. The story of his life and times in Ancient Greece emerges today as a web of apocrypha and legend, derived from such scant sources.

In this poem, written for children as much as adults, Charles Causley weaves a colourful bedtime story from some of that portraiture. As its title suggests, fittingly, the lively verse rounds itself into a fable.

Its lesson? That even after we are long gone, the stories we tell each other survive. In Aesop's case, whoever he may have been, outliving him by some two thousand five hundred years.

Fable
by Charles Causley

I was a slave on Samos, a small man
Carelessly put together; face a mask
So frightful that at first the people ran
Away from me, especially at dusk.

I was possessed, too, of a rattling tongue
That only now and then would let words pass
As they should properly be said or sung.
In general, you could say I was a mess.

One thing redeemed me. People marvelled at
The brilliance with which my speech was woven.
It was, they said, as if a toad had spat
Diamonds. And my ugliness was forgiven.

Soon I was freed, and sooner was the friend
Of kings and commoners who came a-calling.
Of my bright hoard of wit there seemed no end,
Nor of the tales that I rejoiced in telling.

But there were heads and hearts where, green and
    cold,
The seeds of envy and of hate were lying.
From our most sacred shrine, a cup of gold
Was hidden in my store, myself unknowing.

'Sacrilege! He is a thief!' my accusers swore,
And to the cliffs of Delphi I was taken,

Hurled to the myrtle-scented valley floor
And on its whitest stones my body broken.

'This is the end of him and his poor fame!'
I heard them cry upon the gleaming air.
Stranger, now tell me if you know my name,
My story of the Tortoise and the Hare?

★

The Rematch
by B. J. Novak

In the aftermath of an athletic humiliation on an unprece-
dented scale – a loss to a tortoise in a footrace so staggering
that, his tormentors teased, it would not only live on in
the record books, but would transcend sport itself, and be
taught to children around the world in textbooks and bed-
time stories for centuries; that hundreds of years from now,
children who had never heard of a 'tortoise' would learn
that it was basically a fancy type of turtle from hearing about
this very race – the hare retreated, understandably, into a
substantial period of depression and self-doubt.

The hare gained weight, then lost weight; turned to reli-
gion, then another less specific religion. The hare got into
yoga; shut himself indoors on a self-imposed program to
read all the world's great novels; then traveled the world;
then did some volunteer work. Everything helped a little
bit, at first; but nothing really helped. After a while, the
hare realized what the simplest part of him had known from
the beginning: he was going to have to rematch the tortoise.

'No,' came the word from the tortoise's spokesperson.

'The tortoise prefers to focus on the future, not relive the past. The tortoise is focused full time on inspiring a new generation with the lessons of dedication and persistence through his popular speaking tours and his charitable work with the Slow and Steady Foundation.'

The smugness and sanctimony of the tortoise's response infuriated the hare. *'The lessons of dedication and persistence'*? Had everyone forgotten that the hare had taken six naps throughout the race (!) – unequivocally guaranteeing victory to anyone – a horse, a dog, a worm, *a leaf*, depending on the wind – *anyone* lucky enough to be matched against the hare at this reckless, perspectiveless, and now-forever-lost peak phase of his career, an offensive period of his own life that he had obsessed about and tried in vain to forgive himself for ever since? How could anyone think the tortoise was relevant to any of this? A minor detail of the race, known to few but obsessives (of which there were still plenty), was that there had been a gnat clinging to the leg of the tortoise throughout the entire contest: was this gnat, too, worthy of being celebrated as a hero, full of counterlogical lessons and nonsensical insight like 'Right place, right time takes down talent in its prime'? Or 'Hang on to a tortoise's leg, who knows where it will lead'?

No – the lesson of this story has nothing to do with the tortoise, thought the hare, and everything to do with the hare. How he had let himself become so intoxicated with the aspects of his talent that were rare that he had neglected the much more common aspects of his character that also, it so happened, were more important – things like always doing your best, and never taking success for granted, and keeping enough pride burning inside to fuel your success but not so much to burn it down. Now, the hare knew these things. Now. Now that it was too late.

Or was it? What was the lesson again? Slow and steady?

The hare started running again, every day, even though there was no race planned. He ran a mile every morning, then two, then ten.

Before long, he added an afternoon run to his training routine – a slower one, with a different goal in mind. On this run, he made a point to start a conversation with everyone he came across. 'Boy, I sure would love to race that tortoise again someday. You think anyone would want to watch it, though?' Then he would shrug it off and jog along to the next stranger. 'Hey, what do you think would happen if I raced that tortoise again? Ya think I'd win this time? Or do you think pride would get the better of me all over again?' Then he'd shrug and run off again, at a provocatively medium pace.

Slowly, steadily, anticipation built for a tortoise-hare rematch. After a while it became all that anyone could talk about, and eventually, the questions made their way to the tortoise.

'No,' said the tortoise, but this time his 'no' just led to more questions. 'No' now, or 'no' ever? Would he *ever* rematch the hare? If so, when, and under what conditions? If not, why? Could he at least say 'maybe'?

No, said the tortoise again; never. They kept asking, and he kept saying no, until eventually, everyone gave up and stopped asking. And that's when the tortoise, sad and dizzy at having all this attention given to him and then taken away, impulsively said, Yes, okay, I bet I can beat this hare again. Yes.

I'm undefeated against the hare, thought the tortoise.

Actually, I'm 1—0 — I'm undefeated in my entire racing career! How do you win a race? Slow and steady, that's what they say, right? Well, I invented slow and steady. This is good. This will be good. One time could have been a fluke. Twice, there'll be no question.

The race was set for ten days' time. The tortoise set out to replicate what seemed to have worked the first time, which was nothing in particular: simple diet, some walking around. A little of this, a little of that. He didn't want to overthink it. He was going to mainly just focus on being slow and steady.

The hare trained like no one had ever trained for anything. He ran fifteen miles every morning and fifteen every afternoon. He watched tapes of his old races. He slept eight hours every night, which is practically unheard of for a hare, and he did it all under a wall taped full of the mean, vicious things everyone had said about him in all the years since the legendary race that had ruined his life.

On the day of the race, the tortoise and the hare met for the first time in five years at the starting line, and shared a brief, private conversation as their whole world watched.

'Good luck, hare,' said the tortoise, as casual as ever. 'Whoa! You know what's funny — do that again — huh, from this angle you look like a duck. Now you look like a hare again. Funny. Anyway, good luck, hare!'

'And good luck to you, tortoise,' whispered the hare, leaning in close. 'And just so you know — nobody knows this, and if you tell anyone I said it, I'll deny it — but I'm not really a hare. I'm a rabbit.'

This wasn't true — the hare just said it to fuck with him.

'On your mark, get set, *GO!*'

There was a loud bang, and the tortoise and hare both took off from the starting line.

Never, in the history of competition – athletic or otherwise, human or otherwise, mythical or otherwise – has anyone ever kicked anyone's ass by the order of magnitude that the hare kicked the ass of that goddamn fucking tortoise that afternoon.

Within seconds, the hare was in the lead by hundreds of yards. Within minutes, the hare had taken the lead by more than a mile. The tortoise crawled on, slow and steady, but as he became anxious at having lost sight of his competitor and panicked over what he seemed to have done to his legacy, he started speeding up: less slow, less steady. But it hardly mattered. Before long – less than twenty minutes after the seven-mile race had begun – word worked its way back to the beginning of the race that the hare had not only won the contest, and had not only recorded a time that was a personal best, but had also set world records not only for all hares but also for leporids and indeed all mammals under twenty pounds. When news reached the tortoise, still essentially under the banner of the starting line, he fainted. 'Oh, now *he's* napping?! Isn't *that* rich,' heckled a nearby goat, drunk on radish wine.

Those who didn't know the context – who hadn't heard about the first race – never realized what was so important about this one. 'A tortoise raced a hare, and the hare won? Okay.' They didn't understand the story, so they didn't repeat it, and it never became known. But those who were there for both contests knew what was so special about what they had witnessed: slow and steady wins the race, till truth and talent claim their place.

(2014)

★

The Moth and the Star
by James Thurber

A young and impressionable moth once set his heart on a certain star. He told his mother about this and she counselled him to set his heart on a bridge lamp instead. 'Stars aren't the thing to hang around,' she said; 'lamps are the thing to hang around.' 'You get somewhere that way,' said the moth's father. 'You don't get anywhere chasing stars.' But the moth would not heed the words of either parent. Every evening at dusk when the star came out he would start flying toward it and every morning at dawn he would crawl back home worn out with his endeavor. One day his father said to him, 'You haven't burned a wing in months, boy, and it looks to me as if you were never going to. All your brothers have been badly burned flying around street lamps and all your sisters have been terribly singed flying around house lamps. Come on, now, get out of here and get yourself scorched! A big strapping moth like you without a mark on him!'

The moth left his father's house, but he would not fly around street lamps and he would not fly around house lamps. He went right on trying to reach the star, which was four and one-third light years, or twenty-five trillion miles, away. The moth thought it was just caught in the top branches of an elm. He never did reach the star, but he went right on trying, night after night, and when he was a very, very old moth he began to think that he really had reached the star and he went around saying so. This gave him a deep and lasting pleasure, and he lived to a great old age. His parents and his brothers and his sisters had all been burned to death when they were quite young.

Moral: Who flies afar from the sphere of our sorrow is here today and here tomorrow.

(1940)

★

Escape at Bedtime
by Robert Louis Stevenson

The lights from the parlour and kitchen shone out
    Through the blinds and the windows and bars;
And high overhead and all moving about,
    There were thousands of millions of stars.
There ne'er were such thousands of leaves on a tree,
    Nor of people in church or the Park,
As the crowds of the stars that looked down on me,
    And that glittered and winked in the dark.

The Dog, and the Plough, and the Hunter, and all,
    And the star of the sailor, and Mars,
These shown in the sky, and the pail by the wall
    Would be half full of water and stars.
They saw me at last, and they chased me with cries,
    And they soon had me packed into bed;
But the glory kept shining and bright in my eyes,
    And the stars going round in my head.

(1885)

★

80

The Sultan Shahriar has vowed to kill a new wife every morning after their 'wedding' but his latest, the vizier's daughter Shahrazad, has a plan: she will distract him from his purpose by telling him stories. Night after night – over a thousand and one nights – Shahriar postpones her execution because he wants to hear more. In this way Shahrazad uses her wits and her tongue to save her life and that of all other women condemned by her husband.

The Arabian Nights is primarily a book about storytelling. It's a collection that celebrates the power of stories to lead experience, and many of them, like the story of the Greek King and the Physician Duban, issue warnings about comeuppances of dishonest brokers and the punishments that will befall them. As with fairy tales, the stories warn against bad faith, cruelty and capriciousness, promising that eventually, fortune will favour the downtrodden, the poor, and the wrongfully accused. But this narrative therapy isn't soothing. These aren't sleepy-making bedtime stories, and they don't shrink from scenes of violence and horror. This particular tale of posthumous vengeance is a story of cunning rough justice and one of the shapeliest in the *Nights*: revenge is wishful thinking, as well as a powerful source of reader and listener's pleasure (though some disapprove of this effect). The plot has had a long afterlife, and inspired, for example, Umberto Eco's *The Name of the Rose*. In the world of the story, at least, the treacherous tyrant gets his due.

The Tale of King Yunan and the Sage Duban
(from The Arabian Nights)

There was once a king called Yunan, who reigned in one of the cities of Persia, in the province of Zuman. This king was afflicted with leprosy, which had defied the physicians and the sages, who, for all the medicines they gave him to drink and all the ointments they applied, were unable to cure him. One day there came to the city of King Yunan a sage called Duban. This sage had read all sorts of books, Greek, Persian, Turkish, Arabic, Byzantine, Syriac, and Hebrew, had studied the sciences, and had learned their groundwork, as well as their principles and basic benefits. Thus he was versed in all the sciences, from philosophy to the lore of plants and herbs, the harmful as well as the beneficial. A few days after he arrived in the city of King Yunan, the sage heard about the king and his leprosy and the fact that the physicians and the sages were unable to cure him. On the following day, when God's morning dawned and His sun rose, the sage Duban put on his best clothes, went to King Yunan and, introducing himself, said, 'Your Majesty, I have heard of that which has afflicted your body and heard that many physicians have treated you without finding a way to cure you. Your Majesty, I can treat you without giving you any medicine to drink or ointment to apply.' When the king heard this, he said, 'If you succeed, I will bestow on you riches that would be enough for you and your grandchildren. I will bestow favours on you, and I will make you my companion and friend.' The king bestowed robes of honour on the sage, treated him kindly, and then asked him, 'Can you really cure me from my leprosy without any medicine to drink or ointment to apply?' The sage replied, 'Yes, I will cure you externally.' The king was astonished, and he began to feel respect as well as great affection for the sage. He said, 'Now, sage, do what you have promised.' The sage replied, 'I hear and obey. I will do it tomorrow morning, the Almighty God willing.' Then the sage went to the city, rented a house, and there he distilled and extracted medicines and drugs. Then with his great knowledge and skill, he fashioned a mallet with a curved end, hollowed the mallet, as well as the handle, and filled the handle with his medicines and drugs. He likewise made a ball. When he had perfected and prepared everything, he went on the following day to King Yunan and kissed the ground before him . . .

He asked him to ride to the playground to play with the ball and mallet. The king rode out, attended by his chamberlains, princes, viziers, and lords and eminent men of the realm. When the king was seated, the sage Duban entered, offered him the mallet, and said, 'O happy King, take this mallet, hold it in your hand, and as you race on the playground, hold the grip tightly in your fist, and hit the ball. Race until you perspire, and the medicine will ooze from the grip into your perspiring hand, spread to your wrist, and circulate through your entire body. After you perspire and the medicine spreads in your body, return to your royal palace, take a bath, and go to sleep. You will wake up cured, and that is all there is to it.' King Yunan took the mallet from the sage Duban and mounted his horse. The attendants threw the ball before the king, who, holding the grip tightly in his fist, followed it and struggled excitedly to catch up with it and hit it. He kept galloping after the ball and hitting it until his palm and the rest of his body began to perspire, and the medicine began to ooze from the handle and flow through his entire body. When the sage Duban was certain that the medicine had oozed and spread through the king's body, he advised him to return to his palace and go immediately to the bath. The king went to the bath and washed himself thoroughly. Then he put on his clothes, left the bath, and returned to his palace.

As for the sage Duban, he spent the night at home, and early in the morning, he went to the palace and asked for permission to see the king. When he was allowed in, he entered and kissed the ground before the king; then, pointing toward him with his hand, he began to recite the following verses:

> The virtues you fostered are great;
> For who but you could sire them?
> Yours is the face whose radiant light
> Effaces the night dark and grim.
> Forever beams your radiant face;
> That of the world is still in gloom.
> You rained on us with ample grace,
> As the clouds rain on thirsty hills,
> Expending your munificence,
> Attaining your magnificence.

When the sage Duban finished reciting these verses, the king stood up and embraced him. Then he seated the sage beside him, and with attentiveness and smiles, engaged him in conversation. Then the king bestowed on the sage robes of honour, gave him gifts and endowments, and granted his wishes. For when the king had looked at himself the morning after the bath, he found that his body was clear of leprosy, as clear and pure as silver. He therefore felt exceedingly happy and in a very generous mood. Thus when he went in the morning to the reception hall and sat on his throne, attended by the Mamluks and chamberlains, in the company of the viziers and the lords of the realm, and the sage Duban presented himself, as we have mentioned, the king stood up, embraced him, and seated him beside him. He treated him attentively and drank and ate with him . . .

King Yunan bestowed favours on the sage, gave him robes of honour, and granted his wishes. At the end of the day he gave the sage a thousand dinars and sent him home. The king, who was amazed at the skill of the sage Duban, said to himself, 'This man has treated me externally, without giving me any draught to drink or ointment to apply. His is indeed a great wisdom for which he deserves to be honoured and rewarded. He shall become my companion, confidant, and close friend.' Then the king spent the night, happy at his recovery from his illness, at his good health, and at the soundness of his body . . .

In the morning, the king went to the royal reception hall, and the princes and viziers came to stand in attendance. It happened that King Yunan had a vizier who was sinister, greedy, envious, and fretful, and when he saw that the sage had found favour with the king, who bestowed on him much money and many robes of honour, he feared that the king would dismiss him and appoint the sage in his place; therefore, he envied the sage and harboured ill will against him, for nobody is free from envy. The envious vizier approached the king and, kissing the ground before him, said, 'O excellent King and glorious Lord, it was by your kindness and with your blessing that I rose to prominence; therefore, if I fail to advise you on a grave matter, I am not my father's son. If the great

King and noble Lord commands, I shall disclose the matter to him.' The king was upset and asked, 'Damn you, what advice have you got?' The vizier replied, 'Your Majesty, "He who considers not the end, fortune is not his friend." I have seen your Majesty make a mistake, for you have bestowed favours on your enemy who has come to destroy your power and steal your wealth. Indeed, you have pampered him and shown him many favours, but I fear that he will do you harm.' The king asked, 'Whom do you accuse, whom do you have in mind, and at whom do you point the finger?' The vizier replied, 'If you are asleep, wake up, for I point the finger at the sage Duban, who has come from Byzantium.' The king replied, 'Damn you, is he my enemy? To me he is the most faithful, the dearest, and the most favoured of people, for this sage has treated me simply by making me hold something in my hand and has cured me from the disease that had defied the physician and the sages and rendered them helpless. In all the world, east and west, near and far, there is no one like him, yet you accuse him of such a thing. From this day onward, I will give him every month a thousand dinars, in addition to his rations and regular salary. Even if I were to share my wealth and my kingdom with him, it would be less than he deserves. I think that you have said what you said because you envy him . . . you, being envious of this wise man, would like me to kill him and regret it afterward.'

When the vizier heard what King Yunan said, he replied, 'O great King, what harm has this sage done to me? Why, he has not harmed me in any way. I am telling you all this out of love and fear for you.' . . . The vizier added, 'Your Majesty, if you trust, befriend, and bestow favours on this sage, he will plot to destroy you and cause your death. Your Majesty should realize that I know for certain that he is a foreign agent who has come to destroy you. Haven't you seen that he cured you externally, simply with something you held in your hand?' King Yunan, who was beginning to feel angry, replied, 'You are right, vizier. The sage may well be what you say and may have come to destroy me. He who has cured me with something to hold can kill me with something to smell.' Then the king asked the vizier, 'My vizier and good counsellor, how should I deal with him?' The vizier replied, 'Send for him now and have him brought before you, and when he arrives, strikes off his head. In this way, you will attain your aim and fulfil your wish.' The king said, 'This is good and sound advice.' Then he sent for the sage Duban, who came immediately, still feeling happy at the favours, the money, and the robes the king had bestowed on him. When he entered, he pointed with his hand toward the king and began to recite the following verses:

If I have been remiss in thanking you,
For whom then have I made my verse and prose?
You granted me your gifts before I asked,
Without deferment and without excuse.
How can I fail to praise your noble deeds,
Inspired in private and in public by my muse?
I thank you for your deeds and for your gifts,
Which, though they bend my back, my care reduce.

The king asked, 'Sage, do you know why I have had you brought before me?' The sage replied, 'No, your Majesty.' The king said, 'I brought you here to have you killed and to destroy the breath of life within you.' In astonishment,

Duban asked, 'Why does your Majesty wish to have me put to death, and for what crime?' The king replied, 'I have been told that you are a spy and that you have come to kill me. Today I will have you killed before you kill me. "I will have you for lunch before you have me for dinner." Then the king called for the executioner and ordered him, saying, 'Strike off the head of this sage and rid me of him! Strike!'

When the sage heard what the king said, he knew that because he had been favoured by the king, someone had envied him, plotted against him, and lied to the king, in order to have him killed and get rid of him. The sage realized then that the king had little wisdom, judgment, or good sense, and he was filled with regret, when it was useless to regret. He said to himself, 'There is no power and no strength, save in God the Almighty, the Magnificent. I did a good deed but was rewarded with an evil one.' In the meantime, the king was shouting at the executioner, 'Strike off his head.' The sage implored, 'Spare me, your Majesty, and God will spare you; destroy me and God will destroy you.' King Yunan said to the sage, 'Sage, you must die, for you have cured me with a mere handle, and I fear that you can kill me with anything.' The sage replied, 'This is my reward from your Majesty. You reward good with evil.' The king said, 'Don't stall; you must die today without delay.' When the sage Duban became convinced that he was going to die, he was filled with grief and sorrow, and his eyes overflowed with tears. He blamed himself for doing a favour for one who does not deserve it and for sowing seeds in a barren soil.

Then the sage added, 'Is this my reward from your Majesty? It is like the reward of the crocodile.' The king asked, 'What is the story of the crocodile?' The sage replied, 'I am in no condition to tell you a story. For God's sake, spare me, and God will spare you. Destroy me, and God will destroy you,' and he wept bitterly.

Then several noblemen approached the king and said, 'We beg your Majesty to forgive him for our sake, for in our view, he has done nothing to deserve this.' The king replied, 'You do not know the reason why I wish to have him killed. I tell you that if I spare him, I will surely perish, for I fear that he who has cured me externally from my affliction, which had defied the Greek sages, simply by having me hold a handle, can kill me with anything I touch. I must kill him, in order to protect myself from him.' The sage Duban implored again, 'For God's sake, your Majesty, spare me, and God will spare you. Destroy me, and God will destroy you.' The king insisted, 'I must kill you.'

When the sage realized that he was surely going to die, he said, 'I beg your Majesty to postpone my execution until I return home, leave instructions for my burial, discharge my obligations, distribute alms, and donate my scientific and medical books to one who deserves them. I have in particular a book entitled *The Secret of Secrets*, which I should like to give you for safekeeping in your library.' The king asked, 'What is the secret of this book?' The sage replied, 'It contains countless secrets, but the chief one is that if your Majesty has my head struck off, opens the book on the sixth leaf, reads three lines from the left page, and speaks to me, my head will speak and answer whatever you ask.'

The king was greatly amazed and said, 'Is it possible that if I cut off your head and, as you say, open the book, read the third line, and speak to your head, it will speak to me?

This is the wonder of wonders.' Then the king allowed the sage to go and sent him home under guard. The sage settled his affairs and on the following day returned to the royal palace and found assembled there the princes, viziers, chamberlains, lords of the realm, and military officers, as well as the king's retinue, servants, and many of his citizens. The sage Duban entered, carrying an old book and kohl jar containing powder. He sat down, ordered a platter, and poured out the powder and smoothed it on the platter. Then he said to the king, 'Take this book, your Majesty, and don't open it until after my execution. When my head is cut off, let it be placed on the platter and order that it be pressed on the powder. Then open the book and begin to ask my head a question, for it will then answer you. There is no power and no strength save in God, the Almighty, the Magnificent. For God's sake, spare me, and God will spare you; destroy me, and God will destroy you.' The king replied, 'I must kill you, especially to see how your head will speak to me.' Then the king took the book and ordered the executioner to strike off the sage's head. The executioner drew his sword and, with one stroke, dropped the head in the middle of the platter, and when he pressed the head on the powder, the bleeding stopped. Then the sage Duban opened his eyes and said, 'Now, your Majesty, open the book.' When the king opened the book, he found the pages stuck. So he put his finger in his mouth, wetted it with his saliva, and opened the first page, and he kept opening the pages with difficulty until he turned seven leaves. But when he looked in the book, he found nothing written inside, and he exclaimed, 'Sage, I see nothing written in this book.' The sage replied, 'Open some more pages.' The king opened some more pages but still found nothing, and while he was doing this, the drug spread through his body – for the book had been poisoned – and he began to heave, sway, and twitch.

When the sage Duban saw that the drug had spread through the king's body and that the king was heaving and swaying, he began to recite the following verses:

For long they ruled us arbitrarily,
But suddenly vanished their powerful rule.
Had they been just, they would have happily
Lived, but they oppressed, and punishing fate
Afflicted them with ruin deservedly,
And on the morrow the world taunted them,
''Tis tit for tat; blame not just destiny.'

As the sage's head finished reciting the verses, the king fell dead, and at that very moment the head too succumbed to death.

(14th century)
Translated by Husain Haddawy

Marina Warner is known for her work in mythology and feminism. Her many books range from *Alone of All Her Sex: The Cult of the Virgin Mary* (1976) to *From the Beast to the Blonde: On Fairy Tales and Their Tellers* (1996) and *Stranger Magic: Charmed States and the Arabian Nights* (2012). Professor of English and Creative Writing at Birkbeck, University of London, she was appointed DBE in 2015.

★

When I was recently asked what my favourite story was while growing up, I had no hesitation in choosing Oscar Wilde's 'The Happy Prince'. It continues to move me immeasurably, now that I'm a grown-up and have read it to my own children at bedtime.

The Happy Prince
by Oscar Wilde

High above the city, on a tall column, stood the statue of the Happy Prince. He was gilded all over with thin leaves of fine gold, for eyes he had two bright sapphires, and a large red ruby glowed on his sword-hilt.

He was very much admired indeed. 'He is as beautiful as a weathercock,' remarked one of the Town Councillors who wished to gain a reputation for having artistic tastes; 'only not quite so useful,' he added, fearing lest people should think him unpractical, which he really was not.

'Why can't you be like the Happy Prince?' asked a sensible mother of her little boy who was crying for the moon. 'The Happy Prince never dreams of crying for anything.'

'I am glad there is someone in the world who is quite happy,' muttered a disappointed man as he gazed at the wonderful statue.

'He looks just like an angel,' said the Charity Children as they came out of the cathedral in their bright scarlet cloaks, and their clean white pinafores.

'How do you know?' said the Mathematical Master, 'you have never seen one.'

'Ah! but we have, in our dreams,' answered the children; and the Mathematical Master frowned and looked very severe, for he did not approve of children dreaming.

One night there flew over the city a little Swallow. His friends had gone away to Egypt six weeks before, but he had stayed behind, for he was in love with the most beautiful Reed. He had met her early in the spring as he was flying down the river after a big yellow moth, and had been so attracted by her slender waist that he had stopped to talk to her.

'Shall I love you?' said the Swallow, who liked to come to the point at once, and the Reed made him a low bow. So he flew round and round her, touching the water with his wings, and making silver ripples. This was his courtship, and it lasted all through the summer.

'It is a ridiculous attachment,' twittered the other Swallows, 'she has no money, and far too many relations;' and indeed the river was quite full of Reeds. Then, when the autumn came, they all flew away.

After they had gone he felt lonely, and began to tire of his lady-love. 'She has no conversation,' he said, 'and I am afraid that she is a coquette, for she is always flirting with the wind.' And certainly, whenever the wind blew, the Reed made the most graceful curtsies. 'I admit that she is domestic,' he continued, 'but I love travelling, and my wife, consequently, should love travelling also.'

'Will you come away with me?' he said finally to her; but the Reed shook her head, she was so attached to her home.

'You have been trifling with me,' he cried, 'I am off to the Pyramids. Good-bye!' and he flew away.

All day long he flew, and at night-time he arrived at the city. 'Where shall I put up?' he said; 'I hope the town has made preparations.'

Then he saw the statue on the tall column. 'I will put up

there,' he cried; 'it is a fine position with plenty of fresh air.' So he alighted just between the feet of the Happy Prince.

'I have a golden bedroom,' he said softly to himself as he looked round, and he prepared to go to sleep; but just as he was putting his head under his wing a large drop of water fell on him. 'What a curious thing!' he cried, 'there is not a single cloud in the sky, the stars are quite clear and bright, and yet it is raining. The climate in the north of Europe is really dreadful. The Reed used to like the rain, but that was merely her selfishness.'

Then another drop fell.

'What is the use of a statue if it cannot keep the rain off?' he said; 'I must look for a good chimney-pot,' and he determined to fly away.

But before he had opened his wings, a third drop fell, and he looked up, and saw – Ah! what did he see?

The eyes of the Happy Prince were filled with tears, and tears were running down his golden cheeks. His face was so beautiful in the moonlight that the little Swallow was filled with pity.

'Who are you?' he said.

'I am the Happy Prince.'

'Why are you weeping then?' asked the Swallow; 'you have quite drenched me.'

'When I was alive and had a human heart,' answered the statue, 'I did not know what tears were, for I lived in the palace of Sans-Souci, where sorrow is not allowed to enter. In the daytime I played with my companions in the garden, and in the evening I led the dance in the Great Hall. Round the garden ran a very lofty wall, but I never cared to ask what lay beyond it, everything about me was so beautiful. My courtiers called me the Happy Prince, and happy indeed I was, if pleasure be happiness. So I lived, and so I died. And now that I am dead they have set me up here so high that I can see all the ugliness and all the misery of my city, and though my heart is made of lead yet I cannot choose but weep.'

'What, is he not solid gold?' said the Swallow to himself. He was too polite to make any personal remarks out loud.

'Far away,' continued the statue in a low musical voice, 'far away in a little street there is a poor house. One of the windows is open, and through it I can see a woman seated at a table. Her face is thin and worn, and she has coarse, red hands, all pricked by the needle, for she is a seamstress. She is embroidering passion-flowers on a satin gown for the loveliest of the Queen's maids-of-honour to wear at the next Court-ball. In a bed in the corner of the room her little boy is lying ill. He has a fever, and is asking for oranges. His mother has nothing to give him but river water, so he is crying. Swallow, Swallow, little Swallow, will you not bring her the ruby out of my sword-hilt? My feet are fastened to this pedestal and I cannot move.'

'I am waited for in Egypt,' said the Swallow. 'My friends are flying up and down the Nile, and talking to the large lotus-flowers. Soon they will go to sleep in the tomb of the great King. The King is there himself in his painted coffin. He is wrapped in yellow linen, and embalmed with spices. Round his neck is a chain of pale green jade, and his hands are like withered leaves.'

'Swallow, Swallow, little Swallow,' said the Prince, 'will you not stay with me for one night, and be my messenger? The boy is so thirsty, and the mother so sad.'

'I don't think I like boys,' answered the Swallow. 'Last

summer, when I was staying on the river, there were two rude boys, the miller's sons, who were always throwing stones at me. They never hit me, of course; we swallows fly far too well for that, and besides, I come of a family famous for its agility; but still, it was a mark of disrespect.'

But the Happy Prince looked so sad that the little Swallow was sorry. 'It is very cold here,' he said; 'but I will stay with you for one night, and be your messenger.'

'Thank you, little Swallow,' said the Prince.

So the Swallow picked out the great ruby from the Prince's sword, and flew away with it in his beak over the roofs of the town.

He passed by the cathedral tower, where the white marble angels were sculptured. He passed by the palace and heard the sound of dancing. A beautiful girl came out on the balcony with her lover. 'How wonderful the stars are,' he said to her, 'and how wonderful is the power of love!'

'I hope my dress will be ready in time for the State-ball,' she answered; 'I have ordered passion-flowers to be embroidered on it; but the seamstresses are so lazy.'

He passed over the river, and saw the lanterns hanging to the masts of the ships. He passed over the Ghetto, and saw the old Jews bargaining with each other, and weighing out money in copper scales. At last he came to the poor house and looked in. The boy was tossing feverishly on his bed, and the mother had fallen asleep, she was so tired. In he hopped, and laid the great ruby on the table beside the woman's thimble. Then he flew gently round the bed, fanning the boy's forehead with his wings. 'How cool I feel,' said the boy, 'I must be getting better;' and he sank into a delicious slumber.

Then the Swallow flew back to the Happy Prince, and

told him what he had done. 'It is curious,' he remarked, 'but I feel quite warm now, although it is so cold.'

'That is because you have done a good action,' said the Prince. And the little Swallow began to think, and then he fell asleep. Thinking always made him sleepy.

When day broke he flew down to the river and had a bath. 'What a remarkable phenomenon,' said the Professor of Ornithology as he was passing over the bridge. 'A swallow in winter!' And he wrote a long letter about it to the local newspaper. Every one quoted it, it was full of so many words that they could not understand.

'To-night I go to Egypt,' said the Swallow, and he was in high spirits at the prospect. He visited all the public monuments, and sat a long time on top of the church steeple. Wherever he went the Sparrows chirruped, and said to each other, 'What a distinguished stranger!' so he enjoyed himself very much.

When the moon rose he flew back to the Happy Prince. 'Have you any commissions for Egypt?' he cried; 'I am just starting.'

'Swallow, Swallow, little Swallow,' said the Prince, 'will you not stay with me one night longer?'

'I am waited for in Egypt,' answered the Swallow. 'To-morrow my friends will fly up to the Second Cataract. The river-horse couches there among the bulrushes, and on a great granite throne sits the God Memnon. All night long he watches the stars, and when the morning star shines he utters one cry of joy, and then he is silent. At noon the yellow lions come down to the water's edge to drink. They have eyes like green beryls, and their roar is louder than the roar of the cataract.'

'Swallow, Swallow, little Swallow,' said the Prince, 'far away across the city I see a young man in a garret. He is leaning over a desk covered with papers, and in a tumbler by his side there is a bunch of withered violets. His hair is brown and crisp, and his lips are red as a pomegranate, and he has large and dreamy eyes. He is trying to finish a play for the Director of the Theatre, but he is too cold to write any more. There is no fire in the grate, and hunger has made him faint.'

'I will wait with you one night longer,' said the Swallow, who really had a good heart. 'Shall I take him another ruby?'

'Alas! I have no ruby now,' said the Prince; 'my eyes are all that I have left. They are made of rare sapphires, which were brought out of India a thousand years ago. Pluck out one of them and take it to him. He will sell it to the jeweller, and buy food and firewood, and finish his play.'

'Dear Prince,' said the Swallow, 'I cannot do that;' and he began to weep.

'Swallow, Swallow, little Swallow,' said the Prince, 'do as I command you.'

So the Swallow plucked out the Prince's eye, and flew away to the student's garret. It was easy enough to get in, as there was a hole in the roof. Through this he darted, and came into the room. The young man had his head buried in his hands, so he did not hear the flutter of the bird's wings, and when he looked up he found the beautiful sapphire lying on the withered violets.

'I am beginning to be appreciated,' he cried; 'this is from some great admirer. Now I can finish my play,' and he looked quite happy.

The next day the Swallow flew down to the harbour.

He sat on the mast of a large vessel and watched the sailors hauling big chests out of the hold with ropes. 'Heave a-hoy!' they shouted as each chest came up. 'I am going to Egypt!' cried the Swallow, but nobody minded, and when the moon rose he flew back to the Happy Prince.

'I am come to bid you good-bye,' he cried.

'Swallow, Swallow, little Swallow,' said the Prince, 'will you not stay with me one night longer?'

'It is winter,' answered the Swallow, 'and the chill snow will soon be here. In Egypt the sun is warm on the green palm-trees, and the crocodiles lie in the mud and look lazily about them. My companions are building a nest in the Temple of Baalbec, and the pink and white doves are watching them, and cooing to each other. Dear Prince, I must leave you, but I will never forget you, and next spring I will bring you back two beautiful jewels in place of those you have given away. The ruby shall be redder than a red rose, and the sapphire shall be as blue as the great sea.'

'In the square below,' said the Happy Prince, 'there stands a little match-girl. She has let her matches fall in the gutter, and they are all spoiled. Her father will beat her if she does not bring home some money, and she is crying. She has no shoes or stockings, and her little head is bare. Pluck out my other eye, and give it to her, and her father will not beat her.'

'I will stay with you one night longer,' said the Swallow, 'but I cannot pluck out your eye. You would be quite blind then.'

'Swallow, Swallow, little Swallow,' said the Prince, 'do as I command you.'

So he plucked out the Prince's other eye, and darted

down with it. He swooped past the match-girl, and slipped the jewel into the palm of her hand. 'What a lovely bit of glass,' cried the little girl; and she ran home, laughing.

Then the Swallow came back to the Prince. 'You are blind now,' he said, 'so I will stay with you always.'

'No, little Swallow,' said the poor Prince, 'you must go away to Egypt.'

'I will stay with you always,' said the Swallow, and he slept at the Prince's feet.

All the next day he sat on the Prince's shoulder, and told him stories of what he had seen in strange lands. He told him of the red ibises, who stand in long rows on the banks of the Nile, and catch goldfish in their beaks; of the Sphinx, who is as old as the world itself and lives in the desert, and knows everything; of the merchants, who walk slowly by the side of their camels, and carry amber beads in their hands; of the King of the Mountains of the Moon, who is as black as ebony, and worships a large crystal; of the great green snake that sleeps in a palm-tree, and has twenty priests to feed it with honey-cakes; and of the pygmies who sail over a big lake on large flat leaves, and are always at war with the butterflies.

'Dear little Swallow,' said the Prince, 'you tell me of marvellous things, but more marvellous than anything is the suffering of men and of women. There is no Mystery so great as Misery. Fly over my city, little Swallow, and tell me what you see there.'

So the Swallow flew over the great city, and saw the rich making merry in their beautiful houses, while the beggars were sitting at the gates. He flew into dark lanes, and saw the white faces of starving children looking out listlessly at the black streets. Under the archway of a bridge two little boys were lying in one another's arms to try and keep themselves warm. 'How hungry we are!' they said. 'You must not lie here,' shouted the Watchman, and they wandered out into the rain.

Then he flew back and told the Prince what he had seen.

'I am covered with fine gold,' said the Prince, 'you must take it off, leaf by leaf, and give it to my poor; the living always think that gold can make them happy.'

Leaf after leaf of the fine gold the Swallow picked off, till the Happy Prince looked quite dull and grey. Leaf after leaf of the fine gold he brought to the poor, and the children's faces grew rosier, and they laughed and played games in the street. 'We have bread now!' they cried.

Then the snow came, and after the snow came the frost. The streets looked as if they were made of silver, they were so bright and glistening; long icicles like crystal daggers hung down from the eaves of the houses, everybody went about in furs, and the little boys wore scarlet caps and skated on the ice.

The poor little Swallow grew colder and colder, but he would not leave the Prince, he loved him too well. He picked up crumbs outside the baker's door where the baker was not looking, and tried to keep himself warm by flapping his wings.

But at last he knew that he was going to die. He had just strength to fly up to the Prince's shoulder once more. 'Good-bye, dear Prince!' he murmured, 'will you let me kiss your hand?'

'I am glad that you are going to Egypt at last, little Swallow,' said the Prince, 'you have stayed too long here; but you must kiss me on the lips, for I love you.'

'It is not to Egypt that I am going,' said the Swallow. 'I am going to the House of Death. Death is the brother of Sleep, is he not?'

And he kissed the Happy Prince on the lips, and fell down dead at his feet.

At that moment a curious crack sounded inside the statue, as if something had broken. The fact is that the leaden heart had snapped right in two. It certainly was a dreadfully hard frost. Early the next morning the Mayor was walking in the square below in company with the Town Councillors. As they passed the column he looked up at the statue: 'Dear me! how shabby the Happy Prince looks!' he said.

'How shabby indeed!' cried the Town Councillors, who always agreed with the Mayor, and they went up to look at it.

'The ruby has fallen out of his sword, his eyes are gone, and he is golden no longer,' said the Mayor; 'in fact, he is little better than a beggar!'

'Little better than a beggar,' said the Town Councillors.

'And here is actually a dead bird at his feet!' continued the Mayor. 'We must really issue a proclamation that birds are not to be allowed to die here.' And the Town Clerk made a note of the suggestion.

So they pulled down the statue of the Happy Prince. 'As he is no longer beautiful he is no longer useful,' said the Art Professor at the University.

Then they melted the statue in a furnace, and the Mayor held a meeting of the Corporation to decide what was to be done with the metal. 'We must have another statue, of course,' he said, 'and it shall be a statue of myself.'

'Of myself,' said each of the Town Councillors, and they

quarrelled. When I last heard of them they were quarrelling still.

'What a strange thing!' said the overseer of the workmen at the foundry. 'This broken lead heart will not melt in the furnace. We must throw it away.' So they threw it on a dust-heap where the dead Swallow was also lying.

'Bring me the two most precious things in the city,' said God to one of His Angels; and the Angel brought Him the leaden heart and the dead bird.

'You have rightly chosen,' said God, 'for in my garden of Paradise this little bird shall sing for evermore, and in my city of gold the Happy Prince shall praise me.'

(1888)

In 1841, Hans Christian Andersen published the tale of master storyteller Ole Lukøje. To ready his young charges for a story, Lukøje – Danish for 'shut-eye' – would first waft magic dust into children's eyes, sending them peacefully off to sleep. This minstrel would next blow softly on their necks, until their young heads would loll down. Asleep, Lukøje was then free to work his real magic – storytelling. In Andersen's words: 'There is nobody in the world who knows so many stories as Ole Lukøje, or who can relate them so nicely.'

Of course, the proverbial sand that Lukøje blows into children's eyes has been around since before time began. During the day, as we blink, our eyelids flush out the rheum that would otherwise cluster. In sleep, of course, with our eyes closed, this sluicing does not occur. Meaning that we have sleep in our eyes on waking up, especially when children.

American poet Susan Holton recast Ole Lukøje as 'the Sandman', in 1928, in a short poem – and he has stalked popular culture's subconscious ever since, leaping from one artist's reverie into another visionary's nightmares.

Roy Orbison had the idea for his 1963 hit song 'In Dreams', which features the sandman, while 'half-asleep'. He heard a radio disc jockey announce the song as Elvis Presley's newest offering but then, frustratingly, didn't catch the end of the track, thinking to himself, 'Boy, that's good. I need to finish that. Too bad things don't happen in my dreams.' Except Orbison then woke up. He wiped the sleep from his eyes and, within twenty feverish minutes, had finished writing the song of his dreams. 'In Dreams' is today considered a classic, its instrumentation underscoring a 'magic night' of unconsciousness, dreamily evoked by Orbison's ethereal vocals.

By all accounts, Orbison was alarmed when, twenty-three years later, David Lynch's film *Blue Velvet* (1986) nightmarishly appropriated his ballad. A grotesque rendition of 'In Dreams', and its account of the tiptoeing, whispering, 'candy coloured-clown they call the sandman' sends the demonic Frank Booth, played by Dennis Hopper, into a tailspin. Lynch had twisted Orbison's lovelorn, little night music into a sinister phantasm.

Yet, today, the sandman is probably more associated in the popular cultural consciousness with Neil Gaiman than with Lynch, Orbison or Andersen. Gaiman's graphic novel *The Sandman* is a seminal classic of its genre. Its writer has since continually enchanted readers the world over, weaving webs over grown-ups and children alike, for instance in 2014's *The Sleeper and the Spindle* (with Chris Riddell).

In *The Sandman*, Gaiman and his artists tell the story of Morpheus, the King of Dreams, and his kin, the Endless. In the first volume, 'Preludes and Nocturnes', this oneiromancer – his angular frame covered head-to-toe by black, much like Gaiman himself – must quest through hell and back to retrieve his pouch of sand, his helm and his ruby. Indeed, the narratives of both *The Sandman* and *The Sleeper and the Spindle* are bedecked with rubies. They blush within the plots – as in 'The Happy Prince' – and glow also in this next tale from Neil Gaiman.

'Tales and dreams are the shadow-truths that will endure when mere facts are dust and ashes, and forgot,' says Morpheus in 'Dream Country', volume three of *The Sandman*.

Mr Gaiman, bring me a dream . . .

Diamonds and Pearls: A Fairy Tale
by Neil Gaiman

Once upon the olden times, when the trees walked and the stars danced, there was a girl whose mother died, and a new mother came and married her father, bringing her own daughter with her. Soon enough the father followed his first wife to the grave, leaving his daughter behind him.

The new mother did not like the girl and treated her badly, always favouring her own daughter, who was indolent and rude. One day, her stepmother gave the girl, who was only eighteen, twenty dollars to buy her drugs. 'Don't stop on the way,' she said.

So the girl took the twenty-dollar bill, and put an apple into her purse, for the way was long, and she walked out of the house and down to the end of the street, where the wrong side of town began.

She saw a dog tied to a lamppost, panting and uncomfortable in the heat, and the girl said, 'Poor thing.' She gave it water.

The elevator was out of service. The elevator there was always out of service. Halfway up the stairs she saw a hooker, with a swollen face, who stared up at her with yellow eyes. 'Here,' said the girl. She gave the hooker the apple.

She went up to the dealer's floor and she knocked on the door three times. The dealer opened the door and stared at her and said nothing. She showed him the twenty-dollar bill.

Then she said, 'Look at the state of this place,' and she bustled in. 'Don't you ever clean up in here? Where are your cleaning supplies?'

The dealer shrugged. Then he pointed to a closet. The girl opened it and found a broom and a rag. She filled the bathroom sink with water and she began to clean the place.

When the rooms were cleaner, the girl said, 'Give me the stuff for my mother.'

He went into the bedroom, came back with a plastic bag. The girl pocketed the bag and walked down the stairs.

'Lady,' said the hooker. 'The apple was good. But I'm hurting real bad. You got anything?'

The girl said, 'It's for my mother.'

'Please?'

'You poor thing.'

The girl hesitated, then she gave her the packet. 'I'm sure my stepmother will understand,' she said.

She left the building. As she passed, the dog said, 'You shine like a diamond, girl.'

She got home. Her mother was waiting in the front room. 'Where is it?' she demanded.

'I'm sorry,' said the girl. Diamonds dropped from her lips, rattled across the floor.

Her stepmother hit her.

'Ow!' said the girl, a ruby-red cry of pain, and a ruby fell from her mouth.

Her stepmother fell to her knees, picked up the jewels. 'Pretty,' she said. 'Did you steal them?'

The girl shook her head, scared to speak.

'Do you have any more in there?'

The girl shook her head, mouth tightly closed.

The stepmother took the girl's tender arm between her finger and her thumb and pinched as hard as she could, squeezed until the tears glistened in the girl's eyes, but she said nothing. So her stepmother locked the girl in her windowless bedroom, so she could not get away.

The woman took the diamonds and the ruby to Al's Pawn and Gun, on the corner, where Al gave her five hundred dollars no questions asked.

Then she sent her other daughter off to buy drugs for her.

The girl was selfish. She saw the dog panting in the sun, and, once she was certain that it was chained up and could not follow, she kicked at it. She pushed past the hooker on the stair. She reached the dealer's apartment and knocked on the door. He looked at her, and she handed him the twenty without speaking. On her way back down, the hooker on the stair said, 'Please . . .?' but the girl did not even slow.

'Bitch!' called the hooker.

'Snake,' said the dog, when she passed it on the sidewalk.

Back home, the girl took out the drugs, then opened her mouth to say, 'Here,' to her mother. A small frog, brightly coloured, slipped from her lips. It leapt from her arm to the wall, where it hung and stared at them unblinking.

'Oh my god,' said the girl. 'That's just disgusting.' Five

more coloured tree frogs, and one small red, black and yellow-banded snake.

'Black against red,' said the girl. 'Is that poisonous?' (Three more tree frogs, a cane toad, a small blind white snake, and a baby iguana.) She backed away from them.

Her mother, who was not afraid of snakes or of anything, kicked at the banded snake, which bit her leg. The woman screamed and flailed, and her daughter also began to scream, a long loud scream which fell from her lips as a healthy adult python.

The girl, the first girl, whose name was Amanda, heard the screams and then the silence but she could do nothing to find out what was happening.

She knocked on the door. No one opened it. No one said anything. The only sounds she could hear were rustlings, as if of something huge and legless slipping across the carpet.

When Amanda got hungry, too hungry for words, she began to speak.

'Thou still unravish'd bride of quietness,' she began. 'Thou foster child of Silence and slow Time . . .'

She spoke, although the words were choking her.

'Beauty is truth, truth beauty, – that is all ye know on earth, and all ye need to know . . .' A final sapphire clicked across the wooden floor of Amanda's closet room.

The silence was absolute.

(2008)

★

Jacked
by Michael Cunningham

This is not a smart boy we're taking about. This is not a kid who can be trusted to remember to take his mother to her chemo appointment, or to close the windows when it rains.

Never mind asking him to sell the cow, when he and his mother are out of cash, and the cow is their last asset.

We're talking about a boy who doesn't get halfway to town with his mother's sole remaining possession before he's sold the cow to some stranger for a handful of beans. The guy claims they're magic beans, and that, it seems, is enough for Jack. He doesn't even ask what variety of magic the beans supposedly deliver. Maybe they'll transform themselves into seven beautiful wives for him. Maybe they'll turn into the seven deadly sins, and buzz around him like flies for the rest of his life.

Jack isn't doubtful. Jack isn't big on questions. Jack is the boy who says, *Wow, dude, magic beans, really?*

There are any number of boys like Jack. Boys who prefer the crazy promise, the long shot, who insist that they're natural-born winners. They have a great idea for a screenplay – they just need, you know, someone to write it for them. They DJ at friends' parties, believing a club owner will wander in sooner or later and hire them to spin for multitudes. They drop out of vocational school because they can see, after a semester or two, that it's a direct path to loserdom – better to live in their childhood bedrooms, temporarily unemployed, until fame and prosperity arrive.

Is Jack's mother upset when he strides back into the

house, holds out his hand, and shows her what he's gotten for the cow? She is.

What have I done, how exactly have all the sacrifices I've made, all the dinners I put together out of nothing and ate hardly any of myself, how exactly did I raise you to be this cavalier and unreliable, could you please explain that to me, please?

Is Jack disappointed by his mother's poverty of imagination, her lack of nerve in the face of life's gambles, her continued belief in the budget-conscious, off-brand caution that's gotten her exactly nowhere? He is.

I mean, Mom, look at this house. Don't you think thrift is some kind of death? Ask yourself. Since Dad died, why hasn't anyone come around? Not even Hungry Hank. Not even Half-Wit Willie.

Jack doesn't want, or need, to hear her answer, though it runs silently through her mind.

I have my beautiful boy, I see strong young shoulders bent over the washbasin every morning. What would I want with Hungry Hank's yellow teeth, or Half-Wit Willie's bent-up body?

Nevertheless, her son has sold the cow for a handful of beans. Jack's mother tosses the beans out the window, and sends him to bed without supper.

Fairy tales are generally moral tales. In the bleaker version of this one, mother and son both starve to death.

That lesson would be: Mothers, try to be realistic about your imbecilic sons, no matter how charming their sly little grins, no matter how heartbreaking the dark-gold tousle of their hair. If you romanticize them, if you insist on virtues they clearly lack, if you persist in your blind desire to have raised a wise child, one who'll be helpful in your old age . . . don't be surprised if you find that you've fallen on the bathroom floor, and end up spending the night there, because he's out drinking with his friends until dawn.

That is not, however, the story of 'Jack and the Beanstalk'.

The implication of this particular tale is: Trust strangers. Believe in magic.

In 'Jack and the Beanstalk', the stranger has not lied. The next morning, Jack's bedroom window is obscured by rampant green. He looks out into leaves the size of skillets, and a stalk as thick as an oak's trunk. When he cranes his neck upward, he sees that the beanstalk is so tall it vanishes into the clouds.

Right. Invest in desert real estate, where an interstate high-way is certain to be built soon. Get in on the ground floor of your uncle's revolutionary new age-reversal system. Use half the grocery money to buy lottery tickets every week.

Jack, being Jack, does not ask questions, nor does he wonder if climbing the beanstalk is the best possible idea.

At the beanstalk's apex, on the upper side of the cloud-bank, he finds himself standing before a giant's castle, built on a particularly fleecy rise of cloud. The castle is dizzyingly white, prone to a hint of tremble, as if built of concentrated clouds; as if a proper rainstorm could reduce it to an enormous, pearly puddle.

Being Jack, he walks right up to the titanic snow-colored door. Who, after all, wouldn't be glad to see him?

Before he can knock, though, he hears his name called by a voice so soft it might merely be a gust of wind that's taught itself to say, *Jaaaaack*.

The wind coalesces into a cloud-girl; a maiden of the mist.

She tells Jack that the giant who lives in the castle killed Jack's father, years ago. The giant would have killed the infant Jack as well, but Jack's mother so ardently pled her case, holding the baby to her bosom, that the giant spared Jack, on the condition that Jack's mother never reveal the cause of his father's death.

Maybe that's why Jack's mother has always treated him as if he were bounty and hope, incarnate.

The mist-girl tells Jack that everything the giant owns belongs rightfully to him. Then she vanishes, as quickly as the wisp of an exhaled cigarette.

Jack, however, being Jack, had assumed already that everything the giant owns – everything everybody owns – rightfully belongs to him. And he'd never really believed that story about his father getting dysentery on a business trip to Brazil.

He raps on the door, which is opened by the giant's wife. The wife may once have been pretty, but no trace of loveliness remains. Her hair is thinning, her housecoat stained. She's as offhandedly careworn as a fifty-foot tall version of Jack's mother.

Jack announces he's hungry, that he comes from a place where the world fails to provide.

The giant's wife, who rarely receives visitors of any kind, is happy to see a handsome, miniature man-child standing at her door. She invites him in, feeds him breakfast, though she warns him that if her husband comes home, he'll eat *Jack* for breakfast.

Does Jack stick around anyway? Of course he does. Does the giant arrive home unexpectedly? He does.

He booms from the vastness of the hallway:

Fe fi fo fum
I smell the blood of an Englishman.
Be he alive or be he dead,
I'll grind his bones to make my bread.

The giant's wife conceals Jack in, of all places, the very saucepan in which her husband would cook him. She's barely got the lid put down when the giant lumbers in.

The giant is robustly corpulent, thundering, strident, dangerous in the way of barroom thugs, of any figure who is comical in theory (he wears a jerkin and tights) but truly threatening in fact, simply because he's fool enough and drunk enough to do serious harm; simply because he's a stranger to reason, because killing a man with a pool cue seems like a justifiable response to some vaguely insulting remark.

The giantess assures her husband that he merely smells the ox she's cooked him for lunch.

Really?

Here we move, briefly, into farce. There's nowhere else for us to go.

> Giant: *I know what ox smells like. I know what the blood of*
> *an Englishman smells like.*
> Giantess: *Well, this is a new kind of ox. It's flavored.*
> Giant: *What?*
> Giantess: *It's brand new. You can also get Tears of a Princess*
> *Ox. You can get Wicked Queen Envy Ox.*

She serves him the ox. A whole ox.

Giant: *Hm. Tastes like regular ox to me.*

Giantess: *Maybe I won't get this kind anymore.*

Giant: *There's nothing wrong with regular ox.*

Giantess: *But a little variety, every now and then . . .*

Giant: *You get suckered in too easily.*

Giantess: *I know. No one knows that better than I do.*

After the giant has eaten the ox, he commands his wife to bring him his bags of gold, so he can perform the day's tally. This is a ritual, a comforting reminder that he's just as rich today as he was yesterday, and the day before.

Once he's content that he still has all the gold he's ever had, he lays his colossal head down on the tabletop and falls into the kind of deep, wheezing nap anybody would want to take after eating an ox.

Which is Jack's cue to climb back out of the saucepan, grab the bags of gold, and take off.

And which would be the giantess's cue to resuscitate her marriage. It would be the time for her to holler, 'Thief,' and claim never to have seen Jack before.

By evening, she and her husband could have sat laughing at the table, each holding aloft one of Jack's testicles on a toothpick before popping them in their mouths. They could have declared to each other, It's enough. It's enough to be rich, and live on a cloud together; to age companionably; to want nothing more than they've got already.

The giant's wife seems to agree, however, that robbing her husband is a good move.

We all know couples like this. Couples who've been waging the battle for decades; who seem to believe that if finally, someday, one of them can prove the other wrong – deeply wrong, soul-wrong – they'll be exonerated, and released. Amassing the evidence, working toward the proof, can swallow an entire life.

Jack and his mother, wealthy now (Jack's mother has invested the gold in stocks and real estate), don't move to a better neighborhood. They can't abandon the beanstalk. So they rebuild. Seven fireplaces, cathedral ceilings, indoor and outdoor pools.

They continue living together, mother and son. Jack doesn't date. Who knows what succession of girls and boys sneak in through the sliding glass doors at night, after the mother has sunk to the bottom of her own private lake, with the help of Absolut and Klonopin?

Jack and his mother are doing fine. Especially considering that, recently, they were down to their last cow.

But as we all know, it's never enough. No matter how much it is.

Jack and his mother still don't have a black American Express card. They don't have a private plane. They don't own an island.

And so, Jack goes up to the beanstalk again. He knocks for a second time at the towering cloud-door.

The giantess answers again. She seems not to recognize Jack, and it's true that he's no longer dressed in the cheap lounge lizard outfit – the tight pants and synthetic shirt he boosted at the mall. He's all Marc Jacobs now. He has a shockingly expensive haircut.

But still. Does the giantess really believe a different, better-dressed boy has appeared at her door, one with the same sly grin and the same dark-gold hair, however improved the cut?

115

There is, after all, the well-known inclination to continue to sabotage our marriages, without ever leaving them. And there's this, too. There's the appeal of the young thief who robs you, and climbs back down off your cloud. It's possible to love that boy, in a wistful and hopeless way. It's possible to love his greed and narcissism, to grant him that which is beyond your own capacities: heedlessness, cockiness, a self-devotion so pure it borders on the divine.

The scenario plays itself out again. This time, when the fifty-foot-tall dim-witted thug *Fi fi fo fums*, early and unexpected, from the hallway, the giantess hides Jack in the oven.

We don't need advanced degrees to understand something about her habit of flirtation with eating Jack.

The second exchange between giant and giantess – the one about how he smells the blood of an Englishman, and she assures him it's just the bullock she's fixed for lunch – is too absurd even for farce.

Let's imagine an unconscious collusion between husband and wife, then. He knows something's up. He knows she's hiding something, or someone. Let's imagine he prefers a wife who's capable of deceit. A wife who can manage something more interesting than drudgery and peevish, drowsy fidelity.

This time, after polishing off the bullock, the giant demands to be shown the hen that lays the golden eggs. And, a moment later, there she is: a prizewinning pullet, as regal and self-important as it's possible for a chicken to be. She stands before the giant, her claw-tipped, bluish feet firmly planted on the tabletop, and, with a low cackle of triumph, lays another golden egg.

Which the giant picks up and examines. It's the daily egg. They never vary. The giant, however, maintains his attachment to the revisiting of his own bounty, as he does to his postprandial snooze, face down on the tabletop, wheezing out blasts of bullock-reeking breath, emitting a lake of drool.

Again, Jack emerges (this time from the oven), and makes off with the hen. Again, the giantess watches him steal her husband's joy and fortune. Again, she adores the meanness of Jack, a small-time crook dressed now in two-hundred-dollar jeans. She envies him his rapaciousness, his insatiability. She who has let herself go, who prepares the meals and does the dishes and wanders, with no particular purpose, from room to room. She who finds herself strangely glad to be in the presence of someone avaricious and heartless and uncaring.

Are we surprised to learn that, a year or so later, Jack goes up the beanstalk one more time?

By now, there's nothing left for him and his mother to buy. They've got the car and driver, they've got the private plane, they own that small, otherwise-uninhabited island in the Lesser Antilles, where they've built a house that's staffed year-round, in anticipation of their single annual visit.

We always want more, though. Some of us want more than others, it's true, but we always want more of . . . something. More love, more youth, more . . .

On his third visit, Jack decides not to press his luck with the giantess. This time, he sneaks in through the back.

He finds the giant and giantess unaltered, though it would seem they've had to cut back, having lost their gold and their magic hen. The castle has dissolved a bit – sky knifes in through gaps in the cloud-walls. The daily lunch of an entire animal runs more along the lines of an antelope or an ibex, sinewy and dark-tasting, no longer the fattened, farm-tender ox or bullock of their salad days.

Still, habits resist change. The giant devours his creature, spits out horns and hooves, and demands his last remaining treasure: a magic harp.

The harp is a prize of a different order entirely. Who knows about its market value? It's nothing so simple as gold coins or golden eggs. It too is made of gold but it's not prosaic in the way of actual currency.

It's a harp like any harp – strings, knee, neck, tuning pins – but its head is the head of a woman, slightly smaller than an apple, more stern than beautiful; more Athena than Botticelli Venus. And it can play itself.

The giant commands the harp to play. The harp obliges. It plays a tune unknown on the earth below; a melody that emanates from clouds and stars, a song of celestial movements, the music of the spheres, that which composers like Bach and Chopin came close to approximating but which, being ethereal, cannot be produced by instruments made of brass or wood, cannot be summoned by human breath or fingering.

The harp plays the giant into his nap. That gargantuan head makes its thudding daily contact with the tabletop.

What must the giantess think, when Jack creeps in and grabs the harp? *Again? You're kidding? You actually want the very last of our treasures?*

Is she appalled, or relieved, or both? Does she experience some ecstasy of total loss? Or has she had enough? Is she going to put an end, at last, to Jack's voracity?

We'll never know. Because it's the harp, not the giantess, who finally protests. As Jack makes for the door, the harp calls out, 'Master, help me, I'm being stolen.'

The giant wakes, looks around uncertainly. He's been dreaming. Can this be his life, his kitchen, his haggard and grudging wife?

By the time he's up and after Jack, Jack has already traversed the cloud-field and reached the top of the bean-stalk, holding firm to the harp as the harp cries out for rescue.

It's a race down the beanstalk. Jack is hampered by his grip on the harp – he can only climb one-handed – but the giant has far more trouble than Jack in negotiating the stalk itself, which, for the giant, is thin and unsteady, like the rope he was forced to climb in gym class when he was a weepy, lonely boy.

As Jack nears the ground, he calls to his mother to bring him an axe. He's lucky – she's semi-sober today. She rushes out with an axe. Jack chops the beanstalk down, while the giant is still as high as a hawk circling for rabbits.

The beanstalk falls like a redwood. The giant hits the earth so hard his body crashes through the topsoil, imbeds itself ten feet deep, leaves a giant-shaped chasm in the middle of a cornfield.

It's a mercy, of sorts. What, after all, did the giant have left, with his gold and his hen and his harp all gone?

Jack has had the giant-hole filled in, right over the giant's body, and in a rare act of piety he's ordered a grove of lilac bushes planted over the giant's resting-place. If you were to

119

look down at the lilac grove from above, you'd see that it's shaped like an enormous man, arms and legs akimbo; a man frozen in an attitude of oddly voluptuous surrender.

Jack and his mother prosper. Jack, in his rare moments of self-questioning, remembers what the mist-girl told him, years earlier. The giant committed a crime. Jack has, since infancy, been entitled to everything the giant owned. This salves the stripling conscience that's been growing feebly within Jack as he's gotten older.

Jack's mother has started collecting handbags (she especially prizes her limited-edition Murakami Cherry Blossom by Louis Vuitton), and meeting her girlfriends for lunches that can go on until four or five p.m. Jack sometimes acquires girls and boys in neighbouring towns, sometimes rents them, but always arranges for them to arrive late at night, in secret. Jack is not, as we know, the brightest bulb on the Christmas tree, but he's canny enough to understand that only his mother will uncritically adore him forever; that if one of the girls or boys were suffered to stay, the fits of mysterious frustration, the critiques, would set in soon enough.

The hen, who cares only for the eggs she produces, lays a gold one every day, and lives contentedly in her concrete coop with her twenty-four-hour guard, Jack's attempt at exterminating all the local foxes having proven futile.

Only the harp is restive and sorrowful. Only the harp looks yearningly out through the window of the room in which it resides, a room that affords it a view of the lilac grove planted over the giant's imbedded body. The harp, long mute, dreams of the time when it lived on a cloud and played music too beautiful for anyone but the giant to hear.

(2015)

★

Les Murray, often called the 'Bush Bard', is widely recognized as Australia's greatest living poet. Murray's poetry is dexterous, down-to-earth and laconic: in these ways, his ballads sing a quintessentially Australian 'dirt music'.

Murray has framed his poem 'The Sleepout' in particularly personal terms, by explaining his own origins: 'I come from a verandah on a dairy farm between Foster and Gloucester on the north coast of New South Wales – forest and farming country. People up there still, to some extent, sleep in verandah rooms, known as sleepouts.'

However homespun Murray's introduction, 'The Sleepout' is far from simple. It conjures the timelessness of childhood dreams, with all its tactile minutiae and sensual specificity ('splinters picked lint off warm linen'), before spinning out into the encroaching outback night ('the never-fenced country'), crescendoing into a transcendent rhapsody, immutable and irresistible.

The Sleepout
by Les Murray

Childhood sleeps in a verandah room
in an iron bed close to the wall
where the winter over the railing
swelled the blind on its timber boom

and splinters picked lint off warm linen
and the stars were out over the hill;
then one wall of the room was forest
and all things in there were to come.

Breathings climbed up on the verandah
when dark cattle rubbed at the corner
and sometimes dim towering rain stood
for forest, and the dry cave hunched woollen.

Inside the forest was lamplit
along tracks to a starry creek bed
and beyond lay the never-fenced country,
its full billabongs all surrounded

by animals and birds, in loud crustings,
and something kept leaping up amongst them.
And out there, to kindle whenever
dark found it, hung the daylight moon.

                                                    (1987)

This next story, which was at one point entitled 'I Dropped Off', depicts a coming of age amid an English pastoral.

A middle-aged woman drifts off (adult energies do trough markedly in the mid-afternoon and so short cat naps (of 10–30 minutes) are advisable, as the brain's alertness can thereby be renewed for between two and three hours afterwards).

Our nearby narrator – then a child – is, in contrast, abuzz with stories, and all the formative hopes and fears that they conjure. Soon her musings take flight, like butterflies. The girl's imaginings give way to vivid daydream. Images cascade through her mind, and our own as reader, charting a dreamscape of internalized wanderings . . .

The pair's semi-conscious states eventually comingle and commune somehow, despite the age gap. When the grown-up

122

awakes, she tells the child – who has been neither seen nor heard – that 'only young people should be seen asleep'.

True enough. Although, some might say, we are all children when we sleep.

The Idea of Age
by Elizabeth Taylor

When I was a child, people's ages did not matter; but age mattered. Against the serious idea of age I did not match the grown-ups I knew – who had all an ageless quality – though time unspun itself from year to year. Christmases lay far apart from one another, birthdays even farther; but that time was running on was shown in many ways. I 'shot out' of my frocks, as my mother put it. By the time that I was ten, I had begun to discard things from my heart and to fasten my attention on certain people whose personalities affected me in a heady and delicious way.

Though the years drew me upwards at a great pace, as if they were full of a hurried, *growing* warmth, the seasons still held. Summers netted me in bliss, endlessly. Winter did not promise spring. But when the spring came, I felt that it was there for ever. I had no dread that a few days would filch it from me, and in fact a few days were much when every day was endless.

In the summer holidays, when we went to the country, the spell of the long August days were coloured, intensified, by the fascinations of Mrs Vivaldi. My first thought when we arrived at the guest-house in Buckinghamshire was to look for some sign of *her* arrival – a garden hat hanging in the porch, or books from Mudie's. She came there, she made it clear, to rusticate (a word she herself used, which put a little flushed constraint upon the ladies who kept the guest-house, who felt it to be derogatory); she came to rest from the demands of London; and she did seem to be always very tired.

I remember so many of the clothes she wore, for they seemed to me unusual and beautiful. A large hat of coarse hessian sacking was surprisingly lined under the brim with gold lamé, which threw a light over her pale face. In the evenings, panels heavy with steel-bead embroidery swung away from her as she walked. She was not content to appeal only to one's sight, with her floating scarves, her fringes and tassels, but made claims upon the other senses, with scents of carnations and jasmine, with the rustling of moiré petticoats and the more solid sound of heavy amber and ivory bracelets sliding together on her wrists. Once, when we were sitting in the garden on a still afternoon, she narrowed her hand and wriggled it out of the bracelets and tried them on me. They were warm and heavy, alive like flesh. I felt this to be one of the situations I would enjoy in retrospect but find unendurable at the time. Embarrassed, inadequate, I turned the bracelets on my arm; but she had closed her eyes in the sun.

I realize now that she was not very young. Her pretty ash-blond hair had begun to have less blond, more ash; her powdered-over face was lined. Then I did not think of her as being any age. I drifted after her about house and garden, beset by her magic, endeavouring to make my mark on her.

One evening in the drawing-room she recited, for the guests, the Balcony Scene from *Romeo and Juliet* – all three parts – sitting on the end of the sofa, with her pearls laced through her fingers, her bronze shoes with pointed toes neatly together. Another evening, in that same room, she turned on the wireless and fixed the headphones over my ears (pieces of sponge lessened the pressure), and very far off, through a tinkling, scuffling, crackling atmosphere, I heard Edith Sitwell reciting through a megaphone. Mrs Vivaldi impressed me with the historical nature of the occasion. She made historical occasions seem very rare and to be fastened on to. Since then, life has been one historical occasion after another, but I remember that scene clearly and the lamplight in the room with all the beautiful china. The two ladies who kept the guest-house had come down in the world and brought cupboards full of Crown Derby with them. The wireless-set, with its coils and wires, was on a mosaic-topped table that, one day, my brother stumbled against and broke. It disintegrated almost into powder, and my mother wept. Mrs Vivaldi walked with her in the garden. I saw them going under the rose-arches – the fair head and the dark – both very tall. I thought they looked like ladies in a book by Miss Braddon.

One afternoon I was alone in the drawing-room when Mrs Vivaldi came in from the garden with a basketful of sweet-peas. As if the heat were suddenly too much for her, she sat down quite upright, in a chair, with the basket beside her, and closed her eyes.

The room was cool and shadowy, with blinds half-drawn to spare the threadbare carpet. The house seemed like a hollow shell; its subfusc life had flowed out into the garden, to the croquet lawn, to the shade of the mulberry tree, where elderly shapes sagged in deck chairs, half-covered with newspapers.

I knew that Mrs Vivaldi had not seen me. I was reading, sitting in my ungainly way on the floor, with my body slewed round so that my elbows and my book rested on the seat of a chair. Down there among the legs of furniture, I seemed only part of the overcrowded room. As I read, I ate sweets out of a rather grubby paper bag. Nothing could, I felt, have been more peaceful than that afternoon. The clock ticked, sweets dissolved in my cheek. The scent of the flowers Mrs Vivaldi had brought in began to mix with the clove smell of pinks outside. From the lawn came only an occasional grim word or two – the word 'partner' most of all, in tones of exhortation or apology – and the solid sound of the mallet on the ball. The last smells of luncheon had faded, and the last distant clatter of washing-up. Alone in the room with Mrs Vivaldi, I enjoyed the drowsy afternoon with every sense and also with peaceful feelings of devotion. I liked to be there while she slept. I had her presence without needing to make her love me, which was tiring.

Her presence must have been enough, for I remember that I sat with my back to her and only once or twice turned to glance in her direction. My book was about a large family of motherless children. I did not grudge children in books their mothers, but I did not want them to run the risk, which haunted me, of losing them. It was safer if their mother had already gone before the book began, and the wound healed, and I always tried to choose stories in which this had happened.

From time to time I glanced a little beyond the book and fell into reverie. I tried to imagine my own mother, who had gone out walking that afternoon, alone in the cherry orchard that ran down from hilltop to valley. Her restlessness often sent her off on long walks, too long for me to enjoy. I always lagged behind, thinking of my book, of the large, motherless family. In the cherry orchard it would be hot and scented, with bees scrambling into flowers, and faded-blue butterflies all over the chicory and heliotrope. But I found that I could not imagine her walking there alone; it seemed an incomplete picture that did not contain me. The reality was in this room, with its half-drawn blinds, its large gros-point picture of a cavalier saying good-bye to his lady. (Behind him, a soldier said good-bye in a less affecting way to a servant.) The plush-covered chairs, the Sèvres urns were so familiar to me, so present, as never to fade. It was one of those stamped scenes, heeled down onto my experience, which cannot link up with others, or move forward, or change. Like a dream, it was separate, inviolable, and could be preserved. Then I suddenly thought that I should not have let my mother go out alone. It was a revolutionary thought, suggesting that children have some protection to offer to grown-ups. I did not know from what I should have protected her; perhaps just from her lonely walk that hot afternoon. I felt an unwelcome stir of pity. Until now I had thought that being adult put one beyond the slur of being pitiable.

I tried to return to my book, to draw all those children round me for safety, but in my disturbed mind I began to feel that Mrs Vivaldi was not asleep. A wasp zigzagged round the room and went abruptly, accidentally, out of the window. It did not leave the same peace behind, but unease.

I could see myself – with *her* eyes – hunched up over my book, my frock crumpled under me, as I endlessly sorted out and chose and ate and brooded over my bag of sweets. I felt that I had intruded and it was no longer a natural thing to be indoors on such a day. If she was awake, I must get up and speak to her.

Her hand supported her head, her white elbow was on the plush arm of the chair. In that dark red chair she seemed very white and fair and I could see long blue veins branching down the inside of her arm.

As I went towards her, I saw, through the slats of her parted fingers, her lashes move. I stood in front of her, holding out the bag of sweets, but she did not stir. Yet so sure was I that she was awake that I did not know how to move away or leave her. Just as my hand wavered uncertainly, her hand fell from her face. She opened her eyes and made a little movement of her mouth, too delicate to be called a yawn. She smiled. 'I must have dropped off for a moment,' she said. She glanced at the basket of flowers, at the clock, then at my bag of sweets.

'How kind of you!' she murmured, shaking her head, increasing my awkwardness. I took a few steps to one side, feeling I was looming over her.

'So you were here all the time?' she asked. 'And I asleep. How dreadful I must have looked.' She put her hand to the plaited hair at the nape of her neck. 'Only young people should be seen asleep.'

She was always underlining my youth, emphasising her own age. I wanted to say, 'You looked beautiful,' but I felt clumsy and absurd. I smiled foolishly and wandered out into the garden, leaving my book in the room. The painted balls lay over the lawn. The syringa made the paths untidy with dropped blossom. Everyone's afternoon was going forward but mine. Interrupted, I did not know where to take it up. I began to wonder how old Mrs Vivaldi was. Standing by the buddleia tree, I watched the drunken butterflies clinging to the flowers, staggering about the branches. Why did she pretend? I asked myself. I knew that children were not worth acting for. No one bothered to keep it up before us; the voices changed, the faces yielded. We were a worthless audience. That she should dissemble for me made me feel very sad and responsible. I was burdened with what I had not said to comfort her.

I hid there by the buddleia a long time, until I heard my mother coming up the path, back from her walk. I dreaded now more than ever that her step would drag, as sometimes it did, or that she would sigh. I came out half-fearfully from behind the buddleia tree.

She was humming to herself, and when she saw me, she handed me a large bunch of wild strawberries, the stalks warm from her hand. She sat down on the grass under the tree, and, lifting her long arms, smoothed her hair, pressing in the hair-pins more firmly. She said: 'So you crept out of that stuffy little room after all?'

I ate the warm, gritty strawberries one by one, and my thoughts hovered all over her as the butterflies hovered over the tree. My shadow bent across her, as my love did.

(1952)

129

Dream Children: A Reverie
by Charles Lamb

Children love to listen to stories about their elders, when *they* were children; to stretch their imagination to the conception of a traditionary great-uncle or grandame, whom they never saw. It was in this spirit that my little ones crept about me the other evening to hear about their great-grandmother Field, who lived in a great house in Norfolk (a hundred times bigger than that in which they and papa lived) which had been the scene – so at least it was generally believed in that part of the country – of the tragic incidents which they had lately become familiar with from the ballad of the Children in the Wood. Certain it is that the whole story of the children and their cruel uncle was to be seen fairly carved out in wood upon the chimney-piece of the great hall, the whole story down to the Robin Redbreasts; till a foolish rich person pulled it down to set up a marble one of modern invention in its stead, with no story upon it. Here Alice put out one of her dear mother's looks, too tender to be called upbraiding. Then I went on to say, how religious and how good their great-grandmother Field was, how beloved and respected by everybody, though she was not indeed the mistress of this great house, but had only the charge of it (and yet in some respects she might be said to be the mistress of it too) committed to her by the owner, who preferred living in a newer and more fashionable mansion which he had purchased somewhere in the adjoining county; but still she lived in it in a manner as if it had been her own, and kept up the dignity of the great house in a sort while she lived, which afterward came to decay, and was nearly pulled down, and all its old ornaments stripped and carried away to the owner's other house, where they were set up, and looked as awkward as if some one were to carry away the old tombs they had seen lately at the Abbey, and stick them up in Lady C.'s tawdry gilt drawing-room. Here John smiled, as much as to say, 'that would be foolish indeed.' And then I told how, when she came to die, her funeral was attended by a concourse of all the poor, and some of the gentry too, of the neighbourhood for many miles round, to show their respect for her memory, because she had been such a good and religious woman; so good indeed that she knew all the Psaltery by heart, ay, and a great part of the Testament besides. Here little Alice spread her hands. Then I told what a tall, upright, graceful person their great-grandmother Field once was; and how in her youth she was esteemed the best dancer – here Alice's little right foot played an involuntary movement, till upon my looking grave, it desisted – the best dancer, I was saying, in the county, till a cruel disease, called a cancer, came, and bowed her down with pain; but it could never bend her good spirits, or make them stoop, but they were still upright, because she was so good and religious. Then I told how she was used to sleep by herself in a lone chamber of the great lone house; and how she believed that an apparition of two infants was to be seen at midnight gliding up and down the great staircase near where she slept, but she said 'those innocents would do her no harm'; and how frightened I used to be, though in those days I had my maid to sleep with me, because I was never half so good or religious as she – and yet I never saw the infants. Here John expanded all his eyebrows and tried to look courageous. Then I told how good she was to all her grand-children, having us to the great house in the holydays, where I in particular used to spend many hours by myself, in gazing upon the old busts of the twelve Cæsars, that had been Emperors of Rome, till the old marble heads would seem to live again, or I to be turned into marble with them; how I never could be tired with roaming about that huge mansion, with its vast empty rooms, with their worn-out hangings, fluttering tapestry, and carved oaken panels, with the gilding almost rubbed out – sometimes in the spacious old-fashioned gardens, which I had almost to myself, unless when now and then a solitary gardening man would cross me – and how the nectarines and peaches hung upon the walls, without my ever offering to pluck them, because they were forbidden fruit, unless now and then, – and because I had more pleasure in strolling about among the old melancholy-looking yew trees, or the firs, and picking up the red berries, and the fir apples, which were good for nothing but to look at – or in lying about upon the fresh grass, with all the fine garden smells around me – or basking in the orangery, till I could almost fancy myself ripening, too, along with the oranges and the limes in that grateful warmth – or in watching the dace that darted to and fro in the fish-pond, at the bottom of the garden, with here and there a great sulky pike hanging midway down the water in silent state, as if it mocked at their impertinent friskings, – I had more pleasure in these busy-idle diversions than in all the sweet flavours of peaches, nectarines, oranges, and such like common baits of children. Here John slyly deposited back upon the plate a bunch of grapes, which, not unobserved by Alice, he had meditated dividing with her, and both seemed willing to relinquish them for the present as irrelevant. Then, in somewhat a more heightened tone, I told how, though their great-grandmother Field loved all her grandchildren, yet in an especial manner she might be said to love their uncle, John L——, because he was so handsome and spirited a youth, and a king to the rest of us; and, instead of moping about in solitary corners, like some of us, he would mount the most mettlesome horse he could get, when but an imp no bigger than themselves, and make it carry him half over the county in a morning, and join the hunters when there were any out – and yet he loved the old great house and gardens too, but had too much spirit to be always pent up within their boundaries – and how their uncle grew up to man's estate as brave as he was handsome, to the admiration of every-body, but of their great-grandmother Field most especially; and how he used to carry me upon his back when I was a lame-footed boy – for he was a good bit older than me – many a mile when I could not walk for pain; – and how in after life he became lame-footed too, and I did not always (I fear) make allowances enough for him when he was impa-tient and in pain, nor remember sufficiently how considerate he had been to me when I was lame-footed; and how when he died, though he had not been dead an hour, it seemed as if he had died a great while ago, such a distance there is betwixt life and death; and how I bore his death as I thought pretty well at first, but afterward it haunted and haunted me; and though I did not cry or take it to heart as some do, and as I think he would have done if I had died, yet I missed him all day long, and knew not till then how much I had loved him. I missed his kindness, and I missed his crossness, and wished him to be alive again, to be quarrelling with him (for we quarrelled sometimes), rather than not have him again, and was as uneasy without him, as he, their poor uncle, must have been when the doctor took off his limb. Here the children fell a-crying, and asked if their little mourning which they had on was not for uncle John, and they looked up, and prayed me not to go on about their uncle, but to tell them some stories about their pretty, dead mother. Then I told them how for seven long years, in hope sometimes, sometimes in despair, yet persisting ever, I courted the fair Alice W———n; and, as much as children could understand, I explained to them what coyness, and difficulty, and denial meant in maidens – when suddenly, turning to Alice, the soul of the first Alice looked out at her eyes with such a reality of re-presentment, that I became in doubt which of them stood there before me, or whose that bright hair was; and while I stood gazing, both the children gradually grew fainter to my view, receding, and still receding, till nothing at last but two mournful features were seen in the uttermost distance, which, without speech, strangely impressed upon me the effects of speech: 'We are not of Alice, nor of thee, nor are we children at all. The children of Alice call Bartrum father. We are nothing; less than nothing, and dreams. We are only what might have been, and must wait upon the tedious shores of Lethe millions of ages before we have existence, and a name' – and immediately awaking, I found myself quietly seated in my bachelor armchair, where I had fallen asleep, with the faithful Bridget unchanged by my side – but John L. (or James Elia) was gone forever.

(1822)

134

Of the many treasures I have read to my children, Philip Pullman's refashioned *Grimm Tales* have perhaps brought us all the most joy. The fact that my mother gave my wife the book for her birthday corroborates its headline, 'For Young and Old'. The kids hang on my (Pullman's/Grimms') every word, as do I even as I read them aloud.

I also love reading the coda to each tale, in which its literary context is framed succinctly.

The book is an embarrassment of riches but my then six-year-old daughter Ione herself read 'The Mouse, the Bird and the Sausage' *to me*, while I dozed in bed early one Saturday morning. It was bliss. We immediately agreed, together with her brother, George, that this was the right story to include in this anthology.

The Mouse, the Bird and the Sausage

A mouse, a bird and a sausage decided to set up home together. For a long time they carried on happily, within their means and even managing to save a little. The bird's job was to go into the forest every day and bring back wood for the fire, the mouse had to get water from the well, make the fire and lay the table, and the sausage did the cooking.

But we're never content with living well if we think we can live better. One day, as the bird was in the forest, he met another bird and boasted about his pleasant way of life. The other bird only called him a poor dupe.

'What d'you mean?'

'Well, who's doing the lion's share of the work? You are. You have to fly back and forth carrying heavy bits of wood, while the other two take it easy. They're taking advantage of you, make no mistake about it.'

The bird thought about it. It was true that after the mouse had lit the fire and carried the water in, she usually went to her little room and had a snooze before getting up in time to lay the table. The sausage stayed by the pot most of the time, keeping an eye on the vegetables, and time to time he'd slither through the water to give it a bit of flavouring. If it needed seasoning, he'd swim more slowly. That was more or less all he did. When the bird came home with the wood, they'd stack it neatly by the fire, sit down to eat, and then sleep soundly till the next day. That was how they lived, and a fine way of life it was.

However, the bird couldn't help thinking about what the other bird had said, and next day he refused to go and gather wood.

'I've been your slave long enough,' he declared. 'You must have taken me for a fool. It's high time we tried a better arrangement.'

'But this works so well!' said the mouse.

'You would say that, wouldn't you?'

'Besides,' said the sausage, 'this suits our different talents.'

'Only because we've never tried to do it any other way.'

The mouse and the sausage argued, but the bird wouldn't be denied. Finally they gave in and drew lots, and the job of gathering wood fell to the sausage, of cooking to the mouse, and of fetching water and making the fire to the bird.

What happened?

After the sausage went out to gather wood, the bird lit the fire and the mouse put the saucepan on the stove. Then they waited for the sausage to come back with the first load of wood, but he was gone so long that they began to worry about him, so the bird went out to see if he was all right.

Not far from the house he came across a dog licking his lips.

'You haven't seen a sausage, have you?'

'Yeah, I just ate him. Delicious.'

'What d'you mean? You can't do that! That's appalling! I'll have you up before the law!'

'He was fair game. There's no sausage season that I know of.'

'He certainly was not fair game! He was innocently going about his business! This is outright murder!'

'Well, that's just where you're wrong, chum. He was carrying forged papers, and that's a capital crime.'

'Forged papers – I've never heard such nonsense. Where are they? Where's your proof?'

'I ate them too.'

There was nothing the bird could do. In a fight between a dog and a bird, there's only one winner, and it isn't the bird. He turned back home and told the mouse what had happened.

'Eaten?' she said. 'Oh, that's dreadful! I shall miss him terribly.'

'It's very sad. We'll just have to do the best we can without him,' said the bird.

The bird laid the table while the mouse put the finishing touches to the stew. She remembered how easily the sausage had managed to swim round and round to season it, and thought she could do the same, so she clambered on to the saucepan handle and launched herself in; but either it was too hot and she suffocated, or else she couldn't swim at all and she drowned, but at all events she never came out.

When the bird saw the vegetable stew coming to the boil with a dead mouse in it, he panicked. He was making up the fire at the time, and in his shock and alarm he scattered the burning logs all over the place and set fire to the house. He raced to the well to get some water to put it out, but got his foot caught in the rope; and when the bucket plunged down the well, down he went with it. So he was drowned, and that was the end of them all.

Unlike the cat and mouse, these housemates are not fundamentally ill-matched. They could have lived happily together for a long time, if the bird's satisfaction had not been fatally undermined. That's the only moral of this story, but it is a sort of fable, like the tale of the cat and the mouse, so a moral is only to be expected.

Some enquiring readers might like to know what sort of sausage it was. After all, according to the internet, Germany has over 1,500 kinds of sausage: from which could we expect this sort of selfless domesticity? Well, it – I mean he – was a bratwurst. But somehow the word 'bratwurst' isn't as funny as the word 'sausage'. According to a famous comedian whose name has slipped my mind, 'sausage' is the funniest word in the English language. This story would certainly have a different kind of poignancy if it had been about a mouse, a bird and a lamb chop.

(2013)

★

A couple of years ago, within the space of a few months, I attended a relative's funeral and then another relative's wedding. The same clan was gathered at both events. As is ever the way, during such gatherings of humans at which public emotion is pitched feverishly, we turned to poetry and music to express what we, as a family, were failing to articulate.

There was one poem that was, independently, selected by the children of the deceased for their funeral oration and, later, also chosen by the bride and groom for a reading at their nuptials.

What poem could possibly have such resonance, such versatility?

It was one they had all learned as children. The bereaved had it read to them by their late mother at bedtime. The bride and groom invited our children to perform it at their ceremony. The sing-song synchronicity of the piece made everyone cry (twice over).

All thanks to a little, dreamy tale about two animals voyaging together into the moonlight . . .

The Owl and the Pussycat
by Edward Lear

The Owl and the Pussycat went to sea
    In a beautiful pea-green boat,
They took some honey, and plenty of money,
    Wrapped up in a five-pound note.
The Owl looked up to the stars above,
    And sang to a small guitar,
'O lovely Pussy! O Pussy, my love,

What a beautiful Pussy you are,
        You are,
        You are!
What a beautiful Pussy you are!'

II

Pussy said to the Owl, 'You elegant fowl!
        How charmingly sweet you sing!
O let us be married! too long we have tarried:
        But what shall we do for a ring?'
They sailed away, for a year and a day,
        To the land where the Bong-tree grows
And there in a wood a Piggy-wig stood
        With a ring at the end of his nose,
        His nose,
        His nose,
With a ring at the end of his nose.

III

'Dear Pig, are you willing to sell for one shilling
        Your ring?' Said the Piggy, 'I will.'
So they took it away, and were married next day
        By the Turkey who lives on the hill.
They dined on mince, and slices of quince,
        Which they ate with a runcible spoon;
And hand in hand, on the edge of the sand,
        They danced by the light of the moon,
        The moon,
        The moon,
They danced by the light of the moon.

(1871)

3

HOOK, LINE AND SINKER

S *leep latency* is the name given to the period between the point that you put down this book and turn off the light, and the moment of falling asleep. In other words, how long the journey is for a person to *go to* sleep. In principle, the shorter that time period, the better. Readiness is all. A bedtime story can help reduce the timespan. Soon that soporific siren-call, with its mantic entreaties, seduces. No longer latent, sleep itself is awake.

The Sleep Gate then swings open, as our circadian rhythms combine with measures of melatonin. Perhaps for around 10–15 minutes, we will inhabit *hypnagogic sleep,* known in Italy as 'sleep-waking', during which we (literally sometimes) nod off. Our bodies are freed of any responsibility. Their temperature plunges. Physicality slipstreams away, drifting into inertia, manoeuvred by the currents of our minds.

We enter a liminal state, suspended somewhere between conscience and consciousness, on the edges of the deepest cycle of sleep. We may experience fluttering, shorter dreams during this limbo.

The preternatural imagery and discombobulated delights such dream-states bring were enough to push Edgar Allan Poe into jerking himself awake by sheer will amid such states, feverishly writing down what visions they had brought with them. This variety of hallucination, which can be prompted by opium, too, was a reservoir of inspiration for nineteenth-century Romantic writers – notably De Quincey but also Coleridge and Wordsworth.

During these furtive first paddles into sleep, *alpha waves* crest our brain. We are on a cusp. As we pass the tide's reach and wade into the eddies, a threshold swells and then bursts into a watershed (within our sleep cycle).

Assuming we have not snapped back awake during those initial throes of somnolence, these currents are soon subsumed by much deeper *theta* and *delta waves*. These roll against the banks of our minds, crashing ever deeper, low in frequency but high in amplitude. As the waves carouse ashore, our eyes roll beneath their lids.

Like sandy footprints during high tide, any impressions left behind by the day's conscious state are washed away by this slow surge. The tideline retreats as those parts of our cortex that harbour emotional responses or social awareness are flooded. We cross the threshold of consciousness and are soon all at sea – freediving into the unknown – or, more simply, as an anaesthetist might say, we are 'under'.

Along the way, the *sleep spindle* will have pricked our brain's electric charge. It spikes this state of mind; marking a new high-point in electro activity amid these phases, demarcating the peak of such initial cycles of *shallow sleep*. It lances only after our muscles have become comfortably numb. No wonder that the nomenclature in English for this transitional state of sleep oozes with a zoned-out, drowsy ease: 'snooze' and 'doze', 'zizz' and 'zeez'.

And so the brain continues waving – in every sense – while the body drowns.

Extract from Speak, Memory
by Vladimir Nabokov

It was at night, however that the *Compagnie Internationale des Wagons-Lits et des Grands Express Européens* lived up to the magic of its name. From my bed under my brother's bunk (Was he asleep? Was he there at all?), in the semidarkness of our compartment, I watched things, and parts of things, and shadows, and sections of shadows cautiously moving about and getting nowhere. The woodwork gently creaked and crackled. Near the door that led to the toilet, a dim garment on a peg and, higher up, the tassel of the blue, bivalved nightlight swung rhythmically. It was hard to correlate those halting approaches, that hooded stealth, with the headlong rush of the outside night, which I knew *was* rushing by, spark-streaked, illegible.

I would put myself to sleep by the simple act of identifying myself with the engine driver. A sense of drowsy well-being invaded my veins as soon as I had everything nicely arranged – the carefree passengers in their rooms enjoying the ride I was giving them, smoking, exchanging knowing smiles, nodding, dozing; the waiters and cooks and train guards (whom I had to place somewhere) carousing in the diner; and myself, goggled and begrimed, peering out of the engine cab at the tapering track, at the ruby or emerald point in the black distance. And then, in my sleep, I would see something totally different – a glass marble rolling under a grand piano or a toy engine on its side with its wheels still working gamely.

(1947)

★

My wife, Salome, is half-Greek and, during summer, we vacate London and head for the Greek Islands. We have spent a lot of time in Hydra, an island a few hours' ferry ride from Athens. Once there, we always head to our favourite restaurant, Xeri Elia — also known, to those in the know, as 'Douskos'. We consider it 'our place', I suppose.

The restaurant is not on the seafront. It takes a little finding, at first. You must walk the gleaming, brecciated limestone cobbles uphill from the harbour, through white-washed narrow passageways, alongside donkeys humping hay bales (no motors are allowed in Hydra), under the beady gaze of street-corner alley cats, past the school-turned-open-air-cinema . . . and into a small square. There, tables radiate in a courtyard: spoked, like moonbeams, around an indomitable pine tree.

The Douskos family has been serving food in this square for almost two hundred years. The fisherman's catch, washed down with their homemade wine, is my recommendation. A ceiling of trellised wisteria provides welcome shade during lunchtime, but try to go when the moon begins to gleam, so that you can catch the local musicians striking up.

Of course, Douskos Taverna is not 'our place' any more than it was once local resident Leonard Cohen's. Its charms, as timeless as a fixed star, are for everyone. Just like Cohen's poetry and music.

Dusko's Taverna 1967
by Leonard Cohen

They are still singing down at Dusko's,
sitting under the ancient pine tree,
in the deep night of fixed and falling stars.
If you go to your window you can hear them.
It is the end of someone's wedding,
or perhaps a boy is leaving on a boat in the morning.
There is a place for you at the table,
wine for you, and apples from the mainland,
a space in the songs for your voice.
Throw something on,
and whoever it is you must tell
that you are leaving,
tell them, or take them, but hurry:
they have sent for you—
the call has come—
they will not wait forever.
They are not even waiting now.

(2006)

Harbour (from Running in the Family)
by Michael Ondaatje

I arrived in a plane but love the harbour. Dusk. And the
turning on of electricity in ships, portholes of moon, the
blue glide of a tug, the harbour road and its ship chandlers,
soap makers, ice on bicycles, the hidden anonymous barber
shops behind the pink dirt walls of Reclamation Street.

One frail memory dragged up out of the past – going to the harbour to say goodbye to a sister or mother, dusk. For years I loved the song 'Harbour Lights', and later in my teens danced disgracefully with girls, humming 'Sea of Heartbreak'.

There is nothing wise about a harbour, but it is real life. It is as sincere as a Singapore cassette. Infinite waters cohabit with flotsam on this side of the breakwater and luxury liners and Maldive fishing vessels steam out to erase calm sea. Who was I saying goodbye to? Automatically as I travel on the tug with my brother-in-law, a pilot in the harbour, I sing, 'The lights in the harbour don't shine for me . . .' but I love it here, skimming out into the night anonymous among the lazy commerce, my nieces dancing on the breakwater as they wait, the lovely swallowing of thick night as it carves around my brain, blunt, cleaning itself with nothing but this anonymity, with the magic word. *Harbour. Lost ship. Chandler. Estuary.*

(1982)

New Zealander Katherine Mansfield died aged just thirty-four.

Told from the perspective of little Fenella, this tale of Mansfield's shows life to be as transitory as sleep. We feel with and for Fenella. We cringe when she is embarrassed by her sad father. We look away too from Dad's childish clinging to his mother, her grandma. Yet then it is our turn to cling on – to his lapels. We are not ready for him to go. For his part, her father hides his sadness and fumbles a goodbye, disappearing before we can know it, melding into a distant memory. The gangplank to familiarity is raised. The estuaries of Fenella's young mind – wise yet immature – recede.

This watershed journey is billeted as passage away from sadness. Yet life is but the briefest of dreams, over in a flash, like Fenella's sleep (this apparent rapidity suggesting that the child, unsurprisingly under the circumstances, has accrued a severe sleep deficit amid her grief).

Transit complete, the same gangplank is lowered through dawn mist, over a slumbering sea.

'It's land, Grandma.'

The Voyage
by Katherine Mansfield

The Picton boat was due to leave at half past seven. It was a beautiful night, mild, starry, only when they got out of the cab and started to walk down the Old Wharf that jutted out into the harbour, a faint wind blowing off the water ruffled under Fenella's hat, and she put up her hand to keep it on. It was dark on the Old Wharf, very dark; the wool sheds, the cattle trucks, the cranes standing up so high, the little squat railway engine, all seemed carved out of solid darkness. Here and there on a rounded wood-pile, that was like the stalk of a huge black mushroom, there hung a lantern, but it seemed afraid to unfurl its timid, quivering light in all that blackness; it burned softly, as if for itself.

Fenella's father pushed on with quick, nervous strides. Beside him her grandma bustled along in her crackling black ulster; they went so fast that she had now and again to give an undignified little skip to keep up with them. As well as her luggage strapped into a neat sausage, Fenella carried clasped to her grandma's umbrella, and the handle, which was a swan's head, kept giving her shoulder a sharp little peck as if it too wanted her to hurry . . . Men, their caps pulled down, their collars turned up, swung by; a few women all muffled scurried along; and one tiny boy, only his little black arms and legs showing out of a white woolly shawl, was jerked along angrily between his father and mother; he looked like a baby fly that had fallen into the cream.

Then suddenly, so suddenly that Fenella and her grandma both leapt, there sounded from behind the largest wool shed, that had a trail of smoke hanging over it, *Mia-oo-oo-O-O*!

'First whistle,' said her father briefly, and at that moment they came in sight of the Picton boat. Lying beside the dark wharf, all strung, all beaded with round golden lights, the Picton boat looked as if she was more ready to sail among stars than out into the cold sea. People pressed along the gangway. First went her grandma, then her father, then Fenella. There was a high step down on to the deck, and an old sailor in a jersey standing by gave her his dry, hard hand. They were there; they stepped out of the way of the hurrying people, and standing under a little iron stairway that led to the upper deck they began to say good-bye.

'There, Mother, there's your luggage!' said Fenella's father, giving Grandma another strapped-up sausage.

'Thank you, Frank.'

'And you've got your cabin tickets safe?'

'Yes, dear.'

'And your other tickets?'

Grandma felt for them inside her glove and showed him the tips.

'That's right.'

He sounded stern, but Fenella, eagerly watching him,

150

saw that he looked tired and sad. *Mia-oo-oo-O-O!* The second whistle blared just above their heads, and a voice like a cry shouted, 'Any more for the gangway?'

'You'll give my love to Father,' Fenella saw her father's lips say. And her grandma, very agitated, answered, 'Of course I will, dear. Go now. You'll be left. Go now, Frank. Go now.'

'It's all right, Mother. I've got another three minutes.' To her surprise Fenella saw her father take off his hat. He clasped Grandma in his arms and pressed her to him. 'God bless you, Mother!' she heard him say.

And Grandma put her hand, with the black thread glove that was worn through on her ring finger, against his cheek, and she sobbed, 'God bless you, my own brave son!'

This was so awful that Fenella quickly turned her back on them, swallowed once, twice, and frowned terribly at a little green star on a mast head. But she had to turn round again; her father was going.

'Good-bye, Fenella. Be a good girl.' His cold wet moustache brushed her cheek. But Fenella caught the lapels of his coat.

'How long am I going to stay?' she whispered anxiously. He wouldn't look at her. He shook her off gently, and gently said, 'We'll see about that. Here! Where's your hand?' He pressed something into her palm. 'Here's a shilling in case you should need it.'

A shilling! She must be going away for ever! 'Father!' cried Fenella. But he was gone. He was the last off the ship. The sailors put their shoulders to the gangway. A huge coil of dark rope went flying through the air and fell 'thump' on the wharf. A bell rang; a whistle shrilled. Silently the dark wharf began to slip, to slide, to edge away from them. Fenella strained to see with all her might. 'Was that Father turning round?' – or waving? – or standing alone? – walking off by himself? The strip of water grew broader, darker. Now the Picton boat began to swing round steady, pointing out to sea. It was no good looking any longer. There was nothing to be seen but a few lights, the face of the town clock hanging in the air, and more lights, little patches of them, on the dark hills.

The freshening wind tugged at Fenella's skirts; she went back to her grandma. To her relief Grandma seemed no longer sad. She had put the two sausages of luggage one on top of the other, and she was sitting on them, her hands folded, her head a little on one side. There was an intent, bright look on her face. Then Fenella saw that her lips were moving and guessed that she was praying. But the old woman gave her a bright nod as if to say that the prayer was nearly over. She unclasped her hands, sighed, clasped them again, bent forward, and at last gave herself a soft shake.

'And now, child,' she said, fingering the bow of her bonnet-strings, 'I think we ought to see about our cabins. Keep close to me, and mind you don't slip.'

'Yes, Grandma!'

'And be careful the umbrellas aren't caught in the stair rail. I saw a beautiful umbrella broken in half like that on my way over.'

'Yes, Grandma.'

Dark figures of men lounged against the rails. In the glow of their pipes a nose shone out, or the peak of a cap, or a pair of surprised-looking eyebrows. Fenella glanced up. High in the air, a little figure, his hand thrust in his short jacket pockets, stood staring out to sea. The ship rocked ever so little, and she thought the stars rocked too. And now a pale steward in a linen coat, holding a tray high in the palm of his hand, stepped out of a lighted doorway and skimmed past them. They went through that doorway. Carefully over the high brass-bound step on to the rubber mat and then down such a terribly steep flight of stairs that Grandma had to put both feet on each step, and Fenella clutched the clammy brass rail and forgot all about the swan-necked umbrella.

At the bottom Grandma stopped; Fenella was rather afraid she was going to pray again. But no, it was only to get out the cabin tickets. They were in the saloon. It was glaring bright and stifling; the air smelled of paint and burnt chop-bones and india-rubber. Fenella wished her grandma would go on, but the old woman was not to be hurried. An immense basket of ham sandwiches caught her eye. She went up to them and touched the top one delicately with her finger.

'How much are the sandwiches?' she asked.

'Tuppence!' bawled a rude steward, slamming down a knife and fork.

Grandma could hardly believe it.

'Twopence *each*?' she asked.

'That's right,' said the steward, and he winked at his companion.

Grandma made a small, astonished face. Then she whispered primly to Fenella. 'What wickedness!' And they sailed out at the further door and along a passage that had cabins on either side. Such a very nice stewardess came to meet them. She was dressed all in blue, and her collar and cuffs were fastened with large brass buttons. She seemed to know Grandma well.

'Well, Mrs Crane,' said she, unlocking their washstand. 'We've got you back again. It's not often you give yourself a cabin.'

'No,' said Grandma. 'But this time my dear son's thoughtfulness—'

'I hope—' began the stewardess. Then she turned round and took a long mournful look at Grandma's blackness and at Fenella's black coat and skirt, black blouse, and hat with a crape rose.

Grandma nodded. 'It was God's will,' said she.

The stewardess shut her lips and, taking a deep breath, she seemed to expand.

'What I always say is,' she said, as though it was her own discovery, 'sooner or later each of us has to go, and that's a certainty.' She paused. 'Now, can I bring you anything, Mrs Crane? A cup of tea? I know it's no good offering you a little something to keep the cold out.'

Grandma shook her head. 'Nothing, thank you. We've got a few wine biscuits, and Fenella has a very nice banana.'

'Then I'll give you a look later on,' said the stewardess, and she went out, shutting the door.

What a very small cabin it was! It was like being shut up in a box with Grandma. The dark round eye above the washstand gleamed at them dully. Fenella felt shy. She stood against the door, still clasping her luggage and the umbrella. Were they going to get undressed in here? Already her grandma had taken off her bonnet, and, rolling up the strings, she fixed each with a pin to the lining before she hung the bonnet up. Her white hair shone like silk; the little bun at the back was covered with a black net. Fenella hardly ever saw her grandma with her head uncovered; she looked strange.

'I shall put on the woollen fascinator your dear mother crocheted for me,' said Grandma, and, unstrapping the sausage, she took it out and wound it round her head; the fringe of grey bobbles danced at her eyebrows as she smiled tenderly and mournfully at Fenella. Then she undid her bodice, and something under that, and something else underneath that. Then there seemed a short, sharp tussle, and Grandma flushed faintly. Snip! Snap! She had undone her stays. She breathed a sigh of relief, and sitting on the plush couch, she slowly and carefully pulled off her elastic-sided boots and stood them side by side.

By the time Fenella had taken off her coat and skirt and put on her flannel dressing-gown Grandma was quite ready.

'Must I take off my boots, Grandma? They're lace.'

Grandma gave them a moment's deep consideration. 'You'd feel a great deal more comfortable if you did, child,' said she. She kissed Fenella. 'Don't forget to say your prayers. Our dear Lord is with us when we are at sea even more than when we are on dry land. And because I am an experienced traveller,' said Grandma briskly, 'I shall take the upper berth.'

'But, Grandma, however will you get up there?'

Three little spider-like steps were all Fenella saw. The old woman gave a small silent laugh before she mounted them nimbly, and she peered over the high bunk at the astonished Fenella.

'You didn't think your grandma could do that, did you?' said she. And as she sank back Fenella heard her light laugh again.

155

The hard square of brown soap would not lather, and the water in the bottle was like a kind of blue jelly. How hard it was, too, to turn down those stiff sheets; you simply had to tear you way in. If everything had been different, Fenella might have got the giggles . . . At last she was inside, and while she lay there panting, there sounded from above a long, soft whispering, as though someone was gently, gently rustling among tissue paper to find something. It was Grandma saying her prayers . . .

A long time passed. Then the stewardess came in; she trod softly and leaned her hand on Grandma's bunk.

'We're just entering the Straits,' she said.

'Oh!'

'It's a fine night, but we're rather empty. We may pitch a little.'

And indeed at that moment the Picton boat rose and rose and hung in the air just long enough to give a shiver before she swung down again, and there was the sound of heavy water slapping against her sides. Fenella remembered she had left that swan-necked umbrella standing up on the little couch. If it fell over, would it break? But Grandma remembered too, at the same time.

'I wonder if you'd mind, stewardess, laying down my umbrella,' she whispered.

'Not at all, Mrs Crane.' And the stewardess, coming back to Grandma, breathed, 'Your little granddaughter's in such a beautiful sleep.'

'God be praised for that,' said Grandma.

'Poor little motherless mite!' said the stewardess. And Grandma was still telling the stewardess all about what happened when Fenella fell asleep.

But she hadn't been asleep long enough to dream before she woke up again to see something waving in the air above her head. What was it? What could it be? It was a small grey foot. Now another joined it. They seemed to be feeling about for something; there came a sigh.

'I'm awake, Grandma,' said Fenella.

'Oh, dear, am I near the ladder?' asked Grandma. 'I thought it was this end.'

'No, Grandma, it's the other. I'll put your foot on it. Are we there?' asked Fenella.

'In the harbour,' said Grandma. 'We must get up, child. You'd better have a biscuit to steady yourself before you move.'

But Fenella had hopped out of her bunk. The lamp was still burning, but night was over, and it was cold. Peering through that round eye, she could see far off some rocks. Now they were scattered over with foam; now a gull flipped by; and now there came a long piece of real land.

'It's land, Grandma,' said Fenella, wonderingly, as though they had been at sea for weeks together. She hugged herself; she stood on one leg and rubbed it with the toes of the other foot; she was trembling. Oh, it had all been so sad lately. Was it going to change? But all her grandma said was, 'Make haste, child. I should leave your nice banana for the stewardess as you haven't eaten it.' And Fenella put on her black clothes again, and a button sprang off one of her gloves and rolled to where she couldn't reach it. They went up on deck.

But if it had been cold in the cabin, on deck it was like ice. The sun was not up yet, but the stars were dim, and the cold pale sky was the same colour as the cold pale sea. On the land a white mist rose and fell. Now they could see quite plainly dark bush. Even the shapes of the umbrella ferns showed, and those strange silvery withered trees that are like skeletons . . . Now they could see the landing-stage and some little houses, pale too, clustered together, like shells on the lid of a box. The other passengers tramped up and down, but more slowly than they had the night before, and they looked gloomy.

And now the landing-stage came out to meet them. Slowly it swam towards the Picton boat, and a man holding a coil of rope, and a cart with a small drooping horse and another man sitting on the step, came too.

'It's Mr Penreddy, Fenella, come for us,' said Grandma. She sounded pleased. Her white waxen cheeks were blue with cold, her chin trembled, and she had to keep wiping her eyes and her little pink nose.

'You've got my—'

'Yes, Grandma.' Fenella showed it to her.

The rope came flying through the air, and 'smack' it fell on to the deck. The gangway was lowered. Again Fenella followed her grandma on to the wharf over to the little cart, and a moment later they were bowling away. The hooves of the little horse drummed over the wooden piles, then sank softly into the sandy road. Not a soul was to be seen; there was not even a feather of smoke. The mist rose and fell, and the sea still sounded asleep as slowly it turned on the beach.

'I seen Mr Crane yestiddy,' said Mr Penreddy. 'He looked himself then. Missus knocked him up a batch of scones last week.'

And now the little horse pulled up before one of the shell-like houses. They got down. Fenella put her hand on the gate, and the big, trembling dewdrops soaked through her glove-tips. Up a little path of round white pebbles they went, with drenched sleeping flowers on either side. Grandma's delicate white picotees were so heavy with dew that they were fallen, but their sweet smell was part of the cold morning. The blinds were down in the little house; they mounted the steps on to the veranda. A pair of old bluchers was on one side of the door, and a large red water-can on the other.

'Tut! Tut! Your grandpa,' said Grandma. She turned the handle. Not a sound. She called, 'Walter!' And immediately a deep voice that sounded half stifled called back, 'Is that you, Mary?'

'Wait, dear,' said Grandma. 'Go in there.' She pushed Fenella gently into a small dusky sitting-room.

On the table a white cat, that had been folded up like a camel, rose, stretched itself, yawned, and then sprang on to the tips of its toes. Fenella buried one cold little hand in the white, warm fur, and smiled timidly while she stroked and listened to Grandma's gentle voice and the rolling tones of Grandpa.

A door creaked. 'Come in, dear.' The old woman beckoned, Fenella followed. There, lying to one side of an immense bed, lay Grandpa. Just his head with a white tuft, and his rosy face and long silver beard showed over the quilt. He was like a very old wide-awake bird.

'Well, my girl!' said Grandpa. 'Give us a kiss!' Fenella kissed him. 'Ugh!' said Grandpa. 'Her little nose is as cold as a button. What's that she holding? Her grandma's umbrella?'

Fenella smiled again, and crooked the swan neck over the bed-rail. Above the bed there was a big text in a deep-black frame:

Lost! One Golden Hour
Set with Sixty Diamond Minutes.
No Reward Is Offered
For It Is GONE FOR EVER!

'Yer grandma painted that,' said Grandpa. And he ruffled his white tuft and looked at Fenella so merrily she almost thought he winked at her.

(1921)

★

The Pipe
by Stéphane Mallarmé

Yesterday I found my pipe while pondering a long evening of work, of fine winter work. Thrown aside were my cigarettes, with all the childish joys of summer, into the past which the leaves shining blue in the sun, the muslins, illuminate, and taken up once again was the grave pipe of a serious man who wants to smoke for a long while without being disturbed, so as better to work; but I was not prepared for the surprise that this abandoned object had in store for me; for hardly had I drawn the first puff when I forgot the grand books I was planning to write, and, amazed, moved to a feeling of tenderness, I breathed in the air of the previous winter which was now coming back to me. I had not been in contact with my faithful sweetheart since returning to France, and now all of London, London as I had lived it a year ago entirely alone, appeared before my eyes: first the dear fogs that muffle one's brains and have an odour of their own there when they penetrate beneath the casements. My

160

tobacco had the scent of a sombre room with leather furniture sprinkled by coal dust, on which the thin black cat would curl and stretch; the big fires! and the maid with red arms pouring coals, and the noise of those coals falling from the sheet-iron bucket into the iron scuttle in the morning – when the postman gave the solemn double knock that kept me alive! Once again I saw through the windows those sickly trees of the deserted square – I saw the open sea, crossed so often that winter, shivering on the deck of the steamer wet with drizzle and blackened from the fumes – with my poor wandering beloved, decked out in traveller's clothes, a long dress, dull as the dust of the roads, a coat clinging damply to her cold shoulders, one of those straw hats with no feather and hardly any ribbons that wealthy ladies throw away upon arrival, mangled as they are by the sea, and that poor loved ones refurbish for many another season. Around her neck was wound the terrible handkerchief that one waves when saying goodbye forever.

(1864)
Translated by Henry Weinfield

One Sail at Sea
by Edward Thomas

This is a simple world. On either hand the shore sweeps out in a long curve and ends in a perpendicular, ash-coloured cliff, carving the misty air as with a hatchet-stroke. The shore is of tawny, terraced sand, like hammered metal from the prints of the retreating waves; and here and there a group of wildly carved and tragic stones – *unde homines nati, durum genus* – such as must have been those stones from which Deucalion made the stony race of men to arise. Up over the sand, and among these stones the water slides in tracery like May blossom or silver mail. A little way out, the long wave lifts itself up laboriously into a shadowy cliff, nods proudly and crumbles, vain and swift, into a thousand sparks of foam. Far out the desolate, ridgy leagues vibrate and murmur with an unintelligible voice, not less intelligible than when one man says, 'I believe,' or another man, 'I love,' or another, 'I am your friend.' Almost at the horizon a sharp white sail sways, invisibly controlled. In a minute it does not move; in half an hour it has moved. It fascinates and becomes the image of the watcher's hopes, as when in some tranquil grief we wait, with faint curiosity and sad foretelling, to see how our plans will travel, smiling a little even when they stray or stop, because we have foretold it. Will the sail sink? Will it take wing into the sky? Will it go straight and far, and overcome and celebrate its success? But it only fades away, and presently another is there unasked, yet not surprising, and it also fades away, and the night has come, and still the sea speaks with tongues. In the moonlight one strange flower glistens, white as a campanula, like a sweet-pea in shape – the bleached thigh-bone of a rat – and we forget the rest.

(1916)

MARGARET DRABBLE

We three Drabble girls, Susan, Margaret and Helen, were given a copy of Walter de la Mare's *Songs of Childhood* for Christmas 1943 by our mother and father. I was four years old, and learning to read. I loved these poems, and 'The Isle of Lone' in particular haunted me. The names of the dwarfs would repeat themselves to me throughout the day and as I fell asleep, like the words of a lullaby. Much of de la Mare's work has this incantatory, onomatopoeic, drowsy magic. As I grew older I learned that he was not rated as a great poet, but he has a timeless genius which has survived many shifts of fashion. I know many of his songs by heart, most of them soporific and melancholy. The story of the dwarfs and the apes and the quarrel by the sea had a profound meaning for me. How could the dwarfs have died so sadly, in their exotic island paradise? I even loved the grey apes, with their guttural groan.

There is no moral to this tale. There is mystery, beauty, an elegiac yearning, and a kind of comfort for the almost enjoyable loneliness that children (and adults) suffer so frequently.

The Isle of Lone
by Walter de la Mare

Three dwarfs there were which lived on an isle,
    And the name of that isle was Lone,
And the names of the dwarfs were Alliolyle,
    Lallerie, Muziomone.

Alliolye was green of een,
    Lallerie light of locks,
Muziomone was mild of mien,
    As ewes in April flocks.

Their house was small and sweet of the sea,
    And pale as the Malmsey wine;

Their bowls were three, and their beds were three,
    And their nightcaps white were nine.

Their beds they were made of the holly-wood,
    Their combs of the tortoise's shell,
Three basins of silver in corners there stood,
    And three little ewers as well.

Green rushes, green rushes lay thick on the floor,
    For light beamed a gobbet of wax;
There were three wooden stools for whatever they
      wore
    On their humpity-dumpity backs.

So each would lie on a drowsy pillow
    And watch the moon in the sky—
And hear the parrot scream to the billow,
    The billow roar reply.—

Parrots of sapphire and sulphur and amber,
    Scarlet, and flame, and green,
While five-foot apes did scramble and clamber,
    In the feathery-tufted treen.

All night long with bubbles a-glisten
    The ocean cried under the moon,
Till ape and parrot, too sleepy to listen,
    To sleep and slumber were gone.

Then from three small beds the dark hours' while
    In a house in the Island of Lone
Rose the snoring of Lallerie, Alliolyle,
    The snoring of Muziomone.

But soon as ever came peep of sun
    On coral and feathery tree,
Three night-capped dwarfs to the surf would run
    And soon were a-bob in the sea.

At six they went fishing, at nine they snared
    Young foxes in the dells,
At noon on sweet berries and honey they fared,
    And blew in their twisted shells.

Dark was the sea they gambolled in,
    And thick with silver fish,
Dark as green glass blown clear and thin
    To be a monarch's dish.

They sate to sup in a jasmine bower,
    Lit pale with flies of fire,
Their bowls the hue of the iris-flower,
    And lemon their attire.

Sweet wine in little cups they sipped,
    And golden honeycomb
Into their bowls of cream they dipped,
    Whipt light and white as foam.

Now Alliolyle, where the sand-flower blows,
    Taught three old apes to sing—
Taught three old apes to dance on their toes
    And caper around in a ring.

They yelled them hoarse and they croaked them sweet,
    They twirled them about and around,
To the noise of their voices they danced with their feet,
    They stamped with their feet on the ground.

But down to the shore skipped Lallerie,
    His parrot on his thumb,
And the twain they scotched in mockery,
    While the dancers go and come.

And, alas! in the evening, rosy and still,
    Light-haired Lallerie
Bitterly quarrelled with Alliolyle
    By the yellow-sanded sea.

The rising moon swam sweet and large
    Before their furious eyes,
And they rolled and rolled to the coral marge
    Where the surf for ever cries.

Too late, too late, comes Muziomone:
    Clear in the clear green sea
Alliolyle lies not alone,
    But clasped with Lallerie.

He blows on his shell plaintiff notes;
    Ape, parraquito, bee
Flock where a shoe on the salt wave floats,—
    The shoe of Lallerie.

He fetches nightcaps, one and nine,
    Grey apes he dowers three,
His house as fair as the Malmsey wine
    Seems sad as cypress-tree.

Three bowls he brims with sweet honeycomb
    To feast the bumble bees,
Saying, 'O bees, be this your home,
    For grief is on the seas!'

He sate him lone in a coral grot,
    At the flowing in of the tide;
When ebbed the billow, there was not,
    Save coral, aught beside.

So hairy apes in three white beds,
    And nightcaps, one and nine,
On moonlit pillows lay three heads
    Bemused with dwarfish wine.

A tomb of coral, the dirge of bee,
    The grey apes' guttural groan
For Alliolyle, for Lallerie,
    For thee, O Muziomone!

                                        (1902)

Margaret Drabble has published eighteen novels, notably *A Summer Bird-Cage* (1963), *The Millstone* (1965) and *The Pure Gold Baby* (2013). She has also written one volume of short stories and several works of non-fiction, including studies of Wordsworth, Arnold Bennett and Angus Wilson. She edited two editions of *The Oxford Companion to English Literature* (1985, 2000). She was appointed DBE in 2008.

★

Phosphorescence – or bioluminescence – requires a network of billions of tiny organisms to blaze trails in the water in unison: algae and plankton; just as dreams require the flicker and fire of countless neurons.

The effect of phosphorescence – swirls and shimmers of colour – is not unlike those dilatory, transcendental moments after sleep latency, as we fall asleep and the insides of our eyelids swim. People experience this state with differing frequency and facility but such hallucinations are commonplace.

I remember being a teenager giddy on an acid trip, on a moonlit English beach, marvelling at the trails that followed my arms when I waved them aloft. Time had become distended. My limbs were wands.

This whirling zoetrope effect is of course different from the shimmer of colour that pulses from phosphorescence. Yet I can still see in flashback my phantasmagorical limb chasing itself, blazing trails as bright as a sparkler's light-doodles – or the pulses of light from bioluminescence.

Those sorts of extra-sensory hallucinations are common not just to those who have dabbled with tabs, but to anyone who has entered shallow sleep. There is no emotional response to these sightings: that part of the brain has tuned out. Furtive and fugitive, shapes dance not immediately before us but deeper afield in our semi-conscious perspective. A multifocal whirligig of constellations bursts before us.

We are all prone to such hypnagogia – these hollowed hallucinations – once we, like Lucy, open wide shut our kalei-doscope eyes.

Fireflies of the Sea
by James Fenton

Dip your hand in the water.
Watch the current shine.
See the blaze trail from your fingers,
Trail from your fingers,
Trail from mine.
There are fireflies on the island
And they cluster in one tree
And in the coral shallows
There are fireflies of the sea.

Look at the stars reflected
Now the sea is calm
And the phosphorus exploding,
Flashing like a starburst
When you stretch your arm.
When you reach down in the water
It's like reaching up to a tree,
To a tree clustered with fireflies,
Fireflies of the sea.

Dip your hand in the water.
Watch the current shine.
See the blaze trail from your fingers,
Trail from your fingers,
Trail from mine
And as you reach down in the water,
As you turn away from me,
As you gaze down at the coral
And the fireflies of the sea.

(1987)

From *The Princess*
by Alfred, Lord Tennyson

Now sleeps the crimson petal, now the white;
Nor waves the cypress in the palace walk;
Nor winks the gold fin in the porphyry font:
The firefly wakens: waken thou with me.

Now droops the milk-white peacock like a ghost,
And like a ghost she glimmers on to me.

Now lies the Earth all Danaë to the stars,
And all thy heart lies open unto me.

Now slides the silent meteor on, and leaves
A shining furrow, as thy thoughts in me.

Now folds the lily all her sweetness up,
And slips into the bosom of the lake:

So fold thyself, my dearest, thou, and slip
Into my bosom and be lost in me.

(1847)

★

As our bodies are submerged by sleep, our shipwrecked brains drown in psychogeography.

J. G. Ballard's stories deluge their readers with desires and dislocations. In this luminous tale, 'Now Wakes the Sea', sodden in subconscious and as salty as any old shanty, his protagonist, Mason — a name that incongruously conjures stone and utility, joints and joinery — proves an adventurous avatar.

Now Wakes the Sea
by J. G. Ballard

Again at night Mason heard the sounds of the approaching sea, the muffled thunder of breakers rolling up the near-by streets. Roused from his sleep, he ran out into the moonlight, where the white-framed houses stood like sepulchres among the washed concrete courts. Two hundred yards away the waves plunged and boiled, sluicing in and out across the pavement. Foam seethed through the picket fences, and the broken spray filled the air with the wine-sharp tang of brine.

Off-shore the deeper swells of the open sea rode across the roofs of the submerged houses, the white-caps cleft by isolated chimneys. Leaping back as the cold foam stung his feet, Mason glanced at the house where his wife lay sleeping. Each night the sea moved a few yards nearer, a hissing guillotine across the empty lawns.

For half an hour Mason watched the waves vault among the rooftops. The luminous surf cast a pale nimbus on the clouds racing overhead on the dark wind, and covered his hands with a waxy sheen.

At last the waves began to recede, and the deep bowl of illuminated water withdrew down the emptying streets, disgorging the lines of houses in the moonlight. Mason ran forwards across the expiring bubbles, but the sea shrank away from him, disappearing around the corners of the houses, sliding below the garage doors. He sprinted to the end of the road as a last glow was carried across the sky beyond the spire of the church. Exhausted, Mason returned to his bed, the sound of the dying waves filling his head as he slept.

'I saw the sea again last night,' he told his wife at breakfast.

Quietly, Miriam said: 'Richard, the nearest sea is a thousand miles away.' She watched her husband for a moment, her pale fingers straying to the coil of black hair lying against her neck. 'Go out into the drive and look. There's no sea.'

'Darling, I *saw* it.'

'Richard— !'

Mason stood up, and with slow deliberation raised his palms. 'Miriam, I felt the spray on my hands. The waves were breaking around my feet. I wasn't dreaming.'

'You must have been.' Miriam leaned against the door, as if trying to exclude the strange nightworld of her husband. With her long raven hair framing her oval face, and the scarlet dressing-gown open to reveal her slender neck and white breast, she reminded Mason of a Pre-Raphaelite heroine in an Arthurian pose. 'Richard, you must see Dr Clifton. It's beginning to frighten me.'

Mason smiled, his eyes searching the distant rooftops above the trees. 'I shouldn't worry. What's happening is really very simple. At night I hear the sounds of the sea, I go out and watch the waves in the moonlight, and then come back to bed.' He paused, a flush of fatigue on his face. Tall and slimly built, Mason was still convalescing from the illness which had kept him at home for the previous six months. 'It's curious, though,' he resumed, 'the water is remarkably luminous. I should guess its salinity is well above normal—'

'But Richard . . .' Miriam looked around helplessly, her husband's calmness exhausting her. 'The sea isn't *there*; it's only in your mind. No one else can see it.'

Mason nodded, hands lost in his pockets. 'Perhaps no one else has heard it yet.'

Leaving the breakfast-room, he went into his study. The couch on which he had slept during his illness still stood against the corner, his bookcase beside it. Mason sat down, taking a large fossil mollusc from a shelf. During the winter, when he had been confined to bed, the smooth trumpet-shaped conch, with its endless associations of ancient seas and drowned strands, had provided him with unlimited pleasure, a bottomless cornucopia of image and reverie. Cradling it reassuringly in his hands, as exquisite and ambiguous as a fragment of Greek sculpture found in a dry riverbed, he reflected that it seemed like a capsule of time, the condensation of another universe. He could almost believe that the midnight sea which haunted his sleep had been released from the shell when he had inadvertently scratched one of its helixes.

Miriam followed him into the room and briskly drew

the curtains, as if aware that Mason was returning to the twilight world of his sick-bed. She took his shoulders in her hands.

'Richard, listen. Tonight, when you hear the waves, wake me and we'll go out together.'

Gently, Mason disengaged himself. 'Whether you see it or not is irrelevant, Miriam. The fact is that I see it.'

Later, walking down the street, Mason reached the point where he had stood the previous night, watching the waves break and roll towards him. The sounds of placid domestic activity came from the houses he had seen submerged. The grass on the lawns was bleached by the July heat, and sprays rotated in the bright sunlight, casting rainbows in the vivid air. Undisturbed since the rainstorms in the early spring, the long summer's dust lay between the wooden fences and water hydrants.

The street, one of a dozen suburban boulevards on the perimeter of the town, ran north-west for some three hundred yards and then joined the open square of the neighbourhood shopping centre. Mason shielded his eyes and looked out at the clock tower of the library and the church spire, identifying the protuberances which had risen from the steep swells of the open sea. All were in exactly the positions he remembered.

The road shelved slightly as it approached the shopping centre, and by a curious coincidence marked the margins of the beach which would have existed if the area had been flooded. A mile or so from the town, this shallow ridge, which formed part of the rim of a large natural basin enclosing the alluvial plain below, culminated in a small chalk outcropping.

Although it was partly hidden by the intervening houses, Mason now recognized it clearly as the promontory which had reared like a citadel above the sea. The deep swells had rolled against its flanks, sending up immense plumes of spray that fell back with almost hypnotic slowness upon the receding water. At night the promontory seemed larger and more gaunt, an uneroded bastion against the sea. One evening, Mason promised himself, he would go out to the promontory and let the waves wake him as he slept on the peak.

A car moved past, the driver watching Mason curiously as he stood in the middle of the road, head raised to the air. Not wishing to appear any more eccentric than he was already considered – the solitary, abstracted husband of the beautiful but childless Mrs Mason – Mason turned into the avenue which ran along the ridge. As he approached the distant outcropping he glanced over the hedges for any signs of water-logged gardens or stranded cars. The houses had been inundated by floodwater.

The first visions of the sea had come to Mason only three weeks earlier, but he was already convinced of their absolute validity. He recognized that after its nightly withdrawal the water failed to leave any mark on the hundreds of houses it submerged, and he felt no alarm for the drowned people who were sleeping undisturbed in the sea's immense liquid locker as he watched the luminous waves break across the roof-tops. Despite this paradox, it was his complete conviction of the sea's reality that had made him admit to Miriam that he had woken one night to the sound of waves outside the window and gone out to find the sea rolling across the neighbourhood streets and houses. At first she had merely smiled at him, accepting this illustration of his strange private world. Then, three nights later, she had woken to the sound of him latching the door on his return, bewildered by his pumping chest and perspiring face.

From then on she spent all day looking over her shoulder through the window for any signs of the sea. What worried her as much as the vision herself was Mason's complete calm in the face of this terrifying unconscious apocalypse.

Tired by his walk, Mason sat down on a low ornamental wall, screened from the surrounding houses by the rhododendron bushes. For a few minutes he played with the dust at his feet, stirring the white grains with a branch. Although formless and passive, the dust shared something of the same evocative qualities of the fossil mollusc, radiating a curious compacted light.

In front of him, the road curved and dipped, the incline carrying it away on to the fields below. The chalk shoulder, covered by a mantle of green turf, rose into the clear sky. A metal shack had been erected on the slope, and a small group of figures moved about the entrance of a mine-shaft, adjusting a wooden hoist. Wishing that he had brought his wife's car, Mason watched the diminutive figures disappear one by one into the shaft.

The image of this elusive pantomime remained with him all day in the library, overlaying his memories of the dark waves rolling across the midnight streets. What sustained Mason was his conviction that others would soon also become aware of the sea.

When he went to bed that night he found Miriam sitting fully dressed in the armchair by the window, her face composed into an expression of calm determination.

'What are you doing?' he asked.

'Waiting.'

'For what?'

'The sea. Don't worry, simply ignore me and go to sleep. I don't mind sitting here with the light out.'

'Miriam . . .' Wearily, Mason took one of her slender hands and tried to draw her from the chair. 'Darling, what on earth will this achieve?'

'Isn't it obvious?'

Mason sat down on the foot of the bed. For some reason, not wholly concerned with the wish to protect her, he wanted to keep his wife from the sea. 'Miriam, don't you understand? I might not actually *see* it, in the literal sense. It might be . . .' he extemporized . . . 'an hallucination, or a dream.'

Miriam shook her head, hands clasped on the arms of the chair. 'I don't think it is. Anyway, I want to find out.'

Mason lay back on the bed. 'I wonder whether you're approaching this the right way—'

Miriam sat forward. 'Richard, you're taking it all so calmly; you accept this vision as if it were a strange head-ache. That's what frightens me. If you were really terrified by this sea I wouldn't worry, but . . .'

Half an hour later he fell asleep in the darkened room, Miriam's slim face watching him from the shadows.

Waves murmured, outside the windows the distant swish of racing foam drew him from sleep, the muffled thunder of rollers and the sounds of deep water drummed at his ears. Mason climbed out of bed, and dressed quickly as the hiss of receding water sounded up the street. In the corner, under the light reflected from the distant foam,

177

Miriam lay asleep in the armchair, a bar of moonlight across her throat.

His bare feet soundless on the pavement, Mason ran towards the waves. He stumbled across the glistening tide-line as one of the breakers struck with a guttural roar. On his knees, Mason felt the cold brilliant water, seething with animalcula, spurt across his chest and shoulders, slacken and then withdraw, sucked like a gleaming floor into the mouth of the next breaker. His wet suit clinging to him like a drowned animal, Mason stared out across the sea. In the moonlight the white houses advanced into the water like the palazzos of a spectral Venice, mausoleums on the causeways of some island necropolis. Only the church spire was still visible. The water rode in to its high tide, a further twenty yards down the street, the spray carried almost to the Masons' house.

Mason waited for an interval between two waves and then waded through the shallows to the avenue which wound towards the distant headland. By now the water had crossed the roadway, swilling over the dark lawns and slapping at the doorsteps.

Half a mile from the headland he heard the great surge and sigh of the deeper water. Out of breath, he leaned against a fence as the cold foam cut across his legs, pulling him with its undertow. Illuminated by the racing clouds, he saw the pale figure of a woman standing above the sea on a stone parapet at the cliff's edge, her black robe lifting behind her in the wind, her long hair white in the moonlight. Far below her feet, the luminous waves leapt and vaulted like acrobats.

Mason ran along the pavement, losing sight of her as the

road curved and the houses intervened. The water slackened and he caught a last glimpse of the woman's icy-white profile through the spray. Turning, the tide began to ebb and fade, and the sea shrank away between the houses, draining the night of its light and motion.

As the last bubbles dissolved on the damp pavement, Mason searched the headland, but the luminous figure had gone. His damp clothes dried themselves as he walked back through the empty streets. A last tang of brine was carried away off the hedges on the midnight air.

The next morning he told Miriam: 'It *was* a dream, after all. I think the sea has gone now. Anyway, I saw nothing last night.'

'Thank heavens, Richard. Are you sure?'

'I'm certain.' Mason smiled encouragingly. 'Thanks for keeping watch over me.'

'I'll sit up tonight as well.' She held up her hand. 'I insist. I feel all right after last night, and I want to drive this thing away, once and for all.' She frowned over the coffee cups. 'It's strange, but once or twice I think I heard the sea too. It sounded very old and blind, like something waking again after millions of years.'

On his way to the library, Mason made a detour towards the chalk outcropping, and parked the car where he had seen the moonlit figure of the white-haired woman watching the sea. The sunlight fell on the pale turf, illuminating the mouth of the mine-shaft, around which the same desultory activity was taking place.

For the next fifteen minutes Mason drove in and out

of the tree-lined avenues, peering over the hedges at the kitchen windows. Almost certainly she would live in one of the nearby houses, still wearing the black robe beneath a housecoat.

Later, at the library, he recognized a car he had seen on the headland. The driver, an elderly tweed-suited man, was examining the display cases of local geological finds.

'Who was that?' he asked Fellowes, the keeper of antiquities, as the car drove off. 'I've seen him on the cliffs.'

'Professor Goodhart, one of the party of palaeontologists. Apparently they've uncovered an interesting bone-bed.' Fellowes gestured at the collection of femurs and jaw-bone fragments. 'With luck we may get a few pieces from them.'

Mason stared at the bones, aware of a sudden closing of the parallax within his mind.

Each night, as the sea emerged from the dark streets and the waves rolled farther towards the Masons' home, he would wake beside his sleeping wife and go out into the surging air, wading through the deep water towards the headland. There he would see the white-haired woman on the cliff's edge, her face raised above the roaring spray. Always he failed to reach her before the tide turned, and would kneel exhausted on the wet pavements as the drowned streets rose around him.

Once a police patrol car found him in its headlights, slumped against a gate-post in an open drive. On another night he forgot to close the front door when he returned. All through breakfast Miriam watched him with her old wariness, noticing the shadows which encircled his eyes like manacles.

'Richard, I think you should stop going to the library. You look worn out. It isn't that sea dream again?'

Mason shook his head, forcing a tired smile. 'No, that's finished with. Perhaps I've been over-working.'

Miriam held his hands. 'Did you fall over yesterday?' She examined Mason's palms. 'Darling, they're still *raw*! You must have grazed them only a few hours ago. Can't you remember?'

Abstracted, Mason invented some tale to satisfy her, then carried his coffee into the study and stared at the morning haze which lay across the rooftops, a soft lake of opacity that followed the same contours as the midnight sea. The mist dissolved in the sunlight, and for a moment the diminishing reality of the normal world reasserted itself, filling him with a poignant nostalgia.

Without thinking, he reached out to the fossil conch on the bookshelf, but involuntarily his hand withdrew before touching it.

Miriam stood beside him. 'Hateful thing,' she commented. 'Tell me, Richard, what do you think caused your dream?'

Mason shrugged. 'Perhaps it was a sort of memory . . .' He wondered whether to tell Miriam of the waves which he still heard in his sleep, and of the white-haired woman on the cliff's edge who seemed to beckon to him. But like all women Miriam believed that there was room for only one enigma in her husband's life. By an inversion of logic he felt that his dependence on his wife's private income, and the loss of self-respect, gave him the right to withhold something of himself from her.

'Richard, what's the matter?'

In his mind the spray opened like a diaphanous fan and the enchantress of the waves turned towards him.

Waist-high, the sea pounded across the lawn in a whirlpool. Mason pulled off his jacket and flung it into the water, and then waded out into the street. Higher than ever before, the waves had at last reached his house, breaking over the doorstep, but Mason had forgotten his wife. His attention was fixed upon the headland, which was lashed by a continuous storm of spray, almost obscuring the figure standing on its crest.

As Mason pressed on, sometimes sinking to his shoulders, shoals of luminous algae swarmed in the water around him. His eyes smarted in the saline air. He reached the lower slopes of the headland almost exhausted, and fell to his knees.

High above, he could hear the spray singing as it cut through the coigns of the cliff's edge, the deep base of the breakers overlaid by the treble of the keening air. Carried by the music, Mason climbed the flank of the headland, a thousand reflections of the moon in the breaking sea. As he reached the crest, the black robe hid the woman's face, but he could see her tall erect carriage and slender hips. Suddenly, without any apparent motion of her limbs, she moved away along the parapet.

'Wait!'

His shout was lost on the air. Mason ran forwards, and the figure turned and stared back at him. Her white hair swirled around her face like a spume of silver steam and then parted to reveal a face with empty eyes and notched mouth. A hand like a bundle of white sticks clawed towards him, and the figure rose through the whirling darkness like a gigantic bird.

Unaware whether the scream came from his own mouth or from this spectre, Mason stumbled back. Before he could catch himself he tripped over the wooden railing, and in a cackle of chains and pulleys fell backwards into the shaft, the sounds of the sea booming in its hurtling darkness.

After listening to the policeman's description, Professor Goodhart shook his head.

'I'm afraid not, sergeant. We've been working on the bed all week. No one's fallen down the shaft.' One of the flimsy wooden rails was swinging loosely in the crisp air. 'But thank you for warning me. I suppose we must build a heavier railing, if this fellow is wandering around in his sleep.'

'I don't think he'll bother to come up here,' the sergeant said. 'It's quite a climb.' As an afterthought he added: 'Down at the library where he works they said you'd found a couple of skeletons in the shaft yesterday. I know it's only two days since he disappeared, but one of them couldn't possibly be his?' The sergeant shrugged. 'If there was some natural acid, say . . .'

Professor Goodhart drove his heel into the chalky turf. 'Pure calcium carbonate, about a mile thick, laid down during the Triassic Period 200 million years ago when there was a large inland sea here. The skeletons we found yesterday, a man's and a woman's, belong to two Cro-Magnon fisher people who lived on the shore just before it dried up. I wish I could oblige you – it's quite a problem to understand how these Cro-Magnon relics found their way into the bonebed. This shaft wasn't sunk until about thirty years ago. Still, that's my problem, not yours.'

Returning to the police car, the sergeant shook his head.

As they drove off he looked out at the endless stretch of placid suburban homes.

'Apparently there was an ancient sea here once. A million years ago.' He picked a crumpled flannel jacket off the back seat. 'That reminds me, I know what Mason's coat smells of – brine.'

(1963)

★

From The Tempest
by William Shakespeare

Full fathom five thy father lies;
Of his bones are coral made;
Those are pearls that were his eyes;
Nothing of him that doth fade,
But doth suffer a sea-change
Into something rich and strange.
Sea-nymphs hourly ring his knell:
Ding-dong.
Hark! now I hear them – Ding-dong, bell.

(1610–11)

4

THE DEAD SPOT

I t is the dead of night.

After the furtive paddling out to sleep's reaches, you are now away. Brainwaves roll with diminished frequency. Slower and slower. Your muscles shot, the body is now at its least responsive to external stimuli. It has given way to the inevitable, deepest of slumbers. This period of sleep is the hardest from which to rouse a person. You are dead to the world.

Indeed, the *dead spot*, as it is known, is the point during our human sleep cycle when, of those who die in their sleep, the sick or elderly, most commonly pass away. Our body temperature and blood pressure are at their lowest. The iced physiological state at this juncture (usually between 2 a.m. and 4 a.m.) lends itself to an easeful death. Our bodies are at their least responsive to sensations, notably pain – no wonder such a mortal slippage is how most of us would wish to 'pass away' (which, after all, sounds so similar to 'drift off') . . . I'd certainly like 'to go' during my secondary life, during sleep. Death probably wouldn't then feel like such an awfully big misadventure.

Death and sleep have, of course, long been bedfellows. It is no wonder. On a physical level, after all (literally), a grave – horizontal, solitary, darkened, confined – is not unlike a bed in design; and on a more metaphorical or figurative footing, how else are we supposed to conjure what death must be like, than liken it to the sweet oblivion of a deep sleep?

In Greek mythology, the goddess of Night, Nyx, had twin sons: Hypnos (Sleep) and Thanatos (Death). Writers through the ages have since extended the parallel and converged these states of being. It is comforting, I think, to picture the end in this way – 'To sleep, perchance to dream' – just as a ghost story, however chilling, is inherently consolatory as it implies an afterlife.

Yet we rarely dream of the moment of our own death. Growing up, there was a playground rumour that if you dreamed you had died, you would indeed not wake up! I later discovered, one feverish night of the soul, that this was most certainly not true. Yet our darker dreams portending death do tend to halt just prior to the moment of truth. We wake up, suddenly, from such a nightmare. It is rare that we vault upright sweatily, as so often seen in movies when a character has a nightmare (cue thunderclap). More likely, as our brain is suddenly roused during deep REM sleep but our body left behind, our musculature still effectively paralysed – we freeze! We can't move. Time zooms in and pans out. We swivel our eyeballs into the half-seen recesses of the room, where our darkling imaginations take flight: the tingling curtain is sinisterly silhouetted, the soft creak of footfall is heard creeping up the stairs . . . In these peripheral ways, crouching in the corners of our minds, our darkest fears jump from one world into another.

Philip Larkin lurked often in such corners of the *dead spot*. For instance, in 'Unfinished Poem' and, here, 'Aubade':

And so it stays just on the edge of vision,
A small, unfocused blur, a standing chill
That slows each impulse down to indecision.

When advising screenwriters of supernatural thrillers, which I have had occasion to do a lot these past few years through my work with the horror studio Hammer Films, I usually say that they are allowed to show just one dream. Otherwise, the lazy screenwriter falls back on the dream sequence as a device to grab a scare. One nightmare provides illuminating characterization and an effective fright, catching the audience unawares (just like the dreamer who suddenly awakens). Two such sequences, however, suggests carelessness and, more worryingly, a lack of cinematic ideas as to how else to frighten us and depict a character's inner life. We risk alienating the audience with the old lie, 'and then he woke up and it was all a dream'. Or nightmare.

The origins of that word *nightmare* lie, as with the word *sleep* (once called *swefn*), in Old English: *mare* meaning demon. The implication of its etymology is that our dreams can somehow be infected. Cultures around the world still believe this to be true: that – during our more lurid, darker dreams – a sort of possession takes place. Talismans, like dreamcatchers, are deposited above beds throughout the world to ward off such malign spirits.

This reminds me of another playground myth – that a person who never has a nightmare will become insane. That one bad dream now and then is healthy, to expunge darker thoughts or baser instincts. This may just be schoolboy chat but Schopenhauer had a point when observing that 'dreams are a brief madness, madness a long dream'. Indeed, who is more sane – or, for that matter, truly 'alive' – the waking drone or the sleeping Queen Bee?

I would like to report back (perhaps in a future dream) to my playground self that a healthy inquisitive mind is reliant not so much on having nightmares as, more basically, on ensuring the brain receives a balanced and good amount of sleep. This will, from time to time, in dream states, lend itself to gothic imaginings: uncanny occurrences and unlikely coincidences; strange meetings, not least astonishing visitations from deceased loved ones; excruciating embarrassments also, when we are the Emperor wearing new clothes (*'Whoops, so sorry, Your Majesty, I seemed to have forgotten to put my trousers on this morning!'*); grotesque animisms, conjurings and happenings. These darker shadows of dream are every bit as magical and crucial as the sweetest, brightest of reveries and should be celebrated. The gothic imagination offers really profound excavations of ourselves – and our *doppelgängers* – by delving into divided states of selfhood, identity, existentialism and consciousness. A chiaroscuro of the soul is brought into relief, under the penumbra of sleep and amid the echoed murmurings of our hearts.

The physiology of the *dead spot* – when we are, on a daily basis, at our most physically relaxed and least susceptible to pain (due to the congealment of metabolic activity and body temperature) – does have a corollary to death, a happier flipside. Those wee hours are also traditionally the appointed time when most babies are born. In this brightly lit modern age, this ratio may statistically be on the wane, and yet it still makes symmetrical sense: that our body clocks should stop ticking at around the same time that they first began, once upon a time.

★

This fabled tale is itself framed by accounts of storytelling, so that it becomes a story within a story, within a book (that you are now holding).

Authorial subterfuge was a trademark of Washington Irving but his story structure in 'Rip Van Winkle' also reminds us of the later gothic literature that so frequently layered its narratives within letters, diaries and such, to lend levels of subjectivity, as well as credence or faux authenticity. There are, accordingly, also moments of the grotesque and uncanny in this story. Irving smuggles a nightmare into a dream into a reality, with a cloak of wit and a dagger of charm, his tone as unprepossessing as the beguiling, eponymous protagonist himself.

Yet 'Rip Van Winkle' operates on so many different levels. Irving also invokes folk traditions, historical fiction and fairy tale in order to beg the age-old question – older than Rip himself – of whether our little life is lived while asleep or awake . . .

Doesn't time fly? The story is one of the longer in this collection and yet over before you know it.

Rip Van Winkle
by Washington Irving

By Woden, God of Saxons,
From whence comes Wensday, that is Wodensday,
Truth is a thing that ever I will keep
Unto thylke day in which I creep into
My sepulchre.

CARTWRIGHT

The following Tale was found among the papers of the late Diedrich Knickerbocker, an old gentleman of New York, who was very curious in the Dutch history of the province, and the manners of the descendants from its primitive settlers. His historical researches, however, did not lie so much among books as among men; for the former are lamentably scanty on his favorite topics; whereas he found the old burghers, and still more their wives, rich in that legendary lore, so invaluable to true history. Whenever, therefore, he happened upon a genuine Dutch family, snugly shut up in its low-roofed farmhouse, under a spreading sycamore, he looked upon it as a little clasped volume of black-letter, and studied it with the zeal of a book-worm.

The result of all these researches was a history of the province during the reign of the Dutch governors, which he published some years since. There have been various opinions as to the literary character of his work, and, to tell the truth, it is not a whit better than it should be. Its chief merit is its scrupulous accuracy, which indeed was a little questioned on its first appearance, but has since been completely established; and it is now admitted into all historical collections, as a book of unquestionable authority.

The old gentleman died shortly after the publication of his work, and now that he is dead and gone, it cannot do much harm to his memory to say that his time might have been better employed in weightier labors. He, however, was apt to ride his hobby his own way; and though it did now and then kick up the dust a little in the eyes of his neighbors, and grieve the spirit of some friends, for whom he felt the truest deference and affection; yet his errors and follies are remembered 'more in sorrow than in anger', and it begins to be suspected, that he never intended to injure or offend. But however his memory may be appreciated by critics, it is still held dear by many folks, whose good opinion is well worth having; particularly by certain biscuit-bakers, who have gone so far as to imprint his likeness on their new-year cakes; and have thus given him a chance for immortality, almost equal to the being stamped on a Waterloo Medal, or a Queen Anne's Farthing.

Whoever has made a voyage up the Hudson must remember the Catskill mountains. They are a dismembered branch of the great Appalachian family, and are seen away to the west of the river, swelling up to a noble height, and lording it over the surrounding country. Every change of season, every change of weather, indeed, every hour of the day, produces some change in the magical hues and shapes of these mountains, and they are regarded by all the good wives, far and near, as perfect barometers. When the weather is fair and settled, they are clothed in blue and purple, and print their bold outlines on the clear evening sky, but, sometimes, when the rest of the landscape is cloudless, they will gather a hood of gray vapors about their summits, which, in the last rays of the setting sun, will glow and light up like a crown of glory.

At the foot of these fairy mountains, the voyager may have descried the light smoke curling up from a village, whose shingle-roofs gleam among the trees, just where the blue tints of the upland melt away into the fresh green of the nearer landscape. It is a little village of great antiquity, having been founded by some of the Dutch colonists, in the early times of the province, just about the beginning of the government of the good Peter Stuyvesant (may he rest in peace!), and there were some of the houses of the original settlers standing within a few years, built of small yellow bricks brought from Holland, having latticed windows and gable fronts, surmounted with weather-cocks.

In that same village, and in one of these very houses (which, to tell the precise truth, was sadly time-worn and weather-beaten), there lived many years since, while the country was yet a province of Great Britain, a simple good-natured fellow of the name of Rip Van Winkle. He was a descendant of the Van Winkles who figured so gallantly in the chivalrous days of Peter Stuyvesant, and accompanied him to the siege of Fort Christina. He inherited, however, but little of the martial character of his ancestors. I have observed that he was a simple good-natured man; he was, moreover, a kind neighbor, and an obedient hen-pecked husband. Indeed, to the latter circumstance might be owing that meekness of spirit which gained him such universal popularity; for those men are most apt to be obsequious and conciliating abroad, who are under the discipline of shrews at home. Their tempers, doubtless, are rendered pliant and malleable in the fiery furnace of domestic tribulation; and a curtain lecture is worth all the sermons in the world for teaching the virtues of patience and long-suffering. A termagant wife may, therefore, in some respects, be considered a tolerable blessing; and if so, Rip Van Winkle was thrice blessed.

Certain it is, that he was a great favorite among all the good wives of the village, who, as usual, with the amiable sex, took his part in all family squabbles; and never failed, whenever they talked those matters over in their evening gossipings, to lay all the blame on Dame Van Winkle. The children of the village, too, would shout with joy whenever he approached. He assisted at their sports, made their playthings, taught them to fly kites and shoot marbles, and told them long stories of ghosts, witches, and Indians. Whenever he went dodging about the village, he was surrounded by a troop of them, hanging on his skirts, clambering on his back, and playing a thousand tricks on him with impunity; and not a dog would bark at him throughout the neighborhood.

The great error in Rip's composition was an insuperable aversion to all kinds of profitable labor. It could not be from the want of assiduity or perseverance; for he would sit on a wet rock, with a rod as long and heavy as a Tartar's lance, and fish all day without a murmur, even though he should not be encouraged by a single nibble. He would carry a fowling-piece on his shoulder for hours together, trudging through woods and swamps, and up hill and down dale, to shoot a few squirrels or wild pigeons. He would never refuse to assist a neighbor even in the roughest toil, and was a foremost man at all country frolics for husking Indian corn, or building stone-fences. The women of the village, too, used to employ him to run their errands, and to do such little odd jobs as their less obliging husbands would not do for them. In a word Rip was ready to attend to anybody's business but his own; but as to doing family duty, and keeping his farm in order, he found it impossible.

In fact, he declared it was of no use to work on his farm; it was the most pestilent little piece of ground in the whole country; every thing about it went wrong, and would go wrong, in spite of him. His fences were continually falling to pieces; his cow would either go astray, or get among the cabbages; weeds were sure to grow quicker in his fields than anywhere else; the rain always made a point of setting in just as he had some out-door work to do; so that though his patrimonial estate had dwindled away under his management, acre by acre, until there was little more left than a mere patch of Indian corn and potatoes, yet it was the worst conditioned farm in the neighborhood.

His children, too, were as ragged and wild as if they belonged to nobody. His son Rip, an urchin begotten in his own likeness, promised to inherit the habits, with the old clothes of his father. He was generally seen trooping like a colt at his mother's heels, equipped in a pair of his father's cast-off galligaskins, which he had much ado to hold up with one hand, as a fine lady does her train in bad weather.

Rip Van Winkle, however, was one of those happy mortals, of foolish, well-oiled dispositions, who take the world easy, eat white bread or brown, whichever can be got with least thought or trouble, and would rather starve on a penny than work for a pound. If left to himself, he would have whistled life away in perfect contentment; but his wife kept continually dinning in his ears about his idleness, his carelessness, and the ruin he was bringing on his family. Morning, noon, and night, her tongue was incessantly going, and everything he said or did was sure to produce a torrent of household eloquence. Rip had but one way of replying to all lectures of the kind, and that, by frequent use, had grown into a habit. He shrugged his shoulders, shook his head, cast up his eyes, but said nothing. This, however, always provoked a fresh volley from his wife; so that he was fain to draw off his forces, and take to the outside of the house – the only side which, in truth, belongs to a hen-pecked husband.

Rip's sole domestic adherent was his dog Wolf, who was as much hen-pecked as his master; for Dame Van Winkle regarded them as companions in idleness, and even looked upon Wolf with an evil eye, as the cause of his master's going so often astray. True it is, in all points of spirit befitting an honorable dog, he was as courageous an animal as ever scoured the woods – but what courage can withstand the ever-during and all-besetting terrors of a woman's tongue? The moment Wolf entered the house his crest fell, his tail drooped to the ground, or curled between his legs; he sneaked about with a gallows air, casting many a sidelong glance at Dame Van Winkle, and at the least flourish of a broom-stick or ladle, he would fly to the door with yelping precipitation.

Times grew worse and worse with Rip Van Winkle as years of matrimony rolled on; a tart temper never mellows with age, and a sharp tongue is the only edged tool that grows keener with constant use. For a long while he used to console himself, when driven from home, by frequenting a kind of perpetual club of the sages, philosophers, and other idle personages of the village; which held its sessions on a bench before a small inn, designated by a rubicund portrait of His Majesty George the Third. Here they used to sit in the shade through a long lazy summer's day, talking listlessly over village gossip, or telling endless sleepy stories about nothing. But it would have been worth any statesman's money to have heard the profound discussions that sometimes took place, when by chance an old newspaper fell into their hands from some passing traveler. How solemnly they would listen to the contents, as drawled out by Derrick Van Bummel, the schoolmaster, a dapper learned little man, who was not to be daunted by the most gigantic word in the dictionary; and how sagely they would deliberate upon public events some months after they had taken place.

The opinions of this junto were completely controlled by Nicholas Vedder, a patriarch of the village, and landlord of the inn, at the door of which he took his seat from morning till night, just moving sufficiently to avoid the sun and keep in the shade of a large tree; so that the neighbors could tell the hour by his movements as accurately as by a sundial. It is true he was rarely heard to speak, but smoked his pipe incessantly. His adherents, however (for every great man has his adherents), perfectly understood him, and knew how to gather his opinions. When anything that was read or related displeased him, he was observed to smoke his pipe vehemently, and to send forth short, frequent and angry puffs; but when pleased, he would inhale the smoke slowly and tranquilly, and emit it in light and placid clouds; and sometimes, taking the pipe from his mouth, and letting the fragrant vapor curl about his nose, would gravely nod his head in token of perfect approbation.

From even this stronghold the unlucky Rip was at length routed by his termagant wife, who would suddenly break in upon the tranquillity of the assemblage and call the members all to naught; nor was that august personage, Nicholas Vedder himself, sacred from the daring tongue of this terrible virago, who charged him outright with encouraging her husband in habits of idleness.

Poor Rip was at last reduced almost to despair; and his

only alternative, to escape from the labor of the farm and clamor of his wife, was to take gun in hand and stroll away into the woods. Here he would sometimes seat himself at the foot of a tree, and share the contents of his wallet with Wolf, with whom he sympathized as a fellow-sufferer in persecution. 'Poor Wolf,' he would say, 'thy mistress leads thee a dog's life of it; but never mind, my lad, whilst I live thou shalt never want a friend to stand by thee!' Wolf would wag his tail, look wistfuly in his master's face, and if dogs can feel pity I verily believe he reciprocated the sentiment with all his heart.

In a long ramble of the kind on a fine autumnal day, Rip had unconsciously scrambled to one of the highest parts of the Catskill mountains. He was after his favorite sport of squirrel shooting, and the still solitudes had echoed and re-echoed with the reports of his gun. Panting and fatigued, he threw himself, late in the afternoon, on a green knoll, covered with mountain herbage, that crowned the brow of a precipice. From an opening between the trees he could overlook all the lower country for many a mile of rich woodland. He saw at a distance the lordly Hudson, far, far below him, moving on its silent but majestic course, with the reflection of a purple cloud, or the sail of a lagging bark, here and there sleeping on its glassy bosom, and at last losing itself in the blue highlands.

On the other side he looked down into a deep mountain glen, wild, lonely, and shagged, the bottom filled with fragments from the impending cliffs, and scarcely lighted by the reflected rays of the setting sun. For some time Rip lay musing on this scene; evening was gradually advancing; the mountains began to throw their long blue shadows over the valleys; he saw that it would be dark long before he could reach the village, and he heaved a heavy sigh when he thought of encountering the terrors of Dame Van Winkle.

As he was about to descend, he heard a voice from a distance, hallooing, 'Rip Van Winkle! Rip Van Winkle!' He looked round, but could see nothing but a crow winging its solitary flight across the mountain. He thought his fancy must have deceived him, and turned again to descend, when he heard the same cry ring through the still evening air: 'Rip Van Winkle! Rip Van Winkle!' — at the same time Wolf bristled up his back, and giving a low growl, skulked to his master's side, looking fearfully down into the glen. Rip now felt a vague apprehension stealing over him; he looked anxiously in the same direction, and perceived a strange figure slowly toiling up the rocks, and bending under the weight of something he carried on his back. He was surprised to see any human being in this lonely and unfrequented place, but supposing it to be some one of the neighborhood in need of his assistance, he hastened down to yield it.

On nearer approach he was still more surprised at the singularity of the stranger's appearance. He was a short square-built old fellow, with thick bushy hair, and a grizzled beard. His dress was of the antique Dutch fashion — a cloth jerkin strapped round the waist — several pair of breeches, the outer one of ample volume, decorated with rows of buttons down the sides, and bunches at the knees. He bore on his shoulder a stout keg, that seemed full of liquor, and made signs for Rip to approach and assist him with the load. Though rather shy and distrustful of this new acquaintance, Rip complied with his usual alacrity; and mutually relieving one another, they clambered up a

narrow gully, apparently the dry bed of a mountain tor-
rent. As they ascended, Rip every now and then heard long
rolling peals, like distant thunder, that seemed to issue
out of a deep ravine, or rather cleft, between lofty rocks,
toward which their rugged path conducted. He paused for
an instant, but supposing it to be the muttering of one of
those transient thunder-showers which often take place
in mountain heights, he proceeded. Passing through the
ravine, they came to a hollow, like a small amphitheatre,
surrounded by perpendicular precipices, over the brinks of
which impending trees shot their branches, so that you only
caught glimpses of the azure sky and the bright evening
cloud. During the whole time Rip and his companion had
labored on in silence; for though the former marvelled
greatly what could be the object of carrying a keg of liquor
up this wild mountain, yet there was something strange
and incomprehensible about the unknown, that inspired
awe and checked familiarity.

On entering the amphitheatre, new objects of wonder
presented themselves. On a level spot in the centre was a
company of odd-looking personages playing at nine-pins.
They were dressed in a quaint outlandish fashion; some
wore short doublets, others jerkins, with long knives in
their belts, and most of them had enormous breeches, of
similar style with that of the guide's. Their visages, too,
were peculiar: one had a large beard, broad face, and small
piggish eyes: the face of another seemed to consist entirely
of nose, and was surmounted by a white sugar-loaf hat
set off with a little red cock's tail. They all had beards, of
various shapes and colors. There was one who seemed to
be the commander. He was a stout old gentleman, with

a weather-beaten countenance; he wore a laced doublet, broad belt and hanger, high-crowned hat and feather, red stockings, and high-heeled shoes, with roses in them. The whole group reminded Rip of the figures in an old Flemish painting, in the parlor of Dominie Van Shaick, the village parson, and which had been brought over from Holland at the time of the settlement.

What seemed particularly odd to Rip was, that though these folks were evidently amusing themselves, yet they maintained the gravest faces, the most mysterious silence, and were, withal, the most melancholy party of pleasure he had ever witnessed. Nothing interrupted the stillness of the scene but the noise of the balls, which, whenever they were rolled, echoed along the mountains like rumbling peals of thunder.

As Rip and his companion approached them, they suddenly desisted from their play, and stared at him with such fixed statue-like gaze, and such strange, uncouth, lack-lustre countenances, that his heart turned within him, and his knees smote together. His companion now emptied the contents of the keg into large flagons, and made signs to him to wait upon the company. He obeyed with fear and trembling; they quaffed the liquor in profound silence, and then returned to their game.

By degrees Rip's awe and apprehension subsided. He even ventured, when no eye was fixed upon him, to taste the beverage, which he found had much of the flavor of excellent Hollands. He was naturally a thirsty soul, and was soon tempted to repeat the draught. One taste provoked another; and he reiterated his visits to the flagon so often that at length his senses were overpowered, his eyes swam in his head, his head gradually declined, and he fell into a deep sleep.

On waking, he found himself on the green knoll whence he had first seen the old man of the glen. He rubbed his eyes – it was a bright sunny morning. The birds were hopping and twittering among the bushes, and the eagle was wheeling aloft, and breasting the pure mountain breeze. 'Surely,' thought Rip, 'I have not slept here all night.' He recalled the occurrences before he fell asleep. The strange man with a keg of liquor – the mountain ravine – the wild retreat among the rocks – the woe-begone party at ninepins – the flagon – 'Oh! that flagon! that wicked flagon!' thought Rip – 'what excuse shall I make to Dame Van Winkle!'

He looked round for his gun, but in place of the clean well-oiled fowling-piece, he found an old firelock lying by him, the barrel incrusted with rust, the lock falling off, and the stock worm-eaten. He now suspected that the grave roysterers of the mountain had put a trick upon him, and having dosed him with liquor, had robbed him of his gun. Wolf, too, had disappeared, but he might have strayed away after a squirrel or partridge. He whistled after him and shouted his name, but all in vain; the echoes repeated his whistle and shout, but no dog was to be seen.

He determined to revisit the scene of the last evening's gambol, and if he met with any of the party, to demand his dog and gun. As he rose to walk, he found himself stiff in the joints, and wanting in his usual activity. 'These mountain beds do not agree with me,' thought Rip; 'and if this frolic should lay me up with a fit of the rheumatism, I shall have a blessed time with Dame Van Winkle.' With some difficulty he got down into the glen: he found the gully up which he and his companion had ascended the preceding evening; but to his astonishment a mountain stream was now foaming down it, leaping from rock to rock, and filling the glen with babbling murmurs. He, however, made shift to scramble up its sides, working his toilsome way through thickets of birch, sassafras, and witch-hazel, and sometimes tripped up or entangled by the wild grapevines that twisted their coils or tendrils from tree to tree, and spread a kind of network in his path.

At length he reached to where the ravine had opened through the cliffs to the amphitheatre; but no traces of such opening remained. The rocks presented a high impenetrable wall over which the torrent came tumbling in a sheet of feathery foam, and fell into a broad deep basin, black from the shadows of the surrounding forest. Here, then, poor Rip was brought to a stand. He again called and whistled after his dog; he was only answered by the cawing of a flock of idle crows, sporting high in air about a dry tree that over-hung a sunny precipice; and who, secure in their elevation, seemed to look down and scoff at the poor man's perplexi-ties. What was to be done? the morning was passing away, and Rip felt famished for want of his breakfast. He grieved to give up his dog and gun; he dreaded to meet his wife; but it would not do to starve among the mountains. He shook his head, shouldered the rusty firelock, and, with a heart full of trouble and anxiety, turned his steps homeward.

As he approached the village he met a number of people, but none whom he knew, which somewhat surprised him, for he had thought himself acquainted with every one in the country round. Their dress, too, was of a different fashion from that to which he was accustomed. They all stared at him with equal marks of surprise, and whenever they cast their eyes upon him, invariably stroked their chins. The constant recurrence of this gesture induced Rip, involuntarily, to do the same, when to his astonishment, he found his beard had grown a foot long!

He had now entered the skirts of the village. A troop of strange children ran at his heels, hooting after him, and pointing at his gray beard. The dogs, too, not one of which he recognized for an old acquaintance, barked at him as he passed. The very village was altered; it was larger and more populous. There were rows of houses which he had never seen before, and those which had been his familiar haunts had disappeared. Strange names were over the doors – strange faces at the windows – every thing was strange. His mind now misgave him; he began to doubt whether both he and the world around him were not bewitched. Surely this was his native village, which he had left but the day before. There stood the Catskill mountains – there ran the silver Hudson at a distance – there was every hill and dale precisely as it had always been – Rip was sorely perplexed – 'That flagon last night,' thought he, 'has addled my poor head sadly!'

It was with some difficulty that he found the way to his own house, which he approached with silent awe, expecting every moment to hear the shrill voice of Dame Van Winkle. He found the house gone to decay – the roof fallen in, the windows shattered, and the doors off the hinges. A half-starved dog that looked like Wolf was skulking about it. Rip called him by name, but the cur snarled, showed his teeth, and passed on. This was an unkind cut indeed – 'My very dog,' sighed poor Rip, 'has forgotten me!'

He entered the house, which, to tell the truth, Dame Van Winkle had always kept in neat order. It was empty, forlorn, and apparently abandoned. This desolateness overcame all his connubial fears – he called loudly for his wife and children – the lonely chambers rang for a moment with his voice, and then all again was silence.

He now hurried forth, and hastened to his old resort, the village inn – but it too was gone. A large rickety wooden building stood in its place, with great gaping windows, some of them broken and mended with old hats and petticoats, and over the door was painted, 'the Union Hotel, by Jonathan Doolittle'. Instead of the great tree that used to shelter the quiet little Dutch inn of yore, there now was reared a tall naked pole, with something on the top that looked like a red night-cap, and from it was fluttering a flag, on which was a singular assemblage of stars and stripes – all this was strange and incomprehensible. He recognized on the sign, however, the ruby face of King George, under which he had smoked so many a peaceful pipe; but even this was singularly metamorphosed. The red coat was changed for one of blue and buff, a sword was held in the hand instead of a sceptre, the head was decorated with a cocked hat, and underneath was painted in large characters, GENERAL WASHINGTON.

There was, as usual, a crowd of folk about the door, but none that Rip recollected. The very character of the people seemed changed. There was a busy, bustling, disputatious tone about it, instead of the accustomed phlegm and drowsy tranquillity. He looked in vain for the sage Nicholas Vedder, with his broad face, double chin, and fair long pipe, uttering clouds of tobacco-smoke instead of idle speeches; or Van Bummel, the schoolmaster, doling forth the contents of an ancient newspaper. In place of these, a lean, bilious-looking fellow, with his pockets full of handbills, was haranguing vehemently about rights of citizens – elections – members of congress – liberty – Bunker's Hill – heroes of seventy-six – and other words, which were a perfect Babylonish jargon to the bewildered Van Winkle.

The appearance of Rip, with his long grizzled beard, his rusty fowling-piece, his uncouth dress, and an army of women and children at his heels, soon attracted the attention of the tavern politicians. They crowded round him, eyeing him from head to foot with great curiosity. The orator bustled up to him, and, drawing him partly aside, inquired 'on which side he voted?' Rip stared in vacant stupidity. Another short but busy little fellow pulled him by the arm, and, rising on tiptoe, inquired in his ear, 'Whether he was Federal or Democrat?' Rip was equally at a loss to comprehend the question; when a knowing, self-important old gentleman, in a sharp cocked hat, made his way through the crowd, putting them to the right and left with his elbows as he passed, and planting himself before Van Winkle, with one arm akimbo, the other resting on his cane, his keen eyes and sharp hat penetrating, as it were, into his very soul, demanded in an austere tone, 'what brought him to the election with a gun on his shoulder, and a mob at his heels, and whether he meant to breed a riot in the village?' – 'Alas! gentlemen,' cried Rip, somewhat dismayed, 'I am a poor quiet man, a native of the place, and a loyal subject of the king, God bless him!'

Here a general shout burst from the by-standers – 'A tory! a tory! a spy! a refugee! hustle him! away with him!' It was with great difficulty that the self-important man in the cocked hat restored order; and, having assumed a tenfold austerity of brow, demanded again of the unknown culprit, what he came there for, and whom he was seeking? The poor man humbly assured him that he meant no harm, but merely came there in search of some of his neighbors, who used to keep about the tavern.

'Well – who are they? – name them.'

Rip bethought himself a moment, and inquired, 'Where's Nicholas Vedder?'

There was a silence for a little while, when an old man replied, in a thin piping voice, 'Nicholas Vedder! why, he is dead and gone these eighteen years! There was a wooden tombstone in the church-yard that used to tell all about him, but that's rotten and gone too.'

'Where's Brom Dutcher?'

'Oh, he went off to the army in the beginning of the war; some say he was killed at the storming of Stony Point – others say he was drowned in a squall at the foot of Antony's Nose. I don't know – he never came back again.'

'Where's Van Bummel, the schoolmaster?'

'He went off to the wars too, was a great militia general, and is now in congress.'

Rip's heart died away at hearing of these sad changes in his home and friends, and finding himself thus alone in the world. Every answer puzzled him too, by treating of such enormous lapses of time, and of matters which he could not understand: war – congress – Stony Point; – he had no courage to ask after any more friends, but cried out in despair, 'Does nobody here know Rip Van Winkle?'

'Oh, Rip Van Winkle!' exclaimed two or three, 'Oh, to be sure! That's Rip Van Winkle yonder, leaning against the tree.'

Rip looked, and beheld a precise counterpart of himself, as he went up the mountain: apparently as lazy, and certainly as ragged. The poor fellow was now completely confounded. He doubted his own identity, and whether he was himself or another man. In the midst of his bewilderment, the man in the cocked hat demanded who he was, and what was his name?

'God knows,' exclaimed he, at his wits' end; 'I'm not myself – I'm somebody else – that's me yonder – no – that's somebody else got into my shoes – I was myself last night, but I fell asleep on the mountain, and they've changed my gun, and every thing's changed, and I'm changed, and I can't tell what's my name, or who I am!'

The by-standers began now to look at each other, nod, wink significantly, and tap their fingers against their foreheads. There was a whisper also, about securing the gun, and keeping the old fellow from doing mischief, at the very suggestion of which the self-important man in the cocked hat retired with some precipitation. At this critical moment a fresh comely woman pressed through the throng to get a peep at the gray-bearded man. She had a chubby child in her arms, which, frightened at his looks, began to cry. 'Hush, Rip,' cried she, 'hush, you little fool; the old man won't hurt you.' The name of the child, the air of the mother, the tone of her voice, all awakened a train of recollections in his mind. 'What is your name, my good woman?' asked he.

'Judith Cardenier.'

'And your father's name?'

'Ah, poor man, Rip Van Winkle was his name, but it's twenty years since he went away from home with his gun, and never has been heard of since – his dog came home without him; but whether he shot himself, or was carried away by the Indians, nobody can tell. I was then but a little girl.'

Rip had but one question more to ask; but he put it with a faltering voice:

'Where's your mother?'

'Oh, she too had died but a short time since; she broke a blood-vessel in a fit of passion at a New-England peddler.'

There was a drop of comfort, at least, in this intelligence. The honest man could contain himself no longer. He caught his daughter and her child in his arms. 'I am your father!' cried he – 'Young Rip Van Winkle once – old Rip Van Winkle now! – Does nobody know poor Rip Van Winkle?'

All stood amazed, until an old woman, tottering out from among the crowd, put her hand to her brow, and peering under it in his face for a moment, exclaimed, 'Sure enough! it is Rip Van Winkle – it is himself! Welcome home again, old neighbor – Why, where have you been these twenty long years?'

Rip's story was soon told, for the whole twenty years had been to him but as one night. The neighbors stared when they heard it; some were seen to wink at each other, and put their tongues in their cheeks: and the self-important man in the cocked hat, who, when the alarm was over, had returned to the field, screwed down the corners of his mouth, and shook his head – upon which there was a general shaking of the head throughout the assemblage.

It was determined, however, to take the opinion of old Peter Vanderdonk, who was seen slowly advancing up the road. He was a descendant of the historian of that name, who wrote one of the earliest accounts of the province.

Peter was the most ancient inhabitant of the village, and well versed in all the wonderful events and traditions of the neighborhood. He recollected Rip at once, and corroborated his story in the most satisfactory manner. He assured the company that it was a fact, handed down from his ancestor the historian, that the Kaatskill mountains had always been haunted by strange beings. That it was affirmed that the great Hendrick Hudson, the first discoverer of the river and country, kept a kind of vigil there every twenty years, with his crew of the Half-Moon; being permitted in this way to revisit the scenes of his enterprise, and keep a guardian eye upon the river, and the great city called by his name. That his father had once seen them in their old Dutch dresses playing at nine-pins in a hollow of the mountain; and that he himself had heard, one summer afternoon, the sound of their balls, like distant peals of thunder.

To make a long story short, the company broke up, and returned to the more important concerns of the election. Rip's daughter took him home to live with her; she had a snug, well-furnished house, and a stout cheery farmer for a husband, whom Rip recollected for one of the urchins that used to climb upon his back. As to Rip's son and heir, who was the ditto of himself, seen leaning against the tree, he was employed to work on the farm; but evinced an hereditary disposition to attend to anything else but his business.

Rip now resumed his old walks and habits; he soon found many of his former cronies, though all rather the worse for the wear and tear of time; and preferred making friends among the rising generation, with whom he soon grew into great favor.

Having nothing to do at home, and being arrived at that

211

happy age when a man can be idle with impunity, he took his place once more on the bench at the inn door, and was reverenced as one of the patriarchs of the village, and a chronicle of the old times 'before the war'. It was some time before he could get into the regular track of gossip, or could be made to comprehend the strange events that had taken place during his torpor. How that there had been a revolutionary war – that the country had thrown off the yoke of old England – and that, instead of being a subject of his Majesty George the Third, he was now a free citizen of the United States. Rip, in fact, was no politician; the changes of states and empires made but little impression on him; but there was one species of despotism under which he had long groaned, and that was – petticoat government. Happily that was at an end; he had got his neck out of the yoke of matrimony, and could go in and out whenever he pleased, without dreading the tyranny of Dame Van Winkle. Whenever her name was mentioned, however, he shook his head, shrugged his shoulders, and cast up his eyes; which might pass either for an expression of resignation to his fate, or joy at his deliverance.

He used to tell his story to every stranger that arrived at Mr Doolittle's hotel. He was observed, at first, to vary on some points every time he told it, which was, doubtless, owing to his having so recently awaked. It at last settled down precisely to the tale I have related, and not a man, woman, or child in the neighborhood, but knew it by heart. Some always pretended to doubt the reality of it, and insisted that Rip had been out of his head, and that this was one point on which he always remained flighty. The old Dutch inhabitants, however, almost universally gave it full credit. Even to this day they never hear a thunderstorm of a summer afternoon about the Catskills, but they say Hendrick Hudson and his crew are at their game of nine-pins; and it is a common wish of all hen-pecked husbands in the neighborhood, when life hangs heavy on their hands, that they might have a quieting draught out of Rip Van Winkle's flagon.

NOTE – The foregoing tale, one would suspect, had been suggested to Mr Knickerbocker by a little German superstition about the Emperor Frederick der Rothbart, and the Kypphauser Mountain: the subjoined note, however, which he had appended to the tale, shows that it is an absolute fact, narrated with his usual fidelity:

'The story of Rip Van Winkle may seem incredible to many, but nevertheless I give it my full belief, for I know the vicinity of our old Dutch settlements to have been very subject to marvellous events and appearances. Indeed, I have heard many stranger stories than this, in the villages along the Hudson; all of which were too well authenticated to admit of a doubt. I have even talked with Rip Van Winkle myself who, when last I saw him, was a very venerable old man, and so perfectly rational and consistent on every other point, that I think no conscientious person could refuse to take this into the bargain; nay, I have seen a certificate on the subject taken before a country justice and signed with a cross, in the justice's own handwriting. The story, therefore, is beyond the possibility of doubt.

'D. K.'

POSTSCRIPT

The following are travelling notes from a memorandum-book of Mr. Knickerbocker:

The Kaatsberg or Catskill mountains have always been a region full of fable. The Indians considered them the abode of spirits, who influenced the weather, spreading sunshine or clouds over the landscape, and sending good or bad hunting seasons. They were ruled by an old squaw spirit, said to be their mother. She dwelt on the highest peak of the Catskills, and had charge of the doors of day and night to open and shut them at the proper hour. She hung up the new moons in the skies, and cut up the old ones into stars. In times of drought, if properly propitiated, she would spin light summer clouds out of cobwebs and morning dew, and send them off from the crest of the mountain, flake after flake, like flakes of carded cotton, to float in the air; until, dissolved by the heat of the sun, they would fall in gentle showers, causing the grass to spring, the fruits to ripen, the corn to grow an inch an hour. If displeased, however, she would brew up clouds as black as ink, sitting in the midst of them like a bottle-bellied spider in the midst of its web; and when these clouds broke, woe betide the valleys!

In old times, say the Indian traditions, there was a kind of Manitou or Spirit, who kept about the wildest recesses of the Catskill mountains, and took a mischievous pleasure in wreaking all kind of evils and vexations upon the red men. Sometimes he would assume the form of a bear, a panther, or a deer, lead the bewildered hunter a weary chase through tangled forests and among ragged rocks, and then spring off with a loud ho! ho! leaving him aghast on the brink of a beetling precipice or raging torrent.

The favorite abode of this Manitou is still shown. It is a rock or cliff on the loneliest port of the mountains, and, from the flowering vines which clamber about it, and the wild flowers which abound in its neighbourhood, is known by the name of the Garden Rock. Near the foot of it is a small lake, the haunt of the solitary bittern, with water-snakes basking in the sun on the leaves of the pond-lilies which lie on the surface. This place was held in great awe by the Indians, insomuch that the boldest hunter would not pursue his game within its precincts. Once upon a time, however, a hunter who had lost his way penetrated to the Garden Rock, where he beheld a number of gourds placed in the crotches of trees. One of these he seized and made off with it, but in the hurry of his retreat he let it fall among the rocks, when a great stream gushed forth, which washed him away and swept him down precipices, where he was dashed to pieces, and the stream made its way to the Hudson, and continues to flow to the present day, being the identical stream known by the name of the Kaaterskill.

(1819)

It is believed that when we sleep the chemical systems within the brain that control short-term memory are switched off, hence why we have next to no recall of our dreams the next morning (unless rudely awakened). This suspension allows the higher cortical brain to download recently acquired experiences into its longer-term memory during sleep. Proving this theory, memory is one of the first faculties to be noticeably impaired by sleep deprivation.

Similarly, some recent US medical studies suggest that there may be links between certain sleep patterns and the prevalence of the dread beta-amyloid plaques that characterize Alzheimer's. Statistically, we sleep more lightly – and so, less — as we grow old. This falling-off coincides with our becoming more absent-minded. More of this anon.

The late Nora Ephron, chronicler of grown-up relationships in many great films (the most pertinent example for us being *Sleepless in Seattle*), also wrote with tremendous wit about ageing.

In this short piece, 'Who Are You?', Ephron mines the sometime nightmarish experience of feeling our age. Amid her social satire, the gentle panic of these vignettes should be familiar to every grown-up. Her triptych culminates with a deliciously grotesque realization. In that instant, Ephron is not only sublimely self-effacing, but also captures the twitchy half-familiarity that can inwardly paralyse us so often in sleep. For in our dreams — even as we re-make old, forgotten acquaintances — deep down, we are only ever getting to know ourselves.

Who Are You?
by Nora Ephron

I Know You

I know you. I know you well. It's true I always have a little trouble with your name, but I do know your name. I just don't know it at this moment. We're at a big party. We've kissed hello. We've had a delightful conversation about how we are the last two people on the face of the earth who don't kiss on both cheeks. Now we're having a conversation about how phony all the people are who do kiss on both cheeks. Ha ha ha ha ha ha. You're so charming. If only I could remember your name. It's inexcusable that I can't. You've been to my house for dinner. I tried to read your last book. I know your girlfriend's name, or I almost know it. It's something like Chanelle. Only it's not. Chantelle? That's not it either. Fortunately, she isn't here, so I haven't forgotten both of your names. I'm becoming desperate. It's something like Larry. Is it Larry? No, it's not. Jerry? No, it's not. But it ends in a *Y*. Your last name: three syllables. Starts with a *C*. Starts with a *G*? I'm losing my mind. But a miracle occurs: the host is about to toast the guest of honor. Thank God. I can escape to the bar.

Have We Met?

Have we met? I think we've met. But I can't be sure. We were introduced, but I didn't catch your name because it's so noisy at this party. I'm going to assume we know each other, and I'm not going to say, 'Nice to meet you.' If I say, 'Nice to meet you,' I know what will happen. You'll say, 'We've met.' You'll say 'We've met' in a sort of aggressive, irritable tone. And you won't even tell me your name so I can recover in some way. So I'm not going to say, 'Nice to meet you.' I'm going to say, 'Nice to see you.' I'll have a big smile on my face. I won't look desperate. But what I'll be thinking is, Please throw me your name. Please, please, please. Give me a hint. My husband is likely to walk up, and I'll have to introduce you, and I won't be able to, and you'll know that I have no idea who you are, even though we probably spent an entire weekend together on a boat in 1984. I have a secret signal with my husband that involves my pinching him very hard on the upper arm. The signal means, 'Throw your name at this person because I have no idea whom I'm talking to.' But my husband always forgets the secret signal and can't be counted on to respond to my pinching, even when it produces a bruise. I would like to chew my husband out about his forgetfulness on this point, but I'm not exactly in a position to do so since I myself have forgotten (if I ever knew it) the name of the person I'm talking to.

Old Friends

Old friends? We must be. You're delighted to see me. I'm delighted to see you. But who are you? Oh, my God, you're Ellen. I can't believe it. Ellen. 'Ellen! How are you? It's been – how long has it been?' I'd like to suggest that the reason I didn't recognize you right off the bat is that you've done something to your hair, but you've done nothing to your hair, nothing that would excuse my not recognizing you. What you've actually done is gotten older. I don't believe it. You used to be my age, and now you're much, much, much older than I am. You could be my mother. Unless, of course, I look as old as you and I don't know it. Which is not possible. Or is it? I'm looking around the room and I notice that everyone in it looks like someone – and when I try to figure out exactly who that someone is, it turns out to be a former version of herself, a thinner version or a healthier version or a pre-plastic-surgery version or a taller version. If this is true of everyone, it must be true of me. Mustn't it? But never mind: you are speaking. 'Maggie,' you say, 'it's been so long.' 'I'm not Maggie,' I say. 'Oh my God,' you say, 'it's you. I didn't recognize you. You've done something to your hair.'

(2010)

★

Nobel Laureate Isaac Bashevis Singer once said, 'When a writer sits down and psychoanalyzes, he's ruining his work!'

The Reencounter
by Isaac Bashevis Singer

The telephone rang and Dr Max Greitzer woke up. On the night table the clock showed fifteen minutes to eight. 'Who could be calling so early?' he murmured. He picked up the phone and a woman's voice said, 'Dr Greitzer, excuse me for calling at this hour. A woman who was once dear to you has died. Liza Nestling.'

'My God!'

'The funeral is today at eleven. I thought you would want to know.'

'You are right. Thank you. Liza Nestling played a major role in my life. May I ask whom I am speaking to?'

'It doesn't matter. Liza and I became friends after you two separated. The service will be in Gutgestalt's funeral parlor. You know the address?'

'Yes, thank you.'

The woman hung up.

Dr Greitzer lay still for a while. So Liza was gone. Twelve years had passed since their breaking up. She had been his great love. Their affair lasted about fifteen years – no, not fifteen; thirteen. The last two had been filled with so many misunderstandings and complications, with so much madness, that words could not describe them. The same powers that built this love destroyed it entirely. Dr Greitzer and Liza Nestling never met again. They never wrote to one another. From a friend of hers he learned that she was having an affair with a would-be theater director, but that was the only word he had about her. He hadn't even known that Liza was still in New York.

Dr Greitzer was so distressed by the bad news that he didn't remember how he got dressed that morning or found his way to the funeral parlor. When he arrived, the clock across the street showed twenty-five to nine. He opened the door, and the receptionist told him that he had come too early. The service would not take place until eleven o'clock.

'Is it possible for me to see her now?' Max Greitzer asked. 'I am a very close friend of hers, and . . .'

'Let me ask if she's ready.' The girl disappeared behind a door.

Dr Greitzer understood what she meant. The dead are elaborately fixed up before they are shown to their families and those who attend the funeral.

Soon the girl returned and said, 'It's all right. Fourth floor, room three.'

A man in a black suit took him up in the elevator and opened the door to room number 3. Liza lay in a coffin opened to her shoulders, her face covered with gauze. He recognized her only because he knew it was she. Her black hair had the dullness of dye. Her cheeks were rouged, and the wrinkles around her closed eyes were hidden under makeup. On her reddened lips there was a hint of a smile. How do they produce a smile? Max Greitzer wondered. Liza had once accused him of being a mechanical person, a robot with no emotion. The accusation was false then, but now, strangely, it seemed to be true. He was neither dejected nor frightened.

The door to the room opened and a woman with an uncanny resemblance to Liza entered. 'It's her sister, Bella,' Max Greitzer said to himself. Liza had often spoken about her younger sister, who lived in California, but he had never met her. He stepped aside as the woman approached the coffin. If she burst out crying, he would be nearby to comfort her. She showed no special emotion, and he decided to leave her with her sister, but it occurred to him that she might be afraid to stay alone with a corpse, even her own sister's.

After a few moments, she turned and said, 'Yes, it's her.'

'I expect you flew in from California,' Max Greitzer said, just to say something.

'From California?'

'Your sister was once close to me. She often spoke about you. My name is Max Greitzer.'

The woman stood silent and seemed to ponder his words Then she said, 'You're mistaken.'

'Mistaken? You aren't her sister, Bella?'

'Don't you know that Max Greitzer died? There was an obituary in the newspapers.'

Max Greitzer tried to smile. 'Probably another Max Greitzer.' The moment he uttered those words, he grasped the truth: he and Liza were both dead – the woman who spoke to him was not Bella but Liza herself. He now realized that if he were still alive he would be shaken with grief. Only someone on the other side of life could accept with such indifference the death of a person he had once loved. Was what he was experiencing the immortality of the soul, he wondered. If he were able, he would laugh now, but the illusion of the body had vanished; he and Lisa no longer had material substance. Yet they were both present. Without a voice he asked, 'Is this possible?'

He heard Liza answer in her smart style, 'If it is so, it must be possible.' She added, 'For your information, your body is lying here too.'

'How did it happen? I went to sleep last night a healthy man.'

'It wasn't last night and you were not healthy. A degree of amnesia seems to accompany this process. It happened to me a day ago and therefore—'

'I had a heart attack?'

'Perhaps.'

'What happened to *you*?' he asked.

'With me, everything takes a long time. How did you hear about me, anyway?' she added.

'I thought I was lying in bed. Fifteen minutes to eight, the telephone rang and a woman told me about you. She refused to give her name.'

'Fifteen minutes to eight, your body was already here. Do you want to go look at yourself? I've seen you. You are in number 5. They made a *krasavetz* out of you.'

He hadn't heard anyone say *krasavetz* for years. It meant a beautiful man. Liza had been born in Russia and she often used this word.

'No. I'm not curious.'

In the chapel it was quiet. A clean-shaven rabbi with curly hair and a gaudy tie made a speech about Liza. 'She was an intellectual woman in the best sense of the word,' he said. 'When she came to America, she worked all day in a shop and at night she attended college, graduating with high honors. She had bad luck and many things in her life went awry, but she remained a lady of high integrity.'

'I never met that man. How could he know about me?' Liza asked.

'Your relatives hired him and gave him the information,' Greitzer said.

'I hate these professional compliments.'

'Who's the fellow with the gray mustache on the first bench?' Max Greitzer asked.

Liza uttered something like a laugh. 'My has-been husband.'

'You were married? I heard only that you had a lover.'

'I tried everything, with no success whatsoever.'

'Where would you like to go?' Max Greitzer asked.

'Perhaps to your service.'

'Absolutely not.'

'What state of being is this?' Liza asked. 'I see everything. I recognize everyone. There is my Aunt Reizl. Right behind her is my Cousin Becky. I once introduced you to her.'

'Yes, true.'

'The chapel is half empty. From the way I acted towards others in such circumstances, it is what I deserve. I'm sure that for you the chapel will be packed. Do you want to wait and see?'

'I haven't the slightest desire to find out.'

The rabbi had finished his eulogy and a cantor recited 'God Full of Mercy'. His chanting was more like crying and Liza said, 'My own father wouldn't have gone into such lamentations.'

'Paid tears.'

'I've had enough of it,' Liza said. 'Let's go.'

They floated from the funeral parlor to the street. There,

six limousines were lined up behind the hearse. One of the chauffeurs was eating a banana.

'Is this what they call death?' Liza asked. 'It's the Same City: the same streets, the same stores. I seem the same, too.'

'Yes, but without a body.'

'What am I then? A soul?'

'Really, I don't know what to tell you,' Max Greitzer said. 'Do you feel any hunger?'

'Hunger? No.'

'Thirst?'

'No. No. What do you say to all this?'

'The unbelievable, the absurd, the most vulgar superstitions are proving to be true,' Max Greitzer said.

'Perhaps we will find there is even a Hell and a Paradise.'

'Anything is possible at this point.'

'Perhaps we will be summoned to the Court on High after the burial and asked to account for our deeds?'

'Even this can be.'

'How does it come about that we are together?'

'Please, don't ask any more questions, I know as little as you.'

'Does this mean that all the philosophic works you read and wrote were one big lie?'

'Worse – they were sheer nonsense.'

At that moment, four pallbearers carried out the coffin holding Liza's body. A wreath lay on top, with an inscription in gold letters: 'To the unforgettable Liza in loving memory.'

'Whose wreath is that?' Liza asked, and she answered herself, 'For this he's not stingy.'

'Would you like to go with them to the cemetery?' Max Greitzer asked.

'No – what for? That phony cantor may recite a whining Kaddish after me.'

'What do you want to do?'

Liza listened to herself. She wanted nothing. What a peculiar state, not to have a single wish. In all the years she could remember, her will, her yearnings, her fears, tormented her without letting up. Her dreams were full of desperation, ecstasy, wild passions. More than any other catastrophe, she dreaded the final day, when all that has been is extinguished and the darkness of the grave begins. But here she was, remembering the past, and Max Greitzer was again with her. She said to him, 'I imagined that the end would be much more dramatic.'

'I don't believe this is the end,' he said. 'Perhaps a transition between two modes of existence.'

'If so, how long will it last?'

'Since time has no validity, duration has no meaning.'

'Well, you've remained the same with your puzzles and paradoxes. Come, we cannot just stay here if you want to avoid seeing your mourners,' Liza said. 'Where should we go?'

'You lead.'

Max Greitzer took her astral arm and they began to rise without purpose, without a destination. As they might have done from an airplane, they looked down at the earth and saw cities, rivers, fields, lakes – everything but human beings.

'Did you say something?' Liza asked.

And Max Greitzer answered. 'Of all my disenchantments, immortality is the greatest.'

(1979)

225

★

E. B. White, the author of children's classics *Charlotte's Web* (about a literate spider) and *Stuart Little* (concerning a talking mouse), was also famously a contributor to *The New Yorker* magazine. When discussing his relationship with nature in 1969, and the apparent contradiction with his urbane work for the magazine, White said: 'There is no contradiction. New York is part of the natural world. I love the city, I love the country, and for the same reasons . . . It is not just a question of birds and animals. The urban scene is a spectacle that fascinates me. People are animals, and the city is full of people in strange plumage, defending their territorial rights, digging for their supper.'

The Second Tree from the Corner
by E. B. White

'Ever have any bizarre thoughts?' asked the doctor.

Mr Trexler failed to catch the word. 'What kind?' he said.

'Bizarre,' repeated the doctor, his voice steady. He watched his patient for any slight change of expression, any wince. It seemed to Trexler that the doctor was not only watching him closely but was creeping slowly toward him, like a lizard toward a bug. Trexler shoved his chair back an inch and gathered himself for a reply. He was about to say 'Yes' when he realized that if he said yes the next question would be unanswerable. Bizarre thoughts, bizarre thoughts? Ever have any bizarre thoughts? What kind of thoughts *except* bizarre had he had since the age of two?

Trexler felt the time passing, the necessity for an answer. These psychiatrists were busy men, overloaded, not to be kept waiting. The next patient was probably already perched out there in the waiting room, lonely, worried, shifting around on the sofa, his mind stuffed with bizarre thouths and amorphous fears. Poor bastard, thought Trexler. Out there all alone in that misshapen antechamber, staring at the filing cabinet and wondering whether to tell the doctor about that day on the Madison Avenue bus.

Let's see, bizarre thoughts. Trexler dodged back along the dreadful corridor of the years to see what he could find. He felt the doctor's eyes upon him and knew that time was running out. Don't be so conscientious, he said to himself. If a bizarre thought is indicated here, just reach into the bag and pick anything at all. A man as well supplied with bizarre thoughts as you are should have no difficulty producing one for the record. Trexler darted into the bag, hung for a moment before one of his thoughts, as a humming bird pauses in the delphinium. No, he said, not that one. He darted to another (the one about the rhesus monkey), paused, considered. No, he said, not that.

Trexler knew he must hurry. He had already used up pretty nearly four seconds since the question had been put. But it was an impossible situation – just one more lousy, impossible situation such as he was always getting himself into. When, he asked himself, are you going to quit maneuvering yourself into a pocket? He made one more effort. This time he stopped at the asylum, only the bars were lucite – fluted, retractable. Not here, he said. Not this one.

He looked straight ahead at the doctor. 'No,' he said quietly. 'I never have any bizarre thoughts.'

The doctor sucked in on his pipe, blew a plume of smoke toward the rows of medical books. Trexler's gaze followed the smoke. He managed to make out one of the titles, 'The Genito-Urinary System.' A bright wave of fear swept cleanly over him, and he winced under the first pain of kidney stones. He remembered when he was a child, the first time he ever entered a doctor's office, sneaking a look at the titles of the books – and the flush of fear, the shirt wet under the arms, the book on t.b., the sudden knowledge that he was in the advanced stages of consumption, the quick vision of hemorrhage. Trexler sighed wearily. Forty years, he thought, and I still get thrown by the title of a medical book. Forty years and I still can't stay on life's little bucky horse. No wonder I'm sitting here in this dreary joint at the end of this woebegone afternoon, lying about my bizarre thoughts to a doctor who looked, come to think of it, rather tired.

The session dragged on. After about twenty minutes, the doctor rose and knocked his pipe out. Texler got up, knocked the ashes out of his brain, and waited. The doctor smiled warmly and stuck out his hands. 'There's nothing the matter with you – you're just scared. Want to know how I know you're scared?'

'How?' asked Trexler.

'Look at the chair you've been sitting in! See how it has moved back away from my desk. You kept inching away from me while I asked you questions. That means you're scared.'

'Does it?' said Trexler, faking a grin. 'Yeah, I suppose it does.'

They finished shaking hands. Trexler turned and walked out uncertainly along the passage, then into the waiting room and out past the next patient, a ruddy pin-striped man who was seated on the sofa twirling his hat nervously and staring straight ahead at the files. Poor, frightened guy, thought Trexler, he's probably read in the *Times* that one American male out of every two is going to die of heart disease by twelve o'clock next Thursday. It says that in the paper almost every morning. And he's also probably thinking about that day on the Madison Avenue bus.

A week later, Trexler was back in the patient's chair. And for several weeks thereafter he continued to visit the doctor, always toward the end of the afternoon, when the vapors hung thick above the pool of the mind and darkened the whole region of the East Seventies. He felt no better as time went on, and he found it impossible to work. He discovered that the visits were becoming routine and that although the routine was one to which he certainly did not look forward, at least he could accept it with cool resignation, as once, years ago, he had accepted a long spell with a dentist who had settled down to a steady footing with a couple of dead teeth. The visits, moreover, were now assuming a pattern recognizable to the patient.

Each session would begin with a résumé of symptoms — dizziness in the streets, the constricting pain in the back of the neck, the apprehensions, the tightness of the scalp, the inability to concentrate, the despondency and the melancholy times, the feeling of pressure and tension, the anger at not being able to work, the anxiety over work not done, the gas on the stomach. Dullest set of neurotic symptoms in the world, Trexler would think, as he obediently trudged back over them for the doctor's benefit. And then, having listened attentively to the recital, the doctor would spring his question: 'Have you ever found anything that gives you relief?' And Trexler would answer, 'Yes. A drink.' And the doctor would nod his head knowingly.

As he became familiar with the pattern Trexler found that he increasingly tended to identify himself with the doctor, transferring himself into the doctor's seat – probably (he thought) some rather slick form of escapism. At any rate, it was nothing new for Trexler to identify himself with other people. Whenever he got into a cab, he instantly became the driver, saw everything from the hackman's angle (and the reaching over with the right hand, the nudging of the flag, the pushing it down, all the way down along the side of the meter), saw everything – traffic, fare, everything – through the eyes of Anthony Rocco, or Isidore Freedman, or Matthew Scott. In a barbershop, Trexler was the barber, his fingers curled around the comb, his hand on the tonic. Perfectly natural, then, that Trexler should soon be occupying the doctor's chair, asking the questions, waiting for the answers. He got quite interested in the doctor, in this way. He liked him, and he found him a not too difficult patient.

It was on his fifth visit, about halfway through, that the doctor turned to Trexler and said, suddenly, 'What do you want?' He gave the word 'want' special emphasis.

'I d'know,' replied Trexler uneasily. 'I guess nobody knows the answer to that one.'

'Sure they do,' replied the doctor.

'Do *you* know what *you* want?' asked Trexler narrowly.

'Certainly,' said the doctor. Trexler noticed that at this point the doctor's chair slid slightly backward, away from him. Trexler stifled a small, internal smile. Scared as a rabbit, he said to himself. Look at him scoot!

'What *do* you want?' continued Trexler, pressing his advantage, pressing it hard.

The doctor glided back another inch away from his

inquisitor. 'I want a wing on the small house I own in Westport. I want more money, and more leisure to do the things I want to do.'

Trexler was just about to say, 'And what are those things you want to do, Doctor?' when he caught himself. Better not go too far, he mused. Better not lose possession of the ball. And besides, he thought, what the hell goes on here, anyway – me paying fifteen bucks a throw for these séances and then doing the work myself, asking the questions, weighing the answers. So he wants a new wing! There's a fine piece of theatrical gauze for you! A new wing.

Trexler settled down again and resumed the role of patient for the rest of the visit. It ended on a kindly, friendly note. The doctor reassured him that his fears were the cause of his sickness, and that his fears were unsubstantial. They shook hands, smiling.

Trexler walked dizzily through the empty waiting room and the doctor followed along to let him out. It was late; the secretary had shut up shop and gone home. Another day over the dam. 'Good-bye,' said Trexler. He stepped into the street, turned west toward Madison, and thought of the doctor all alone there, after hours, in that desolate hole – a man who worked longer hours than his secretary. Poor, scared, overworked bastard, thought Trexler. And that new wing!

It was an evening of clearing weather, the Park showing green and desirable in the distance, the last daylight applying a high lacquer to the brick and brownstone walls and giving the street scene a luminous and intoxicating splendor. Trexler meditated, as he walked, on what he wanted. 'What do you want?' he heard again. Trexler knew what he wanted, and what, in general all men wanted; and he was glad, in a way, that it was both inexpressible and unattainable, and that it wasn't a wing. He was satisfied to remember that it was deep, formless, enduring, and impossible of fulfillment, and that it made men sick, and that when you sauntered along Third Avenue and looked through the doorways into the dim saloons, you could sometimes pick out from the unregenerate the ranks who had not forgotten, gazing steadily into the bottoms of the glasses on the long chance that they could get another little peek at it. Trexler found himself renewed by the remembrance that what he wanted was at once great and microscopic, and that although it borrowed from the nature of large deeds and of youthful love and of old songs and early intimations, it was not any one of these things, and that it had not been isolated or pinned down, and that a man who attempted to define it in the privacy of a doctor's office would fall flat on his face.

Trexler felt invigorated. Suddenly his sickness seemed health, his dizziness stability. A small tree, rising between him and the light, stood there saturated with the evening, each gilt-edged leaf perfectly drunk with excellence and delicacy. Trexler's spine registered an ever so slight tremor as it picked up this natural disturbance in the lovely scene. 'I want the second tree from the corner, just as it stands,' he said, answering an imaginary question from an imaginary physician. And he felt a slow pride in realizing that what he wanted none could bestow, and that what he had none could take away. He felt content to be sick, unembarrassed at being afraid; and in the jungle of his fear he glimpsed (as he had so often glimpsed them before) the flashy tail feathers of the bird courage.

Then he thought once again of the doctor, and of his being left there all alone, tired, frightened. (The poor, scared guy, thought Trexler.) Trexler began humming. 'Moonshine Lullaby', his spirit reacting instantly to the hypodermic of Merman's healthy voice. He crossed Madison, boarded a downtown bus, and rode all the way to Fifty-second Street before he had a thought that could rightly have been called bizarre.

(1948)

★

Is it coincidence that White's story mentions 'Moonshine Lullaby', which also features earlier in this collection?

Everyone has been surprised by unbelievable coincidences in daily life, ones that defy explanation. I don't believe in luck (you make that stuff) – but I respect that others, who swerve towards spirituality, like to interpret deeper, hidden truths of inner-connectivity. Symbiosis, synchronicity and serendipity . . . rather than mere circumstance.

Dreams too are ripe for extrapolations and interpretations. Freud, for one, championed such an attitude towards them.

Read into them – dreams, coincidences – what you will, I say.

By Chance
by Wendy Cope

About fifteen years ago while I was teaching a summer course at the Skyros Centre in Greece I picked up a discarded paperback copy of *An Evil Cradling* by Brian Keenan. It's his account of his four and a half years as a hostage in Beirut and his friendship with fellow hostage John McCarthy. I might not have thought of buying it because I thought I knew enough about this episode from newspapers, radio and television. And I had no reason to think that Keenan was an especially good writer – I must have missed the reviews. By the time I'd read twenty or thirty pages I was glad to have come across it by chance. It's a powerful and moving book, very well written. In 1991 it won the *Irish Times* Literature Prize for non-fiction. By the time I finished it I felt warm admiration for the author.

A few months later, having parked my car in a London street, I came back to find a motorcycle parked so close to it that there was no way I was going to get out of the space. As I stood there wondering what to do, a man came out of a nearby theatre and saw the problem. He picked up the motorbike and moved it several yards down the street. I thanked him. He nodded, smiled and went on his way. I recognised the man from his photographs. It was Brian Keenan.

(2014)

Extract from *An Evil Cradling*
by Brian Keenan

I knew they had a motor-generator to light the prison at night whilst bringing in new prisoners. On one occasion the generator was running, though there was no light, and the ventilation pipe was blowing in dusty hot air as usual. I could not see the dust falling. I wasn't bothered by it. But I remember listening to the noise of the machine and the air as it passed through this long vent of piping. My mind seemed to be pulled into the noise until the noise became music. And I listened entranced in the dark to the music that was coming from this pipe. I knew that there was no music and yet I heard it. And flowing out melodiously was all the music that I had ever loved or half remembered. All at once, all simultaneously playing especially for me. It seemed I sat alone in a great concert hall in which this music was being played for me alone. I heard the ethnic chant music of Africa. The rhythmic music of bone and skin. I heard the swirl and squeal of bagpipes. I heard voices chanting in a tribal chant; great orchestras of violins; and flutes filling the air like bird flight, while quiet voices sang some Gregorian chant. All the music of the world was there, playing incessantly into my cell. I lay at first smiling and listening and enjoying this aural feast. I kept telling myself 'There is no music, Brian, it's in your head.' But still I heard it and the music played on and on ever-changing, ever-colourful. I heard the uilleann pipes' lilting drone. I heard fingers strum and pluck a classical flamenco. I heard ancient musics of ancient civilisations coming all at once to fill my cell and from simply smiling and laughing I fell into a musical delirium and began to tap and dance and beat softly upon the walls the different rhythms offered to me.

For how long I did this, I cannot tell, but then suddenly I was fearful. This music that was not there but that I heard had taken hold of me and would not let me go. I could not silence it. It was carrying me away. I called for it to stop. I pressed my hands over my ears foolishly trying to block out a music that was already thumping in my head and it would not go away. I could not end this or silence it. The more I tried the louder it swirled about me, the more it filled the room. And in its loudness I was gripped with a fear that was new to me. I did not know how to contain myself or how to end this thing. My fight against it was defeating me. It was crushing out every part of me and filling me with fear itself. I could not bear it.

I fumbled under my mattress to find the stubs of candles that I had squirrelled away. I took out one candle and lit it in the hope that light would dispel the music that filled the room, but it did not. With my mind only half conscious, I lit another and another candle until I had filled the cell with candlelight, bright, dazzling, soft, alluring light. But still the music played around me. Everywhere the bright burning of the small candles and me waiting and hoping that this imagined music would stop. And then I remembered again you do not overcome by fighting, you only concede the victory to the madness within. You overcome by going beyond it.

Like a somnambulist, I got up from my mattress and in that tiny cell, naked and wet with sweat, I began to dance. Slowly, slowly at first then going with the music, faster I danced and faster until I went beyond, and beyond the music's hold on me. I danced every dance I knew and dances unknown to me. I danced and danced until the music had to keep up with me, I was a dancing dervish. I was the master of this music and I danced and danced. The sweat rolled off me and I bathed myself in the luxury of it. I felt myself alive and unfearful. I was the pied piper who was calling this tune. A tiny cell, a dozen candle stubs and a madman dancing naked. I was laughing. The laughter was part of the music around me. Not the laugh of hysteria, but the laugh of self-possession, the laugh that comes with the moment of victory. Every part of me, every limb, every muscle energized in this dance. For how long I danced or how long I laughed I cannot tell. But it seemed that I would be dancing forever.

(1992)

A Barred Owl
by Richard Wilbur

The warping night air having brought the boom
Of an owl's voice into her darkened room,
We tell the wakened child that all she heard
Was an odd question from a forest bird,
Asking of us, if rightly listened to,
'Who cooks for you?' and then 'Who cooks for you?'

Words, which can make our terrors bravely clear,
Can also thus domesticate a fear,
And send a small child back to sleep at night
Not listening for the sound of stealthy flight
Or dreaming of some small thing in a claw
Borne up to some dark branch and eaten raw.

(2000)

The Haunted Mind
by Nathaniel Hawthorne

What a singular moment is the first one, when you have hardly begun to recollect yourself, after starting from midnight slumber! By unclosing your eyes so suddenly, you seem to have surprised the personages of your dream in full convocation round your bed, and catch one broad glance at them before they can flit into obscurity. Or, to vary the metaphor, you find yourself, for a single instant, wide awake in that realm of illusions, whither sleep has been the passport, and behold its ghostly inhabitants and wondrous scenery, with a perception of their strangeness, such as you never attain while the dream is undisturbed. The distant sound of a church clock is borne faintly on the wind. You question with yourself, half seriously, whether it has stolen to your waking ear from some gray tower, that stood within the precincts of your dream. While yet in suspense, another clock flings its heavy clang over the slumbering town, with so full and distinct a sound, and such a long murmur in the neighboring air, that you are certain it must proceed from the steeple at the nearest corner. You count the strokes — one — two — and there they cease, with a booming sound, like the gathering of a third stroke within the bell.

If you could choose an hour of wakefulness out of the whole night, it would be this. Since your sober bedtime, at eleven, you have had rest enough to take off the pressure of yesterday's fatigue; while before you, till the sun comes from 'far Cathay' to brighten your window, there is almost the space of a summer night; one hour to be spent in thought, with the mind's eye half shut, and two in pleasant dreams, and two in that strangest of enjoyments, the forgetfulness alike of joy and woe. The moment of rising belongs to another period of time, and appears so distant, that the plunge out of a warm bed into the frosty air cannot yet be anticipated with dismay. Yesterday has already vanished among the shadows of the past; to-morrow has not yet emerged from the future. You have found an intermediate space, where the business of life does not intrude; where the passing moment lingers, and becomes truly the present; a spot where Father Time, when he thinks nobody is watching him, sits down by the way side to take breath. Oh, that he would fall asleep, and let mortals live on without growing older!

Hitherto you have lain perfectly still, because the slightest motion would dissipate the fragments of your slumber. Now, being irrevocably awake, you peep through the half-drawn window-curtain, and observe that the glass is ornamented with fanciful devices in frostwork, and that each pane presents something like a frozen dream. There will be time enough to trace out the analogy, while waiting the summons to breakfast. Seen through the clear portion of the glass, where the silvery mountain peaks of the frost scenery do not ascend, the most conspicuous object is the steeple; the white spire of which directs you to the wintry lustre of the firmament. You may almost distinguish the figures on the clock that has just told the hour. Such a frosty sky, and the snow-covered roofs, and the long vista of the frozen street, all white, and the distant water hardened into rock, might make you shiver, even under four blankets and a woolen comforter. Yet look at that one glorious star! Its beams are distinguishable from all the rest, and actually cast the shadow of the casement on the bed, with a radiance of deeper hue than moonlight, though not so accurate an outline.

You sink down and muffle your head in the clothes, shivering all the while, but less from bodily chill, than the bare idea of a polar atmosphere. It is too cold even for the thoughts to venture abroad. You speculate on the luxury of wearing out a whole existence in bed, like an oyster in its shell, content with the sluggish ecstasy of inaction, and drowsily conscious of nothing but delicious warmth, such as you now feel again. Ah! that idea has brought a hideous one in its train. You think how the dead are lying in their cold shrouds and narrow coffins, through the drear winter of the grave, and cannot persuade your fancy that they neither shrink nor shiver, when the snow is drifting over their little hillocks, and the bitter blast howls against the door of the tomb. That gloomy thought will collect a gloomy multitude, and throw its complexion over your wakeful hour.

In the depths of every heart, there is a tomb and a dungeon, though the lights, the music, and revelry above may cause us to forget their existence, and the buried ones, or prisoners whom they hide. But sometimes, and oftenest at midnight, those dark receptacles are flung wide open. In an hour like this, when the mind has a passive sensibility, but no active strength; when the imagination is a mirror, imparting vividness to all ideas, without the power of selecting or controlling them; then pray that your griefs may slumber, and the brotherhood of remorse not break their chain. It is too late! A funeral train comes gliding by your bed, in which Passion and Feeling assume bodily shape, and things of the mind become dim spectres to the eye. There is your earliest Sorrow, a pale young mourner, wearing a sister's likeness to first love, sadly beautiful, with a hallowed sweetness in her melancholy features, and grace in the flow of her sable robe. Next appears a shade of ruined loveliness, with dust among her golden hair, and her bright garments all faded and defaced, stealing from your glance with drooping head, as fearful of reproach; she was your fondest Hope, but a delusive one; so call her Disappointment now. A sterner form succeeds, with a brow of wrinkles, a look and gesture of iron authority; there is no name for him unless it be Fatality, an emblem of the evil influence that rules your fortunes; a demon to whom you subjected yourself by some error at the outset of life, and were bound his slave forever, by once obeying him. See! those fiendish lineaments graven on the darkness, the writhed lip of scorn, the mockery of that living eye, the pointed finger, touching the sore place in your heart! Do you remember any act of enormous folly, at which you would blush, even in the remotest cavern of the earth? Then recognize your Shame.

Pass, wretched band! Well for the wakeful one, if, riotously miserable, a fiercer tribe do not surround him, the devils of a guilty heart, that holds its hell within itself. What if Remorse should assume the features of an injured friend? What if the fiend should come in woman's garments, with a pale beauty amid sin and desolation, and lie down by your side? What if he should stand at your bed's foot, in the likeness of a corpse, with a bloody stain upon the shroud? Sufficient without such guilt, is this nightmare of the soul; this heavy, heavy sinking of the spirits; this wintry gloom about the heart; this indistinct horror of the mind, blending itself with the darkness of the chamber.

By a desperate effort, you start upright, breaking from a sort of conscious sleep, and gazing wildly round the bed, as if the fiends were anywhere but in your haunted mind. At the same moment, the slumbering embers on the hearth send forth a gleam which palely illuminates the whole outer room, and flickers through the door of the bed-chamber, but cannot quite dispel its obscurity. Your eye searches for whatever may remind you of the living world. With eager minuteness, you take note of the table near the fire-place, the book with an ivory knife between its leaves, the unfolded letter, the hat and the fallen glove. Soon the flame vanishes, and with it the whole scene is gone, though its image remains an instant in your mind's eye, when darkness has swallowed the reality. Throughout the chamber, there is the same obscurity as before, but not the same gloom within your breast. As your head falls back upon the pillow, you think – in a whisper be it spoken – how pleasant in these night solitudes would be the rise and fall of a softer breath-ing than your own, the slight pressure of a tenderer bosom, the quiet throb of a purer heart, imparting its peacefulness to your troubled one, as if the fond sleeper were involving you in her dream.

Her influence is over you, though she have no existence but in that momentary image. You sink down in a flowery spot, on the borders of sleep and wakefulness, while your thoughts rise before you in pictures, all disconnected, yet all assimilated by a pervading gladsomeness and beauty. The wheeling of gorgeous squadrons, that glitter in the sun, is succeeded by the merriment of children round the door of a school-house, beneath the glimmering shadow of old trees, at the corner of a rustic lane. You stand in the sunny rain of a summer shower, and wander among the sunny trees of an autumnal wood, and look upward at the brightest of all rainbows, over-arching the unbroken sheet of snow, on the American side of Niagara. Your mind struggles pleasantly between the dancing radiance round the hearth of a young man and his recent bride, and tile twittering flight of birds in spring, about their new-made nest. You feel the merry bounding of a ship before the breeze; and watch the tuneful feet of rosy girls, as they twine their last and merriest dance, in a splendid ballroom; and find yourself in the brilliant circle of a crowded theatre, as the curtain falls over a light and airy scene.

With an involuntary start, you seize hold on consciousness, and prove yourself but half awake, by running a doubtful parallel between human life and the hour which has now elapsed. In both you emerge from mystery, pass through a vicissitude that you can but imperfectly control, and are borne onward to another mystery. Now comes the peal of the distant clock, with fainter and fainter strokes as you plunge farther into the wilderness of sleep. It is the knell of a temporary death. Your spirit has departed, and strays like a free citizen, among the people of a shadowy world, beholding strange sights, yet without wonder or dismay. So calm, perhaps, will be the final change; so undisturbed, as if among familiar things, the entrance of the soul to its Eternal home!

(1835)

A Haunted House
by Virginia Woolf

Whatever hour you woke there was a door shutting. From room to room they went, hand in hand, lifting here, opening there, making sure – a ghostly couple.

'Here we left it,' she said. And he added, 'Oh, but here

too!' 'It's upstairs,' she murmured. 'And in the garden,' he whispered. 'Quietly,' they said, 'or we shall wake them.'

But it wasn't that you woke us. Oh, no. 'They're looking for it; they're drawing the curtain,' one might say, and so read on a page or two. 'Now they've found it,' one would be certain, stopping the pencil on the margin. And then, tired of reading, one might rise and see for oneself, the house all empty, the doors standing open, only the wood pigeons bubbling with content and the hum of the threshing machine sounding from the farm. 'What did I come in here for? What did I want to find?' My hands were empty. 'Perhaps it's upstairs then?' The apples were in the loft. And so down again, the garden still as ever, only the book had slipped into the grass.

But they had found it in the drawing room. Not that one could ever see them. The windowpanes reflected apples, reflected roses; all the leaves green in the glass. If they moved in the drawing room, the apple only turned its yellow side. Yet, the moment after, if the door was opened, spread about the floor, hung upon the walls, pendant from the ceiling – what? My hands were empty. The shadow of a thrush crossed the carpet; from the deepest wells of silence the wood pigeon drew its bubble of sounds. 'Safe, safe, safe,' the pulse of the house beat softly. 'The treasure buried; the room . . .' the pulse stopped short. Oh, was that the buried treasure?

A moment later the light faded. Out in the garden then? But the trees spun darkness for a wandering beam of sun. So fine, so rare, coolly sunk beneath the surface the beam I sought always burned behind the glass. Death was the glass; death was between us, coming to the woman first, hundreds of years ago, leaving the house, sealing the windows; the rooms were darkened. He left it, left her, went North, went East, saw the stars turned in the Southern sky; sought the house, found it dropped beneath the Downs. 'Safe, safe, safe,' the pulse of the house beat gladly. 'The Treasure yours.'

The wind roars up the avenue. Trees stoop and bend this way and that. Moonbeams splash and spill wildly in the rain. But the beam of the lamp falls straight from the window. The candle burns stiff and still. Wandering through the house, opening the windows, whispering not to wake us, the ghostly couple seek their joy.

'Here we slept,' she says. And he adds, 'Kisses without number.' 'Waking in the morning—' 'Silver between the trees—' 'Upstairs—' 'In the garden—' 'When summer came—' 'In winter snowtime—' The doors go shutting far in the distance, gently knocking like the pulse of a heart.

Nearer they come, cease at the doorway. The wind falls, the rain slides silver down the glass. Our eyes darken, we hear no steps beside us; we see no lady spread her ghostly cloak. His hands shield the lantern. 'Look,' he breathes. 'Sound asleep. Love upon their lips.'

Stooping, holding their silver lamp above us, long they look and deeply. Long they pause. The wind drives straightly; the flame stoops slightly. Wild beams of moonlight cross both floor and wall, and, meeting, stain the faces bent; the faces pondering; the faces that search the sleepers and seek their joy.

'Safe, safe, safe,' the heart of the house beats proudly. 'Long years—' he sighs. 'Again you found me.' 'Here,' she murmurs, 'sleeping; in the garden reading; laughing, rolling apples in the loft. Here we left our treasure—' Stooping, their light lifts the lids upon my eyes. 'Safe! Safe! Safe!' the pulse of the house beats wildly. Waking, I cry, 'Oh, is this your buried treasure? The light in the heart.'

(1921)

★

Joanne Harris

The margin between reality and delusion has rarely been as narrow as in 'The Haunting of Hill House', by Shirley Jackson, mistress of the waking dream. In this passage, Eleanor drives to the haunted house through a shifting landscape of fairy tales, tableaux and omens, glimpsed through a distorting lens of domestic disquiet and suburban unease . . .

Extract from *The Haunting of Hill House*
by Shirley Jackson

At one spot she stopped altogether beside the road to stare in disbelief and wonder. Along the road for perhaps a quarter of a mile she had been passing and admiring a row of splendid tended oleanders, blooming pink and white in a steady row. Now she had come to the gateway they protected, and past the gateway the trees continued. The gateway was no more than a pair of ruined stone pillars, with a road leading away between them into empty fields. She could see that the oleander trees cut away from the road and ran up each side of a great square, and she could see all the way to the farther side of the square, which was a line of oleander trees seemingly going along a little river.

Inside the oleander square there was nothing, no house, no building, nothing but the straight road going across and ending at the stream. Now what was here, she wondered, what was here and is gone, or what was going to be here and never came? Was it going to be a house or a garden or an orchard; were they driven away forever or are they coming back? Oleanders are poisonous, she remembered; could they be guarding something? Will I, she thought, will I get out of my car and go between the ruined gates and then, once I am in the magic oleander square, find that I have wandered into a fairyland, protected poisonously from the eyes of people passing? Once I have stepped between the magic gateposts, will I find myself through the protective barrier, the spell broken? I will go into a sweet garden, with fountains and low benches and roses trained over arbors, and find one path – jeweled, perhaps, with rubies and emeralds, soft enough for a king's daughter to walk upon with her little sandaled feet – and it will lead me directly to the palace which lies under a spell. I will walk up low stone steps past stone lions guarding and into a courtyard where a fountain plays and the queen waits, weeping, for the princess to return. She will drop her embroidery when she sees me, and cry out to the palace servants – stirring at last after their long sleep – to prepare a great feast, because the enchantment is ended and the palace is itself again. And we shall live happily ever after.

No, of course, she thought, turning to start her car again, once the palace becomes visible and the spell is broken, the *whole* spell will be broken and all this countryside outside the oleanders will return to its proper form, fading away, towns and signs and cows, into a soft green picture from a fairy tale. Then, coming down from the hills there will be a prince riding, bright in green and silver with a hundred bowmen riding behind him, pennants stirring, horses tossing, jewels flashing . . .

She laughed and turned to smile good-bye at the magic oleanders. Another day, she told them, another day I'll come back and break your spell.

She stopped for lunch after she had driven a hundred miles and a mile. She found a country restaurant which advertised itself as an old mill and found herself seated, incredibly, upon a balcony over a dashing stream, looking down upon wet rocks and the intoxicating sparkle of moving water, with a cut-glass bowl of cottage cheese on the table before her, and corn sticks in a napkin. Because this was a time and a land where enchantments were swiftly made and broken she wanted to linger over her lunch, knowing that Hill House always waited for her at the end of her day. The only other people in the dining room were a family party, a mother and father with a small boy and girl, and they talked to one another softly and gently, and once the little girl turned and regarded Eleanor with frank curiosity and, after a minute, smiled. The lights from the stream below touched the ceiling and the polished tabled and glanced along the little girl's curls, and the little girl's mother said, 'She wants her cup of stars.'

Eleanor looked up, surprised; the little girl was sliding back in her chair, sullenly refusing her milk, while her father frowned and her brother giggled and her mother said calmly, 'She wants her cup of stars.'

Indeed yes, Eleanor thought; indeed, so do I; a cup of stars, of course.

'Her little cup,' the mother was explaining, smiling apologetically at the waitress, who was thunderstruck at the thought that the mill's good country milk was not rich enough for the little girl. 'It has stars in the bottom, and she always drinks her milk from it at home. She calls it her cup of stars because she can see the stars while she drinks her milk.' The waitress nodded, unconvinced, and the mother told the little girl, 'You'll have your milk from your cup of stars tonight when we get home. But just for now, just to be a very good little girl, will you take a little milk from this glass?'

Don't do it, Eleanor told the little girl; insist on your cup of stars; once they have trapped you into being like everyone else you will never see your cup of stars again; don't do it; and the little girl glanced at her, and smiled a little subtle, dimpling, wholly comprehending smile, and shook her head stubbornly at the glass. Brave girl, Eleanor thought; wise, brave girl.

'You're spoiling her,' the father said. 'She ought not to be allowed these whims.'

'Just this once,' the mother said. She put down the glass of milk and touched the little girl gently on the hand. 'Eat your ice cream,' she said.

When they left, the little girl waved good-by to Eleanor, and Eleanor waved back, sitting in joyful loneliness to finish her coffee while the gay stream tumbled along below her. I have not very much farther to go, Eleanor thought; I am more than halfway there. Journey's end, she thought, and far back in her mind, sparkling like the little stream, a tag end of a tune danced through her head, bringing distantly a word or so; 'In delay there lies no plenty,' she thought, 'in delay there lies no plenty.'

She nearly stopped forever just outside Ashton, because she came to a tiny cottage buried in a garden. I could live there all alone, she thought, slowing the car to look down the winding garden path to the small blue front door with, perfectly, a white cat on the step. No one would ever find me there, either, behind all those roses, and just to make sure I would plant oleanders by the road. I will light a fire in the cool evenings and toast apples at my own hearth. I will raise white cats and sew white curtains for the windows and sometimes come out of my door to go to the store to buy cinnamon and tea and thread. People will come to me to have their fortunes told, and I will brew love potions for sad maidens; I will have a robin . . . But the cottage was far behind, and it was time to look for her new road, so carefully charted by Dr Montague.

'Turn left onto Route 5 going west,' his letter said, and, as efficiently and promptly as though he has been guiding her from some spot far away, moving her car with controls in her hands, it was done; she was on Route 5 going west, and her journey was nearly done. In spite of what he said, though, she thought, I will stop in Hillsdale for a minute, just for a cup of coffee, because I cannot bear to have my long trip end so soon. It was not really disobeying, anyway; the letter said it was inadvisable to stop in Hillsdale to ask the way, not forbidden to stop for coffee, and perhaps if I don't mention Hill House I will not be doing wrong. Anyway, she thought obscurely, it's my last chance.

(1959)

The nineteen novels by **Joanne Harris** include *Chocolat* (1999), which was turned into an Academy Award-nominated film, *Blackberry Wine* (2000), *Five Quarters of the Orange* (2001) and the *Rune* series of fantasy novels. She has also published two collections of short stories and co-written two French cookery books.

★

'I had been telling my small daughters a story in bed at nights about a peach that went on growing and growing until it got as big as a house. They liked that story. Mind you, up until then, I had been writing stories only for grown-ups. I'd been doing it for twenty years. But why, I asked, shouldn't I try to write a book for children?'

Roald Dahl's first children's novel, *James and the Giant Peach*, followed in 1961, and the modern master of children's story-telling was born, thanks to the bedtime stories he'd been making up for Olivia and Tessa, who were just five and three years old.

A night owl, Dahl's motto was:

My candle burns at both ends
It will not last the night
But oh my foes and oh my friends
It gives a lovely light.

Towards the end of his life, Dahl would recount his years of service in the RAF during the Second World War in *Going Solo*, his memoir for young adult readers, including his crash in the Western Desert of North Africa. He would spend six months in hospital recovering from his injuries.

Later in the war years, once recovered and working also as a part-time writer, he would support fellow wounded servicemen by giving them the proceeds of the stories he sold: for example, he donated a handsome $1,000 fee received for a story called 'Bedtime' to the widow of an RAF colleague killed the previous week.

This anthology's Dahl offering, 'Only This', which relates a night's raid with startling detail, is therefore not so fanciful a flight of the imagination. Dahl melds the waking and sleeping worlds, navigating – for protagonist and reader alike – a night of the soul as long as his story is short. His story weaves the fates of a mother and her pilot son. (Dahl was very close to his own mother, Sofie, writing that when he was a child she 'was undoubtedly the absolute primary influence on my own life. She was the matriarch, the materfamilias, and her children radiated round her like planets round a sun.')

Like all ghost stories, 'Only This' is really about loss. Of course, Dahl being Dahl, there is also a 'stingaling' in the tale's tail. One that is dark, sure – but also heartbreakingly full of love.

Only This
by Roald Dahl

That night the frost was very heavy. It covered the hedges and whitened the grass in the fields so that it seemed almost as though it had been snowing. But the night was clear and beautiful and bright with stars, and the moon was nearly full.

The cottage stood alone in a corner of the big field. There was a path from the front door which led across the field to a stile and on over the next field to a gate which opened on to the lane about three miles from the village. There were no other houses in sight and the country around was open and flat and many of the fields were under the plough because of the war.

The light of the moon shone upon the cottage. It shone through the open window into the bedroom where the woman was asleep. She slept lying on her back, with her face upturned to the ceiling, with her long hair spread out around her on the pillow, and although she was asleep, her face was not the face of someone who is resting. Once she had been beautiful, but now there were thin furrows running across her forehead and there was a tightness about the way in which her skin was stretched over the cheekbones. But her mouth was still gentle, and as she slept, she did not close her lips.

The bedroom was small, with a low ceiling, and for furniture there was a dressing-table and an armchair. The clothes of the woman lay over the back of the armchair where she had put them when she undressed. Her black shoes were on the floor beside the chair. On the dressing-table there was a hairbrush, a letter and a large photograph of a young boy in uniform who wore a pair of wings on the left side of his tunic. It was a smiling photograph, the kind that one likes to send to one's mother and it had a thin, black frame made of wood. The moon shone through the open window and the woman slept her restless sleep. There was no noise anywhere save for the soft, regular noise of her breathing and the rustle of the bedclothes as she stirred in her sleep.

Then, from far away, there came a deep, gentle rumble which grew and grew and became louder and louder until soon the whole sky seemed to be filled with a great noise which throbbed and throbbed and kept on throbbing and did not stop.

Right at the beginning, even before it came close, the

253

woman had heard the noise. In her sleep she had been waiting for it, listening for the noise and dreading the moment when it would come. When she heard it, she opened her eyes and for a while lay quite still, listening. Then she sat up, pushed the bedclothes aside and got out of bed. She went over to the window and placing her hands on the window sill, she leaned out, looking up into the sky; and her long hair fell down over her shoulders, over the thin cotton nightdress which she wore. For many minutes she stood there in the cold, leaning out of the window, hearing the noise, looking up and searching the sky; but she saw only the bright moon and the stars.

'God keep you,' she said aloud. 'Oh dear God keep you safe.'

Then she turned and went quickly over to the bed, pulled the blankets away and wrapped them round her shoulders like a shawl. She slipped her bare feet into the black shoes and walked over to the armchair and pushed it forward so that it was right up in front of the window. Then she sat down.

The noise and the throbbing overhead was very great. For a long time it continued as the huge procession of bombers moved towards the south. All the while the woman sat huddled in her blankets, looking out of the window into the sky.

Then it was over. Once more the night became silent. The frost lay heavy on the field and on the hedges and it seemed as though the whole countryside was holding its breath. An army was marching in the sky. All along the route people had heard the noise and knew what it was; they knew that soon, even before they had gone to sleep, there would be a battle. Men drinking beer in the pubs had stopped their talking in order to listen. Families in their houses had turned off the radio and gone out in their gardens, where they stood looking up into the sky. Soldiers arguing in their tents had stopped their shouting, and men and women walking home at night from the factories had stood still on the road, listening to the noise.

It is always the same. As the bombers move south across the country at night, the people who hear them become strangely silent. For those women whose men are with the planes, the moment is not an easy one to bear.

Now they had gone, and the woman lay back in the armchair and closed her eyes, but she did not sleep. Her face was white and the skin seemed to have been drawn tightly over her cheeks and gathered up in wrinkles around her eyes. Her lips were parted and it was as though she were listening to someone talking. Almost she could hear the sound of his voice as he used to call to her from outside the window when he came back from working in the fields. She could hear him saying he was hungry and asking what there was for supper, and then when he came in he would put his arm around her shoulder and talk to her about what he had been doing all day. She would bring in the supper and he would sit down and start to eat and always he would say, why don't you have some and she never knew what to answer except that she wasn't hungry. She would sit and watch him and pour out his tea, and after a while take his plate and go out into the kitchen to get him some more.

It was not easy having only one child. The emptiness when he was not there and the knowing all the time that something might happen; the deep conscious knowing that there was nothing else to live for except this; that if something did happen, then you too would be dead. There would be no use sweeping the floor or washing the dishes or cleaning the house; there would be no use in gathering wood for the fire or in feeding the hens; there would be no use in living.

Now, as she sat there by the open window she did not feel the cold; she felt only a great loneliness and a great fear. The fear took hold of her and grew upon her so that she could not bear it, and she got up from the chair and leaned out of the window again, looking up into the sky. And as she looked the night was no longer beautiful; it was cold and clear and immensely dangerous. She did not see the fields or the hedges or the carpet of frost upon the countryside; she saw only the depths of the sky and the danger was there.

Slowly she turned and sank down again into her chair. Now the fear was great. She could think of nothing at all except that she must see him now because tomorrow would be too late. She let her head rest against the back of the chair and when she closed her eyes she saw the aircraft; she saw it clearly in the moonlight, moving forward through the night like a great, black bird. She was so close to it and she could see the way in which the nose of the machine reached out far ahead of everything, as though the bird was craning its neck in the eagerness of its passage. She could see the markings on the wings and on the body and she knew that he was inside. Twice she called to him, but there was no answer; then the fear and the longing welled up within her so that she could stand it no longer and it carried her forward through the night and on and on until she was with him, beside him, so close that she could have touched him had she put out her hand.

He was sitting at the controls with gloves on his hands, dressed in a great bulky flying-suit which made his body look huge and shapeless and twice its normal size. He was looking straight ahead at the instruments on the panel, concentrating upon what he was doing and thinking of nothing except flying the machine.

Now she called to him again and he heard her. He looked around and when he saw her, he smiled and stretched out a hand and touched her shoulder, and then all the fear and the loneliness and the longing went out of her and she was happy.

For a long time she stood beside him watching him as he flew the machine. Every now and then he would look around and smile at her, and once he said something, but she could not hear what it was because of the noise of the engines. Suddenly he pointed ahead through the glass windshield of the aeroplane and she saw that the sky was full of searchlights. There were many hundreds of them; long white fingers of light travelling lazily across the sky, swaying this way and that, working in unison so that sometimes several of them would come together and meet in the same spot and after a while they would separate and meet again somewhere else, all the time searching the night for the bombers which were moving in on the target.

Behind the searchlights she saw the flak. It was coming up from the town in a thick many-coloured curtain, and the flash of the shells as they burst in the sky lit up the inside of the bomber.

He was looking straight ahead now, concentrating upon the flying, weaving through the searchlights and going directly into this curtain of flak, and she watched and waited and did not dare to move or to speak lest she distract him from his task.

She knew that they had been hit when she saw the flames from the nearest engine on the left side. She watched them through the glass of the side panel, licking against the surface of the wing as the wind blew them backwards, and she watched them take hold of the wing and come dancing over the black surface until they were right up under the cockpit itself. At first she was not frightened. She could see him sitting there, very cool, glancing continually to one side, watching the flames and flying the machine, and once he looked quickly around and smiled at her and she knew then that there was no danger. All around she saw the searchlights and the flak and the explosions of the flak and the colours of the tracer, and the sky was not a sky but just a small confined space which was so full of lights and explosions that it did not seem possible that one could fly through it.

But the flames were brighter now on the left wing. They had spread over the whole surface. They were alive and active, feeding on the fabric, leaning backwards in the wind which fanned them and encouraged them and gave them no chance of going out.

Then came the explosion. There was a blinding white flash and a hollow *crumph* as though someone had burst a blown-up paper bag; then there was nothing but flames and thick whitish-grey smoke. The flames were coming up through the floor and through the sides of the cockpit; the smoke was so thick that it was difficult to see and almost impossible to breathe. She became terrified and panicky because he was still sitting there at the controls, flying the machine, fighting to keep it on an even keel, turning the wheel first to one side, then to the other, and suddenly there was a blast of cold air and she had a vague impression of urgent crouching figures scrambling past her and throwing themselves away from the burning aircraft.

Now the whole thing was a mass of flames and through the smoke she could see him still sitting there, fighting with the wheel while the crew got out, and as did so he held one arm up over his face because the heat was so great. She rushed forward and took him by the shoulders and shook him and shouted, 'Come on, quickly, you must get out, quickly, quickly.'

Then she saw that his head had fallen forward upon his chest and that he was limp and unconscious. Frantically she tried to pull him out of the seat and towards the door, but he was too limp and heavy. The smoke was filling her lungs and her throat so that she began to retch and gasp for breath. She was hysterical now, fighting against death and against everything and she managed to get her hands under his arms and drag him a little way towards the door. But it was impossible to get him farther. His legs were tangled around the wheel and there was a buckle somewhere which she could not undo. She knew then that it was impossible, that there was no hope because of the smoke and the fire and because there was no time; and suddenly all the strength drained out of her body. She fell down on top of him and began to cry as she had never cried before.

Then came the spin and the fierce rushing drive downwards and she was thrown forward into the fire so that the last she knew was the bright yellow of the flames and the smell of the burning.

Her eyes were closed and her head was resting against the back of the chair. Her hands were clutching the edges of the blankets as though she were trying to pull them tighter around her body and her long hair fell down over her shoulders.

Outside the moon was low in the sky. The frost lay heavier than ever on the fields and on the hedges and there was no noise anywhere. Then from far away in the south came a deep gentle rumble which grew and grew and became louder and louder until soon the whole sky was filled with noise and the singing of those who were coming back.

But the woman who sat by the window never moved. She had been dead for some time.

(1946)

Out on the River
by Guy de Maupassant

Last summer I rented a small country house on the banks of the Seine several leagues downstream from Paris and each evening I travelled down to spend the night there. A few days after settling in, I got to know one of my neighbours who was maybe thirty or forty and far and away the oddest man I ever clapped eyes on. He was not just a practised hand with boats, he was mad about them, and was always near the water or on it or in it. He must have been born in a boat and he'll die in a boat.

One evening as we were strolling quietly along the banks of the Seine, I asked this chap to tell me some tales of his nautical life. He perked up at once, a change came over him, and he started talking fifteen to the dozen, waxing almost lyrical. He had one great passion in him, all-consuming irresistible passion: the river.

Oh yes! (he said) I've a good few memories of that old river you see rolling along there. People like you from city streets have no conception of what the river's like. But just listen to the way a fisherman says the word. For him, a river is something mysterious, deep, and unknown, a place of mirages and ghostly visions where some nights you see things that don't exist, hear sounds you've never heard before, and you shake in your boots as though you were walking through a cemetery. Come to that, a river is the most sinister cemetery there is: a graveyard where the dead don't have graves.

To a fisherman, dry land is confined and circumscribed, but on dark moonless nights the river has no limits. Sailors don't feel the same way about the sea. True enough, the sea can often be merciless and full of spite, but it shrieks and howls and at least the open sea plays fair. But a river is silent and treacherous. It never roars and thunders but just slips quietly on its way, and that never-ending flow of water gliding smoothly along is to me more frightening than any mountainous ocean waves.

People with too much imagination say that the depths of the sea hide vast blue lands where drowned men roam among great fish through strange forests and caves of crystal. The river bottom is just black and full of mud where bodies rot. Yet it can be beautiful when it shines at daybreak and laps quietly at its murmuring reedy banks.

Talking of the ocean, a poet once said:

The foaming waves play host to sombre tales;
O Angry billows, feared by mothers who pray,
You tell those tales with each tide rise
And this no less explains those awful cries
Which roar as beaching rollers surge at end of day.

Well, I believe that stories whispered by quiet-voiced slender reeds are even more sinister than the sombre tales told by the waves' roar.

But since you've asked to hear some of the things I remember, I'll tell you about something odd that happened to me here about ten years ago.

In those days, I had a room – as I still do – in Madame Lafon's house, and one of my best friends, Louis Bernet, who, now he's a member of the Privy Council, has given up boating and all the spit and polish and larking about that go with it, had found somewhere to stay in the village of C— a couple of leagues downstream. We used to have dinner together every day, sometimes at his place, sometimes at mine.

One evening, I was going home alone, feeling pretty tired, having a hard time making headway in my big boat, a sea-going twelve-footer with a drop-keel which I always took out at night. I stopped for a moment to get my wind back just off that spit of reeds over there, a couple of hundred metres below the railway bridge. It was a marvellous night. The moon was bright, the river gleamed, and the air was still and warm. It was so peaceful that I was tempted. I said to myself that nothing could be finer than to smoke a pipe in such a spot. The thought was father to the deed. I got my anchor and dropped it overboard.

With the pull of the current, the boat went the length of the mooring chain and then stopped. I made myself as comfortable as I could on my sheepskin coat in the stern. It was quiet, dead quiet, except now and then I seemed to catch a faint, almost inaudible sound of water lapping the bank, and I saw the tallest clumps of reeds turn into startling shapes which at times appeared to sway and wave.

The river was utterly peaceful but I felt apprehensive sitting there surrounded by extraordinary silence. All the marshy creatures, the frogs and toads which sing at night, were hushed. Then, just to my right, a frog croaked. I jumped. It stopped. Hearing nothing more, I decided to smoke my pipe to give myself something to do. Now I'm second to none at getting a pipe going, but I'm damned if I could make it draw. With my second puff, I started to feel sick and gave up. I began humming a little tune but couldn't stand the sound of my own voice. So I settled down in the bottom of the boat and watched the sky. I lay there quietly for some time, but after a while the rocking of the boat made me feel uneasy. I had this sensation that it was yawing wildly, swinging into one bank and then the other; then I felt that some invisible hand or unseen force was gently pulling it down to the bottom then heaving it out of the water before letting it down again. I was being tossed about as though I'd been caught in a storm. I heard noises all round me. I sat up in a hurry. The water was shining and everywhere was calm.

I came to the conclusion that my nerves must be a bit on edge and decided to clear off. I pulled on the chain; the boat surged forward but I felt some resistance. I pulled harder but the anchor wouldn't come free. It must have fouled something on the bottom and I just couldn't shift it. I started hauling on it again, but it was no good. Seizing the oars, I turned the boat round and moved upstream to change the position of the anchor. It was still no use: it was good and fast. I lost my temper and shook the chain in a rage. It wouldn't budge. I sat down disconsolately and began reflecting on my position. There was no way I could break the chain or slip it off the boat, for it was heavy and bolted to a block of wood on the prow that was thicker than my arm; but since the weather continued very fine, I imagined it wouldn't be long before I met up with some fisherman or other who would come to the rescue. The whole business had calmed my nerves and now I managed a smoke of my pipe. I had a bottle of rum with me, drank a couple of glasses, and then laughed as I saw that my predicament was really rather funny. It was very warm and if the worst came to the worst I'd be able to spend the night under the stars without coming to much harm.

All at once, something thudded faintly against the side of the boat. I jumped and broke out all over in a cold sweat. The sound had probably been caused by a piece of timber floating down on the current, but it was enough to set my nerves oddly on edge once more. I took hold of the chain and arched my back in a desperate attempt to haul it up. But the anchor held fast. I sat down again, exhausted.

Meanwhile, the river had become wreathed in a very thick, white mist which hung very low over the water so that when I stood up I couldn't see the river or my feet or my boat, and all I could make out were the top of the reeds and, beyond them, the plain stretching away all pale in the moonlight with great black smudges reaching up to the

264

sky here and there where clumps of poplars grew. I was so to speak swathed up to my middle in a cotton sheet of singular whiteness, and I began imagining the most fantastic things. I thought that someone was trying to clamber into the boat which I could no longer see, and that beneath the opaque mist the river teemed with strange creatures swimming round and round me. I was horribly uneasy, my head felt as though it had been clamped in a vice, and my heart beat so fast I thought I'd choke. I got a bit flustered then and considered swimming to the bank, but the very idea made me shake in my shoes. I could see myself getting lost, floundering about in the thick mist, getting entangled in the unavoidable reeds and rushes half-dead with fear, not knowing where the bank was, not being able to find my boat again, and I seemed to sense that there'd be something trying to pull me down to the bottom of the inky water.

Anyway, since I'd have had to swim upstream for at least five hundred metres before finding a pot free of reeds and rushes, where I could scramble ashore, I had one chance in ten of navigating my way through the fog and making it without drowning, good swimmer though I was.

I tried to talk some sense into myself. I felt my will was telling me not to be afraid, but there was something else at work other than my will, and that something else was scared. I wondered what I had to be frightened of. My courageous self jeered at my cowardly self and never more clearly than at that moment did I understand the struggle that goes on between the two opposing forces that lie within us, one wanting, the other resisting, with each taking turns to win the battle.

My idiotic, inexplicable fears went on growing until they

tuned into terror. I stood there absolutely still, eyes staring and ears cocked, waiting. What was I expecting? I had absolutely no idea, but I was certain it would be something horrible. I do believe that if a fish had taken it into its head to jump out of the water, as they often do, it would have been more than enough to make me fall down in a heap unconscious.

Yet in the end, by making a supreme effort, I managed to reclaim most of my wits which were on the point of turning completely. I reached for the rum-bottle again and took a few good swigs.

Then I got an idea and began yelling as loud as I could to all the points of the compass. When my throat finally seized up, I listened. In the distance, a dog barked.

I took another drink and then stretched out full length in the bottom of the boat. I stayed like that for perhaps an hour, maybe two, not sleeping and not closing my eyes and with nightmares zooming all around me. I didn't dare stand up and yet oh! how I longed to! I kept putting it off from one minute to the next. I kept saying: 'On your feet!' but I was too afraid to move a muscle. In the end, taking every care not to make the slightest sound, as though my very life depended on it, I sat up and looked over the side.

I was dazzled by the most marvellous, the most astounding spectacle anybody could ever possibly expect to see. It was the weirdest sight – like something out of a fairy-tale, or one of those wonders that travellers just back from far-off lands prattle on about while you listen and don't really believe.

The mist which had been clinging to the surface of the water two hours before had lifted slowly and collected all along the banks. Leaving the river quite clear, it had formed into an unbroken ridge which stretched along each side to a height of six metres and shone in the moonlight as blindingly brilliant as a snowscape. As a result all I could see was the river streaked with fire between two white mountains. And high up, above my head, full and looming, a huge shining moon hung in a milky, blue-washed sky.

All the creatures of pond and marsh were now awake. The frogs were making a tremendous row and against it, throbbing away to right and left, I could make out the squat, unvarying, melancholy croaking which the brass-voiced toads blare at the stars. Oddly enough, I wasn't afraid any more. I was sitting right in the middle of such extraordinary scenic splendour that the weirdest things could have happened and left me cold.

How long it lasted I couldn't say, because in the end I dozed off. When I opened my eyes again, the moon had set and the sky was overcast. The water lapped lugubriously, the wind had got up, it was cold and very dark.

I drank what was left of the rum, then sat shivering, listening to the swish of the reeds and the ominous sound of the river. I peered around but could not make out my boat or even my hands, even when I held them up in front of my face.

Gradually, however, the blackness thinned. Suddenly I thought I sensed a shadow gliding just by me. I gave a cry and a voice answered: it was a fisherman. I called him, he rowed across, and I explained what had happened. He pulled alongside and we both heaved on the chain. The anchor would not shift. Day was breaking, grim, grey, rainy, and bitterly cold, the sort of day that brings sorrow and grief. Then I spotted another boat and we hailed it. The man at the oars joined forces with us and only then, little by little, did the anchor give. It came up slowly, very slowly, weighed down by something very heavy. Finally, we made out a black bulky mass which we manhandled into my boat.

It was the body of an old woman. There was a large stone tied around her neck.

(1876)

Translated by David Coward

Can A Corn
by Jess Walter

Ken took dialysis Tuesdays and Thursdays. It fell to Tommy after his mom passed to check his stepdad out of the Pine Lodge Correctional Facility. Drop him at the hospital. Take him back three hours later.

Ken groaned as he climbed up the truck. —Whatcha got there, Tom?

Tommy looked over the back seat. —Pole and tackle.

—You goin' fishin' this weekend?

—I ain't skydivin'.

Ken stared out his window. —You stop me by a store?

There was a downtown grocery sold Lotto, fortified wines, and forties. Ken hopped out. Tommy spun radio stations until Ken came back with a can a corn.

—Oh, no you ain't, Ken.

—So got-damn tired, Tom. Can't sit on that blood machine today.

—You'd rather die?

—I'd rather fish.

—No way, Ken.

He drove toward Sacred Heart. But when Tommy stopped at a red light Ken reached back, got the pole, and jumped out. Fine, Tommy thought. Die. I don't care. The old man walked toward the Spokane River. Tommy pulled up next to him, reached over, and popped the passenger door.

—Get in the damn truck, Ken.

Ken ignored him.

—That pole ain't even geared.

Ken walked, facing away.

Tommy drove alongside for another block. —Get in the truck, Ken.

Ken turned down a one-way. Tommy couldn't follow.

Fine. Stupid bastard. Tommy went back to work, but the only thing in the pit was a brake job on some old lady's Lincoln: six hundred in repairs on a shit-bucket worth three. Right. Pissed, Tommy gave the Lincoln to Miguel and drove back downtown.

He parked, got his tackle box from the truck, and walked back along the river. Found his stepfather under a bridge, dry pole next to him.

Tommy gave him hook and weight.

Ken's gray fingers shook.

—Give it here. Tommy weighted and hooked the line. He pulled a can opener from the tackle box and opened Ken's corn. Carefully, Tommy pushed the steel hook into the corn's paper skin until, with a tiny spurt, it gave way.

He handed the old man back the pole. Ken cast it.

Half-hour later, Ken reeled in a dull catfish, yellow-eyed and spiny. No fight in it. Almost like it didn't mind.

Ken held it up. —Well I will be got-damned.

Tommy released the fish. It just sort of sank.

He dropped the old man at the front gate of the prison, his breathing already shallow. Rusty. He was so weak Tommy had to reach over and pop his door again.

—Hey that wadn't a bad got-damn fish. All things considered. His eyes were filming over already. —We should go again Tuesday.

—We gonna start playin' catch now, too? Tommy asked.

Ken laughed.

Tommy watched the old man pass through the metal gate. The fucker.

(2013)

5

BE NOT AFEARD

A fter about an hour of sleep, a dramatic shift in brain activity occurs. A swell storms our systems. Those leviathan delta waves are splashed aside by a flotilla of new wavelets, leaping frenetically over and over, skimming wildly within your brain.

This new pattern of slumbers is often called *Paradoxical Sleep* because outwardly we still seem discombobulated and suspended in the depths of sleep – and yet inwardly, science has shown us (via such mechanisms as an EEG or *electroencephalogram*), our brains are as awhirl as when we are awake. Indeed, we are now whirring with energy, expending a huge amount more metabolism than during those prior, deeper-slung and slower-wave sections of sleep; our blood pressure and pulse rate have also markedly risen – and yet our muscles are totally paralysed.

Welcome to *Dream Sleep* (another term for it). This is the province of REM, as discovered in 1953 by Nathaniel Kleinman and Eugene Aserinsky while the latter was monitoring his eight-year-old son, Armond's, sleep patterns. Had he not been studying his child, the science of sleep might have been delayed yet longer – children experience REM sleep earlier in the sleep cycle than adults. Kleinman and Aserinksy deduced that oculomotor activity (the up-down and left-right continuous movements of the eye) were linked to periods of intense brain activity and, as it occurred intermittently but regularly during sleep, vivid dreaming.

Many sleep experts believe that during REM sleep, the flicker of our eyes is the tracking of our own visions as depicted in our dreams. In which case, the mind's eye itself becomes an aperture, as our little lives unspool like a roll of film and play themselves out, complete with shutter speed and forty-wink frame rate.

In other words, we tell ourselves a story.

Activity is particularly intense within the *lateral hypothalamus* and *amygdaloid complex* of the brain: our chambers of memory. The harbour from which our dreams are launched is our own past history. Memories ripple outwards from a childhood echo chamber, projecting the ultimate home movies.

As we trip down memory's lanes, meanwhile, the brain continues its churn. *Cerebrospinal fluid* is pumped through it, in and around the blood vessels, rushing and sluicing the brain's circuitry. The *pineal cells* (so-called because the pineal gland resembles a tiny pine cone), meanwhile, deliver *melatonin* (during REM and its obverse NREM state), which oils the cogs of your body clock. It is sometimes called the *Dracula hormone*, due to its elixir qualities being vampiric, in that it is only produced at night. It chronometers the body, internally, and is pumped from the *pineal gland* mainly, which operates like a lock-keeper for your brain — its cells piping melatonin to order — all helmed by the *suprachiasmatic nuclei* in the brain. This opening of the byways during deep sleep, allowing mel-atonin to rush up and down the spinal cord, is particularly pronounced during the *dead spot*. Its production not only chronicles the length of night, but is also varied in line with the different seasons.

Our body clock pendulums back to childhood rhythms when we hit late middle-age. While teenagers are genuinely marooned on a different time zone, adult circadian rhythms plateau from about the age of fifty-five, returning to roughly the same cycle as when we were ten and younger (most of us wake up earlier again, basically).

During our dotage, we are more likely to find ourselves awake during the small hours. This lighter sleeping is attributable to our increased susceptibility to light, as the eyeball's lens sepias over time, dimming the key photosensitive receptors in the retina, called *ganglion cells*, and also as melatonin is produced less and less. Plasticity in the brain is slowly but surely reduced.

In Holland, some old-people's homes have found cognitive and behavioural improvements in their residents by over-lighting the interior between 9 a.m. and 6 p.m. The over-compensation in brightness of lighting during the day has helped the elderly sleep at night, floodlighting their circadian receptors.

The brain also loosens in terms of charge and activity over time. While half of a two-week-old baby's sleep will consist of REM, the elderly spend the least time in such an emblazoned state. Those crucial cleansing processes that the brain conducts on itself during this type of sleep are curtailed.

Sometimes the result of such weakened sleep patterns is the accumulation of amyloid beta, the dread plaque that is a hallmark of Alzheimer's disease. It should be no surprise, when we talk of dreams as echoing memories, that such weakened sleep patterns can contribute to this condition's depleting the mind's ability to remember. The symptoms of Alzheimer's are directly analogous with the functionality during sleep of the brain's *aminergic* (switched off) and *cholinergic* (live-wired) systems. We should not be surprised when we discover that often what linger on for the advanced Alzheimer's patient are childhood memories. A song or poem learned during early youth can be perfectly rendered, even while a spouse's name is forgotten.

In such ways, we tick to the rhythm of our chronobiology. Yet, whatever our age, mysteries of sleep remain. The cartography of our dreamscapes, the journeys undertaken in oneiric life, is less easily charted. Many have tried, from Aristotle to Freud, from your friendly dream-diarist to the highest-tech sleep scientist. Even the most banal dream seems awesome to me. Let's not explain away the spectacular atavism that allows us, cumulatively during our nightly flights of fancy, to map the human heart – or, rather, the ever-active brain, lit up by a total eclipse. Those exilic explorations of our inner space – our cosmic consciousness, whole firmaments of our very being – fire us into the next waking day. Now, you might say that I'm a dreamer . . . but I'm not the only one. This wonderment is common to us all, each night, as the time-and-space continuum is left far behind, in sleep's exuberant wake, and we safari past that second star on the right, taking fabulous wing 'straight on till morning'.

From *The Tempest*
by William Shakespeare

Be not afeard; the isle is full of noises,
Sounds, and sweet airs, that give delight and hurt not.
Sometimes a thousand twangling instruments
Will hum about mine ears; and sometime voices,
That, if I then had waked after long sleep,
Will make me sleep again; and then in dreaming,
The clouds methought would open, and show riches
Ready to drop upon me, that when I waked
I cried to dream again.

(1610–11)

Tove Jansson, Finnish writer of the cherished Moomins series,
here weaves a rainbow of a story, fresh and mysterious. She
overcomes the nightmarish and, with a child's innocent real-
ism, decides to soar above her night-terrors (or parasomnia).
She soon describes dreams coming true. Flights of fancy
become commonplace. The grown-ups are schooled. We must
all dare to dream, for pigs really can fly – and we can too, as
long as we muster that crucial first leap of inner faith.

Flying (from *Sculptor's Daughter*)
by Tove Jansson

I dreamed that thousands of people were running in the
street. They weren't shouting but you could hear the sounds
of their boots on the pavement, many thousands of boots,
and there was a red glow in the studio from outside. After a

277

while there weren't so many of them running and in the end there were only the steps of the last one, who was running in such a way that he fell over and then picked himself up and ran on.

Then everything started shrinking. Every piece of furniture became elongated and narrow and disappeared towards the ceiling. There was something crawling under the rag rugs in the hall. It was also narrow and thin and wriggled in the middle, sometimes very quickly and sometimes very slowly.

I tried to get into the bedroom where Mummy had lit the oil lamp but the door was shut. Then I ran up the steps to the bunk. The door of Poppolino's cage was open and I could hear him padding round somewhere in the dark and whining, which is something he always does when it is very cold or when he feels lonely.

Now it came up the steps, grey and limping. One of its legs had come off. It was the ghost of the dead crow. I flew into the sitting-room and bumped about on the ceiling like a fly. I could see the sitting-room and the studio underneath me in a deep well that sank deeper and deeper.

I thought more about that dream afterwards, particularly about the flying part, and decided to fly as often as possible.

But it didn't work and I dreamed about all the wrong things, and in the end I made up my own dreams myself just before I went to sleep or just after I had woken up. I started by thinking up the most awful things I could, which wasn't particularly difficult. When I had made things as awful as possible I took a run and bounced off the floor and flew away from everything, leaving it all behind me in a deep well. Down there the whole town was burning. Down there

Poppolino was padding around in the studio in the dark screaming with loneliness. Down there sat the crow saying: it was your fault that I died. And the Unmentionable Thing crawled under the mat.

But I just went on flying. In the beginning I bumped about on the ceiling like a fly, but then I ventured out the window. Straight across the street was the farthest I could fly. But if I glided I could go on as long as I wanted, right down to the bottom of the well. There I took another leap and flew up again.

It wasn't long before they caught sight of me. At first they just stopped and stared, then they started to shout and point and came running from all directions. But before they could reach me I had taken another leap and was up in the air again laughing and waving at them. They tried to jump after me. They ran to fetch step-ladders and fishing-rods but nothing helped. There they were, left behind below me, longing to be able to fly. Then they went slowly home and got on with their work.

Sometimes they had too much work to do and sometimes they just couldn't work which was horrid for them. I felt sorry for them and made it possible for them all to fly.

Next morning they all woke up with no idea of what had happened and sat up and said: another miserable day begins! They climbed down from their bunks and drank some warm milk and had to eat the skin too. Then they put on their coats and hats and went downstairs and off to their work, dragging their legs and wondering whether they should take the tram. But then they decided to walk in any case because one is allowed to take a tram for seven stops but not really for five, and in any case fresh air is healthy.

One of them came down Wharf Road and a lot of wet snow stuck to her boots. So she stamped a little to get rid of the snow – and sure enough, she flew into the air! Only about six feet, and then came down again and stood wondering what had happened to her. Then she noticed a gentleman running to catch the tram. It rang its bell and was off so he ran even faster and the next moment he was flying too. He took off from the ground and described an arc in the air up to the roof of the tram and there he sat!

Then Mummy began to laugh as hard as she could and immediately understood what had happened and cried ha! ha! ha! and flew onto Victor Ek's roof in a single beautiful curve. There she caught sight of Daddy in the studio window rattling nails and coins in the pockets of his overall and she shouted: jump out! Come flying with me!'

But Daddy daren't until Mummy flew over and sat on the window-sill. Then he opened the window and took hold of her hand and flew out and said: well I'll be damned!

By that time the whole of Helsinki was full of amazed people flying. No one did any work. Windows were open all over the place and down in the street the trams and the cars were empty and it stopped snowing and the sun came out.

All the new-born babies were flying and all the very old people and their cats and dogs and guinea-pigs and monkeys – just everybody!

Even the President was out flying!

The roofs were crowded with picnickers undoing their sandwiches and opening bottles and shouting cheers! to one another across the street and everyone was doing precisely what he or she wanted to do.

I stood in the bedroom window watching the whole thing and enjoying myself no end and wondering how long I should let them go on flying. And I thought that if I now made everything normal again it might be dangerous. Imagine what would happen if the following morning they all opened their windows and jumped out! Therefore I decided that they could be allowed to go on flying until the end of the world in Helsinki.

Then I opened my bedroom window and climbed onto the window-ledge together with the crow and Poppolino. Don't be afraid! I said. And so off we flew.

(1969)

Translated by Kingsley Hart

★

In 2015, Canadian novelist and poet Margaret Atwood became the first contributor to the Future Library Project, a Norwegian public artwork devised by artist Katie Paterson.

The initiative is a fairy tale all of its own. Future Library intends to collect one original story each year from a popular writer until the year 2114, at which point all the manuscripts will be published for the first time, together in an anthology.

There is even a fairy-tale forest: one thousand trees have been planted in Nordmarka, near Oslo; they will be harvested in 100 years' time, in order to print 1,000 copies of the limited-edition anthology.

And so Atwood's story, 'Scribbler Moon', will be dormant for a century or so. 'There's something magical about it,' she has said. 'It's like Sleeping Beauty. The texts are going to slumber for 100 years and then they'll wake up, come to life again . . .'

Adventure Story
by Margaret Atwood

This is a story told by our ancestors, and those before them. It is not just a story, but something they once did, and at last there is proof.

Those who are to go must prepare first. They must be strong and well nourished and they must possess also a sense of purpose, a faith, a determination to persevere to the end, because the way is long and arduous and there are many dangers.

At the right time they gather together in the appointed place. Here there is much confusion and milling around, as yet there is no order, no groups of sworn companions have separated themselves from the rest. The atmosphere is tense, anticipation stirs among them, and now, before some are ready, the adventure has been launched. Through the dark tunnel, faintly lit with lurid gleams of reddish light, shoots the intrepid band, how many I cannot say; only that there are many: a band now, for all are headed in the same direction. The safety of the home country falls behind, the sea between is crossed more quickly than you can think, and now they are in alien territory, a tropical estuary with many coves and hidden bays. The water is salt, the vegetation Amazonian, the land ahead shrouded and obscure, thickened with fog. Monstrous animals, or are they fish, lurk here, pouncing upon the stragglers, slaying many. Others are lost, and wander until they weaken and perish in misery.

Now the way narrows, and those who have survived have reached the gate. It is shut, but they try one password and then another, and look! the gate has softened, melted, turned to jelly, and they pass through. Magic still works; an unseen force is on their side. Another tunnel; here they must crowd together, swimming upstream, between shores curving and fluid as lava, helping one another. Only together can they succeed.

(You may think I'm talking about male bonding, or war, but no: half of these are female, and they swim and help and sacrifice their lives in the same way as the rest.)

And now there is a widening out, and the night sky arches above them, or are we in outer space and all the rocket movies you've ever seen? It's still warm, whatever, and the team, its number sadly diminished, forges onward, driven by what? Greed for treasure, desire for a new home, worlds to conquer, a raid on an enemy citadel, a quest for the Grail? Now it is each alone, and the mission becomes a race which only one may win, as, ahead of them, vast and luminous, the longed-for, the loved planet swims into view, like a moon, a sun, an image of God, round and perfect. A target.

Farewell, my comrades, my sisters! You have died that I may live. I alone will enter the garden, while you must wilt and shrivel in outer darkness. So saying – and you know, because now this is less like a story than a memory – the victorious one reaches the immense perimeter and is engulfed in the soft pink atmosphere of paradise, sinks, enters, casts the imprisoning skin of the self, merges, disappears . . . and the world slowly explodes, doubles, revolves, changes forever, and there, in the desert heaven, shines a fresh-laid star, exile and promised land in one, harbinger of a new order, a new birth, possibly holy; and the animals will be named again.

(1992)

Nietzsche observed that we are all – involuntarily – writers when we dream. This is partly due to the sense that we mostly *see* our dreams (as opposed to hear, touch, taste or smell them). Just as the greatest storytellers must conjure visions for their readers – Joseph Conrad famously proclaimed his task as a writer was 'to make you hear, to make you feel – it is, before all, to make you see' – so must our dreams paint us pictures.

And so when Czesław Miłosz describes poetry below, he might as well be writing about dreams.

Our revolving doors of perception swing open in dream – reasoning is ejected; physical impossibility is welcomed; emotion is intensified, sometimes to manic degrees; and improbable events are accepted unquestioningly, discontinuity and incongruity ushered inside with open arms.

In these next pieces about dreams, a tigerish lucidity abounds. They cumulatively beg the question, as Leonardo da Vinci framed it: 'why does the eye see a thing more clearly in dreams than when awake?'

From *Ars Poetica?*
by Czesław Miłosz

a thing is brought forth which we didn't know we had
    in us,
so we blink our eyes, as if a tiger had sprung out
and stood in the light, lashing his tail . . .

The purpose of poetry is to remind us
how difficult it is to remain just one person,

For our house is open, there are no keys in the doors,
and invisible guests come in and out at will.

(1968)

Translated by Miłosz and Lillian Valee

Dreamtigers
by Jorge Luis Borges

In my childhood I was a fervent worshiper of the tiger – not
the jaguar, that spotted "tiger" that inhabits the floating islands
of water hyacinths along the Paraná and the tangled wilderness
of the Amazon, but the true tiger, the striped Asian breed that
can be faced only by men of war, in a castle atop an elephant. I
would stand for hours on end before one of the cages at the zoo;
I would rank vast encyclopaedias and natural history books by
the splendor of their tigers. (I still remember those pictures,
I who cannot recall without error a woman's brow or smile.)
My childhood outgrown, the tigers and my passion for them
faded, but they are still in my dreams. In that underground sea
or chaos, they still endure. As I sleep I am drawn into some
dream or other, and suddenly I realize that it's a dream. At those
moments, I often think: *This is a dream, a pure diversion of my will,
and since I have unlimited power, I am going to bring forth a tiger.*

Oh, incompetence! My dreams never seem to engender
the creature I so hunger for. The tiger does appear, but it is
all dried up, or it's flimsy-looking, or it has impure vagaries
of shape or an unacceptable size, or it's altogether too ephem-
eral, or it looks more like a dog or bird than like a tiger.

(1960)

Translated by Andrew Hurley

★

The Tyger
by William Blake

Tyger! Tyger! burning bright,
In the forest of the night;
What immortal hand or eye,
Could frame thy fearful symmetry?

In what distant deeps or skies
Burnt the fire of thine eyes?
On what wings dare he aspire?
What the hand dare seize the fire?

And what shoulder, and what art,
Could twist the sinews of thy heart?
And when thy heart began to beat,
What dread hand? and what dread feet?

What the hammer? what the chain?
In what furnace was thy brain?
What the anvil? what dread grasp
Dare its deadly terrors clasp?

When the stars threw down their spears,
And water'd heaven with their tears:
Did he smile his work to see?
Did he who made the lamb make thee?

Tyger! Tyger! burning bright
In the forests of the night:

What immortal hand or eye,
Dare frame thy fearful symmetry?

(1794)

Tony Robinson

When Laura's mum and I split up, sleep became a bit of a problem. I yawned all day, and lay awake staring miserably at the ceiling all night. So, Laura, who was eleven at the time, decided to sort me out.

Late in the evening when she heard me clamber into bed, she'd creep into my room with a copy of *The Colour of Magic*, snuggle up, and read to me. The rolling cadences of Terry Pratchett's prose, his wit, his imagination and his gentle passion, were a balm to my troubled and speedy mind. His words and my daughter's tenderness, invariably sent me to sleep within minutes, and the following night she'd have to start at the same place all over again.

Terry died in 2015 of early-onset Alzheimer's. It was only latterly that he began to get the respect he deserved as a writer. He'd be really chuffed to know he'd been included in an anthology like this, and particularly proud that he had the ability to send at least one of his readers to sleep so efficiently!

The Colour of Magic – Prologue
by Terry Pratchett

In a distant and second-hand set of dimensions, in an astral plane that was never meant to fly, the curling star-mists waver and part . . .

See . . .

Great A'Tuin the Turtle comes, swimming slowly through the interstellar gulf, hydrogen frost on his ponderous limbs, his huge and ancient shell pocked with meteor craters. Through sea-sized eyes that are crusted with rheum and asteroid dust He stares fixedly at the Destination.

In a brain bigger than a city, with geological slowness, He thinks only of the Weight.

Most of the weight is of course accounted for by Berilia, Tubul, Great T'Phon and Jerakeen, the four giant elephants upon whose broad and star-tanned shoulders the disc of the World rests, garlanded by the long waterfall at its vast circumference and domed by the baby-blue vault of Heaven.

Astropsychology has been, as yet, unable to establish what they think about.

The Great Turtle was a mere hypothesis until the day the small and secretive kingdom of Krull, whose rim-most mountains project out over the Rimfall, built a gantry and pulley arrangements at the tip of the most precipitous crag and lowered several observers over the Edge in a quartz-windowed brass vessel to peer through the mist veils.

The early astrozoologists, hauled back from their long dangle by enormous teams of slaves, were able to bring back much information about the shape and nature of A'Tuin and the elephants but this did not resolve fundamental questions about the nature and purpose of the universe.

For example, what was A'Tuin's actual sex? This vital question, said the astrozoologists with mounting authority, would not be answered until a larger and more powerful gantry was constructed for a deep-space vessel. In the meantime, they could only speculate about the revealed cosmos.

There was, for example, the theory that A'Tuin had come

from nowhere and would continue at a uniform crawl, or steady gait, into nowhere, for all time. This theory was popular among academics.

An alternative, favoured by those of a religious persuasion, was that A'Tuin was crawling from the Birthplace to the Time of Mating, as were all the stars in the sky which were, obviously, also carried by giant turtles. When they arrived they would briefly and passionately mate, for the first and only time, and from that fiery union new turtles would be born to carry a new pattern of worlds. This was known as the Big Bang hypothesis.

Thus it was that a young cosmochelonian of the Steady Gait faction, testing a new telescope with which he hoped to make measurements of the precise albedo of Great A'Tuin's right eye, was on this eventful evening the first outsider to see the smoke rise hubward from the burning of the oldest city in the world.

Later that night he became so engrossed in his studies he completely forgot about it. Nevertheless, he was the first.

There were others . . .

(1983)

Tony Robinson is known as Britain's foremost face of popular history, after presenting twenty seasons of Channel 4's archaeology series *Time Team*, and also as the creator of the globally beloved character Baldrick in *Blackadder*. He is an award-winning television writer, and has published over thirty children's books as well as several works for adult readers. Other varied television includes an acclaimed documentary about the elderly, entitled *Me and My Mum*. An ambassador for the Alzheimer's Society since 2008 and Patron of Readathon, Robinson was appointed KBE in 2013.

★

Dreamwood
by Adrienne Rich

In the old, scratched, cheap wood of the typing stand
there is a landscape, veined, which only a child can see
or the child's older self, a poet,
a woman dreaming when she should be typing
the last report of the day. If this were a map,
she thinks, a map laid down to memorize
because she might be walking it, it shows
ridge upon ridge fading into hazed desert
here and there a sign of aquifers
and one possible watering-hole. If this were a map
it would be the map of the last age of her life,
not a map of choices but a map of variations
on the one great choice. It would be the map by which
she could see the end of touristic choices,
of distances blued and purpled by romance,
by which she would recognize that poetry
isn't revolution but a way of knowing
why it must come. If this cheap, mass-produced
wooden stand from the Brooklyn Union Gas Co.,
mass-produced yet durable, being here now,
is what is yet a dream-map
so obdurate, so plain,
she thinks, the material and the dream can join
and that is the poem and that is the late report.

(1987)

★

Extract from *The Wild Places*
by Robert Macfarlane

The poet and musician Ivor Gurney was born and brought up in rural Gloucestershire at around the end of the nine-teenth century. For his family, as for many at that time, the long country walk was a habit and a pleasure. Like the poet Edward Thomas – whom Gurney admired – he grew up as a natural historian, exploring Gloucestershire's riverbanks, woods and hedges.

The loving intensity of Gurney's relationship with the Gloucestershire landscape rings throughout the poetry and letters he wrote as a young man, and the journals he kept. He observed how the fields enjoyed a 'clear shining after the rain', and wrote of the wide River Severn 'homing to the sea'. Of all aspects of the countryside it was woodland he loved best, with its 'avenues of green and gold'. A com-poser as well as a poet, timber and timbre were to Gurney closely grown together: among the many poems he set to music were his own 'Song of the Summer Woods' and A. E. Housman's 'Loveliest of Trees'.

In 1915, Gurney joined up to fight in the Great War. His first posting was to Sarras, on the Ypres Salient. When Gurney arrived at Ypres, the Salient had been a battle area for two years, and the landscape he found there was a dark travesty of the countryside he had left behind. Before the war, Sarras with its rivers, orchards, woods and pastures might have resembled Gurney's Gloucestershire. But two years of conflict had transformed it. Mud, midway between fluid and solid, threatened to drown men and entomb them simultaneously. On the military maps of the area that Gurney used, some of the old names of the landscape remained. But many of the new names spoke of the avoidance of death, or of its arrival. Shrapnel Corner, Crump Farm, Hellfire Corner, Halfway House, Dead Dog Farm, Battle Wood, Sanctuary Wood. The woods were no longer there, however; these were ghost names only. The trees had been felled for revetting, or blasted from the earth by shells. The only evidence of the forest that remained were upright bare dead trunks, stripped of leaves, branches and bark by shrapnel and gunfire. At their bases, human bones protruded from the mud like roots, and blood salted the earth.

To Gurney, writing home, it seemed he had come to an anti-landscape, whose featurelessness was a form of assault: 'Masses of unburied dead strewn over the battle fields; no sign of organized trenches, but merely shell holes joined up to one another . . . and no landmarks anywhere.' The Salient denied the permanence, the rich and complicated pasts of the trees that Gurney cherished: their consoling constancy, their rootedness.

In the trenches, he was seized often by what he called a 'hot heart desire' for his Gloucestershire landscape. He was 'clutched at and heart-grieved' by 'desperate home thoughts' of 'Cotswold, her spinnies'. 'We suffer pain out here,' he wrote home, 'and for myself it sometimes comes that death would be preferable to such a life.'

But Gurney survived the war. He was injured – shot in the chest, and gassed – and invalided home. Shortly after the Armistice, he entered upon a period of frenzied creativity. Between 1919 and 1922, he wrote some nine hundred poems and two hundred and fifty songs. Walking and inspiration became intertwined for Gurney. He strode the countryside both day and night, often for hours. The letters he sent during these years speak of how much he 'needed' the night-walking in particular. At night, he was able to follow what he called 'the white ways . . . unvisited by most', which was, he said, a form of 'discovery'. 'O that night!', he wrote to a friend. 'Meteors flashed like sudden inspirations of song down the sky. The air was too still to set firs or beeches sighing, but – O the depth of it!' He spoke of 'brambles beautiful in wind', of the 'black greenery of beech against the moon', of how a low moon threw into relief the 'still sky-rims . . . high above the valley', and of 'bronzed cloud-bar at cold dawn'. 'Earth, air, and water,' he wrote late in that period of his life, 'are the true sources of song or speaking.'

By 1922, Gurney's mental state, always precarious, had tilted into unbalance. He took to eating in binges, and then fasting for days. He lost weight quickly, and his behaviour became increasingly unpredictable. His family reluctantly committed him to the care of the asylum system. He went first to an institution in Gloucester, and then to one at Dartford in Kent. In both asylums, he was not permitted to walk outside the perimeter of the grounds.

It was to the Dartford asylum that Helen Thomas, the widow of Edward Thomas – who had been killed at the Battle of Arras – travelled on several occasions in the late 1920s to visit Gurney. She later reported that, when she first saw him, his madness was so acute that he was able to communicate only briefly with her, and showed little interest in her presence, or her association with Edward.

The next time she travelled to Dartford, however, Helen

took with her one of her husband's Ordnance Survey maps of the Gloucestershire landscape which both Thomas and Gurney had walked. She recalled afterwards that Gurney, on being shown the map, took it at once from her, and spread it out on his bed, in his hot little white-tiled room in the asylum, with the sunlight falling in patterns upon the floor. Then the two of them kneeled together by the bed and traced out, with their fingers, walks that they and Edward had taken in the past.

For an hour or more this dream-walking went on, Gurney seeing not the map, but looking through its prompts to see land itself. 'He spent that hour,' Helen remembered, 'revisiting his beloved home ... spotting ... a track, a hill, or a wood, and seeing it all in his mind's eye, a mental vision sharper and more actual for his heightened intensity. He trod, in a way we who were sane could not emulate, the lands and fields he knew and loved so well, his guide being his finger tracing the way on the map ... He had Edward as his companion in this strange perambulation ... I became for a while the element which brought Edward back to life for him and the country where the two could wander together.'

Helen returned to visit Gurney several times after this, and on each occasion she brought the map that had been made soft and creased by her husband's hands, and she and Gurney knelt at the bed and together walked through their imagined country.

(2007)

★

The Songs I Had
by Ivor Gurney

The songs I had are withered
Or vanished clean,
Yet there are bright tracks
Where I have been,

And there grow flowers
For other's delight.
Think well, O singer,
Soon comes night.

(C. 1920—1922)

★

ANNE FINE

I live in rural County Durham and walk my dog through an enormous river-field in which a gentle spring occasionally becomes a torrent. I've watched the farmer try to block the spring. I've watched him attempt to re-route it. And I've watched him give up.

It's always cheering to see the countryside outsmart a landowner with fine ideas, and I can imagine a present-day Hobden grinning each time he strolls past.

The Land
by Rudyard Kipling

When Julius Fabricius, Sub-Prefect of the Weald,
In the days of Diocletian owned our Lower River-field,

He called to him Hobdenius – a Briton of the Clay,
Saying: 'What about that River-piece for layin' in to
     hay?'

And the aged Hobden answered: 'I remember as a lad
My father told your father that she wanted dreenin'
     bad.
An' the more that you neglect her the less you'll get her
     clean.
Have it jest as you've a mind to, but, if I was you, I'd
     dreen.'

So they drained it long and crossways in the lavish
     Roman style—
Still we find among the river-drift their flakes of ancient
     tile,
And in drouthy middle August, when the bones of
     meadows show,
We can trace the lines they followed sixteen hundred
     years ago.

Then Julius Fabricius died as even Prefects do,
And after certain centuries, Imperial Rome died too.
Then did robbers enter Britain from across the
     Northern main
And our Lower River-field was won by Ogier the Dane.

Well could Ogier work his war-boat – well could Ogier
     wield his brand—
Much he knew of foaming waters – not so much of
     farming land.

So he called to him a Hobden of the old unaltered blood,
Saying: 'What about that River-piece; she doesn't look
    no good?'

And that aged Hobden answered "Tain't for me to
    interfere,
But I've known that bit o' meadow now for five and fifty
    year.
Have it jest as you've a mind to, but I've proved it time
    on time,
If you want to change her nature you have got to give
    her lime!'

Ogier sent his wains to Lewes, twenty hours' solemn walk,
And drew back great abundance of the cool, grey,
    healing chalk.
And old Hobden spread it broadcast, never heeding
    what was in't,—
Which is why in cleaning ditches, now and then we find
    a flint.

Ogier died. His sons grew English – Anglo-Saxon was
    their name—
Till out of blossomed Normandy another pirate came;
For Duke William conquered England and divided with
    his men,
And our Lower River-field he gave to William of
    Warenne.

But the Brook (you know her habit) rose one rainy
    autumn night

And tore down sodden flitches of the bank to left and
    right.
So, said William to his Bailiff as they rode their
    dripping rounds:
'Hob, what about that River-bit – the Brook's got up no
    bounds?'

And that aged Hobden answered: ''Tain't my business
    to advise,
But ye might ha' known 'twould happen from the way
    the valley lies.
Where ye can't hold back the water you must try and
    save the sile.
Hev it jest as you've a mind to, but, if I was you, I'
    spile!'

They spiled along the water-course with trunks of
    willow-trees,
And planks of elms behind 'em and immortal oaken
    knees.
And when the spates of Autumn whirl the gravel-beds
    away
You can see their faithful fragments, iron-hard in iron
    clay.

*

Georgii Quinti Anno Sexto, I, who own the River-field,
Am fortified with title-deeds, attested, signed and
    sealed,
Guaranteeing me, my assigns, my executors and heirs
All sorts of powers and profits which – are neither
    mine nor theirs.

I have rights of chase and warren, as my dignity
   requires.
I can fish – but Hobden tickles. I can shoot – but
   Hobden wires.
I repair, but he reopens, certain gaps which, men
   allege,
Have been used by every Hobden since a Hobden
   swapped a hedge.

Shall I dog his morning progress o'er the track-
   betraying dew?
Demand his dinner-basket into which my pheasant
   flew?
Confiscate his evening faggot under which my conies ran,
And summons him to judgement? I would sooner
   summons Pan.

His dead are in the churchyard – thirty generations
   laid.
Their names were old in history when Domesday Book
   was made;
And the passion and the piety and prowess of his line
Have seeded, rooted, fruited in some land the Law calls
   mine.

Not for any beast that burrows, not for any bird that
   flies,
Would I lose his large sound council, miss his keen
   amending eyes.
He is bailiff, woodman, wheelwright, field-surveyor,
   engineer,

And if flagrantly a poacher – 'tain't for me to
    interfere.

'Hob, what about that River-bit?' I turn to him again,
With Fabricius and Ogier and William of Warenne.
'Hev it jest as you've a mind to, but' – and here he takes
    command.
For whoever pays the taxes old Mus' Hobden owns the
    land.

(1917)

Anne Fine published her first novel, *The Summer House Loon*,
in 1978 and has been writing for both adults and children
ever since, winning numerous prizes including the Guardian
Award and both the Carnegie Medal and the Whitbread (now
Costa) Award twice over. Her novels include *Goggle-Eyes* (1989),
Bill's New Frock (1990), *Flour Babies* (1992), *The Tulip Touch*
(1996) and *Blood Family* (2013). Her novel *Madame Doubtfire*
(1987) was adapted into the 1993 film *Mrs Doubtfire,* starring
Robin Williams. Fine was the second Children's Laureate
(2001–2003).

Delay
by Elizabeth Jennings

The radiance of the star that leans on me
Was shining years ago. The light that now
Glitters up there my eyes may never see,
And so the time lag teases me with how

Love that loves now may not reach me until
Its first desire is spent. The star's impulse
Must wait for eyes to claim it beautiful
And love arrived may find us somewhere else.

(1953)

★

Letter to The Cosmos
by Jimmy Carter

Jimmy Carter, thirty-ninth US president, sent this state-
ment – recorded in electronic impulses which could in turn
be converted into printed words – into the cosmos, aboard
the space probe *Voyager*. Along with it went a gold-plated
phonograph record featuring music and greetings in fifty-five
languages, as well as the sounds of animals, volcanoes, rain,
laughter and a mother's kiss.

The President launched that kiss into a solar system in
which many of the planets have, revealingly, been named after
characters from timeless stories or myths – Orion and Jupiter,
Mars and Venus.

THE WHITE HOUSE
June 16, 1977

This *Voyager* spacecraft was constructed by the United
States of America. We are a community of 240 million
human beings among the more than 4 billion who inhabit
the planet Earth. We human beings are still divided into
nation states, but these states are rapidly becoming a single
global civilization.

We cast this message into the cosmos. It is likely to survive a billion years into our future, when our civilization is profoundly altered and the surface of the Earth may be vastly changed.

Of the 200 billion stars in the Milky Way galaxy some – perhaps many – may have inhabited planets and spacefaring civilizations. If one such civilization intercepts *Voyager* and can understand these recorded contents, here is our message:

This is a present from a small distant world, a token of our sounds, our science, our images, our music, our thoughts and our feelings. We are attempting to survive our time so we may live into yours.

We hope someday, having solved the problems we face, to join a community of galactic civilizations. This record represents our hope and our determination, and our good will in a vast and awesome universe.

Jimmy Carter
President
United States of America

The following story, by cartographer and author Tim Robinson, first appeared as a work of art, in the Royal Academy's 2015 Summer Exhibition – together with a washer.

The Tale of the Washer
by Tim Robinson

In April 1990, after decades of planning and construction, the Hubble Space Telescope was loaded into the cargo hold of a space shuttle and blasted on the back of a rocket to a height of 559 km, where it was put into orbit around the Earth. At that height the atmosphere is so tenuous that it does not interfere with the Hubble's view of astronomical objects so faint and faraway as to be beyond the ken of all previous telescopes. The heart of the Hubble is a bowl-shaped mirror, nearly eight feet across and polished to within a hundred-millionths of a millimetre of a perfect hyperboloid, which collects the light from whatever stars and galaxies lie within its field of view and focuses it on a camera of exquisite sensitivity. The prime purpose of this wonderful construction is to pierce the distances curtaining the birth scene of spacetime itself.

Having followed the space shuttle's blazing ascent, the telescope's successful injection into the correct orbit, the unfurling of its dragonfly wings of solar cells and the initiation of its functions, no doubt the teams of scientists and technicians responsible for various aspects of this technological triumph sat back with a sigh of relief, and waited for the first sublime starscapes to appear on the monitors in the Goddard Space Flight Centre. And when they came, what did the stars look like? Squashed spiders! So said one astronomer I have seen quoted. An anguished analysis of the blurry images indicated that the great mirror was slightly too flat (by 2.2 thousandths of a millimetre) near its perimeter. Who was to blame? It seems that the error was due to a fault in an optical gadget used to check the curvature of the mirror. In this instrument a certain lens was out of position, by 1.3 mm. Somebody had omitted to insert a washer, or so it was rumoured.

The Hubble is designed to be serviced in orbit as needs arise, by space-walking technicians tethered to a space shuttle, for the cost of bringing it back to Earth for refitting would be prohibitive. Three years after the initial launch a team of seven astronauts, trained in the use of some hundred specialist implements, were space-shuttled up, and over ten days installed a number of optical devices designed to correct the spherical aberration of the primary mirror. The cost of those washers must have mounted into the hundreds of millions of dollars. Since then, however, the Hubble has been an astounding success and still posts home avalanches of information on star formation and many other research topics, and especially on the early history of the universe, the unfurling of time and space.

Such questions interest me deeply, but my wandering mind is as often drawn to a question that has been left behind, being a triviality. What about the fabled washer? I imagine one slipping from the fingers and then from the memory of some technician harassed by the everyday pressures of life on Earth as well as the Hubble project's problems of schedule-slippage and cost-overrun? Did it lie, its glints and gleam unnoticed, on the floor of some 'clean room', until it was swept up and dumped with other waste into a dustbin? Or might some time-ridden space-stepper like myself have noticed it and carried it off as a memento?

(2015)

The Evening Star
by Louise Glück

Tonight, for the first time in many years,
there appeared to me again
a vision of the earth's splendor:

in the evening sky
the first star seemed
to increase in brilliance
as the earth darkened

until at last it could grow no darker.
And the light, which was the light of death,
seemed to restore to earth

its power to console. There were
no other stars. Only the one
whose name I knew

as in my other life I did her
injury: Venus,
star of the early evening,

to you I dedicate
my vision, since on this blank surface

you have cast enough light
to make my thought
visible again.

(2006)

★

WARSAN SHIRE

Myesha Jenkins is an American poet and activist living in
Johannesburg. This poem is from her collection, aptly titled
Dreams of Flight. I read it to myself before going to sleep at night;

the poem comforts me and allows me to reimagine the dream and sleep state as restorative and transformative. A tender mantra-like poem, short enough to memorize and pass on to others as prayer, affirmation, as a prelude to dream healing. It is powerful in the way that it conjures childlike excitement for tomorrow, and for the future, a feeling that so many of us lose as we grow older.

Transformation
by Myesha Jenkins

Who I was
is not who I am.
And who I am
is not who I will be.
Some bits falling off
other parts sprouting.
Inside this cocoon
I dream of flight.

(2011)

Warsan Shire released her debut pamphlet, 'Teaching My Mother How to Give Birth', in 2011, and went on to win the inaugural Brunel University African Poetry Prize in 2013. In 2014, she was appointed as the first Young Poet Laureate for London and was selected as Poet in Residence for Queensland, Australia. Extracts from her poem 'Home' were read during 2015 by Benedict Cumberbatch both onstage as well as for a music single for Save the Children. In 2016, Warsan collaborated with Beyoncé Knowles Carter on the visual album *Lemonade*. Warsan's debut collection will be published during 2016/2017.

★

TAN TWAN ENG

Despite its morbid title, I have always found this to be a comforting poem, entreating us to appreciate every moment of our lives. The poem is a short story by itself, a story of a man's entire life glimpsed in one brief instant. The unknown airman has lived by his own rules all his life, and he will die doing the very thing he loves most. He knows it; he has accepted it. Every time I finish reading the last line, I breathe, I exhale, and I feel ready to drift away to a dreamless, peaceful sleep.

An Irish Airman Foresees his Death
by W. B. Yeats

I know that I shall meet my fate
Somewhere among the clouds above;
Those that I fight I do not hate,
Those that I guard I do not love;
My country is Kiltartan Cross,
My countrymen Kiltartan's poor,
No likely end could bring them loss
Or leave them happier than before.
Nor law, nor duty bade me fight,
Nor public men, nor cheering crowds,
A lonely impulse of delight
Drove to this tumult in the clouds;
I balanced all, brought all to mind,
The years to come seemed waste of breath,

A waste of breath the years behind
In balance with this life, this death.

(1918)

Tan Twan Eng was born in Penang, Malaysia. His debut novel, *The Gift of Rain*, was longlisted for the Man Booker Prize. His second novel, *The Garden of Evening Mists*, was shortlisted for the Man Booker Prize and won the Man Asian Prize and the Walter Scott Prize for Historical Fiction. It was also short-listed for the IMPAC Dublin Literary Award. He is currently working on his third novel.

ROBERT MACFARLANE

Antoine de Saint-Exupéry was a French airman in the heroic age of flight. He piloted small planes by day and night across astonishing landscapes, including the Sahara and the Andes. *Wind, Sand and Stars* is his unforgettable memoir of those years. I first read the book twenty years or so ago, and one passage above all others has sung around my brain ever since: his description of finding his way by accident, in darkness, into a field of meteors. Nocturnal, dreamy, astral – it leads the waking mind into marvels, starlight and black space.

Extract from *Wind, Sand and Stars*
by Antoine de Saint-Exupéry

By the grace of the airplane I have known an extraordinary experience . . . and have been made to ponder with . . .

bewilderment the fact that this earth that is our home is yet in truth a wandering star.

A minor accident had forced me down in the Rio de Oro region, in Spanish Africa. Landing on one of those table-lands of the Sahara which fall away steeply at the sides, I found myself on the flat top of the frustum of a cone, an isolated vestige of a plateau that had crumbled round the edges. In this part of the Sahara such truncated cones are visible from the air every hundred miles or so, their smooth surfaces always at about the same altitude above the desert and their geologic substance always identical. The surface sand is composed of minute and distinct shells; but progres-sively as you dig along a vertical section, the shells become more fragmentary, tend to cohere, and at the base of the cone form a pure calcareous deposit.

Without question, I was the first human being ever to wander over this . . . this iceberg: its sides were remarkably steep, no Arab could have climbed them, and no European had as yet ventured into this wild region.

I was thrilled by the virginity of a soil which no step of man or beast had sullied. I lingered there, startled by this silence that never had been broken. The first star began to shine, and I said to myself that this pure surface had lain here thousands of years in sight only of the stars.

But suddenly my musings on this white sheet and these shining stars were endowed with a singular significance. I had kicked against a hard, black stone, the size of a man's fist, a sort of moulded rock of lava incredibly present on the surface of a bed of shells a thousand feet deep. A sheet spread beneath an apple-tree can receive only apples; a sheet spread beneath the stars can receive only star-dust. Never had a stone fallen from the skies made known its origin so unmistakably.

And very naturally, raising my eyes, I said to myself that from the height of this celestial apple-tree there must have dropped other fruits, and that I should find them exactly where they fell, since never from the beginning of time had anything been present to displace them.

Excited by my adventure, I picked up one and then a second and then a third of these stones, finding them at about the rate of one stone to the acre. And here is where my adventure became magical, for in a striking foreshortening of time that embraced thousands of years, I had become the witness of this miserly rain from the stars. The marvel of marvels was that there on the rounded back of the planet, between this magnetic sheet and those stars, a human consciousness was present in which as in a mirror that rain could be reflected.

(1939)
Translated by Lewis Galantière

Robert Macfarlane is the author of a trilogy of books about landscape and the human heart: *Mountains of the Mind* (2003), *The Wild Places* (2007) and *The Old Ways* (2012), as well as *Landmarks* (2015), a celebration of landscape and language. His writing has won many prizes and has been widely adapted for television and radio. He is currently at work on *Underland*, a book about the worlds beneath our feet. He is a Fellow of Emmanuel College, Cambridge.

6

TREAD SOFTLY

We change our posture some thirty to forty times on average during a night's sleep, without realizing it. These stirrings fashion our innate need to 'get snuggly', as my young son adroitly calls it. It never ceased to amaze me, when he was two or three and would find his way into our bed of a night, how his tiny frame could exert utter dominance, apparently through a combination of wriggling and automatic dominion, over the kingdom of our ample bed.

Sharing our bed – and putting up with someone else's revolutions and manoeuvrings – is an act of true intimacy. Our bedstead is the domain of sleep, after all, a uniquely solitary affair. It is unsurprising then that the act of sleeping together is the precursor or natural follow-up to sharing our bodies. Indeed, the term *sleeping with someone* is now synonymous with sex itself, not catching forty winks.

Our bodies are aroused during REM sleep, whether the dream we're having is of a sexual nature or not. Boys and men, from infancy through to middle-age and beyond, host erections three to four times a night; women are similarly aroused during sleep, at least physiologically. Nobody has adequately been able yet to explain why the body vaults into such states during the night. They are mechanical commonplaces.

If ever such tumescence should tip over, into a sexualised *wet dream*, it is as rude an awakening as we're ever likely to have while fast asleep. More commonplace than such lustful visions are the romantic, lovelorn dreams that express our heart's deepest longings. Sure, dreams are often more banal than that, especially once we pass the hormonal swerves of adolescence. Yet we have all been guilty of crimes of passion, while dreaming (if not in waking life). No wonder the object of a person's affections is often called *dreamy* or a *dreamboat*.

Once such intimacies have become familiar, we are about ready to share not just our beds and bodies with another, but also – accessing our truest vulnerabilities – our dearest dreams. And I don't mean our reveries – however crude, rude, sublime or ridiculous – so much as our life-long ambitions. Our dreams have in this way come to mean also our goals, aspirations, the end-points for a lifetime's toils. A *dream-come-true* expresses the height of human exultation.

Yet *dream* originally meant none of this, but *joy and music* (as it, in large part, derives from the Old English *dréam*). So forget the workaday! In time to a circadian rhythm, dreaming is nature's happy, sweet song. All of which sounds an awful lot like love.

Play on!

I read this poem to my wife on our wedding day — just the two of us, taking vows on a hazy sunlit clifftop overlooking the Pacific Ocean, our life-ahead glimmering.

He Wishes for the Cloths of Heaven
by W. B. Yeats

Had I the heavens' embroidered cloths,
Enwrought with golden and silver light,
The blue and the dim and the dark cloths
Of night and light and the half-light,
I would spread the cloths under your feet:
But I, being poor, have only my dreams;
I have spread my dreams under your feet;
Tread softly because you tread on my dreams.

(1899)

My children, as toddlers, used to clamour to throw a coin into the fountain of our local park whenever we passed near it. I would hand them a copper each and then, once they had slung it into the water and tottered on towards the playground, wonder what on earth they had wished for (much as I used to wonder what they dreamed of as babies, especially as that is the time of life when REM, and dream, abounds at its most prolific).

Yet I never once asked them. It really didn't seem any of my business.

Moreover, if they had told me, I feared that the wish — be it elementary or fantastical — had considerably less chance of coming true . . .

Nicholson Baker is a master observer of life's minutiae,

315

rendering the everyday exquisite. In his essay 'Coins', Baker's descriptions initially seem hum-drum but, as the piece progresses, a whole world opens up. It seems almost as if he is trawling a brainscape, not a fountain – fishing dreams like the sandman, not coins, and then depositing them safely into buckets. Those cents, nickels and dimes are like the tiniest plish-plashes of our consciousness. They reflect those dreams – whether sleeping or waking – that shimmer just beneath the mind's surface, in all of us.

Make no mistake, there is magic in Midtown Plaza: not least residing in that one coin for which he reserves the portentous syntax, 'black it was . . .'

Watch out for it.

Or perhaps it was you that flung it there?

Coins
by Nicholson Baker

In 1973, when I was sixteen, I got a job in building maintenance at Midtown Plaza, Rochester's then flourishing downtown shopping mall. I spent a day pulling nails from two-by-fours – loudly whistling Ravel's *Boléro* while I worked, so that the secretaries would know that I knew a few things about French music – and then Rocky, the boss, a dapper man with a mustache, apprenticed me to the mall's odd-job man, Bradway. Bradway taught me the right way to move filing cabinets (you walk with them on alternating corners, as if you're slow dancing with them, and when you have one of them roughly in position in its row, just put the ball of your foot low against a corner and step down, and the cabinet will slide into place as if pulled there by a magnet);

and he taught me how to snap a chalk line, how to cut curves in Sheetrock, how to dig a hole for a 'No Parking' sign, how to adjust the hydraulic tension on an automatic door, the right way to use a sledgehammer, and how to change the fluorescent bulbs in the ceiling of the elevator. He wore funny-looking glasses, and he sang 'Pretty, Pretty Paper Doll' to the secretaries, embarrassing them and me, but he was a decent person and a good teacher. For reasons I still don't understand he was disliked by one of the carpenters in the maintenance department, who referred to him as a 'proctologist's delight'.

One afternoon Bradway gave me a beeper and told me he was going to teach me how to sweep up the pennies in the fountain. Midtown Plaza's fountain had a fifteen-foot-high inward-curving spray, and there were four or five low mushroom fountains to one side, lit from below; the water went around and under a set of stairs rising up to the mall's second level. People threw pennies in from the landing on the stairs and while standing at the railing on the second level, but mostly they tossed them in as they walked past. I had thrown in pennies myself. The thing to do when you wished on a penny was to thumb-flip it very high – the more air time it had, the more opportunity it had to become an important penny, a singular good-luck penny – and then watch it plunge into the water and twirl down to the tiled bottom of the pool. You had to memorize where it landed. It was the penny with the two very tarnished pennies just to the left of it – or no, was it one of the ones in that very similar constellation a foot away? Every day you could check on your penny, or the penny you had decided must be your penny, to see how it was doing, whether it was accumulating wish-fulfilling powers.

So when Bradway said that I – a maintenance worker earning $2.50 an hour – was going to be sweeping up all the pennies, I experienced a magisterial shiver. We went down to the basement and got a pair of rubber fly-fishing boots, a black bucket with some holes in it, a dustpan, and a squeegee broom. Bradway showed me the switch that turned off the pump for the fountains. I pressed it. There was a clunk.

Back upstairs the water was almost still. I stepped over the marble ledge and, handed the long pole of the squeegee, I began pushing around other people's good luck. The bottom of the pool was covered with small blue tiles, and it was somewhat slimy, so that the pennies, moved along by the squeegee, formed planar sheets of copper, arranging themselves to fit into one another's adjoining curves, until finally a row of pennies would push up, make peaks, and flip back, forming a second layer, and then another layer would form, and eventually there was a sunken reef of loose change – including some nickels and dimes, but no quarters – in one corner of the pool. 'That's it, just keep sweeping them toward the pile,' Bradway said. He gave me the black bucket with the holes in it, and, rolling up my sleeves as high as I could, I used the dustpan to scoop up the change and pour it, entirely underwater, into the bucket. The sound was of anchor chains at the bottom of the sea. By doing as much of it as possible below the surface, we kept the penny removal somewhat discreet.

Bradway went away while I swept further afield, and I looked out with a haughty but weary look at the people walking by: I was the maintenance man, standing in the water; they were just pedestrians in a mall. 'Are you going to keep all that money?' a man said to me. I said no, it was going to charity. 'I'm a good charity, man,' he said. The trickiest area to sweep was along the row of mushroom fountains (which were just stalks when the water was turned off), but even there it wasn't too hard, and when I got the strays out into the open tilework and scooted the change along in a cloud of pale, sluggish dirt, I felt like a seasoned cowboy, bringing the herd home.

Bradway came back and together we pulled the black bucket out, letting the water pour from the holes. It was extremely heavy. We set it on a two-wheeled dolly. 'Feel that slime?' said Bradway. I nodded. 'The bank won't take the money this way.' We went down the freight elevator to the basement and he showed me a room with an old yellow washing machine in it. Together we dumped the money in and Bradway turned the dial to regular wash; the coins went through a slushy-sounding cycle. After lunch, I scooped out the clean money and wheeled it to the bank. As told, I asked to see Diane. Diane led me back to the vault, and I slid the black bucket off the dolly next to some dirty sacks of quarters.

Every week that summer I cleaned the fountain. Every week there was new money there to sweep up. I flipped more coins in myself; one nickel I deliberately left in place for a few weeks while I maneuvered away all the pennies around it, so that my wish-money would have more time to gather momentum. The next time, though, I swept it along with the rest, trying, however, to follow its progress as a crowd of coins lined up like piglets on the sow of the rubber blade. There were momentary collisions and overturnings, and the wavelets of the water added a confusion. My coin slid over another coin and fell to the right, and then, as I

pushed them all into the corner pile, a mass of money ava-
lanched over it and it was lost to view.

Once I came across a penny that had lain in the water
under the stairs, unswept, for a very long time – perhaps
years. Black it was and full of power. I pushed it into the
heap with the others, dumped it into the washing machine,
and delivered it to Diane at the bank.

(2001)

★

The Student
by Anton Chekhov

At first the weather was fine and still. The thrushes were
calling, and in the swamps close by something alive droned
pitifully with a sound like blowing into an empty bottle. A
snipe flew by, and the shot aimed at it rang out with a gay,
resounding note in the spring air. But when it began to get
dark in the forest a cold, penetrating wind blew inappro-
priately from the east, and everything sank into silence.
Needles of ice stretched across the pools, and it felt cheer-
less, remote, and lonely in the forest. There was a whiff of
winter.

Ivan Velikopolsky, the son of a sacristan, and a student of
the clerical academy, returning home from shooting, walked
all the time by the path in the water-side meadow. His fin-
gers were numb and his face was burning with the wind. It
seemed to him that the cold that had suddenly come on had
destroyed the order and harmony of things, that nature itself
felt ill at ease, and that was why the evening darkness was
falling more rapidly than usual. All around it was deserted

and peculiarly gloomy. The only light was one gleaming in the widows' gardens near the river; the village, over three miles away, and everything in the distance all round was plunged in the cold evening mist. The student remembered that, as he went out from the house, his mother was sitting barefoot on the floor in the entry, cleaning the samovar, while his father lay on the stove coughing; as it was Good Friday nothing had been cooked, and the student was terribly hungry. And now, shrinking from the cold, he thought that just such a wind had blown in the days of Rurik and in the time of Ivan the Terrible and Peter, and in their time there had been just the same desperate poverty and hunger, the same thatched roofs with holes in them, ignorance, misery, the same desolation around, the same darkness, the same feeling of oppression – all these had existed, did exist, and would exist, and the lapse of a thousand years would make life no better. And he did not want to go home.

The gardens were called the widows' because they were kept by two widows, mother and daughter. A camp fire was burning brightly with a crackling sound, throwing out light far around on the ploughed earth. The widow Vasilisa, a tall, fat old woman in a man's coat, was standing by and looking thoughtfully into the fire; her daughter Lukerya, a little pock-marked woman with a stupid-looking face, was sitting on the ground, washing a caldron and spoons. Apparently they had just had supper. There was a sound of men's voices; it was the labourers watering their horses at the river.

'Here you have winter back again,' said the student, going up to the camp fire. 'Good evening.'

Vasilisa started, but at once recognized him and smiled cordially.

'I did not know you; God bless you,' she said.

'You'll be rich.'

They talked. Vasilisa, a woman of experience, who had been in service with the gentry, first as a wet-nurse, afterwards as a children's nurse, expressed herself with refinement, and a soft, sedate smile never left her face; her daughter Lukerya, a village peasant woman, who had been beaten by her husband, simply screwed up her eyes at the student and said nothing, and she had a strange expression like that of a deaf mute.

'At just such a fire the Apostle Peter warmed himself,' said the student, stretching out his hands to the fire, 'so it must have been cold then, too. Ah, what a terrible night it must have been, granny! An utterly dismal long night!'

He looked round at the darkness, shook his head abruptly and asked:

'No doubt you have been at the reading of the Twelve Gospels?'

'Yes, I have,' answered Vasilisa.

'If you remember at the Last Supper Peter said to Jesus, "I am ready to go with Thee into darkness and unto death." And our Lord answered him thus: "I say unto thee, Peter, before the cock croweth thou wilt have denied Me thrice." After the supper Jesus went through the agony of death in the garden and prayed, and poor Peter was weary in spirit and faint, his eyelids were heavy and he could not struggle against sleep. He fell asleep. Then you heard how Judas the same night kissed Jesus and betrayed Him to His tormentors. They took Him bound to the high priest and beat Him, while Peter, exhausted, worn out with misery and alarm, hardly awake, you know, feeling that something awful was just going to happen on earth, followed behind . . . He loved Jesus passionately, intensely, and now he saw from far off how He was beaten . . .'

Lukerya left the spoons and fixed an immovable stare upon the student.

'They came to the high priest's,' he went on; 'they began to question Jesus, and meantime the labourers made a fire in the yard as it was cold, and warmed themselves. Peter, too, stood with them near the fire and warmed himself as I am doing. A woman, seeing him, said: "He was with Jesus, too" – that is as much as to say that he, too, should be taken to be questioned. And all the labourers that were standing near the fire must have looked sourly and suspiciously at him, because he was confused and said: "I don't know Him." A little while after again someone recognized him as one of Jesus' disciples and said: "Thou, too, art one of them," but again he denied it. And for the third time someone turned to him: "Why, did I not see thee with Him in the garden to-day?" For the third time he denied it. And immediately after that time the cock crowed, and Peter, looking from afar off at Jesus, remembered the words He had said to him in the evening . . . He remembered, he came to himself, went out of the yard and wept bitterly – bitterly. In the Gospel it is written: "He went out and wept bitterly." I imagine it: the still, still, dark, dark garden, and in the stillness, faintly audible, smothered sobbing . . .'

The student sighed and sank into thought. Still smiling, Vasilisa suddenly gave a gulp, big tears flowed freely down her cheeks, and she screened her face from the fire with her sleeve as though ashamed of her tears, and Lukerya, staring immovably at the student, flushed crimson, and her expression became strained and heavy like that of someone enduring intense pain.

The labourers came back from the river, and one of them riding a horse was quite near, and the light from the fire quivered upon him. The student said good-night to the widows and went on. And again the darkness was about him and his fingers began to be numb. A cruel wind was blowing, winter really had come back and it did not feel as though Easter would be the day after to-morrow.

Now the student was thinking about Vasilisa: since she had shed tears all that had happened to Peter the night before the Crucifixion must have some relation to her . . .

He looked round. The solitary light was still gleaming in the darkness and no figures could be seen near it now. The student thought again that if Vasilisa had shed tears, and her daughter had been troubled, it was evident that what he had just been telling them about, which had happened nineteen centuries ago, had a relation to the present – to both women, to the desolate village, to himself, to all people. The old woman had wept, not because he could tell the story touchingly, but because Peter was near to her, because her whole being was interested in what was passing in Peter's soul.

And joy suddenly stirred in his soul, and he even stopped for a minute to take breath. 'The past,' he thought, 'is linked with the present by an unbroken chain of events flowing one out of another.' And it seemed to him that he had just seen both ends of that chain; that when he touched one end the other quivered.

When he crossed the river by the ferry boat and afterwards, mounting the hill, looked at his village and towards the west where the cold crimson sunset lay a narrow streak of light, he thought that truth and beauty which had guided human life there in the garden and in the yard of the high priest had continued without interruption to this day, and had evidently always been the chief thing in human life and in all earthly life, indeed; and the feeling of youth, health, vigour – he was only twenty-two – and the inexpressible sweet expectation of happiness, of unknown mysterious happiness, took possession of him little by little, and life seemed to him enchanting, marvellous, and full of lofty meaning.

(1894)

Translated by Constance Garnett

Nuptial Sleep
by Dante Gabriel Rossetti

At length their long kiss severed, with sweet smart:
And as the last slow sudden drops are shed
From sparkling eaves when all the storm has fled,
So singly flagged the pulses of each heart.
Their bosoms sundered, with the opening start
Of married flowers to either side outspread
From the knit stem; yet still their mouths, burnt red,
Fawned on each other where they lay apart.

Sleep sank them lower than the tide of dreams,
And their dreams watched them sink, and slid away.
Slowly their souls swam up again, through gleams
Of watered light and dull drowned waifs of day;

Till from some wonder of new woods and streams
He woke, and wondered more: for there she lay.

(1870)

★

One night, back when I was falling in love with my future wife,
I couldn't get to sleep. She was still half-awake. To lull me to
sleep, Salome started to tell me about her childhood in Africa.
Mundane details – where she and her family lived, their daily
routine – but I savoured every word. There was a simplicity to
the tale. It sang, like a lullaby. My mind was taken off whatever
things it had got stuck on. I slept well.

This extract from Joseph O'Neill's novel *Netherland* has
a similar effect. It beguiles. The passage serves as a song of
childhood, a dreamy remembrance, and a romantic bedtime
story all at once.

Extract from *Netherland*
by Joseph O'Neill

I pressed the flashlight's rubber button. I was looking
upward. Everything blacked out except stars and a memory
of stars.

I was twelve. I was on a summer holiday with my mother
and old friends of hers – Floris and Denise Wassenaar,
a married couple. We travelled along the south coast of
Italy. We drove from place to place, stayed in cheap hotels
and took in sights, an itinerary banged together, from my
youthful perspective, with a heavy hammer of boredom.
Then, over dinner one night, Floris announced that he'd
organized a spear-fishing expedition. 'Just for the men,' he

said, ganging up with me. 'The women will stay on land, where it's safe.'

We went out on a wooden motorboat – Floris and I and a local man with dense white body hair. The two men were armed with full-sized spearguns. I was given a smaller speargun requiring only boyish strength to pull back the rubber catapult that fired the spear. For hours the boat bumbled parallel to the shore. We passed two or three headlands and came to a stretch of the coast that was mountainous and truly wild, with no roads for many miles inland. We moored in the beryl of a small bay. There was a beach with white pebbles. A pine forest grew right down to the beach. This was where we would fish and spend the night.

I had never snorkelled before. It was astounding to discover how a simple glass mask made clear and magnified a blue-green water amid its frightening inhabitants: when a ray glided towards me, I scrambled ashore, flippers and all. Snorkelling was hard. Gianni, the Italian, and pale and enormous Floris seemed to be able to hold their breath forever – you needed to, to find the big fish; the big fish lurked in shadows beneath rocks and had to be staked out – but with my small lungs I could only dive for a short while, and shallowly. It hurt my ears to go down deep. As the day wore on, however, a predatory boldness overtook me. A whippersnapper Neptune, I lorded it over the grassy, glistening inlet sending my matte iron thunderbolt through startled groups of small silver and brown fishes. I grew fierce and began to hunt with intent. Stalking one particular fish, I followed the rocks out of the little bay. The fish twisted into a crevice, and I dived after it. Then I became aware that the water had become cold and dark.

I was swimming at the foot of a mountain. From thousands of feet in the air the mountain plunged directly into water and sank into an endless dimness beneath me.

Like a chump in a horror movie, I slowly turned around. Confronting me was the vast green gloom of the open sea.

In a panic I bolted back to the cove.

'Catch anything?' Floris asked. I shook my head shamefully. 'No problem, *jongen,*' Floris said. 'Gianni and I got lucky.'

The killed fish was cooked over a campfire and seasoned with thyme growing wild in the pine forest. Afterwards it was time to sleep. The men lay down under the pines. The most comfortable sleeping berth, in the boat, was reserved for me.

What happened next, on the little wooden boat, was what came back to me on the synagogue roof – and what I once told Rachel about, with the result that she fell in love with me.

She revealed this in the week after Jake was born. We were up in the middle of the night. Jake was having trouble falling asleep. I held him in my arms.

'Do you want to know exactly when I fell in love with you?' Rachel said.

'Yes,' I said. I wanted to know about the moment my wife fell in love with me.

'In that hotel in Cornwall. The Something Inn.'

'The Shipwrecker's Arms,' I said. I could not forget that name and what it called before the imagination: treacherous lights on the land, the salvage of goods at the expense of the drowned.

My wife, on the point of sleep, murmured, 'Remember

328

when you told me about being in that boat at night, when you were little? That's when I fell in love with you. When you told me that story. At that exact moment.'

A small anchor fixed the boat to the bed of the cove. I lay on my side and closed my eyes. The rocking of the boat by the waves was soothing but unknown. The men on the shore were asleep. Not the twelve-year-old though. He shifted and lay on his back and decided to look up at the sky. What he saw took him by surprise. He was basically a city kid. He had never really seen the night sky for what it is. As he stared up at millions of stars, he was filled with a dread he had never known before.

I was just a boy, I said to my wife in a hotel room in Cornwall. I was just a boy on a boat in the universe.

(2008)

★

written, she
may be this
ish-language
to say what
ent hesitated
rassment and
d eaten duck
would have
her trip, and
the eating of the duck.

(2001)

329

★

DANIEL HAHN

From its title, you might expect 'She Frequented Cemeteries' by Dorthe Nors (brilliantly translated by Martin Aitken) to be ghoulish, but it is not. It has its darknesses, but is, in fact, a story about love; about being alone and not being alone. It's delicate and quiet but also filled with insight and wisdom and detail, and in its few pages manages quite magically to reach an extraordinary stillness, a feeling of rightness, of reassurance, of calm. It is also, in its own curious way, immensely alive.

So – very quiet now – breathe deeply, follow her in . . .

She Frequented Cemeteries
by Dorthe Nors

She started frequenting cemeteries that summer, preferring the ones others rarely visited. She could go straight from social events with white wine, canapés, and peripheral acquaintances, cycle to the nearest cemetery, and find the corner where no one ever really went. At the far end of Vestre Cemetery, by the Inuit and the Faeroese and the war graves, down by the disused chapel was a quiet spot. Well away from the plots where brewers, publishers, and prime ministers lay shoulder to shoulder and were dead. There was no edged grass, no small ponds with specially purchased ducks. Most of all, it resembled the hinterland of Jutland, depopulated and with plywood boards across the windows, and through it all a diagonal tunnel of willow trees. No one ever went there, so that was where she liked to go. In the same way, she was fond of the Jewish cemetery and the Catholic cemetery, and, provided she chose the right times and the right spots, Assistens Cemetery could be quiet, too.

Her favorite, though, was just between Frederiksberg and Valby. It was best in the twilight. In late July the evenings were still long and the place was like an overgrown park. Walking along the paths in the cemetery she found the unkempt graves of long-forgotten painters and poets, and at the northern end she came across a section where roses grew everywhere. The bushes had grown over the stones, weeds had tangled up in them, and they were the same roses her mother had at home. Pink, with small flowers, and no one bothered to cut them back. When she got to this part of the cemetery she would stroll peacefully around the paths as if she was drawing arabesques with her feet.

She was thirty-five years old and that summer she was avoiding her girlfriends. Now and then they would call her and ask about meeting up, but she would decline whenever possible. She knew they would be troubled by her situation, and that her way of dealing with what she claimed had happened would excite them and cause them to speculate impulsively. On a few occasions she tried to explain the situation to them, but it had not been pleasant. A few of them had tried to talk her out of it, suggesting her condition was the result of loneliness or biology. One had interrogated her. Was she quite sure, was it wise, wouldn't it be better if . . . All of them wanted to give her advice, even if she didn't need any. She knew why she was going to the cemeteries, why she continued to walk back and forth, and around and about, eating ice cream and rolling rose petals between her fingers. She was waiting, and while she was waiting she was putting something behind her and trying to find a new way of looking at the future. She walked slowly and if not devoutly then at least pensively and with a sense for the little things she didn't feel she'd noticed for years. She saw the wild cats that lived in the bushes. She saw how they drank water from the pond in the middle of the cemetery. She saw the magpie's young and the graves that had fallen in and the gravestones that had tipped over so it looked like the dead and their monuments were about to change places. As summer passed she saw the plants grown and fade, and some evenings she would pick a few of the pink roses and take them home with her to put in a vase on the bedside table. She thought mostly about how hard it was to be allowed to believe that good would arrive and how things would be when in spite of everything it did.

What had happened wasn't exactly spectacular. She had met a man. That was all. She loved him, and the way she loved him made her settle into a place inside her where intangible things took on natural substance. She felt at home there and she knew at some point she would look back on this summer as the one when she stopped holding back. Her feelings were strong and reciprocated. She sensed it, yet she knew also it would take some time before they could be together. He was in mourning for things he'd lost, and his mourning was unhurried. She could see that when he looked up at her from the table. But she was all right with it, because when he looked at her she was in no doubt and could abandon herself to the hope that he would bring all the good with him when he came.

But there was no way she could explain this to her girl-friends. They demanded evidence. They wanted to know who had died, why he kept crying, and if it really wasn't just his own fault. They wanted to know if she'd looked into him and if she knew what laying down arms involved. She mustn't get her heart broken, they said. And all the time they jumped from floe to floe with their dreams of disappearing into the current, losing control, abandoning themselves. Always trying to fill in the empty spaces and keep things moving in the meantime. Doing their best to avoid going home too early to their little apartments that reminded them of coffee bars and bus shelters every time they stepped through the door. Love, nothing less. That was what they wanted. That was what they craved, unconditionally. It was what they talked about when they put their arms under hers and dragged her through the parks, as though the parks were eyes in a storm that had to be sat out, and now she had found it. But she couldn't tell them. There was no way she could share it with them, so that summer she frequented cemeteries.

She would focus on her job, including her hospitality duties, but when it was done she would get on her bike and be gone. In the early evening she would pass through the iron gates into Park Cemetery, stroll past the dead painters, the poets, and head for the place where the pink roses were. When she got there she would walk between the graves, and as she went she closed her eyes to the parts of reality the others were keeping a watch on and imagined the man, who could only be with her in spirit, lacing his fingers in hers. They would walk there in various scenarios, sometimes silently, but together. They would be walking there when he said he loved her. Things like that would be said as they walked side by side through the cemeteries in the various stages of their as-yet-uninitiated time together. She had no trouble picturing the man zigzagging in between the small plots with a child on his shoulders. She could see the man and the child leap out from among the bushes where the wild cats lived. She could feel him kiss her behind the cemetery toilets, see the child fall and hurt itself, hear the wheels of the buggy squeak. Often he would sit down on one of the benches a little farther on and pat the space beside him so she would sit there with him, and that was what she did.

There was nothing secretive about it. She was in love with someone, and while it was going on she thought about the good that had happened and the good that was going to happen. The noise of traffic on Søndre Fasanvej and Roskildevej remained a distant hum as she stole names for the child from the gravestones, and it felt nice, the same way it felt nice to let her thoughts sink into the earth where one day they themselves would lie, white through to the bone and tangled up in each other while the world carried on above them. That was okay, she thought. That kind of death was a good thing, and she would tell him that when he came, and she would tell the child when it was old enough, and perhaps a particularly distraught girlfriend one day. Until then she would keep it to herself, frequent the cemeteries, waiting and occasionally squatting down to see the cats stretch their necks toward the water.

(2008)

Translated by Martin Aitken

Daniel Hahn has over forty books to his name, as a writer, editor or translator. He is the co-editor of the award-winning *Ultimate Book Guide* series of reading guides for children and teenagers, and of *The Oxford Companion to Children's Literature* (the latter with Humphrey Carpenter (1946–2005) and Mari Prichard). He is currently chair of the Society of Authors.

★

The Hug
by Thom Gunn

It was your birthday, we had drunk and dined
Half of the night with our old friend
Who'd showed us in the end
To a bed I reached in one drunk stride.
Already I lay snug,
And drowsy with the wine dozed on one side.

I dozed, I slept. My sleep broke on a hug,
Suddenly, from behind,
In which the full lengths of our bodies pressed:
Your instep to my heel,
My shoulder-blades against your chest.
It was not sex, but I could feel
The whole strength of your body set,
Or braced, to mine,
And locking me to you
As if we were still twenty-two
When our grand passion had not yet
Become familial.
My quick sleep had deleted all
Of intervening time and place.
I only knew
The stay of your secure firm dry embrace.

(1992)

★

Going Up and Coming Down
by Muriel Spark

How many couples have met in an elevator (lift, *ascenseur, ascensore* or whatever you call it) throughout the world? How many marriages have resulted?

In their elevator there is usually an attendant, sometimes not.

She goes up and down every weekday. At the 1.05 crush and the 2.35 return she generally finds him in the crowded box; looking up at the floor number display, looking down at the floor. Sometimes they are alone. He, she discovers, comes down from the twenty-first.

His office? On the board downstairs six offices are listed on the twenty-first floor: a law firm, a real estate office, an ophthalmologist, a Swiss chemicals association, a Palestine Potassium (believe it or not) agency, a rheumatologist. Which of these offices could he belong to? She doesn't look at him direct, but always, at a glance, tests the ramifying possibilities inherent in all six concerns.

He is polite. He stands well back when the crowd presses. They are like coins in a purse.

One day she catches his eye and looks away.

He notices her briefcase while she has her eyes on the floor numbers. Going down. Out she pours with the chattering human throng, turns left (the lobby has two entrances) and is gone. On the board down there are listed four offices on Floor 16, her floor. Two law firms, a literary agency and an office named W. H. Gilbert without further designation. Does she work for Mr Gilbert, he wonders.

Is Gilbert a private detective? W. H. Gilbert may well be something furtive.

Day by day she keeps her eyes on his briefcase of pale brown leather and wonders what he does. The lift stops at Floor 9, and in sidles the grey-haired stoutish man with the extremely cheerful smile. On we go; down, down. She wonders about the young man's daily life, where does he live, where and what does he eat, has he ever read the Bible? She knows nothing, absolutely nothing except one thing, which is this: he tries to catch a glimpse of her when she is looking elsewhere or leaving the elevator.

On the ground floor – seconds, and he's gone. It is like looking out of the window of a train, he flashes by so quickly. She thinks he might be poorly paid up there on the twenty-first, possibly in the real estate office or with the expert on rheumatism. He must be barely twenty-five. He might be working towards a better job, but at the moment with very little left in his pocket after paying out for his rent, food, clothes and insect spray.

Her long fair hair falls over her shoulders, outside her dark green coat. Perhaps she spends her days sending out membership renewal forms for Mr Gilbert's arcane activ-ity: 'Yes, I want to confirm my steadfast support for the Cosmic Paranormal Apostolic Movement by renewing my subscription', followed by different rates to be filled in for the categories: Individual Member, Couple, and Senior Citizen/Unwaged/Student.

Suppose there is a power failure?

She looks at his briefcase, his tie. Everything begins in a dream. In a daydream she has even envisaged an inevitable meeting in a room in some place where only two could be, far from intrusions, such as in a barn, taking shelter from a storm, snowed up. Surely there is some film to that effect.

He does not have the married look. That look, impossible to define apart from a wedding ring, absent in his case, is far from his look. All the same, he could be married, peeling potatoes for two at the weekend. What sign of the zodiac is his? Has there been an orchard somewhere in his past life as there has in hers? What TV channels does he watch?

Her hair hangs over her shoulders. He wonders if she dyes it blonde; her pubic hairs are possibly dark. Is she one of those girls who doesn't eat, so that you pay an enormous restaurant bill for food she has only picked at?

One night the attendant is missing. They are alone. Homicidal? – Could it possibly be? He would only have to take off his tie if his hands alone weren't enough. But his hands could strangle her. When they get out at the ground floor he says, 'Good night,' and is lost in the crowd.

Here in the enclosed space is almost like bundling. He considers how, in remote parts, when it was impossible for a courting man to get home at night, the elders would bundle a couple; they would bundle them together in their clothes. The pair breathed over each other but were mutually inaccessible, in an impotent rehearsal of the intimacy to come. Perhaps, he flounders in his mind, she goes to church and is better than me. This idea of her being morally better hangs about him all night, and he brings it to the elevator next morning.

She is not there. Surely she has flu, alone in her one-room apartment. Her one room with a big bed and a window overlooking the river? Or is Mr Gilbert there with her?

When she appears next day in the elevator he is tempted to follow her home that night. But then she might know;

feel, guess, his presence behind her. Certainly she would. She might well think him a weirdy, a criminal. She might turn and catch sight of him, crossing the park:

> Like one, that on a lonesome road
> Doth walk in fear and dread,
> And having once turned round walks on,
> And turns no more his head;
> Because he knows, a frightful fiend
> Doth close behind him tread.

Does she go to a gym class? She must have caught me looking just now. He knows she does not wear a wedding ring or an engagement ring. But that does not mean very much.

She looks at his briefcase, his tie, the floor, the floor number. Could he be a diamond merchant with a fold of tissue paper, containing five one-carat diamonds, nestling in his inner pocket? One of the names on the board could be a cover.

Other, familiar people join them on every floor. A woman with a white smile that no dentist could warm edges towards him while he edges away.

*

One day at the lunch hour he looks at her and smiles. She is there, too, in the evening with only four other people plus the attendant for the elevator. He takes the plunge. Would she be free for dinner one night? Thursday? Friday?

They have made a date. They eat in a Polish restaurant where the clients are served by waitresses with long hair even blonder and probably more natural than Doreen's.

How long does it take for floating myths and suppositions to form themselves into the separate still digits of reality? Sometimes it is as quick or as slow, according to luck, as fixing the television screen when it has gone haywire. Those stripes and cloudscapes are suddenly furniture and people.

He is employed by one of the law firms up there on the twenty-first, his speciality is marine insurance claims. Doreen, as she is called, remarks that it must be a great responsibility. He realizes she is intelligent even before Doreen Bridges (her full name) tells him she works for W. H. Gilbert, ('Bill'), an independent literary agent, and that she has recently discovered an absolutely brilliant new author called Dak Jan whose forthcoming first novel she has great hopes for. Michael Pivet lives in a bachelor apartment; she shares room with another girl in another part of the city.

And the curious thing is, that all the notions and possibilities that have gone through their minds for the past five weeks or more are totally forgotten by both of them. In the fullness of the plain real facts their speculations disappear into immaterial nothingness, never once to be remembered in the course of their future life together.

(1994)

Patrick Ness

'Dual Balls' by Nicola Barker has nothing to do with sleep or circadian rhythms, but it is the funniest short story ever written and, as such, belongs in every anthology on earth.

It breaks many, many, many rules of comedy – it has a very long build-up, sexual devices aren't at all funny – but by the end, I am, without fail, crying with laughter every single time I read it. In fact, when I teach writing classes, I use it to judge my students. The larger the percentage who think it's hilarious, the more talented I know them all to be. The larger the percentage who think it in bad taste, the longer the hours of impending classroom drudgery for their poor teacher.

Dual Balls
by Nicola Barker

Selina Mitchell had never been particularly free-thinking. Since she was fifteen she had been completely under the sway of her dominant and rather single-minded husband Tom and her dominant and rather light-headed friend Joanna. She had always lived in Grunty Fen. If you grow up somewhere with a name like Grunty Fen you never really see the humour in the name, and Selina was no exception to this rule. She never thought it was a particularly amusing place to live. In fact she hated it most of the time. It was physically small, socially small and intellectually small. It wasn't even close enough to Cambridge to bask in any of the reflected glory; but if ever Selina had cause to write a letter to London or Manchester or Edinburgh for any reason she invariably wrote her address as *Grunty Fen, Cambridgeshire*. She hoped that this created a good impression.

The only scandal that had ever caused real consternation, discussion and debate in Grunty Fen was when Harry Fletcher had started to wear Wellington boots to school (in summer) and the school had been forced to alter their uniform rules in order to acknowledge that Wellingtons were a legitimate item of clothing for school wear. The teachers had seen this new allowance as a victory for the environment over the purity of education, a muddying of the intellectual pursuit. The kids all wore wellies to school for a while and then switched back to mucky trainers after their initial *joie de vivre* had worn off.

Selina had been a quick-witted student – by Grunty Fen standards – and had been one of the few children at the village school bright and determined enough to go to teacher training college. At seventeen she had packed her suitcase and had gone to Reading to learn how to be a teacher; to spread discipline and information.

At seventeen she had thought that she would never return to Grunty Fen again, but inevitably she went home during her vacations to visit her parents and wrote long, emotional letters to her boyfriend Tom, who had tried to stop her going to college in the first place by asking her to marry him.

After three years at college Selina had returned to Grunty Fen, 'Just until I decide where I really want to go.' Eventually she had married Tom and had started teaching at the village primary school.

She disliked children and didn't want any of her own. Tom liked children – probably because he wasn't forced into a classroom with thirty of them every day – but he realized that if he wanted to hang on to Selina (she was one of the intellectual élite) then he would have to bow to her better judgement.

Time rolled by. Selina's life was as flat as the fens and just about as interesting. Nothing much happened at all.

Joanna, Selina's best friend, had lived a very similar sort of life except that she had enjoyed little success at school and had never attended teacher training college. She had got married at sixteen to John Burger whose family owned a large farm to the north of Grunty Fen, and had borne him two children before she reached twenty. She had always been wild and mischievous, but in a quiet way, a way that pretended that nothing serious was ever going on, or at least nothing seriously bad. Joanna was the bale of hay in Selina's field. She made Selina's landscape moderately more entertaining.

Joanna didn't really know the meaning of hard work. Most country women throw in their lot with their husbands and work like automatons on the farm. But Joanna had more sense than that. She preferred to stay at home 'creating a friendly home environment' and cultivating her good looks.

At the age of thirty-nine she aspired to the Dallas lifestyle. She spent many hours growing and painting her nails, making silk-feel shirts and dresses on her automatic sewing machine and throwing or attending Tupperware parties.

Joanna was Grunty Fen's only hedonist, but hedonism wasn't just her way of life, it was her religion, and she tried to spread it like a spoonful of honey on buttery toast.

They were in a café in Ely, a stone's throw from the cathedral, eating a couple of cream eclairs with coffee. Selina was making fun of Joanna but Joanna didn't seem to mind. She pulled the chocolate away from the choux pastry with her cake fork as Selina said laughingly, 'I still can't think of that birthday without smiling. My fortieth, and I thought it would be some sort of great landmark. I was so depressed. I opened Tom's present and it was a home first aid kit. Of course I said how lovely it was. Then, trying to hide my disappointment, I opened your present, firmly believing that it would contain something frivolous and feminine. But inside the parcel there were only ten odd pieces of foam, all neatly and pointlessly sewed up around the edges. Neither of us knew what the hell they were. I thought they might be miniature cushions without covers. Tom thought they were for protecting your knees during cricket games, a sort of knee guard. I even thought they might be falsies.'

Joanna smiled. 'This must be one of the only places in the world where a woman of forty doesn't understand the basics of sophisticated dressing. I thought you could sew the shoulder pads into all your good shirts and dresses. It's a fashionable look, Selina, honestly.'

Selina shrugged her non-padded shoulders. 'I will sew them in eventually, I promise.'

Joanna grinned to herself. She looked rather cheery. Usually before, during and after the consumption of a cream cake Joanna panicked about its calorie content and moaned about its probable effect on her midriff.

As Selina waited for the inevitable outburst she said, 'If we didn't come to Ely every few weeks for a chat and a break I'm sure I'd go mad. Ely. Imagine! This small, insignificant town has come to symbolize freedom and independence to me. It's rather sad; it's like the Americans symbolizing freedom with a sparrow instead of a bald eagle.'

She looked into Joanna's face. Joanna was smiling. It was as if she was listening to a song that no one else could hear. Selina stared at her in silence for a minute or so and then said, 'What is it, Joanna? I'm sure you're up to something.'

Joanna's eyes were vaguely glassy. Selina frowned. 'You've not been taking those tranquillizers again, have you?'

Joanna laughed. It was a sort of throaty, gutsy laugh. 'Oh Selina, if only you knew. If only! What's Tom like in bed at the moment? Has it improved since our last little chat?'

Selina shrugged and her cheeks reddened. 'Nothing much has happened in that department. Are you enjoying that cake?'

She had finished hers several minutes before, but Joanna was still (uncharacteristically) pushing her cake around her plate. Selina added quickly – to distract Joanna from intimate territory – 'School's been awful. Felicity has been sitting in on classes. It's to do with the new assessment rules from the education authority. The classroom is no longer my kingdom. It's been taken over by men in little grey suits. Of course Felicity loves it all. She even had the cheek to offer me a few tips on my teaching technique the other day. I'm surprised she was capable of taking any of the lesson in. Most of it she spent fiddling with her hearing aid. Anyway, everyone knows that Heads are incapable of controlling classes and that's why they become Heads in the first place. Maybe I'm just bitter, but the thought of that old crone deigning to tell me how to handle a class! She said something like, 'Be freer, Selina, be more adventurous, take risks!' I tried to tell her that the syllabus had destroyed all elements of spontaneity in the classroom. If the kids want to cope with the workload nowadays it's all blackboard, chalk and copying.'

As Selina finished speaking Joanna shuddered slightly. Selina smiled. 'Ghost walk over your grave?'

Joanna shook her head and then giggled furtively. 'Look Selina, it's not that I'm not interested in what you are saying about school – God knows, my two did well enough under your tuition and they thought you were a great teacher – it isn't that I'm not interested, but I just must change the subject for a moment.'

As Joanna spoke, she leaned toward Selina conspiratorially and her voice dropped to a whisper, 'Selina, I'm wearing Dual Balls.'

Selina frowned. 'What do you mean? Is it a girdle of some kind, or some sort of skin ointment?'

Joanna never ceased to amaze her with her violent enthusiasms and frivolity. She pushed a slightly greying brown curl behind her ear and thought abstractedly, 'I must have my hair cut, it's almost touching my shoulders now.'

Joanna's chair scraped along the floor as she pulled it up closer to Selina. Selina could smell her perfume – something heady like Opium – which flushed through the air like bleach through water. Joanna whispered again, 'I've got Dual Balls, Selina. I've had them in since I left the house. It's incredible.'

Selina shrugged. 'You're going to have to explain this to me, Joanna. I don't know what Dual Balls are.'

Joanna bit her lip and stared at Selina through her heavily mascaraed lashes for a moment, then she said, 'I got them from an underwear catalogue. I ordered them and they came in the post. John doesn't know anything about them.'

Selina cleared her throat nervously, 'Are they something rude, Joanna?' Joanna winked saucily. 'I should say so. They're like two small round vibrating grapes. Battery operated.'

Selina took a sip of her coffee to try and deflate the tension, then said, 'Have you got them in your bag?'

Joanna snorted loudly and several people at other tables turned and stared at them both for a moment. Selina felt slightly embarrassed. Joanna soon recovered from her fit of hilarity and whispered, 'They're not in my bag, stupid. I've got them in my fanny.'

Selina was not initially so much shocked by the idea of Joanna's little vibrating grapes as by her casual use of the word 'fanny'. It was an old-fashioned word. She had once had a great-aunt called Fanny, a gregarious, light-hearted aunt who had always seemed very old to her as a child; old, frail but charming.

She didn't really know how to reply to Joanna, how to disguise her intense unease and embarrassment. Luckily Joanna had other things on her mind. After a few seconds since she squeezed Selina's arm and said, 'I'm going to nip into the toilets and take them out, then you can have a proper look at them.'

Selina's expression was querulous. Joanna noticed as she stood up, and grinned. 'Don't worry, Selina, I'll give them a good wash before you have to have any contact with them.'

Selina sighed. 'Joanna, please be discreet. This is only Ely after all, not San Francisco.'

Joanna didn't reply.

Once she'd gone Selina relaxed and drank a large mouthful of her coffee. She stared out of the window at the cathedral. She thought, 'God, I feel old. Maybe it's teaching. It just beats all the enthusiasm out of you. I'm sure I never used to feel this way. The kids are no better or no worse than they were twenty years ago. It must be me that's changed.' She sighed and waited for Joanna's return.

After about five minutes Joanna merged from the toilets looking furtive but self-satisfied, like a large tom cat on the prowl, about to spray an unsuspecting territory with his rank odour. Selina thought, 'This room belongs to Joanna. She doesn't give a damn about anything.'

Joanna sat down next to her again and Selina said straight away, 'I don't know where you get these ideas from – or your nerve for that matter – look at you, as bold as brass!'

Joanna smiled and patted her chestnut perm with one of her bright-pink-fingernailed hands. 'Don't look at this hand, look at the other one under the table.'

Selina moved backwards slightly and stared down at Joanna's other hand which held the Dual Balls like a couple of freshly laid eggs. Selina said, 'They're bigger than I thought they'd be and attached to each other. I imagined that they'd be a sort of flesh colour, not that strange off-white.'

Joanna raised her eyebrows, 'Flesh *is* off-white, Selina. Are Tom's balls a very different colour to these?'

She smiled provocatively. Selina shook her head disapprovingly. 'Tom's . . .' – she couldn't use the word – 'Tom's aren't anything unusual, Joanna, and I certainly don't make a habit of trying to use them like you've just used those. Also, his don't use batteries and they aren't attached by a small piece of cord.'

Joanna smirked. 'You wish Tom's balls were like these. They're very effective, and so discreet. I think the thrill of using them is trebled by the fact of wearing them out. It's so arousing.'

Selina grimaced. 'Walking can't be easy with them in. Why don't they just drop out?'

As Selina spoke Joanna switched the balls on. She waited for Selina to finish talking and then said, 'Why don't you try them and see?' The balls vibrated vigorously in her hand. They sounded like a quieter version of an electric razor.

Selina was sure that everyone could hear. She whispered frantically, 'For God's sake, Joanna, switch them off.' Joanna frowned. 'I worry about you, Selina. You're becoming very old-maidish, very schoolmarmish. You don't have any spirit of adventure any more.'

Selina didn't rise to the bait. 'I've never had any spirit of adventure and you know it.'

Joanna nodded. 'I suppose that's true. No backbone, no spontaneity. No interest in what's state of the art . . .'

Selina raised an eyebrow. 'Where did you come across that little phrase? Something on television, something American, I suppose?'

'You wouldn't have the nerve to wear these out, no way,' Joanna interrupted.

Selina smiled. 'I'd have enough nerve, Joanna, just too much sense. I don't need something like those. I think they're horrible. Now switch them off.'

Joanna turned and stared out of the window at people passing by. An old lady staggered past pulling her shopping trolley. Joanna pointed at the woman, 'I bet she'd wear them out. I bet she's got more spunk in her little finger than you've got in your entire body.'

Selina almost smiled at this but then stopped herself. 'Possibly. Look, the waitress is coming over with the bill. Please turn them off.'

Joanna didn't turn them off, but started instead to lift up the hand containing the vibrating balls until they were almost at a level with the surface of the table. Selina was excruciatingly embarrassed. 'Joanna, switch them off and put them away. You're embarrassing me.'

Joanna was staring at the Dual Balls rather thoughtfully.

After a moment she said, 'I dare you to wear these when you're teaching one of your classes. Just for one lesson. I dare you!'

Joanna loved dares. This was principally because she always thought of them and didn't therefore usually do them herself. 'Go on Selina, I dare you!'

Selina laughed. 'You've got to be kidding. Those horrible little things are having no contact with my intimate body whatsoever.'

Joanna lifted the balls slightly higher than the table and said, 'If you don't accept the dare I swear I'm going to put these into your coffee cup when the waitress comes to clear the table. That should be in about twenty seconds.'

Selina saw a couple of people at the nearest table to them discussing something and laughing. She was sure that they had noticed. She said, 'Joanna, put them down, please.'

Joanna held them even higher. The waitress started to walk towards them. When she was about five steps from the table Selina said, 'OK, I promise to wear them, I promise, all right?'

Joanna switched the balls off immediately. It seemed very quiet without their buzzing.

On her way home Joanna passed John in the tractor. He stopped so that she could overtake him then waved his arm so that she would pause for a moment. She wound down her window. 'Yes?'

He shouted from his high seat, not bothering to switch off the tractor's roaring engine, 'Did she take them?'

Joanna nodded emphatically. 'Yes. It worked like a dream. She was really shocked when she thought that I was wearing them. It was a real effort not to laugh.'

He smiled. 'You must be a great actress then.'

She shrugged. 'I did all right.'

She crossed her fingers down by the steering wheel. He frowned – although he couldn't see her hands – 'Joanna, you were just acting?' Joanna guffawed. 'Don't be ridiculous. I'd probably have crashed the car if I'd worn them driving . . . Of course I wouldn't dream of wearing them anyway, why should I?'

She winked. He smiled. He obviously believed her. She uncrossed her fingers, waved at him and then drove on.

She negotiated the turn into their driveway with special care; she'd almost driven off the road there on the trip out.

One of the favourite pastimes in Grunty Fen is Chinese Whispers. People gossip like it's going out of season. They also discuss what's happened in all of the major soaps and mini-series on television. Mostly though they prefer to gossip because it's a tiny place and everyone knows everyone else's business.

John got pissed in the local pub on Saturday night and told several of his cronies about Joanna's dare. The men all laughed loudly at the notion of someone as staid and strait-laced as Selina experimenting with sexual gadgets. They knew she wouldn't do it, but they enjoyed thinking about it just the same. A couple of them went home in their cups and told their wives. The women were shocked, interested and surprised on the whole; a small proportion were slightly jealous.

After Sunday lunch Selina was doing the washing up in the kitchen and Tom was sitting at the dining table in the next room doing the *Sunday Telegraph* crossword. Occasionally he read out loud to Selina any of the clues that had completely eluded him.

Selina washed the soapsuds from the final plate and placed it with the others on the drying rack. Tom seemed busy and preoccupied so she took this opportunity to clean out the sink and refill it with very hot water and a squirt of bleach. She went and found her handbag and took out the Dual Balls which she had placed inside, wrapped up in a tissue. She opened the tissue and removed the Dual Balls then placed them in the hot water and bleach, still wearing her rubber gloves. As she rubbed the balls with her hands she felt like a fetishist.

At the sound of Tom's voice from the next room she jumped guiltily and her heart lurched; then in a split second she had grabbed the washing-up cloth and had dropped it over the balls, covering them completely. Tom was saying, 'Thirty-one across. Vulgar Cockney squeezes ends of these into tube. Six letters. I think it's an anagram. Any ideas, Selina?'

At this exact moment, a mile or so away, Joanna and John were still eating their lunch of beef and roast potatoes. John had a slight hangover. Joanna had prepared a meal for four but neither of the children had bothered hanging around for it. This made John even more ill-tempered and grouchy. He kept saying, 'It's such a waste of good food. Those two don't know what it's like to do without. You spoil them.'

Joanna ignored him. She was thinking about Selina and the Dual Balls. She wondered whether she would use them or not. Selina rarely broke her word, if ever.

She cut into a potato and watched the steam rise from its hot centre. She speared a bit of it on to her fork and prepared

352

to put it into her mouth. Before she had done so, however, John said, 'I told a couple of the fellas about your joke with Selina last night.'

Joanna stared at him, dumbstruck. 'You did what?'

Her voice was sharp and strident. He shrugged. 'I know I promised not to but it sort of slipped out.'

She put down her fork. 'I don't know why I tell you anything. You're totally unreliable. I'm sick of you spreading my business about and sticking your nose into everything. This was none of your affair in the first place.'

He frowned. 'Well, why did you tell me about it then?'

She pushed her chair back from the table and stood up. 'I didn't tell you about it, you opened my bloody mail. You have no right to open letters and parcels that are addressed to me.'

He shook his head, confused. 'You don't have anything to hide from me, Joanna. What's the problem all of a sudden? This isn't like you.'

Joanna slammed her hand down on the table, rattling the plates and glasses and cutlery. 'I am a woman, John, women have secrets. That's one of the few good things about being a woman as far as I can see. Now that you've told everyone about this thing with Selina she'll be a laughing stock. She's my friend, for God's sake.'

John stood up and moved around the table towards Joanna. His head ached with every twitch of his body. 'Everyone knows that Selina won't use those things. She's not like that. It was a silly idea in the first place really.'

Joanna felt tearful. She shouted, 'Well, it seemed like a good excuse at the time!'

Then, grabbing her plate, she marched off into the kitchen, where she threw her lunch into the bin.

John sat down at the table again. He felt somewhat confused.

Felicity Barrow received a telephone call from her friend Janet Street on Sunday afternoon. Janet was extremely excited because she had a bit of amusing gossip to impart about one of the teachers at Felicity's school. Felicity liked to call it 'my school', even though she was only the headmistress.

Janet had a rather puffy, breathy, light voice, and the scandal in her news almost extinguished it altogether. She gasped down the phone, 'Jim told me that Selina Mitchell has been wearing some sort of sexual device to school and using it while she's teaching classes.' Felicity interrupted, putting on her best head-teacherish voice, 'What on earth are you saying, Janet? And do speak clearly, I haven't adjusted my hearing aid yet.' On concluding this sentence she sipped her tea and took a large bite out of a mint-flavoured Viscount biscuit.

Janet gulped. This noise travelled all the way down the telephone line and into Felicity's ear. Then she whispered, 'Well, Jim said that it is a sort of vibrating machine which is shaped like the female sexual organs, but convex. It is attached by elastic to the two thighs, I think the elastic goes around the buttocks at the back . . . anyway Jim says it's very discreet. What happens is that it is battery-operated and it presses into the vagina while methodically rubbing at the clitoris. Apparently after several minutes this stimulates a sexual climax.'

Felicity tried to suppress the impulse to laugh, but finally gave into a throaty chuckle. 'Janet, I think what you're saying is untrue. We both know Selina Mitchell, we've both know her for years. I was headmistress at Grunty Fen Primary when she was a pupil at the school herself. There has never been anyone in the school whose dignity, discretion and professionalism I have held in higher regard. Just the other day I sat in on her class and assessed her performance. My only advice to her was that I thought her techniques too staid, perhaps a jot unimaginative . . .'

Janet interrupted. 'That's all well and good, Felicity, but you know what they say, there's no smoke without fire. She did go away at the end of the sixties, after all. Who knows what sort of habits she picked up then . . .'

Felicity's initial amused indulgence at Janet's news suddenly evaporated. She snapped, 'Stop talking such absolute rubbish, Janet. I'd certainly have expected that you of all people would be the last to surrender your credulity to the clutches of vicious and totally unfounded gossip. I don't want to hear anything more about this subject, and if I do hear anything from a different source I will be forced to presume that it originated with you. Do I make myself clear?' Janet answered breathlessly in the affirmative and the conversation ended abruptly shortly afterwards.

Felicity had been headmistress at Grunty Fen Primary for almost thirty years. The time had come and gone for her to retire but she had ignored suggestions from various departments – chiefly from her husband Donald, who was several years into retirement himself – and had carried on giving her all to the young children of the district.

She took her vocation very seriously. Her main problem was that she couldn't be convinced that anyone else she knew would be suitable for her job. The ideal candidate would be a woman – she thought that women made the best Heads because they were much more frightening than men – and preferably they would originate from Grunty Fen or the surrounding area. She believed that Fen children had to be taught by people who were familiar with the various interests, problems and subtleties of their character. She knew that Selina Mitchell was keen for promotion. She had been coolly vetted for a favourable reference from Selina herself on various occasions, but nothing had come of it.

Felicity put her feet up on to her foot-stool, took out her hearing aid, leaned back in her chair and took another bite out of her biscuit. She had resented Janet's news because she felt that anything bad said about her staff reflected badly on the school and ultimately on herself. She was rather proud and vain but disliked these qualities in other people. Selina, she believed, was far too proud and vain for her own good. She was too closed, not sufficiently free-thinking. Felicity found her distant and arrogant. Selina found Felicity interfering and arrogant. Neither side would bow down to the other. They weren't destined to be good friends, but Felicity often regretted that they had never even managed to become normal friends.

She took another sip of tea and decided to call Selina into her office for a serious chat first thing in the morning. She picked up a copy of the *People's Friend* and ran her finger down the list of contents, muttering. 'No smoke without fire, indeed!'

Selina didn't dare carry the Dual Balls to school in her teaching bag in case any of the children poked around in it looking for a pencil or a book and came across them.

Instead she wore a smart blue blazer with a deep inside pocket in which she carefully placed the Dual Balls before breakfast.

On arriving at school she went straight into her classroom to enjoy five minutes of quiet contemplation before the start of the day. She was keen to avoid Felicity and other members of staff, who on a Monday morning always seemed to try extra hard to be sociable and community spirited. Selina hated all that 'bonding' business. It wasn't her style. She rarely went out for drinks on a Friday night with her colleagues; even so, she always saw them over the weekend because Grunty Fen and the surrounding areas were so sparsely populated that a trip to the shops usually meant a trip to meet everyone from your past, your present and your future that you were keen to avoid.

She sat at her desk and put her hand into her inside pocket to feel the Dual Balls. They felt cold and smooth; highly unerotic. She looked around the classroom and thought, 'I'm so bloody sick of this routine. I'm sick of teaching. I just wish that it was heading somewhere or that something would come of it, but nothing will. I've vegetated, stultified.'

The room smelled clean but of chalk and paper and dust. Her mind turned to Joanna and their conversation at the weekend. This raised a smile. She thought, 'Of course she's right. I don't have any real spirit of adventure.'

The bell rang and the day began.

Felicity had popped into the staff room at the beginning of the day to ask Selina into her office for a chat. Unfortunately Selina didn't materialize so Felicity had to content herself with the idea of meeting her during lunchtime. She checked the wall chart in the staff room to make sure that Selina wasn't on play or dinner duty.

It was a hot day. After several hours Selina became uncomfortable in her blazer and took it off so that she could cool down, hanging it carefully over the top of her chair and keeping a firm eye on it. The morning droned on and eventually it was time for lunch.

All morning she'd had half of her mind on the Dual Balls. A part of her really wanted to fulfil her dare and show Joanna that she was a woman of her word. Another part of her balked at the idea of using the balls in principle. They were crude and revolting. Secretly she was rather interested to know how they would feel, but only in a silly, inquisitive way that took no account of what was right or for the best.

As the last child left her classroom Selina made a firm decision. She resolved to go and 'try on' the Dual Balls and to try them out for several minutes in the privacy of her classroom at the beginning of her lunch hour. Then, if Joanna asked, she could say in all honesty that she had in fact worn the balls at school in the classroom.

The day was very still and warm. She opened the top button on her shirt to let the air circulate more freely around her throat then strolled to her chair and put on her blue blazer. It felt heavy and made her skin feel sticky. She felt ridiculously tense and strung-out. Luckily the toilets were close to her classroom. She worried about walking with the Dual Balls in; Joanna hadn't cleared up that little chestnut during their coffee and eclairs.

The toilets were empty. She chose one of the two cubicles and locked herself in. She as glad that she had opted to wear a skirt and sheer stockings for easier access.

Inserting the Dual Balls gave her a feeling of youthful mischievousness, as though she were one of the children in school doing something secretive and wrong like puffing on a cigarette.

The Dual Balls felt cold, bulky and stupid. She pulled the string that switched them on. In her hyper-sensitive state the buzzing of the Balls seemed like the violent crashing of cymbals. Although the toilets were empty apart from herself, she coughed loudly with embarrassment to try and hide the initial shock of the sound.

After a few moments of acclimatization Selina rearranged her clothing and stepped out of the cubicle. The balls felt like an inordinately large blue-bottle whizzing around, lost inside her knickers. She took a few experimental steps around by the sinks – where she fastidiously washed her hands – and the Dual Balls stayed firmly in place. She breathed a sigh of relief, then steeled her resolve and nerve as she headed for the door.

Once out in the corridor, surrounded by screaming, sweaty, excitable, break-enjoying children, Selina was able to relax. She felt less furtive and guilty out in the public sphere. She reached her classroom without misadventure; though her variation on a John Wayne swagger may easily have aroused interest in any but a child's mind. She pushed open her classroom door and went in.

Her heart sank. Sitting in the front row of desks, dead centre, was Felicity Barrow.

Smiling broadly, Felicity said, 'Oh good, Selina. I was just about to give up my search and return to the staff room.'

Selina's entire body felt stiff and immobile; only the Dual Balls continued on moving naturally inside her. She tried to negotiate the walk to her desk as freely and casually as possible. To distract Felicity's attention she said, 'Lovely day isn't it?', and pointed towards the window. Felicity turned towards the window and stared out through it at the blue sky. 'Yes, it is lovely.'

She was pleased that Selina was trying to be friendly. Selina took these few seconds' leeway to trot over to her desk and plop herself down on to her hard wooden chair. She noisily cleared her throat so that Felicity's silent contemplation of the day's glory wouldn't emphasize the jubilant buzzing of the Dual Balls. Felicity's daze returned to Selina's face. 'You're looking very well, Selina, if I may say so, very bright.' Selina smiled. 'I think I'm actually just a bit warm. Perhaps I should take my blazer off.'

She performed this simple action with as much 'involved noise' as possible, concluding with the scraping up of her chair closer to the table. Her hands were shaking slightly, so she took hold of a pencil and tapped out a tiny, slight rhythm with it on the table top.

Felicity watched these adjustments very closely, then said, 'You seem unusually tense today, Selina, any particular reason?'

Selina shrugged. Inside she was boiling with embarrassment and unease but she endeavoured not to let this show. 'I don't know, Felicity. I feel all right really, just a bit, I don't know, a bit frustrated, rudderless . . .'

She didn't really know what she was saying, but after she had said it she felt as though she was talking about sex, as though she was an actress in a dirty blue film. She pinched herself and blinked her eyes, then looked over at Felicity.

Felicity was still smiling at her. 'Maybe you're upset

about all that ridiculous gossip that was circulating this weekend?'

Selina was still recovering from the tingling pain of her self-inflicted pinch. The pain seemed rather arousing, and the discomfort too. She asked automatically, 'What gossip?'

Felicity's cheeks reddened slightly. She had hoped that Selina would have been willing to make this conversation easy and unembarrassing. She cleared her throat and to hide her discomfort adjusted the position of her hearing aid in her ear. 'Apparently someone has been spreading a rumour about . . . about your purported use of sexual stimulants during school time.'

Selina's face flushed violently and her jaw went slack. 'I . . . I don't know what to say Felicity. What can I say?'

At that moment in time she felt as though her head was clouding over, clouding up, as though she were in a plane that was going through turbulent clouds. She felt quite willing to admit to everything.

Whatever doubts had clouded Felicity's mind evaporated immediately when she saw the strength of Selina's reaction. She had expected Selina to keep her cool and to utter a cold, cynical, stinging reply. Instead her reply was so unguarded and natural, so loose and out of character, almost intimate, that Felicity could not stop herself from smiling warmly at her. 'Of course I knew it was untrue. I just thought you should be aware of the kind of things that a couple of nasty people are saying.'

Selina couldn't meet Felicity's gaze. She looked down at her desk and tried to call on an inner reserve of strength. Unfortunately this moment of introspection only re-emphasized in her mind the furtive activities of the Dual

Balls. She was so tense that her body had become extremely dynamic and excitable. The hard wooden chair wasn't helping matters either. She shuddered, and suddenly her brain felt like sherbet.

The strength of Selina's reaction made Felicity's heart twist in sympathy. She bit her lip for a moment and said nervously, 'Selina, I'm sorry. I didn't think that this would affect you so badly.'

Selina felt as though she was on a roller-coaster ride. She said, 'I feel as though I'm on a roller-coaster ride, Felicity. I don't know what to say.'

She was all gaspy and uncontrolled, her insides churning with a sort of ecstatic violence. In the silence of the room she heard herself breathing heavily. Felicity sat quietly, saying nothing.

After a minute or so Selina began to gasp. She was totally out of control. She threw her head down on the table and shuddered until the shudders turned into enormous, violent, wracking howls.

Felicity froze. She had never seen such a forthright display of uninhibited emotion before and from, of all people, Selina Mitchell. She felt a terrible sense of guilt that she should have provoked such a display, but also a sense of pride that Selina should have chosen to share this wild moment of release and abandon with her, Felicity. She stood up and went over to Selina's side and placed a gentle hand on her back which she moved up and down, up and down, as though comforting a small child or burping a baby.

Selina felt Felicity's hand massaging her back but felt too far gone to respond coherently. She just said, 'Oh God, oh no, oh my!'

Felicity moved her hand from Selina's back and grasped hold of one of her hands. She said, 'Selina, listen to me. This isn't as bad as it seems to you. It doesn't affect the respect and regard that I have for your teaching abilities. You are one of my best members of staff, in fact you are my very best member of staff.'

Selina heard Felicity's words but their sounds washed over her and made very little sense. She was at the edge of a precipice and in the next moment she was falling, flailing, floating. Her ears tingled as the wind rushed by. She steeled herself for a crash landing, but instead her landing was cushioned by a million feather eiderdowns, each as soft as a poodle's belly. Everything solidified again.

Felicity was pleased to note that after a minute or so her piece of encouragement had appeared to get through to Selina. She was calming down. After a while her breathing returned to normal and she raised her head slightly from the desk. Several seconds later she said quietly, 'Felicity, I feel terrible about this, but it was just out of my control. I feel so embarrassed.'

Felicity clucked her tongue and shook her head, 'Don't be silly, Selina. I know how these things build up. I'm just glad that you were able to let go of all that anguish and to share it with me.'

Selina felt as though she was floating in the Red Sea, lifted above the water by the sodium chloride, the sea like a big marshmallow. She blinked several times and sat up straight. She noticed that Felicity was still holding her hand. She smiled at Felicity and said, 'Things have been building up inside me for a long time. I feel so much better now, so buoyant.'

Felicity gave Selina's hand one final squeeze and then let go. She said, 'I know that you are a very controlled person, Selina. I've known you for most of your life and you've never let your emotions rule your head. I think you very much deserved this opportunity to vent your feelings.'

Selina was now fully recovered. She felt stupid but also surprisingly smug. She said, 'I hope you don't think that this silly outburst will have any bearing on my discipline and dignity before my classes.' Felicity shook her head. 'I know that I can always rely on you, Selina. I'm certainly quite positive that you are an indispensable asset to this school.'

Inside Felicity's head an idea was turning. It was as though a light had been switched on or the last piece of a jigsaw puzzle snapped into place. She said, 'Trust me, Selina, you have a great future ahead of you at this school. I'm going to see to that.'

Selina began to smile. She said, 'Felicity, you've been very kind and very understanding. Thank you.'

Felicity shrugged, 'It was nothing. Now clear up your face. Here's a tissue. A bit of spit and polish should do the job.'

Selina took the proffered tissue and applied it to her running mascara. Felicity walked towards the door. 'This has been an invaluable chat, Selina.'

Selina nodded and pushed her hair behind her ears, 'It has, Felicity, and thanks again.'

Felicity smiled and opened the door. Before she closed it behind her, however, she turned and said somewhat distractedly, 'I'm sorry to rush off like this, Selina, but my hearing aid is playing up. I think it's dust or the batteries. It's been driving me mad with its buzzing for the last fifteen minutes or so.'

Selina smiled. 'That's all right.'

As the door closed, she stuffed Felicity's tissue into her mouth and bit down hard.

(1993)

Patrick Ness has written nine books: two novels for adults, *The Crash of Hennington* (2003) and *The Crane Wife* (2013); one short-story collection, also for adults, *Topics About Which I Know Nothing* (2005); and six novels for young adults, including the *Chaos Walking* trilogy and *A Monster Calls* (2011), which he also adapted as a feature film for director Juan Antonio Bayona. His numerous awards include two Carnegie Medals and the Costa Children's Book of the Year.

True Love
by Sharon Olds

In the middle of the night, when we get up
after making love, we look at each other in
complete friendship, we know so fully
what the other has been doing. Bound to each other
like mountaineers coming down from a mountain,
bound with the tie of the delivery-room,
we wander down the hall to the bathroom, I can
hardly walk, I wobble through the granular
shadowless air, I know where you are
with my eyes closed, we are bound to each other
with huge invisible threads, our sexes
muted, exhausted, crushed, the whole
body a sex – surely this

is the most blessed time of my life,
our children asleep in their beds, each fate
like a vein of abiding mineral
not discovered yet. I sit
on the toilet in the night, you are somewhere in the
    room,
I open the window and snow has fallen in a
steep drift, against the pane, I
look up, into it,
a wall of cold crystals, silent
and glistening, I quietly call to you
and you come and hold my hand and I say
I cannot see beyond it. I cannot see beyond it.

(1986)

★

Deborah Treisman

In 'Scheherazade', Haruki Murakami gives us a contemporary version of *A Thousand and One Nights*. His mysterious hero, Nobutaka Habara, has been transported to a house in a small city north of Tokyo, which he cannot leave – whether for his own protection or in punishment for some kind of crime, we are never told and Murakami himself claims not to know. ('Of course, I have a few ideas about what might be the cause, but I expect my readers do as well,' he told me. 'In fact, I think if you took their hypotheses and mine and stacked them on top of each other, you'd have an important form of author–reader communication. Because what's important isn't what caused Habara's situation but, rather, how we ourselves would act in similar circumstances.') In the house, Habara's only contact with the outside world is through bi-weekly visits from a housewife and part-time nurse, who brings him food, books and DVDs, and tends to his sexual needs. Habara nicknames this woman Scheherazade, because after sex she tells him stories, perhaps invented, perhaps true, but always riveting for her lonely listener. 'Scheherazade' is a story about isolation, about obsession, about passion, and about the unlikely connections that can form between people who are thrown together by circumstance. But it is also, and foremost, a story about story-telling, a story about how stories can not only distract, entertain and seduce us but even, sometimes, save our lives.

Scheherazade
by Haruki Murakami

Each time they had sex, she told Habara a strange and gripping story afterward. Like Queen Scheherazade in *A Thousand and One Nights*. Though, of course, Habara, unlike the king, had no plan to chop off her head the next morning. (She never stayed with him till morning, anyway.) She told Habara the stories because she wanted to, because, he guessed, she enjoyed curling up in bed and talking to a man during those languid, intimate moments after making love. And also, probably, because she wished to comfort Habara, who had to spend every day cooped up indoors.

Because of this, Habara had dubbed the woman Scheherazade. He never used the name to her face, but it was how he referred to her in the small diary he kept. 'Scheherazade came today,' he'd note in ballpoint pen. Then he'd record the gist of that day's story in simple, cryptic terms that were sure to baffle anyone who might read the diary later.

Habara didn't know whether her stories were true, invented, or partly true and partly invented. He had no way of telling. Reality and supposition, observation and pure fancy seemed jumbled together in her narratives. Habara therefore enjoyed them as a child might, without questioning too much. What possible difference could it make to him, after all, if they were lies or truth, or a complicated patchwork of the two?

Whatever the case, Scheherazade had a gift for telling stories that touched the heart. No matter what sort of story it was, she made it special. Her voice, her timing, her pacing were all flawless. She captured her listener's attention, tantalized him, drove him to ponder and speculate, and then, in the end, gave him precisely what he'd been seeking. Enthralled, Habara was able to forget the reality that surrounded him, if only for a moment. Like a blackboard wiped with a damp cloth, he was erased of worries, of unpleasant memories. Who could ask for more? At this point in his life, that kind of forgetting was what Habara desired more than anything else.

Scheherazade was thirty-five, four years older than Habara, and a full-time housewife with two children in elementary school (though she was also a registered nurse and was apparently called in for the occasional job). Her husband was a typical company man. Their home was a twenty-minute drive away from Habara's. This was all (or almost all) the personal information she had volunteered. Habara had no way of verifying any of it, but he could think of no particular reason to doubt her. She had never revealed her name. 'There's no need for you to know, is there?' Scheherazade had asked. Nor had she ever called Habara by his name, though of course she knew what it was. She judiciously steered clear of the name, as if it would somehow be unlucky or inappropriate to have it pass her lips.

On the surface, at least, this Scheherazade had nothing in common with the beautiful queen of *A Thousand and One Nights*. She was on the road to middle age and already running to flab, with jowls and lines webbing the corners of her eyes. Her hair style, her makeup, and her manner of dress weren't exactly slapdash, but neither were they likely to receive any compliments. Her features were not unattractive, but her face lacked focus, so that the impression she left was somehow blurry. As a consequence, those who walked by her on the street, or shared the same elevator, probably took little notice of her. Ten years earlier, she might well have been a lively and attractive young woman, perhaps even turned a few heads. At some point, however, the curtain had fallen on that part of her life and it seemed unlikely to rise again.

Scheherazade came to see Habara twice a week. Her days were not fixed, but she never came on weekends. No doubt she spent that time with her family. She always phoned an hour before arriving. She bought groceries at the local supermarket and brought them to him in her car, a small blue Mazda hatchback. An older model, it had a dent in its rear bumper and its wheels were black with grime. Parking it in the reserved space assigned to the house, she would carry the bags to the front door and ring the bell. After checking the peephole, Habara would release the lock, unhook the chain, and let her in. In the kitchen, she'd sort the groceries and arrange them in the refrigerator. Then she'd make a list of things to buy for her next visit. She performed these tasks skillfully, with a minimum of wasted motion, and saying little throughout.

Once she'd finished, the two of them would move wordlessly to the bedroom, as if borne there by an invisible current. Scheherazade quickly removed her clothes and, still silent, joined Habara in bed. She barely spoke during their lovemaking, either, performing each act as if completing an assignment. When she was menstruating, she used her hand to accomplish the same end. Her deft, rather businesslike manner reminded Habara that she was a licensed nurse.

After sex, they lay in bed and talked. More accurately, she talked and he listened, adding an appropriate word here, asking the occasional question there. When the clock said four-thirty, she would break off her story (for some reason, it always seemed to have just reached a climax), jump out of bed, gather up her clothes, and get ready to leave. She had to go home, she said, to prepare dinner.

Habara would see her to the door, replace the chain, and watch through the curtains as the grimy little blue car drove away. At six o' clock, he made a simple dinner and ate it by himself. He had once worked as a cook, so putting a meal together was no great hardship. He drank Perrier with his dinner (he never touched alcohol) and followed it with a cup of coffee, which he sipped while watching a DVD or reading. He liked long books, especially those he had to read several times to understand. There wasn't much else to do. He had no one to talk to. No one to phone. With no computer, he had no way of accessing the Internet. No newspaper was delivered, and he never watched television. (There was a good reason for that.) It went without saying that he couldn't go outside. Should Scheherazade's visits come to a halt for some reason, he would be left all alone.

Habara was not overly concerned about this prospect. If that happens, he thought, it will be hard, but I'll scrape by one way or another. I'm not stranded on a desert island. No, he thought, I *am* a desert island. He had always been comfortable being by himself. What did bother him, though, was the thought of not being able to talk in bed with Scheherazade. Or, more precisely, missing the next installment of her story.

'I was a lamprey eel in a former life,' Scheherazade said once, as they lay in bed together. It was a simple, straight-forward comment, as offhand as if she had announced that the North Pole was in the far north. Habara hadn't a clue what sort of creature a lamprey was, much less what one looked like. So he had no particular opinion on the subject.

'Do you know how a lamprey eats a trout?' she asked.

He didn't. In fact, it was the first time he'd heard that lampreys ate trout.

'Lampreys have no jaws. That's what sets them apart from other eels.'

'Huh? Eels have jaws?'

'Haven't you ever taken a good look at one?' she said, surprised.

'I do eat eel now and then, but I've never had an oppor-tunity to see if they have jaws.'

'Well, you should check it out sometime. Go to an aquar-ium or someplace like that. Regular eels have jaws with teeth.

But lampreys have only suckers, which they use to attach themselves to rocks at the bottom of a river or lake. Then they just kind of float there, waving back and forth, like weeds.'

Habara imagined a bunch of lampreys swaying like weeds at the bottom of a lake. The scene seemed somehow divorced from reality, although reality, he knew, could at times be terribly unreal.

'Lampreys live like that, hidden among the weeds. Lying in wait. Then, when a trout passes overhead, they dart up and fasten on to it with their suckers. Inside their suckers are these tonguelike things with teeth, which rub back and forth against the trout's belly until a hole opens up and they can start eating the flesh, bit by bit.'

'I wouldn't like to be a trout,' Habara said.

'Back in Roman times, they raised lampreys in ponds. Uppity slaves got chucked in and the lampreys ate them alive.'

Habara thought that he wouldn't have enjoyed being a Roman slave, either.

'The first time I saw a lamprey was back in elementary school, on a class trip to the aquarium,' Scheherazade said. 'The moment I read the description of how they lived, I knew that I'd been one in a former life. I mean, I could actually remember – being fastened to a rock, swaying invisibly among the weeds, eyeing the fat trout swimming by above me.'

'Can you remember eating them?'

'No, I can't.'

'That's a relief,' Habara said. 'But is that all you recall from your life as a lamprey – swaying to and fro at the bottom of a river?'

'A former life can't be called up just like that,' she said. 'If you're lucky, you get a flash of what it was like. It's like catching a glimpse through a tiny hole in a wall. Can you recall any of your former lives?'

'No, not one,' Habara said. Truth be told, he had never felt the urge to revisit a former life. He had his hands full with the present one.

'Still, it felt pretty neat at the bottom of the lake. Upside down with my mouth fastened to a rock, watching the fish pass overhead. I saw a really big snapping turtle once, too, a humongous black shape drifting past, like the evil spaceship in *Star Wars*. And big white birds with long, sharp beaks; from below, they looked like white clouds floating across the sky.'

'And you can see all these things now?'

'As clear as day,' Scheherazade said. 'The light, the pull of the current, everything. Sometimes I can even go back there in my mind.'

'To what you were thinking then?'

'Yeah.'

'What do lampreys think about?'

'Lampreys think very lamprey-like thoughts. About lamprey-like topics in a context that's very lamprey-like. There are no words for those thoughts. They belong to the world of water. It's like when we were in the womb. We were thinking things in there, but we can't express those thoughts in the language we use out here. Right?'

'Hold on a second! You can remember what it was like in the womb?'

'Sure,' Scheherazade said, lifting her head to see over his chest. 'Can't you?'

No, he said. He couldn't.

'Then I'll tell you sometime. About life in the womb.'

'Scheherazade, Lamprey, Former Lives' was what Habara recorded in his diary that day. He doubted that anyone who came across it would guess what the words meant.

Habara had met Scheherazade for the first time four months earlier. He had been transported to this house, in a provincial city north of Tokyo, and she had been assigned to him as his 'support liaison'. Since he couldn't go outside, her role was to buy food and other items he required and bring them to the house. She also tracked down whatever books and magazines he wished to read, and any CDs he wanted to listen to. In addition, she chose an assortment of DVDs – though he had a hard time accepting her criteria for selection on this front.

A week after he arrived, as if it were a self-evident next step, Scheherazade had taken him to bed. There had been condoms on the bedside table when he arrived. Habara guessed that sex was one of her assigned duties – or perhaps 'support activities' was the term they used. Whatever the term, and whatever her motivation, he'd gone with the flow and accepted her proposal without hesitation.

Their sex was not exactly obligatory, but neither could it be said that their hearts were entirely in it. She seemed to be on guard, lest they grow too enthusiastic – just as a driving instructor might not want his students to get too excited about their driving. Yet, while the lovemaking was not what you'd call passionate, it wasn't entirely businesslike, either. It may have begun as one of her duties (or, at least, as something that was strongly encouraged), but at a certain point she seemed – if only in a small way – to have found a kind of pleasure in it. Habara could tell this from certain subtle ways in which her body responded, a response that delighted him as well. After all, he was not a wild animal penned up in a cage but a human being equipped with his own range of emotions, and sex for the sole purpose of physical release was hardly fulfilling. Yet to what extent did Scheherazade see their sexual relationship as one of her duties, and how much did it belong to the sphere of her personal life? He couldn't tell.

This was true of other things, too. Habara often found Scheherazade's feelings and intentions hard to read. For example, she wore plain cotton panties most of the time. The kind of panties he imagined housewives in their thirties usually wore – though this was pure conjecture, since he had no experience with housewives of that age. Some days, however, she turned up in colorful, frilly silk panties instead. Why she switched between the two he hadn't a clue.

The other thing that puzzled him was the fact that their lovemaking and her storytelling were so closely linked, making it hard to tell where one ended and the other began. He had never experienced anything like this before: although he didn't love her, and the sex was so-so, he was tightly bound to her physically. It was all rather confusing.

'I was a teenager when I started breaking into empty houses,' she said one day as they lay in bed.

Habara – as was often the case when she told stories – found himself at a loss for words.

'Have you ever broken into somebody's house?' she asked.

'I don't think so,' he answered in a dry voice.

'Do it once and you get addicted.'

'But it's illegal.'

'You betcha. It's dangerous, but you still get hooked.'

Habara waited quietly for her to continue.

'The coolest thing about being in someone else's house when there's no one there,' Scheherazade said, 'is how silent it is. Not a sound. It's like the quietest place in the world. That's how it felt to me, anyway. When I sat on the floor and kept absolutely still, my life as a lamprey came back to me. I told you about my being a lamprey in a former life, right?'

'Yes, you did.'

'It was just like that. My suckers stuck to a rock underwater and my body waving back and forth overhead, like the weeds around me. Everything so quiet. Though that may have been because I had no ears. On sunny days, light shot down from the surface like an arrow. Fish of all colors and shapes drifted by above. And my mind was empty of thoughts. Other than lamprey thoughts, that is. Those were cloudy but very pure. It was a wonderful place to be.'

The first time Scheherazade broke into someone's house, she explained, she was a high-school junior and had a serious crush on a boy in her class. Though he wasn't what you would call handsome, he was tall and clean-cut, a good student who played on the soccer team, and she was powerfully attracted to him. But he apparently liked another girl in their class and took no notice of Scheherazade. In fact, it was possible that he was unaware she existed. Nevertheless, she couldn't get him out of her mind. Just seeing him made her breathless; sometimes she felt as if she were going to throw up. If she didn't do something about it, she thought, she might go crazy. But confessing her love was out of the question.

One day, Scheherazade skipped school and went to the boy's house. It was about a fifteen-minute walk from where she lived. She had researched his family situation before-hand. His mother taught Japanese language at a school in a neighboring town. His father, who had worked at a cement company, had been killed in a car accident some years ear-lier. His sister was a junior-high-school student. This meant that the house should be empty during the day.

Not surprisingly, the front door was locked. Scheherazade checked under the mat for a key. Sure enough, there was one there. Quiet residential communities in provincial cities like theirs had little crime, and a spare key was often left under a mat or a potted plant.

To be safe, Scheherazade rang the bell, waited to make sure there was no answer, scanned the street in case she was being observed, opened the door, and entered. She locked the door again from the inside. Taking off her shoes, she put them in a plastic bag and stuck it in the knapsack on her back. Then she tiptoed up the stairs to the second floor.

His bedroom was there, as she had imagined. His bed was neatly made. On the bookshelf was a small stereo, with a few CDs. On the wall, there was a calendar with a photo of the Barcelona soccer team and, next to it, what looked like a team banner, but nothing else. No posters, no pictures. Just a cream-colored wall. A white curtain hung over the window. The room was tidy, everything in its place. No books strewn about, no clothes on the floor. The room testified to the meticulous personality of its inhabitant. Or else to a mother who kept a perfect house. Or both. It made Scheherazade nervous. Had the room been sloppier, no one would have noticed whatever little messes she might make. Yet, at the same time, the very cleanliness and simplicity of the room, its perfect order, made her happy. It was so like him.

Scheherazade lowered herself into the desk chair and sat there for a while. This is where he studies every night, she thought, her heart pounding. One by one, she picked up the implements on the desk, rolled them between her fingers, smelled them, held them to her lips. His pencils, his scissors, his ruler, his stapler—the most mundane objects became somehow radiant because they were his.

She opened his desk drawers and carefully checked their contents. The uppermost drawer was divided into compartments, each of which contained a small tray with a scattering of objects and souvenirs. The second drawer was largely occupied by notebooks for the classes he was taking at the moment, while the one on the bottom (the deepest drawer) was filled with an assortment of old papers, notebooks, and exams. Almost everything was connected either to school or to soccer. She'd hoped to come across something personal – a diary, perhaps, or letters – but the desk held nothing of that sort. Not even a photograph. That struck Scheherazade as a bit unnatural. Did he have no life outside of school and soccer? Or had he carefully hidden everything of a private nature, where no one would come across it?

Still, just sitting at his desk and running her eyes over his handwriting moved Scheherazade beyond words. To calm herself, she got out of the chair and sat on the floor. She looked up at the ceiling. The quiet around her was absolute. In this way, she returned to the lampreys' world.

'So all you did,' Habara asked, 'was enter his room, go through his stuff, and sit on the floor?'

'No,' Scheherazade said. 'There was more. I wanted something of his to take home. Something that he handled every day or that had been close to his body. But it couldn't be anything important that he would miss. So I stole one of his pencils.'

'A single pencil?'

'Yes. One that he'd been using. But stealing wasn't enough. That would make it a straightforward case of burglary. The fact that *I* had done it would be lost. I was the Love Thief, after all.'

The Love Thief? It sounded to Habara like the title of a silent film.

'So I decided to leave something behind in its place, a token of some sort. As proof that I had been there. A declaration that this was an exchange, not a simple theft. But what should it be? Nothing popped into my head. I searched my knapsack and my pockets, but I couldn't find anything appropriate. I kicked myself for not having thought to bring something suitable. Finally, I decided to leave a tampon behind. An unused one, of course, still in its plastic wrapper. My period was getting close, so I was carrying it around just to be safe. I hid it at the very back of the bottom drawer, where it would be difficult to find. That really turned me on. The fact that a tampon of mine was stashed away in his desk drawer. Maybe it was because I was so turned on that my period started almost immediately after that.'

A tampon for a pencil, Habara thought. Perhaps that was what he should write in his diary that day: 'Love Thief, Pencil, Tampon.' He'd like to see what they'd make of that!

'I was there in his home for only fifteen minutes or so. I couldn't stay any longer than that: it was my first experience of sneaking into a house, and I was scared that someone would turn up while I was there. I checked the street to make sure that the coast was clear, slipped out the door, locked it, and replaced the key under the mat. Then I went to school. Carrying his precious pencil.'

Scheherazade fell silent. From the look of it, she had gone back in time and was picturing the various things that had happened next, one by one.

'That week was the happiest of my life,' she said after a long pause. 'I scribbled random things in my notebook with his pencil. I sniffed it, kissed it, rubbed my cheek with it, rolled it between my fingers. Sometimes I even stuck it in my mouth and sucked on it. Of course, it pained me that the more I wrote the shorter it got, but I couldn't help myself. If it got too short, I thought, I could always go back and get another. There was a whole bunch of used pencils in the pencil holder on his desk. He wouldn't have a clue that one was missing. And he probably still hadn't found the tampon tucked away in his drawer. That idea excited me no end – it gave me a strange ticklish sensation down below. It didn't bother me anymore that in the real world he never looked at me or showed that he was even aware of my existence. Because I secretly possessed something of his—a part of him, as it were.'

Ten days later, Scheherazade skipped school again and paid a second visit to the boy's house. It was eleven o'clock in the morning. As before, she fished the key from under the mat and opened the door. Again, his room was in flawless order. First, she selected a pencil with a lot of use left in it and carefully placed it in her pencil case. Then she gingerly lay down on his bed, her hands clasped on her chest, and looked up at the ceiling. This was the bed where he slept every night. The thought made her heart beat faster, and she found it difficult to breathe normally. Her lungs weren't filling with air and her throat was as dry as a bone, making each breath painful.

Scheherazade got off the bed, straightened the covers, and sat down on the floor, as she had on her first visit. She looked back up at the ceiling. I'm not quite ready for his bed, she told herself. That's still too much to handle.

This time, Scheherazade spent half an hour in the house. She pulled his notebooks from the drawer and glanced through them. She found a book report and read it. It was on *Kokoro*, a novel by Soseki Natsume, that summer's reading assignment. His handwriting was beautiful, as one would expect from a straight-A student, not an error or an omission anywhere. The grade on it was Excellent. What else could it be? Any teacher confronted with penmanship that perfect would automatically give it an Excellent, whether he bothered to read a single line or not.

Scheherazade moved on to the chest of drawers, examining its contents in order. His underwear and socks. Shirts and pants. His soccer uniform. They were all neatly folded. Nothing stained or frayed. Had he done the folding? Or, more likely, had his mother done it for him? She felt a pang of jealousy toward the mother, who could do these things for him each and every day.

Scheherazade leaned over and sniffed the clothes in the

drawers. They all smelled freshly laundered and redolent of the sun. She took out a plain gray T-shirt, unfolded it, and pressed it to her face. Might not a whiff of his sweat remain under the arms? But there was nothing. Nevertheless, she held it there for some time, inhaling through her nose. She wanted to keep the shirt for herself. But that would be too risky. His clothes were so meticulously arranged and maintained. He (or his mother) probably knew the exact number of T-shirts in the drawer. If one went missing, all hell might break loose. Scheherazade carefully refolded the T-shirt and returned it to its proper place. In its stead, she took a small badge, shaped like a soccer ball, that she found in one of the desk drawers. It seemed to date back to a team from his grade-school years. She doubted that he would miss it. At the very least, it would be some time before he noticed that it was gone. While she was at it, she checked the bottom drawer of the desk for the tampon. It was still there.

Scheherazade tried to imagine what would happen if his mother discovered the tampon. What would she think? Would she demand that he explain what on earth a tampon was doing in his desk? Or would she keep her discovery a secret, turning her dark suspicions over and over in her mind? Scheherazade had no idea. But she decided to leave the tampon where it was. After all, it was her very first token.

To commemorate her second visit, Scheherazade left behind three strands of her hair. The night before, she had plucked them out, wrapped them in plastic, and sealed them in a tiny envelope. Now she took this envelope from her knapsack and slipped it into one of the old math notebooks in his drawer. The three hairs were straight and black, neither too long nor too short. No one would know whose they were without a DNA test, though they were clearly a girl's.

She left his house and went straight to school, arriving in time for her first afternoon class. Once again, she was content for about ten days. She felt that he had become that much more hers. But, as you might expect, this chain of events would not end without incident. For, as Scheherazade had said, sneaking into other people's homes is highly addictive.

At this point in the story Scheherazade glanced at the bed-side clock and saw that it was 4:32 p.m. 'Got to get going,' she said, as if to herself. She hopped out of bed and put on her plain white panties, hooked her bra, slipped into her jeans, and pulled her dark-blue Nike sweatshirt over her head. Then she scrubbed her hands in the bathroom, ran a brush through her hair, and drove away in her blue Mazda.

Left alone with nothing in particular to do, Habara lay in bed and ruminated on the story she had just told him, savoring it bit by bit, like a cow chewing its cud. Where was it headed? he wondered. As with all her stories, he hadn't a clue. He found it difficult to picture Scheherazade as a high-school student. Was she slender then, free of the flab she carried today? School uniform, white socks, her hair in braids?

He wasn't hungry yet, so he put off preparing his dinner and went back to the book he had been reading, only to find that he couldn't concentrate. The image of Scheherazade sneaking into her classmate's room and burying her face in his shirt was too fresh in his mind. He was impatient to hear what had happened next.

Scheherazade's next visit to the house was three days later, after the weekend had passed. As always, she came bearing large paper bags stuffed with provisions. She went through

383

the food in the fridge, replacing everything that was past its expiration date, examined the canned and bottled goods in the cupboard, checked the supply of condiments and spices to see what was running low, and wrote up a shopping list. She put some bottles of Perrier in the fridge to chill. Finally, she stacked the new books and DVDs she had brought with her on the table. 'Is there something more you need or want?'

'Can't think of anything,' Habara replied.

Then, as always, the two went to bed and had sex. After an appropriate amount of foreplay, he slipped on his condom, entered her, and, after an appropriate amount of time, ejaculated. After casting a professional eye on the contents of his condom, Scheherazade began the latest installment of her story.

As before, she felt happy and fulfilled for ten days after her second break-in. She tucked the soccer badge away in her pencil case and from time to time fingered it during class. She nibbled on the pencil she had taken and licked the lead. All the time she was thinking of his room. She thought of his desk, the bed where he slept, the chest of drawers packed with his clothes, his pristine white boxer shorts, and the tampon and three strands of hair she had hidden in his drawer.

She had lost all interest in schoolwork. In class, she either fiddled with the badge and the pencil or gave in to daydreams. When she went home, she was in no state of mind to tackle her homework. Scheherazade's grades had never been a problem. She wasn't a top student, but she was a serious girl who always did her assignments. So when her teacher called on her in class and she was unable to give a proper answer, he was more puzzled than angry. Eventually, he summoned her to the staff room during the lunch break. 'What's the problem?' he asked her. 'Is anything bothering you?' She could only mumble something vague about not feeling well. Her secret was too weighty and dark to reveal to anyone – she had to bear it alone.

'I had to keep breaking into his house,' Scheherazade said. 'I was compelled to. As you can imagine, it was a very risky business. Even I could see that. Sooner or later, someone would find me there, and the police would be called. The idea scared me to death. But, once the ball was rolling, there was no way I could stop it. Ten days after my second 'visit', I went there again. I had no choice. I felt that if I didn't I would go off the deep end. Looking back, I think I really was a little crazy.'

'Didn't it cause problems for you at school, skipping class so often?' Habara asked.

'My parents had their own business, so they were too busy to pay much attention to me. I'd never caused any problems up to then, never challenged their authority. So they figured a hands-off approach was best. Forging notes for school was a piece of cake. I explained to my homeroom teacher that I had a medical problem that required me to spend half a day at the hospital from time to time. Since the teachers were racking their brains over what to do about the kids who hadn't come to school in ages, they weren't too concerned about me taking half a day off every now and then.'

Scheherazade shot a quick glance at the clock next to the bed before continuing.

'I got the key from under the mat and entered the house for a third time. It was as quiet as before – no, even quieter for some reason. It rattled me when the refrigerator turned on – it sounded like a huge beast sighing. The phone rang while I was there. The ringing was so loud and harsh that I thought my heart would stop. I was covered with sweat. No one picked up, of course, and it stopped after about ten rings. The house felt even quieter then.'

Scheherazade spent a long time stretched out on his bed that day. This time her heart did not pound so wildly, and she was able to breathe normally. She could imagine him sleeping peacefully beside her, even feel as if she were watching over him as he slept. She felt that, if she reached out, she could touch his muscular arm. He wasn't there next to her, of course. She was just lost in a haze of daydreams.

She felt an overpowering urge to smell him. Rising from the bed, she walked over to his chest of drawers, opened one, and examined the shirts inside. All had been washed and neatly folded. They were pristine, and free of odor, just like before.

Then an idea struck her. She raced down the stairs to the first floor. There, in the room beside the bath, she found the laundry hamper and removed the lid. Mixed together were the soiled clothes of the three family members – mother, daughter, and son. A day's worth, from the looks of it. Scheherazade extracted a piece of male clothing. A white crew-neck T-shirt. She took a whiff. The unmistakable scent of a young man. A mustiness she had smelled before, when her male classmates were close by. Not a scintillating odor, to be sure. But the fact that this smell was *his* brought

Scheherazade unbounded joy. When she put her nose next to the armpits and inhaled, she felt as though she were in his embrace, his arms wrapped firmly about her.

T-shirt in hand, Scheherazade climbed the stairs to the second floor and lay on his bed once more. She buried her face in his shirt and greedily breathed in. Now she could feel a languid sensation in the lower part of her body. Her nipples were stiffening as well. Could her period be on the way? No, it was much too early. Was this sexual desire? If so, then what could she do about it? She had no idea. One thing was for sure, though – there was nothing to be done under these circumstances. Not here in his room, on his bed.

In the end, Scheherazade decided to take the shirt home with her. It was risky, for sure. His mother was likely to figure out that a shirt was missing. Even if she didn't realize that it had been stolen, she would still wonder where it had gone. Any woman who kept her house so spotless was bound to be a neat freak of the first order. When something went missing, she would search the house from top to bottom, like a police dog, until she found it. Undoubtedly, she would uncover the traces of Scheherazade in her precious son's room. But, even as Scheherazade understood this, she didn't want to part with the shirt. Her brain was powerless to persuade her heart.

Instead, she began thinking about what to leave behind. Her panties seemed like the best choice. They were of an ordinary sort, simple, relatively new, and fresh that morning. She could hide them at the very back of his closet. Could there be anything more appropriate to leave in exchange? But, when she took them off, the crotch was damp. I guess this comes from desire, too, she thought. It would hardly do to leave something tainted by her lust in his room. She would only be degrading herself. She slipped them back on and began to think about what else to leave.

Scheherazade broke off her story. For a long time, she didn't say a word. She lay there breathing quietly with her eyes closed. Beside her, Habara followed suit, waiting for her to resume.

At last, she opened her eyes and spoke. 'Hey, Mr Habara,' she said. It was the first time she had addressed him by name.

Habara looked at her.

'Do you think we could do it one more time?'

'I think I could manage that,' he said.

So they made love again. This time, though, was very different from the time before. Violent, passionate, and drawn out. Her climax at the end was unmistakable. A series of powerful spasms that left her trembling. Even her face was transformed. For Habara, it was like catching a brief glimpse of Scheherazade in her youth: the woman in his arms was now a troubled seventeen-year-old girl who had somehow become trapped in the body of a thirty-five-year-old housewife. Habara could feel her in there, her eyes closed, her body quivering, innocently inhaling the aroma of a boy's sweaty T-shirt.

This time, Scheherazade did not tell him a story after sex. Nor did she check the contents of his condom. They lay there quietly next to each other. Her eyes were wide open, and she was staring at the ceiling. Like a lamprey gazing up at the bright surface of the water. How wonderful it would be, Habara thought, if he, too, could inhabit another time or space – leave this single, clearly defined human being named Nobutaka Habara behind and become a nameless lamprey. He pictured himself and Scheherazade side by side, their suckers fastened to a rock, their bodies waving in the current, eying the surface as they waited for a fat trout to swim smugly by.

'So what did you leave in exchange for the shirt?' Habara broke the silence.

She did not reply immediately.

'Nothing,' she said at last. 'Nothing I had brought along could come close to that shirt with his odor. So I just took it and sneaked out. That was when I became a burglar, pure and simple.'

When, twelve days later, Scheherazade went back to the boy's house for the fourth time, there was a new lock on the front door. Its gold color gleamed in the midday sun, as if to boast of its great sturdiness. And there was no key hidden under the mat. Clearly, his mother's suspicions had been aroused by the missing shirt. She must have searched high and low, coming across other signs that told of something strange going on in her house. Her instincts had been unerring, her reaction swift.

Scheherazade was, of course, disappointed by this development, but at the same time she felt relieved. It was as if someone had stepped behind her and removed a great weight from her shoulders. This means I don't have to go on breaking into his house, she thought. There was no doubt that, had the lock not been changed, her invasions would have gone on indefinitely. Nor was there any doubt that her actions would have escalated with each visit. Eventually, a member of the family would have shown up while she was on the second floor. There would have been no avenue of escape. No way to talk herself out of her predicament. This was the future that had been waiting for her, sooner or later, and the outcome would have been devastating. Now she had dodged it. Perhaps she should thank his mother – though she had never met the woman – for having eyes like a hawk.

Scheherazade inhaled the aroma of his T-shirt each night before she went to bed. She slept with it next to her. She would wrap it in paper and hide it before she left for school in the morning. Then, after dinner, she would pull it out to caress and sniff. She worried that the odor might fade as the days went by, but that didn't happen. The smell of his sweat had permeated the shirt for good.

Now that further break-ins were out of the question, Scheherazade's state of mind slowly began to return to normal. She daydreamed less in class, and her teacher's words began to register. Nevertheless, her chief focus was not on her teacher's voice but on her classmate's behavior. She kept her eye discreetly trained on him, trying to detect a change, any indication at all that he might be nervous about something. But he acted exactly the same as always. He threw his head back and laughed as unaffectedly as ever, and answered promptly when called upon. He shouted as loudly in soccer practice and got just as sweaty. She could see no trace of anything out of the ordinary – just an upright young man, leading a seemingly unclouded existence.

Still, Scheherazade knew of one shadow that was hanging over him. Or something close to that. No one else knew, in all likelihood. Just her (and, come to think of it, possibly his mother). On her third break-in, she had come across a number of pornographic magazines cleverly concealed in the farthest recesses of his closet. They were full of pictures of naked women, spreading their legs and offering generous views of their genitals. Some pictures portrayed the act of sex: men inserted rodlike penises into female bodies in the most unnatural of positions. Scheherazade had never laid eyes on photographs like these before. She sat at his desk and flipped slowly through the magazines, studying each photo with great interest. She guessed that he masturbated while viewing them. But the idea did not strike her as especially repulsive. She accepted masturbation as a perfectly normal activity. All those sperm had to go somewhere, just as girls had to have periods. In other words, he was a typical teen-ager. Neither hero nor saint. She found that knowledge something of a relief.

'When my break-ins stopped, my passion for him began to cool. It was gradual, like the tide ebbing from a long, sloping beach. Somehow or other, I found myself smelling his shirt less often and spending less time caressing his pencil and badge. The fever was passing. What I had contracted was not something *like* sickness but the real thing. As long as it lasted, I couldn't think straight. Maybe everybody goes through a crazy period like that at one time or another. Or maybe it was something that happened only to me. How about you? Did you ever have an experience like that?'

Habara tried to remember, but drew a blank. 'No, nothing that extreme, I don't think,' he said.

Scheherazade looked somewhat disappointed by his answer.

'Anyway, I forgot all about him once I graduated. So quickly and easily, it was weird. What was it about him that

391

had made the seventeen-year-old me fall so hard? Try as I might, I couldn't remember. Life is strange, isn't it? You can be totally entranced by something one minute, be willing to sacrifice everything to make it yours, but then a little time passes, or your perspective changes a bit, and all of a sudden you're shocked at how its glow has faded. What was I looking at? you wonder. So that's the story of my 'breaking-and-entering' period.'

She made it sound like Picasso's Blue Period, Habara thought. But he understood what she was trying to convey.

She glanced at the clock next to the bed. It was almost time for her to leave.

'To tell the truth,' she said finally, 'the story doesn't end there. A few years later, when I was in my second year of nursing school, a strange stroke of fate brought us together again. His mother played a big role in it; in fact, there was something spooky about the whole thing – it was like one of those old ghost stories. Events took a rather unbelievable course. Would you like to hear about it?'

'I'd love to,' Habara said.

'It had better wait till my next visit,' Scheherazade said. 'It's getting late. I've got to head home and fix dinner.'

She got out of bed and put on her clothes – panties, stockings, camisole, and, finally, her skirt and blouse. Habara casually watched her movements from the bed. It struck him that the way women put on their clothes could be even more interesting than the way they took them off.

'Any books in particular you'd like me to pick up?' she asked, on her way out the door.

'No, nothing I can think of,' he answered. What he really wanted, he thought, was for her to tell him the rest of her story, but he didn't put that into words. Doing so might jeopardize his chances of ever hearing it.

Habara went to bed early that night and thought about Scheherazade. Perhaps he would never see her again. That worried him. The possibility was just too real. Nothing of a personal nature – no vow, no implicit understanding – held them together. Theirs was a chance relationship created by someone else, and might be terminated on that person's whim. In other words, they were attached by a slender thread. It was likely – no, certain – that that thread would eventually be broken and all the strange and unfamiliar tales she might have told would be lost to him. The only question was when.

It was also possible that he would, at some point, be deprived of his freedom entirely, in which case not only Scheherazade but all women would disappear from his life. Never again would he be able to enter the warm moistness of their bodies. Never again would he feel them quiver in response. Perhaps an even more distressing prospect for Habara than the cessation of sexual activity, however, was the loss of the moments of shared intimacy. What his time spent with women offered was the opportunity to be embraced by reality, on the one hand, while negating it entirely on the other. That was something Scheherazade had provided in abundance – indeed, her gift was inexhaustible. The prospect of losing that made him saddest of all.

Habara closed his eyes and stopped thinking of Scheherazade. Instead, he thought of lampreys. Of jawless lampreys fastened to rocks, hiding among the waterweeds, swaying back and forth in the current. He imagined that he was one of them, waiting for a trout to appear. But no trout passed by, no matter how long he waited. Not a fat one, not a skinny one, no trout at all. Eventually the sun went down, and his world was enfolded in darkness.

(2014)

Translated by Ted Goossen

Deborah Treisman is the Fiction Editor of *The New Yorker* and the host of *The New Yorker* Fiction Podcast.

★

TESSA HADLEY

This story, set probably in the 1910s or 1920s but written much later, through the long perspective of memory, is about an uncomfortable date between two people not at all suited to each other. They begin with high hopes, but quickly realize they don't like each other – don't understand each other at all, don't speak the same language. It's an odd, sideways-on, quirky little fragment. When the narrator gets home at the end of the story, she puts away the new pink underwear she had bought specially for the occasion. At first the women in Rhys's stories seem crushed by the overbearing men. The men are so certain of the rules they live by, the codes. You mustn't, for instance, shoot sitting birds; you mustn't make up stories. And you must either be a lady or a bad girl, there's no space for ambiguity in between. Yet the women are tougher really, they see what the men don't see. They see the absurdity and comedy of the rules: and that nothing in life is actually so clear. At the end of their awful night – how that bed looms, in the corner of the private dining room! – there's such satisfaction for her in putting away the pretty underwear. She's saving it for something better, another time, another man – a better one. And then she falls asleep without a qualm. It's a good story about sleeping alone, the pleasures of sleeping all alone.

On Not Shooting Sitting Birds
by Jean Rhys

There is no control over memory. Quite soon you find your-self being vague about an event which seemed so important at the time that you thought you'd never forget it. Or unable to recall the face of someone whom you could have sworn was there for ever. On the other hand, trivial and meaning-less memories may stay with you for life. I can still shut my eyes and see Victoria grinding coffee on the pantry steps, the glass bookcase and the books in it, my father's pipe-rack, the leaves of the sandbox tree, the wallpaper of the bedroom in some shabby hotel, the hairdresser in Antibes. It's in this way that I remember buying the pink Milanese silk under-clothes, the assistant who sold them to me and coming into the street holding the parcel.

I had started out in life trusting everyone and now I trusted no one. So I had few acquaintances and no close friends. It was perhaps in reaction against the inevitable loneliness of my life that I'd find myself doing bold, risky, even outrageous things without hesitation or surprise. I was usually disappointed in these adventures and they didn't have much effect on me, good or bad, but I never quite lost the hope of something better or different.

One day, I've forgotten now where, I met this young man who smiled at me and when we had talked a bit I agreed to have dinner with him in a couple of days' time. I went home excited, for I'd liked him very much and began to plan what I should wear. I had a dress I quite liked, an evening cloak, stockings, but my underclothes weren't good for the occasion, I decided. Next day I went out and bought the Milanese silk chemise and drawers.

So there we were seated at a table having dinner with a bedroom very obvious in the background. He was younger than I'd thought and stiffer and I didn't like him much at all. He kept eyeing me in such a wary, puzzled way. When we had finished our soup and the waiter had taken the plates away, he said: 'But you're a lady, aren't you?' exactly as he might have said, 'But you're really a snake or a crocodile, aren't you?'

'Oh no, not that you'd notice,' I said, but this didn't work. We looked glumly at each other across the gulf that had yawned between us.

Before I came to England I'd read many English novels and I imagined I knew all about the thoughts and tastes of various sorts of English people. I quickly decided that to distract or interest this man I must talk about shooting.

I asked him if he knew the West Indies at all. He said no, he didn't and I told him a long story of having been lost in the Dominican forest when I was a child. This wasn't true. I'd often been in the woods but never alone. 'There are no parrots now,' I said, 'or very few. There used to be. There's a Dominican parrot in the zoo – have you ever seen it? – a sulky bird, very old I think. However, there are plenty of other birds and we do have shooting parties. Perdrix are very good to eat, but ramiers are rather bitter.'

Then I began describing a fictitious West Indian shooting party and all the time I talked I was remembering the real thing. An old shotgun leaning up in one corner of the room, the round table in the middle where we would sit to make cartridges, putting the shot in, ramming it down with a wad of paper. Gunpowder? There was that too, for I remember the smell. I suppose the boys were trusted to be careful.

The genuine shooting party consisted of my two brothers, who shared the shotgun, some hangers-on and me at the end of the procession, for then I couldn't bear to be left out of anything. As soon as the shooting was about to start I would stroll away casually and when I was out of sight run as hard as I could, crouch down behind a bush and put my fingers in my ears. It wasn't that I was sorry for the birds, but I hated and feared the noise of the gun. When it was all over I'd quietly join the others. I must have done this unobtrusively or probably my brothers thought me too insignificant to worry about, for no one ever remarked on my odd behaviour or teased me about it.

On and on I went, almost believing what I was saying, when he interrupted me, 'Do you mean to say that your brothers shot sitting birds?' His voice was cold and shocked.

I stared at him. How could I convince this man that I hadn't the faintest idea whether my brothers shot sitting birds or not? How could I explain now what really happened? If I did he'd think me a liar. Also a coward and there he'd be right, for I was afraid of many things, not only the sound of gunfire. But by this time I wasn't sure that I liked him at all so I was silent and felt my face growing as stiff and unsmiling as his.

It was a most uncomfortable dinner. We both avoided looking at the bedroom and when the last mouthful was swallowed he announced that he was going to take me home. The way he said this rather puzzled me. Then I told myself that probably he was curious to see where I lived. Neither of us spoke in the taxi except to say, 'Well, good night.' 'Good night.'

I felt regret when it came to taking off my lovely pink chemise, but I could still think: Some other night perhaps, another sort of man.

I slept at once.

(1976)

Tessa Hadley has written six novels, including *Accidents in the Home* (2002), *The London Train* (2011) and *The Past* (2015), and two collections of short stories. She publishes short stories regularly in the *New Yorker*, reviews for the *London Review of Books*, and is Professor of Creative Writing at Bath Spa University. In 2016, she was awarded a Windham-Campbell Literature Prize for her fiction.

The Dream
by Theodore Roethke

I

I met her as a blossom on a stem
Before she ever breathed, and in that dream
The mind remembers from a deeper sleep:
Eye learned from eye, cold lip from sensual lip.
My dream divided on a point of fire;
Light hardened on the water where we were;
A bird sang low; the moonlight sifted in;
The water rippled, and she rippled on.

She came toward me in the flowing air,
A shape of change, encircled by its fire.
I watched her there, between me and the moon;
The bushes and the stones danced on and on;
I touched her shadow when the light delayed;
I turned my face away, and yet she stayed.
A bird sang from the center of a tree;
She loved the wind because the wind loved me.

Love is not love until love's vulnerable.
She slowed to sigh, in that long interval.
A small bird flew in circles where we stood;
The deer came down, out of the dappled wood.
All who remember, doubt. Who calls that strange?
I tossed a stone, and listened to its plunge.
She knew the grammar of least motion, she
Lent me one virtue, and I live thereby.

She held her body steady in the wind;
Our shadows met, and slowly swung around;
She turned the field into a glittering sea;
I played in flame and water like a boy
And I swayed out beyond the white seafoam;
Like a wet log, I sang within a flame.
In that last while, eternity's confine,
I came to love, I came into my own.

(1955)

William Maxwell – an editor at *The New Yorker* for some forty years as well as a distinguished author in his own right – explained the short stories he labelled his 'improvisations' thus: 'I wrote them to please my wife, over a great many years. When we were first married, after we had gone to bed I would tell her a story in the dark. They came from I had no idea where. Sometimes I fell asleep in the middle of a story and she would shake me and say, "What happened next?" and I would struggle up through layers of oblivion and tell her.'

All the days and nights
by William Maxwell

Once upon a time there was a man who asked himself, 'Where have all the days and nights of my life gone?' He was not a young man, or the thought would never have crossed his mind, but neither was he white-haired and bent and dependent on a walker or a cane, and by any reasonable standards one would have to say that his life had been more fortunate than most. He was in excellent health, he had a loving wife, and children and friends, and no financial worries, and an old dog who never failed to welcome him when he came home. But something had taken him by surprise, and it was this: Without actually thinking about it, he had meant to live each day to the full – as he had – and still not let go of it. This was not as foolish as it sounds, because he didn't feel his age. Or rather, he felt seventeen sometimes, and sometimes seven or eight, and sometimes sixty-four, which is what he actually was, and sometimes forty, and sometimes a hundred, depending on whether he was tired or had had enough sleep or on the company he was in or if the place he was in was a place he had been before, and so on. He could think about the past, and did, more than most people, through much of his adult life, and until recently this had sufficed. But now he had a sense of the departure from him not merely of the major events of his life, his marriage, the birth of his children, the death of his mother and father, but of an endless succession of days that were only different from one another insofar as they were subject to accident or chance. And what it felt like was that he had overdrawn his account at the bank or been spending his capital, instead of living comfortably on the income from it.

He found himself doing things that, if he hadn't had the excuse of absentmindedness, would have been simply without rational explanation: for example, he would stand and look around at the clutter in the attic, not with any idea of introducing order but merely taking in what was there; or opening closet doors in rooms he himself did not ordinarily ever go into. Finally he spoke to his wife about it, for he wondered if she felt the same way.

'No,' she said.

'When you go to sleep at night you let go of the day completely?'

'Yes.'

As a rule, he fell asleep immediately and she had to read a while, and even after the light was out she turned and turned and sometimes he knew, even though she didn't move, that she was not asleep yet. If he had taken longer to fall asleep would he also have been able to let go of the – but he knew in his heart that the answer was no, he wouldn't.

And even now when he felt that he was about to leave a large part of his life (and therefore a large part of himself) behind, he couldn't accept it as inevitable and part of growing old. What you do not accept you do not allow to happen, even if you have to have recourse to magic. And so one afternoon he set out, without a word to anybody, to find all the days and nights of his life. When he did not come home by dinnertime, his wife grew worried, telephoned to friends, and finally to the police, who referred her to the Missing Persons Bureau. A description of him – height, color of eyes, color of hair, clothing, scar on the back of his right hand, etc. – was broadcast on the local radio station and the state police were alerted. What began as a counting of days became a counting of weeks. Six months passed, and the family lawyer urged that, because of one financial problem and another, the man's wife consider taking steps to have him pronounced legally dead. This she refused to do, and a year from the day he disappeared, he walked into the house, looking much older, and his first words were 'I'm too tired to talk about it.' He made them a drink and ate a good dinner, and went to bed at the usual time, without having asked a single question about her, about how she had managed without him, not offering a word of apology to her for the suffering he had caused her. He fell asleep immediately, as usual, and she put the light out.

I will never forgive him, she said to herself, *as long as I live*. And when he curled around her, she moved away from him, without waking him and lay on the far side of the bed. And tried to go to sleep and couldn't, and so when he spoke, even though it was hardly louder than a whisper, she heard what he said. What he said was 'They're all there. All the days

402

and all the nights of our life. I don't expect you to believe me,' he went on, 'but—'

To his surprise she turned over and said, 'I do believe you,' and so he was able to tell her about it.

'Think of it as being like a starry night, where every single star is itself a night with its own stars. Or like a book with pages you can turn, and that you can go back and read over again, and also skip ahead to see what's coming. Only it isn't a book. Or a starry night. Think of it as a house, with an infinite number of rooms that you can wander through, one after another after another. And each room is a whole day from morning to evening, with everything that happened, and each day is connected to the one before and the one that comes after, like bars of music. Think of it as a string quartet. And as none of those things. And as nowhere. And right here. And right now.'

A tear ran down the side of her face and he knew it, in the dark, and took her in his arms. 'The reason I didn't miss you,' he said, 'is that we were never separated. You were there. And the children. And this house. And the dogs and the cats and the neighbors, and all our friends, and even what was happening yesterday when I wasn't here. What I can't describe is how it happened. I went out for a walk and left the road and cut across Ned Blackburn's field, and suddenly the light seemed strange – and when I looked up, the sky wasn't just air, it was of a brilliance that seemed to come from thousands and thousands of little mirrors and I felt lightheaded and my heart began to pound and—'

She waited for him to go on and when he didn't, she thought he was trying to say something that was too difficult to put into words. And then she heard his soft regular breathing and realized he was asleep.

In the morning I will hear the rest of it, she thought, and fell asleep herself, much sooner than she usually did. But in the morning he didn't remember a thing he had told her, and she had great trouble making him understand that he had ever been away.

(1988)

7

ASHORE

We have a lot of things for which to thank the Ancient Greeks. Although perhaps the alarm clock is not one of them.

Plato rigged a water organ to blast him awake before dawn lectures (far be it from me, but he would in fact have been better off waiting a few more hours anyway, to allow his brain and those of his charges more time to spark back fully).

The contraptions of the inventor Ctesibius, who effectively invented pneumatics, included a *clepsydra* (water clock) that was timed to trumpet loudly, by compressed air squeezing through a beating reed.

Mechanical alarm clocks first cuckooed in the early fifteenth century.

We shouldn't need an alarm clock, though, nor the sprightly cock's crowings or the morning lark's chirrups. No, our dewy brain should naturally propel our body into motion, in beat with our body clock. As long as our sleep patterns are balanced.

That's not to say that resurgence into waking life is easy. Any resurfacing requires an equalizing and decompression. Sleep is no different. Even ants stretch and yawn upon waking up.

All of us fall victim to a period of *sleep inertia*, as the brain and body reacclimatize to waking life. Judgements are impaired exponentially (rendering Rip Van Winkle's quicksilver awakening veritably Herculean). Just as *hypnagogic hallucinations* can herald sleep's arrival, so can *hypnopompic hallucinations* clarion its departure. In this aftermath, our prodigal senses flare back up: hearing, touch, smell, taste – absent during our dreams – reunite with vision. Even if we have slept long and well, the blood has thickened, its pressure is still low, and muscle tone has been deafened. We have been slowed.

Due to all these adjustments, the crescendo to get going, to launch back into the swing of things, can be taxing. Indeed, the human heart is statistically much more likely to stop beating, to short-circuit into cardiac arrest, during the first few hours of the day (say, between 9 A.M. and 11 A.M.) than at any other time.

Conversely, after an hour or so of such readjustment, our brains are at their most alert – during those very hours that our hearts are at their most vulnerable.

Although the years float by, and morning arrives on the heels of night faster by the day, the horizon is immutable. For as we stretch and elongate out of the foetal crouch, pushing away the folds of our warm, comforting covers, each dawn represents a tiny renaissance.

Morning Song
by Sylvia Plath

Love set you going like a fat gold watch.
The midwife slapped your footsoles, and your bald cry
Took its place among the elements.

Our voices echo, magnifying your arrival. New statue.
In a drafty museum, your nakedness
Shadows our safety. We stand round blankly as walls.

I'm no more your mother
Than the cloud that distils a mirror to reflect its own
    slow
Effacement at the wind's hand.

All night your moth-breath
Flickers among the fat pink roses. I wake to listen:
A far sea moves in my ear.

One cry, and I stumble from bed, cow-heavy and floral
In my Victorian nightgown.
Your mouth opens clean as a cat's. The window square

Whitens and swallows its dull stars. And now you try
Your handful of notes;
The clear vowels rise like balloons.

(1961)

The headstone of Nobel Laureate Seamus Heaney's grave, in County Londonderry, Northern Ireland, is emblazoned with an epitaph that vaults a spring into the step:

'WALK ON AIR AGAINST YOUR BETTER JUDGEMENT'

Heaney referenced the line (from his poem 'The Gravel Walks') – in all its spacewalking splendour – when accepting his Nobel Prize for Literature in 1995. He commenced his address, entitled 'Crediting Poetry', by telling a story and evoking his childhood.

In the 1940s, when I was the eldest child of an ever-growing family in rural County Derry, we crowded together in the three rooms of a traditional thatched farmstead and lived a kind of den-life which was more or less emotionally and intellectually proofed against the outside world. It was an intimate, physical, creaturely existence in which the night sounds of the horse in the stable beyond one bedroom wall mingled with the sounds of adult conversation from the kitchen beyond the other. We took in everything that was going on, of course – rain in the trees, mice on the ceiling, a steam train rumbling along the railway line one field back from the house – but we took it in as if we were in the doze of hibernation. Ahistorical, pre-sexual, in suspension between the archaic and the modern, we were as susceptible and impressionable as the drinking water in a bucket in our scullery: every time a passing train made the earth shake, the surface of that water used to ripple delicately, concentrically and in utter silence.

For all this talk of hermetic hibernation, in this next poem, 'The Rescue', Heaney conjures a coming-together. Romance and reverie flood the soul – into rebirth.

The Rescue
by Seamus Heaney

In drifts of sleep I came upon you
Buried to your waist in snow.
You reached your arms out: I came to
Like water in a dream of thaw.

(1991)

★

The term *making a bed* stems from the Anglo-Saxons, who would form a bed each night from straw and a sack or two. The Ancient Egyptians (not to mention the Ancient Greeks and Romans) had been, unsurprisingly, way ahead of them, crafting beds as fine as those of Renaissance Europe (just thousands of years previously). Several were found in Tutankhamun's tomb when it was uncovered in 1922. They dated to the fourteenth century BC.

Most primates, like us, sleep upstairs (or in higher branches of treetops) – to avoid predators. Pillows are not specific to us humans either (for instance, elephants pile up vegetation on which to lay their heads). We have been using them for millennia. Those Ancient Egyptians even carved headrests of wood or ivory. Ornate, they would be covered in elaborate symbols, designed to fend off malign forces that might trespass the night, such as nightmares or even death.

411

Pillow
by John Updike

Plump mate to my head, you alone absorb,
through your cotton skin, the thoughts behind my bone
skin of skull. When I weep, you grow damp.
When I turn, you comply. In the dark,
you are my only friend, the only kiss
my cheek receives. You are my bowl of dreams.
Your underside is cool, like a second chance,
like a little leap into the air when I turn
you over. Though you would smother me,
properly applied, you are, like the world
with its rotating mass, all I have. You accept
the strange night with me, and are depressed
when the morning discloses your wrinkles.

(1993)

In this tale, John O'Hara (who had more stories published by
The New Yorker than any other author) automatically includes us
in a familiar, familial morning routine – we read unthinkingly
about Mr Jenssen reading unthinkingly, for example – but then
suddenly interrupts proceedings. He provides a rude awaken-
ing via another tale to tell. Something happens out of nothing
and, as a result, the tale sobers the reader up, like the welcome
sting of aftershave in the morning.

The story also operates on another level. Beneath its good
humour and everyday wit, besides the irony of parents packing
off their kids to school so that they are freed up to behave child-
ishly – there is real vulnerability, anxiety in the tone but also

412

improbability in the events. 'The Ideal Man', especially on a second or third reading, feels increasingly unrealistic. Much as a word repeated over and over – I always choose 'yoke' – begins to dissolve itself of meaning and become merely a sound.

Could it be that the real Jenssen breakfast routine is about to commence and this is all taking place in Walter's head? Is he still asleep?

I'm not sure if this is what O'Hara – a chronicler of tender realities – had in mind. He would likely pour scorn on such a fanciful reading of his little tale – and yet I can't help but find the story's paranoia and lurching shifts sweetly dreamy.

The Ideal Man
by John O'Hara

Breakfast in the Jenssen home was not much different from breakfast in a couple of hundred thousand homes in the Greater City. Walter Jenssen had his paper propped up against the vinegar cruet and the sugar bowl. He read expertly, not even taking his eyes off the printed page when he raised his coffee cup to his mouth. Paul Jenssen, seven going on eight, was eating his hot cereal, which had to be sweetened heavily to get him to touch it. Myrna L. Jenssen, Walter's five-year-old daughter, was scratching her towhead with her left hand while she fed herself with her right. Myrna, too, was expert in her fashion: she would put the spoon in her mouth, slide the cereal off, and bring out the spoon upside down. Elsie Jenssen (Mrs Walter) had stopped eating momentarily the better to explore with her tongue a bicuspid that seriously needed attention. That was the only thing she held against the kids – what having them had done to the teeth. Everybody'd warned her, but she wanted—

'Holy hell!' exclaimed Walter Jenssen. He slammed down the coffee cup, splashing the contents on the tablecloth.

'What kind of talk is that in front of the children?' said Elsie.

'In front of the children! A hell of a fine one you are to be worrying about the children,' said Walter. 'Just take a look at this. Take a *look* at it!' He handed her the paper as though he were stabbing her with it.

She took the paper. Her eyes roved about the page and stopped. 'Oh, *that*? Well, I'd like to know what's wrong with that. Hereafter I'll thank you to keep your cursing and swearing—'

'You! You!' said Walter.

'Myrna, Paul, off to school. Get your coats and hats and bring them in here. Hurry now,' said Elsie. The children got up and went to the hall. 'Just hold your temper till the children are where they won't hear you, with your raving like somebody *in*sane.' She buttoned Myrna's coat and made Paul button his and warned him to keep it buttoned and warned Myrna not to let go of Paul's hand; then she shooed them off with a smile that would have been approved by the Good Housekeeping Institute. But as soon as they were out of the apartment, the smile was gone. 'All right, you big baboon, go ahead and curse your head off. I'm used to it.'

Walter said, 'Gimme back that paper.'

'You can have it,' said Elsie. She handed him the paper. 'Go ahead, read it till you get a stroke. You oughta see yourself.'

Walter began to read aloud. 'Is your husband as attentive

to you now that you are married as when he was when he was courting you? Answer: Mrs Elsie Jenssen, West 174th Street, housewife: "Yes, in fact more so. Before we were married my husband was not exactly what would be called the romantic type. He was definitely shy. However, since our marriage he has become the ideal man from the romantic point of view. None of your Tyrone Powers or Clark Gables for me." For God's sake!'

'Well, so what?' said Elsie.

'So *what*? Do you think that's funny or something? What the hell kind of a thing is that you're putting in the paper? Go around blabbing private matters. I guess all the neighbors know how much we owe on the car. I suppose you tell everyone how much I get. How do you think a person's going to have any self-respect if you go running around and shooting off your face to newspaper reporters?'

'I didn't go around anywhere. He stopped me.'

'Who stopped you?'

'The reporter. On Columbus Circle. I was just coming around the corner and he came up and tipped his hat like a gentleman and asked me. It says so there.'

Walter wasn't listening. 'The office,' he said. 'Oh, God. What they're going to do to me at that office. McGonigle. Jeffries. Hall. Wait'll they see it. They prob'ly read it already. I can just see them waiting till I get in. I go to my desk and then they all start calling me Tyrone Power and Clark Gable.' He stared at her. 'You know what's gonna happen, don't you? They'll start kidding till they get too loud, and the boss'll want to know what it's all about, and he'll find out. Maybe they won't come right out and snitch, but he'll find out. And he'll call me in his office and say I'm

415

fired, and he'll be right. I oughta be fired. Listen, when you work for a finance corporation you don't want your employees going around getting a lot of silly publicity. What happens to the public confidence if—'

'It doesn't say a word about you. It says Elsie Jenssen. It doesn't say where you work or anything else. You look in the phone book and there's any number of Walter Jenssens.'

'Three, including Queens, too.'

'Well, it could be another one.'

'Not living on 174th Street. Even if the public doesn't know, they'll know it at the office. What if they don't care about the publicity part? All the boss'll want to know is I have a wife that – that goes blabbing around, and believe you me, they don't want employees with wives that go blabbing around. The public—'

'Oh, you and the public.'

'Yes, me and the public. This paper has a circulation of two million.'

'Oh, hooey,' said Elsie, and began to stack the breakfast dishes.

'Hooey. All right, hooey, but I'm not going to that office today. You call up and tell them I have a cold.'

'You big baby. If you want to stay home, call them up yourself,' said Elsie.

'I said you call them up. I'm not going to that office.'

'You go to the office or I'll – who do you think you are, anyway? The time you had off this year. Your uncle's funeral and your brother's wedding. Go ahead, take the day off, take the week off. Let's take a trip around the world. Just quit your job and I'll go back and ask Mr Fenton to give me back my old job. I'll support you. I'll support you while you sit here, you big baboon.' She put down the dishes and put her apron to her eyes and ran out the room.

Walter took out a cigarette and put it in his mouth but did not light it. He took it out of his mouth and tapped it on the table and lit it. He got up and looked out the window. He stood there a rather long time, with one foot on the radiator and his chin in hand, looking at the wall across the court. Then he went back to his chair and picked the paper off the floor and began to read.

First he reread his wife's interview, and then for the first time he read the other interviews. There were five others. The first, a laughing Mrs Bloomberg, Columbus Avenue, housewife, said her husband was so tired when he came home nights that as far as she was concerned romance was only a word in the dictionary.

A Mrs Petrucelli, East 123rd Street, housewife, said she hadn't noticed any difference between her husband's premarital and present attentiveness. But she had only been married five weeks.

There were three more. The husband of one woman was more attentive, but she did not compare him with Tyrone Power and Clark Gable. The husband of another woman was less attentive, but she did not get sarcastic like Mrs Bloomberg. The last woman said her husband was radio operator on a ship and she didn't really have much way of telling because she only saw him about every five weeks.

Jenssen studied their photographs, and one thing you had to say for Elsie: she was the prettiest. He read the interviews once more, and he reluctantly admitted that – well, if you had to give an interview, Elsie's was the best. Mrs

Bloomberg's was the worst. He certainly would hate to be Bloomberg when his friends saw that one.

He put down the paper and lit another cigarette and stared at his shoes. He began feeling sorry for Mr Bloomberg, who was probably a hard-working guy who really did come home tired. He ended – he ended by beginning to plan what retorts he would have when the gang at the office began to kid him. He began to feel pretty good about it.

He put on his coat and hat and overcoat and then he went to the bedroom. Elsie was lying there, her face deep in the pillow, sobbing.

'Well, I guess I'll go to the office now,' he said. She stopped sobbing.

'What?' she said, but did not let him see her face.

'Going downtown now,' he said.

'What if they start kidding you?'

'Well, what if they do?' he said.

She sat up. 'Are you cross at me any more?' she said.

'Nah, what the hell?' he said.

She smiled and got up and put her arm around his waist and walked down the hall with him to the door. It wasn't a very wide hall, but she kept her arm around him. He opened the door and set his hat on his head. She kissed his cheek and his mouth. He rearranged his hat again. 'Well,' he said. 'See you tonight.' It was the first thing that came into his head. He hadn't said *that* in years.

(1939)

★

418

Stealing Up
by Bernard O'Donoghue

I've always hated gardening: the way
The earth gets under your nails
And in the chevrons of your shoes.
So I don't plan it; I steal up on it,
Casually, until I find—
Hey presto! – the whole lawn's cut
Or the sycamore's wand suddenly
Sports an ungainly, foal-like leaf.

Similarly, I'd have written to you
Sooner, if I'd had the choice.
But morning after morning I woke up
To find the same clouds in the sky,
Disabling the heart. But tomorrow
Maybe I'll get up to find an envelope,
Sealed, addressed to you, propped against
My cup, lit by a slanting sun.

(1995)

'Many bad events originate from just an inch away from the everyday,' observed novelist Richard Ford. Such sentiment can be found also in the work of Ford's direct antecedent in American letters, Richard Yates.

Here, in Yates's story, 'Bells in the Morning', the balance of the future tips into the present. The possibilities of a new dawn bristle bravely amid the lavender mist.

Bells in the Morning
by Richard Yates

At first they were grotesque shapes, nothing more. Then they became drops of acid, cutting the scum of his thick, dreamless sleep. Finally he knew they were words, but they carried no meaning.

'Cramer,' Murphy was saying. 'Let's go, Cramer, wake up. Let's go, Cramer.'

Through sleepy paste in his mouth he swore at Murphy. Then the wind hit him, blue-cold as Murphy pulled the raincoat away from his face and chest.

'You sure like to sleep, don't you, kid.' Murphy was looking at him in that faintly derisive way.

Cramer was awake, moistening the roof of his mouth. 'All right,' he said. 'All right, I'm all right now.' Squirming, he sat up against the dirt wall of the hole slowly, like an old man. His cold legs sprawled out, cramped in their mud-caked pants. He pressed his eyes, then lifted the helmet and scratched his scalp, and the roots of his matted hair were sore. Everything was blue and gray. Cramer dug for a cigarette, embarrassed at having been hard to wake up again. 'Go ahead and get some sleep, Murphy,' he said. 'I'm awake now.'

'No, I'll stay awake too,' Murphy said. 'Six o'clock. Light.'

Cramer wanted to say, 'All right, then, you stay awake and I'll go back to sleep.' Instead he let his shivering come out in a shuddering noise and said, 'Christ, it's cold.'

It was in Germany, in the Ruhr. It was spring, and warm enough to make you sweat as you walked in the afternoon, but still cold at night and in the early morning. Still too cold for a raincoat in a hole.

They stared toward where the enemy was supposed to be. Nothing to see; only a dark area that was the plowed field and then a light one that was the mist.

'They threw in a couple about a half hour ago,' Murphy was saying. 'Way the hell off, over to the left. Ours have been going over right along; don't know why they've quit now. You slept through the whole works.' Then he said, 'Don't you ever clean that?' and he was looking, in the pale light, at Cramer's rifle. 'Bet the son of a bitch won't fire.'

Cramer said he would clean it, and he almost said for Christ's sake lay off. It was better that he didn't, for Murphy would have answered something about only trying to help you, kid. And anyway, Murphy was right.

'Might as well make some coffee,' Murphy said, cramming dirty hands into his pockets. 'Smoke won't show in this mist.'

Cramer found a can of coffee powder, and they both fumbled with clammy web-equipment for their cups and canteens. Murphy scraped out a hollow in the dirt between his boots and put a K-ration box there. He lit it, and they held their cups over the slow, crawling flame.

In a little while they were comfortable, swallowing coffee and smoking, shivering when fingers of the first yellow sunlight caressed their shoulders and necks. The grayness had gone now; things had color. Trees were pencil sketches on the lavender mist. Murphy said he hoped they wouldn't have to move out right away, and Cramer agreed. That was when they heard the bells; church bells, thin and feminine in tone, quavering as the wind changed. A mile, maybe two miles to the rear.

421

'Listen,' Murphy said quietly. 'Don't that sound nice?'
That was the word. Nice. Round and dirty, Murphy's face
was relaxed now. His lips bore two black parallel lines,
marking the place where the mouth closed when Murphy
made it firm. Between the lines the skin was pink and moist;
and these inner lips, Cramer had noticed, were the only part
of a face that always stayed clean. Except the eyes.

'My brother and me used to pull the bells every Sunday
at home,' Murphy said. 'When we was kids, I mean. Used
to get half a dollar apiece for it. Son of a bitch, if that don't
sound just the same.'

Listening, they sat smiling shyly at each other. Church
bells on misty mornings were things you forgot sometimes,
like fragile china cups and women's hands. When you
remembered them you smiled shyly, mostly because you
didn't know what else to do.

'Must be back in that town we came through yesterday,'
Cramer said. 'Seems funny they'd be ringing church bells
there.'

Murphy said it did seem funny, and then it happened.
The eyes got big, and when the voice came it was small,
intense, not Murphy's voice at all. 'Reckon the war's
over?' Something fluttered down Cramer's spine. 'By God,
Murphy. By God, it makes sense. It makes sense, all right.'

'Damned if it don't,' Murphy said, and they gaped at each
other, starting to grin; wanting to laugh and shout, to get
out and run.

'Son of a bitch,' Murphy said.

Cramer heard his own voice, high and babbling: 'That
could be why the artillery stopped.'

Could it be this easy? Could it happen this way? Would the

message come down from headquarters? Would Battalion get it from Regiment? Would Francetti, the platoon runner, come stumbling out across the plowed field with the news? Francetti, waving his pudgy arms and screaming. 'Hey, you guys! Come on back! It's all over! It's all over, you guys!' Crazy. Crazy. But why not?

'By God, Murphy, do you think so?'

'Watch for flares,' Murphy said. 'They might shoot flares.'

'Yeah, that's an idea, they might shoot flares.'

They could see nothing, hear nothing except the faint, silver monotony of the bells. Remember this. Remember every second of it. Remember Murphy's face and the hole and the canteens and the mist. Keep it all.

Watch for flares.

Remember the date. March something. No, April. April something, 1945. What did Meyers say the other day? Day before yesterday? Meyers told you the date then. He said, 'What do you know, this is Good—'

Cramer swallowed, then looked at Murphy quickly. 'Wait a minute wait a minute. We're wrong.' He watched Murphy's smile grow limp as he told him. 'Meyers. Remember what Meyers said about Good Friday? This is Easter Sunday, Murph.'

Murphy eased himself back against the side of the hole. 'Oh yeah,' he said. 'Oh yeah, sure. That's right.'

Cramer swallowed again and said, 'Kraut civilians probably going to church back there.'

Murphy's lips came together in a single black line, and he was quiet for a while. Then, stubbing his cigarette in the dirt, he said, 'Son of a bitch. Easter Sunday.'

(2004)

★

Summer Dawn
by William Morris

Pray but one prayer for me 'twixt thy closed lips,
Think but one thought of me up in the stars.
The summer night waneth, the morning light slips
Faint and grey 'twixt the leaves of the aspen, betwixt
    the cloud-bars,
That are patiently waiting there for the dawn:
Patient and colourless, though Heaven's gold
Waits to float through them along with the sun.
Far out in the meadows, above the young corn,
The heavy elms wait, and restless and cold
The uneasy wind rises; the roses are dun;
Through the long twilight they pray for the dawn,
Round the lone house in the midst of the corn,
Speak but one word to me over the corn,
Over the tender, bow'd locks of the corn.

(1856)

★

KEN FOLLETT

I always have a P. G. Wodehouse novel on the bedside table.
He is one of those authors whose books you can open at any
page, knowing that within a few lines you will be enchanted,
regardless of where you happen to have entered the story. The
same is true of Dickens and Proust, though not of all great
novelists. With George Eliot, you have to know the beginning

to love the end, as with a Beethoven symphony; and if you tried it with Tolstoy, you would be even more than usually confused.

It's partly the sheer exuberance of Wodehouse's prose: the absurd imagery, the verbal cleverness, the barmy hyperbole of the dialogue. There's wit on every page and a couple of hearty chuckles in every chapter. But there is something else, a quality not so often noticed: his plotting is consummate.

Popular fiction is fractal. Not only does the novel have a beginning, a middle and an end; so do every chapter, every scene, and even the longer paragraphs. The dramatic question is posed, the suspense is drawn out, and the resolution suggests a new question. The warp and woof of Wodehouse's story-telling are so closely woven that it rarely takes more than a page for the reader to grasp what is at issue and to engage with the hopes and fears of the characters.

The opening chapter of *The Code of the Woosters* is exceptional even by his standards. In the first two or three thousand words of light-hearted banter, he establishes an astonishing number of story points, including:

- Gussie Fink-Nottle is going to marry Madeline Bassett;
- Bertie Wooster loathes Madeline;
- Madeline believes Bertie is hopelessly in love with her;
- Madeline's father, Sir Watkyn Bassett, is the magistrate who jailed Bertie for stealing a policeman's helmet on Boat Race night;
- Sir Watkyn and Uncle Tom are rival collectors of antique silver;
- Uncle Tom wants to buy a valuable old cream jug in the shape of a cow;

- Aunt Dahlia is hoping to persuade the novelist Pomona Grindle to write a serial for *Milady's Boudoir*;
- Bertie will do anything for an invitation to a meal cooked by Aunt Dahlia's French chef, Anatole;
- Jeeves wants to take Bertie on a world cruise.

Each of these is essential to the plot, but the reader does not actually need to remember them, for Wodehouse the craftsman will meticulously remind us whenever it's important.

The climax of chapter one is a farcical scene of broad comedy into which Wodehouse manages somehow to insert a strain of satire on Fascism (the book was first published in 1938).

Like the mechanism of an Edwardian clock, Wodehouse's plot will whirr and click faultlessly, while the reader notices nothing but the elegance of the dial and the charm of the chime.

Wodehouse himself often said that he is not the man for a reader who wants a book to plumb the depths of human despair. He compared his novels to musical comedy. They are delightful, spellbinding and quite unreal, and just the thing to put me in the frame of mind to slip into dreamland.

Chapter One of *The Code of the Woosters*
by P. G. Wodehouse

I reached out a hand from under the blankets, and rang the bell for Jeeves.

'Good evening, Jeeves.'

'Good morning, sir.'

This surprised me.

'Is it morning?'

'Yes, sir.'

'Are you sure? It seems very dark outside.'

'There is a fog, sir. If you will recollect, we are now in Autumn – season of mists and mellow fruitfulness.'

'Seasons of what?'

'Mists, sir, and mellow fruitfulness.'

'Oh? Yes. Yes, I see. Well, be that as it may, get me one of those bracers of yours, will you?'

'I have one in readiness, sir, in the ice-box.'

He shimmered out, and I sat up in bed with that rather unpleasant feeling you get sometimes that you're going to die in about five minutes. On the previous night, I had given a little dinner at the Drones to Gussie Fink-Nottle as a friendly send-off before his approaching nuptials with Madeline, only daughter of Sir Watkyn Bassett, CBE, and these things take their toll. Indeed, just before Jeeves came in, I had been dreaming that some bounder was driving spikes through my head – not just ordinary spikes, as used by Jael the wife of Heber, but red-hot ones.

He returned with the tissue-restorer. I loosed it down the hatch, and after undergoing the passing discomfort, unavoidable when you drink Jeeves's patent morning revivers, of having the top of the skull fly up to the ceiling and the eyes shoot out of their sockets and rebound from the opposite wall like racquet balls, felt better. It would have been overstating it to say that even now Bertram was back again in mid-season form, but I had at least slid into the convalescent class and was equal to a spot of conversation.

'Ha!' I said, retrieving the eyeballs and replacing them in position. 'Well, Jeeves, what goes on in the great world? Is that the paper you have there?'

'No, sir. It is some literature from the Travel Bureau. I thought that you might care to glance at it.'

'Oh?' I said. 'You did, did you?'

And there was a brief and – if that's the word I want – pregnant silence.

I suppose that when two men of iron will live in close association with one another, there are bound to be occasional clashes, and one of these had recently popped up in the Wooster home. Jeeves was trying to get me to go on a Round-The-World cruise, and I would have none of it. But in spite of my firm statements to this effect, scarcely a day passed without him bringing me a sheaf or nosegay of those illustrated folders which the Ho-for-the-open-spaces birds send out in the hope of drumming up custom. His whole attitude recalled irresistibly to the mind that of some assiduous hound who will persist in laying a dead rat on the drawing-room carpet, though repeatedly apprised by word and gesture that the market for same is sluggish or even non-existent.

'Jeeves,' I said, 'this nuisance must now cease.'

'Travel is highly educational, sir.'

'I can't do with any more education. I was full up years ago. No, Jeeves, I know what's the matter with you. That old Viking strain of yours has come out again. You yearn for the tang of the salt breezes. You see yourself walking the deck in a yachting cap. Possibly someone has been telling you about the Dancing Girls of Bali. I understand, and I sympathise. But not for me. I refuse to be decanted into any blasted ocean-going liner and lugged off round the world.'

'Very good, sir.'

He spoke with a certain what-is-it in his voice, and I could see that, if not actually disgruntled, he was far from being gruntled, so I tactfully changed the subject.

'Well, Jeeves, it was quite a satisfactory binge last night.'

'Indeed, sir?'

'Oh, most. An excellent time was had by all. Gussie sent his regards.'

'I appreciate the kind thought, sir. I trust Mr Fink-Nottle was in good spirits?'

'Extraordinarily good, considering that the sands are running out and that he will shortly have Sir Watkyn Bassett for a father-in-law. Sooner him than me, Jeeves, sooner him than me.'

I spoke with strong feeling, and I'll tell you why. A few months before, while celebrating Boat Race night, I had fallen into the clutches of the Law for trying to separate a policeman from his helmet, and after sleeping fitfully on a plank bed had been hauled up at Bosher Street next morning and fined five of the best. The magistrate who had inflicted this monstrous sentence – to the accompaniment, I may add, of some very offensive remarks from the bench – was none other than old Pop Bassett, father of Gussie's bride-to-be.

As it turned out, I was one of his last customers, for a couple of weeks later he inherited a pot of money from a distant relative and retired to the country. That, at least, was the story that been put about. My own view was that he had got the stuff by sticking like glue to the fines. Five quid here, five quid there – you can see how it would mount up over a period of years.

'You have not forgotten that man of wrath, Jeeves? A hard case, eh?'

'Possibly Sir Watkyn is less formidable in private life, sir.'

'I doubt it. Slice him where you like, a hellhound is always a hellhound. But enough of this Bassett. Any letters today?'

'No, sir.'

'Telephone communications?'

'One, sir. From Mrs Travers.'

'Aunt Dahlia? She's back in town, then?'

'Yes, sir. She expressed a desire that you would ring her up at your earliest convenience.'

'I will do even better,' I said cordially. 'I will call in person.'

And half an hour later I was toddling up the steps of her residence and being admitted by old Seppings, her butler. Little knowing, as I crossed that threshold, that in about two shakes of a duck's tail I was to become involved in an imbroglio that would test the Wooster soul as it had seldom been tested before. I allude to the sinister affair of Gussie Fink-Nottle, Madeline Bassett, old Pop Bassett, Stiffy Byng, the Rev. H. P. ('Stinker') Pinker, the eighteenth-century cow-creamer and the small, brown, leather-covered notebook.

No premonition of an impending doom, however, cast a cloud on my serenity as I buzzed in. I was looking forward with bright anticipation to the coming reunion with this Dahlia – she, as I may have mentioned before, being my good and deserving aunt, not to be confused with Aunt Agatha, who eats broken bottles and wears barbed wire next to the skin. Apart from the mere intellectual pleasure of chewing the fat with her, there was the glittering prospect that I might be able to cadge an invitation to lunch. And owing to the outstanding virtuosity of Anatole, her French cook, the browsing at her trough is always of a nature to lure the gourmet.

The door of the morning-room was open as I went through the hall, and I caught a glimpse of Uncle Tom messing about with his collection of old silver. For a moment I toyed with the idea of pausing to pip-pip and enquire after his indigestion, a malady to which he is extremely subject, but wiser counsels prevailed. This uncle is a bird who, sighting a nephew, is apt to buttonhole him and become a bit informative on the subject of sconces and foliation, not to mention scrolls, ribbon wreaths in high relief and gadroon borders, and it seemed to me that silence was best. I whizzed by, accordingly, with sealed lips, and headed for the library, where I had been informed that Aunt Dahlia was at the moment roosting.

I found the old flesh-and-blood up to her Marcel-wave in proof sheets. As all the world knows, she is the courteous and popular proprietress of a weekly sheet for the delicately nurtured entitled *Milady's Boudoir*. I once contributed an article to it on 'What The Well-Dressed Man Is Wearing'.

My entry caused her to come to the surface, and she greeted me with one of those cheery view-halloos which, in the days when she went in for hunting, used to make her so noticeable a figure of the Quorn, the Pytchley and other organizations for doing the British fox a bit of no good.

'Hullo, ugly,' she said. 'What brings you here?'

'I understood, aged relative, that you wished to confer with me.'

'I didn't want you to come barging in, interrupting my work. A few words on the telephone would have met the case. But I suppose some instinct told you that this was my busy day.'

'If you were wondering if I could come to lunch, have no

anxiety. I shall be delighted, as always. What will Anatole be giving us?'

'He won't be giving you anything, my gay young tape-worm. I am entertaining Pomona Grindle, the novelist, to the midday meal.'

'I should be charmed to meet her.'

'Well, you're not going to. It is to be a strictly *tête-à-tête* affair. I'm trying to get a serial out of her for the *Boudoir*. No, all I wanted was to tell you to go to an antique shop in the Brompton Road – it's just past the Oratory – you can't miss it – and sneer at a cow-creamer.'

I did not get her drift. The impression I received was that of an aunt talking through the back of her neck.

'Do what to a what?'

'They've got an eighteenth-century cow-creamer there that Tom's going to buy this afternoon.'

The scales fell from my eyes.

'Oh, it's a silver whatnot, is it?'

'Yes. A sort of cream jug. Go there and ask them to show it to you, and when they do, register scorn.'

'The idea being what?'

'To sap their confidence, of course, chump. To sow doubts and misgivings in their mind and make them clip the price a bit. The cheaper he gets the thing, the better he will be pleased. And I want him to be in cheery mood, because if I succeed in signing the Grindle up for this serial, I shall be compelled to get into his ribs for a biggish sum of money. It's sinful what these bestselling women novelists want for their stuff. So pop off there without delay and shake your head at the thing.'

I am always anxious to oblige the right sort of aunt, but

I was compelled to put in what Jeeves would have called a *nolle prosequi*. Those morning mixtures of his are practically magical in their effect, but even after partaking of them one does not oscillate the bean.

'I can't shake my head. Not today.'

She gazed at me with a censorious waggle of the right eyebrow.

'Oh, so that's how it is? Well, if your loathsome excesses have left you incapable of headshaking, you can at least curl your lip.'

'Oh, rather.'

'Then carry on. And draw your breath in sharply. Also try clicking the tongue. Oh, yes, and tell them you think it's Modern Dutch.'

'Why?'

'I don't know. Apparently it's something a cow-creamer ought not to be.'

She paused, and allowed her eye to roam thoughtfully over my perhaps somewhat corpse-like face.

'So you were out on the tiles last night, were you, my little chickadee? It's an extraordinary thing – every time I see you, you appear to be recovering from some debauch. Don't you ever stop drinking? How about when you are asleep?'

I rebutted the slur.

'You wrong me, relative. Except at times of special revelry, I am exceedingly moderate in my potations. A brace of cocktails, a glass of wine at dinner and possibly a liqueur with the coffee – that is Bertram Wooster. But last night I gave a small bachelor binge for Gussie Fink-Nottle.'

'You did, did you?' She laughed – a bit louder than I could

have wished in my frail state of health, but then she is always a woman who tends to bring plaster falling from the ceiling when amused. 'Spink-Bottle, eh? Bless his heart! How was the old newt-fancier?'

'Pretty roguish.'

'Did he make a speech at this orgy of yours?'

'Yes. I was astounded. I was all prepared for a blushing refusal. But no. We drank his health, and he rose to his feet as cool as some cucumbers, as Anatole would say, and held us spellbound.'

'Tight as an owl, I suppose?'

'On the contrary. Offensively sober.'

'Well, that's a nice change.'

We fell into a thoughtful silence. We were musing on the summer afternoon down at her place in Worcestershire when Gussie, circumstances having so ordered themselves as to render him full to the back teeth with the right stuff, had addressed the young scholars of Market Snodsbury Grammar School on the occasion of their annual prize giving.

A thing I never know, when I'm starting out to tell a story about a chap I've told a story about before, is how much explanation to bung in at the outset. It's a problem you've got to look at from every angle. I mean to say, in the present case, if I take it for granted that my public knows all about Gussie Fink-Nottle and just breeze ahead, those publicans who weren't hanging on my lips the first time are apt to be fogged. Whereas if before kicking off I give about eight volumes of the man's life and history, other bimbos who were so hanging will stifle yawns and murmur 'Old stuff. Get on with it.'

I suppose the only thing to do is to put the salient facts as briefly as possible in the possession of the first gang, waving an apologetic hand at the second gang the while, to indicate that they had better let their attention wander for a minute or two and that I will be with them shortly.

This Gussie, then, was a fish-faced pal of mine who, on reaching man's estate, had buried himself in the country and devoted himself entirely to the study of newts, keeping the little chaps in a glass tank and observing their habits with a sedulous eye. A confirmed recluse you would have called him, if you had happened to know the word, and you would have been right. By all the rulings of the form book, a less promising prospect for the whispering of tender words into shell-like ears and the subsequent purchase of platinum ring and licence for wedding it would have seemed impossible to discover in a month of Sundays.

But Love will find a way. Meeting Madeline Bassett one day and falling for her like a ton of bricks, he had emerged from his retirement and started to woo, and after numerous vicissitudes had clicked and was slated at no distant date to don the sponge-bag trousers and gardenia for buttonhole and walk up the aisle with the ghastly girl.

I call her a ghastly girl because she was a ghastly girl. The Woosters are chivalrous, but they can speak their minds. A droopy, soupy, sentimental exhibit, with melting eyes and a cooing voice and the most extraordinary views on such things as stars and rabbits. I remember her telling me once that rabbits were gnomes in attendance on the Fairy Queen and that the stars were God's daisy chain. Perfect rot, of course. They're nothing of the sort.

Aunt Dahlia emitted a low, rumbling chuckle, for that

speech of Gussie's down at Market Snodsbury has always been one of her happiest memories.

'Good old Spink-Bottle! Where is he now?'

'Staying at the Bassett's father's place — Totleigh Towers, Totleigh-in-the-Wold, Glos. He went back there this morning. They're having the wedding at the local church.'

'Are you going to it?'

'Definitely no.'

'No, I suppose it would be too painful for you. You being in love with the girl.'

I stared.

'In love? With a female who thinks that every time a fairy blows its wee nose a baby is born?'

'Well, you were certainly engaged to her once.'

'For about five minutes, yes, and through no fault of my own. My dear old relative,' I said, nettled, 'you are perfectly well aware of the inside facts of that frightful affair.'

I winced. It was an incident in my career on which I did not care to dwell. Briefly, what had occurred was this. His nerve sapped by long association with newts, Gussie had shrunk from pleading his cause with Madeline Bassett, and had asked me to plead it for him. And when I did so, the fat-headed girl thought I was pleading mine. With the result that when, after that exhibition of his at the prize giving, she handed Gussie the temporary mitten, she had attached herself to me, and I had had no option but to take the rap. I mean to say, if a girl has got it into her nut that a fellow loves her, and comes and tells him that she is returning her *fiancé* to store and is now prepared to sign up with him, what can a chap do?

Mercifully, things had been straightened out at the eleventh hour by a reconciliation between the two pills, but the thought of my peril was one at which I still shuddered. I wasn't going to feel really easy in my mind till the parson had said: 'Wilt thou, Augustus?' and Gussie had whispered a shy 'Yes.'

'Well, if it is of any interest to you,' said Aunt Dahlia, 'I am not proposing to attend that wedding myself. I disapprove of Sir Watkyn Bassett, and don't think he ought to be encouraged. There's one of the boys, if you want one!'

'You know the old crumb, then?' I said, rather surprised, though of course it bore out what I often say – viz. that it's a small world.

'Yes, I know him. He's a friend of Tom's. They both collect old silver and snarl at one another like wolves about it all the time. We had him staying at Brinkley last month. And would you care to hear how he repaid me for all the loving care I lavished on him while he was my guest? Sneaked round behind my back and tried to steal Anatole!'

'No!'

'That's what he did. Fortunately, Anatole proved staunch – after I had doubled his wages.'

'Double them again,' I said earnestly. 'Keep on doubling them. Pour out money like water rather than lose that superb master of the roasts and hashes.'

I was visibly affected. The thought of Anatole, that peerless disher-up, coming within an ace of ceasing to operate at Brinkley Court, where I could always enjoy his output by inviting myself for a visit, and going off to serve under old Bassett, the last person in the world likely to set out a knife and fork for Bertram, had stirred me profoundly.

'Yes,' said Aunt Dahlia, her eye smouldering as she

437

brooded on the frightful thing, 'that's the sort of horns-woggling high-binder Sir Watkyn Bassett is. You had better warn Spink-Bottle to watch out on the wedding day. The slightest relaxation of vigilance, and the old thug will probably get away with his tie-pin in the vestry. And now,' she said, reaching out for what had the appearance of being a thoughtful essay on the care of the baby in sickness and in health, 'push off. I've got about six tons of proofs to correct. Oh, and give this to Jeeves, when you see him. It's the "Husband's Corner" article. It's full of deep stuff about braid on the side of men's dress trousers, and I'd like him to vet it. For all I know, it may be Red propaganda. And I can rely on you not to bungle that job? Tell me in your own words what it is you're supposed to do.'

'Go to antique shop—'

'—in the Brompton Road—'

'—in, as you say, the Brompton Road. Ask to see cow-creamer—'

'—and sneer. Right. Buzz along. The door is behind you.'

It was with a light heart that I went out into the street and hailed a passing barouche. Many men, no doubt, might have been a bit sick at having their morning cut into in this fashion, but I was conscious only of pleasure at the thought that I had it in my power to perform this little act of kindness. Scratch Bertram Wooster, I often say, and you find a Boy Scout.

The antique shop in the Brompton Road proved, as foreshadowed, to be an antique shop in the Brompton Road and, like all antique shops except the swanky ones in the Bond Street neighbourhood, dingy outside and dark and smelly within. I don't know why it is, but the proprietors of these establishments always seem to be cooking some sort of stew in the back room.

'I say,' I began, entering; then paused as I perceived that the bloke in charge was attending to two other customers.

'Oh, sorry,' I was about to add, to convey the idea that I had horned in inadvertently, when the words froze on my lips.

Quite a slab of misty fruitfulness had drifted into the emporium, obscuring the view, but in spite of the poor light I was able to note that the smaller and elder of these two customers was no stranger to me.

It was old Pop Bassett in person. Himself. Not a picture.

There is a tough, bulldog strain in the Woosters which has often caused comment. It came out in me now. A weaker man, no doubt, would have tiptoed from the scene and headed for the horizon, but I stood firm. After all, I felt, the dead past was the dead past. By forking out that fiver, I had paid my debt to Society and had nothing to fear from this shrimp-faced son of a whatnot. So I remained where I was, giving him the surreptitious once-over.

My entry had caused him to turn and shoot a quick look at me, and at intervals since then he had been peering at me sideways. It was only a question of time, I felt, before the hidden chord in his memory would be touched and he would realise that the slight, distinguished-looking figure leaning on its umbrella in the background was an old acquaintance. And now it was plain that he was hep. The bird in charge of the shop had pottered off into an inner room, and he came across to where I stood, giving me the up-and-down through his wind-shields.

'Hullo, hullo,' he said. 'I know you, young man. I never forget a face. You came up before me once.'

I bowed slightly.

'But not twice. Good! Learned your lesson, eh? Going straight now? Capital. Now, let me see, what was it? Don't tell me. It's coming back. Of course, yes. Bag-snatching.'

'No, no. It was——'

'Bag-snatching,' he repeated firmly. 'I remember it distinctly. Still, it's all past and done with now, eh? We have turned over a new leaf, have we not? Splendid. Roderick, come over here. This is most interesting.'

His buddy, who had been examining a salver, put it down and joined the party.

He was, as I had already been able to perceive, a breathtaking cove. About seven feet in height, and swathed in a plaid ulster which made him look about six feet across, he caught the eye and arrested it. It was as if Nature had intended to make a gorilla, and had changed its mind at the last moment.

But it wasn't merely the sheer expanse of the bird that impressed. Close to, what you noticed more was his face, which was square and powerful and slightly moustached towards the centre. His gaze was keen and piercing. I don't know if you have even seen those pictures in the papers of Dictators with tilted chins and blazing eyes, inflaming the populace with fiery words on the occasion of the opening of a new skittle alley, but that was what he reminded me of.

'Roderick,' said old Bassett, 'I want you to meet this fellow. Here is a case which illustrates exactly what I have so often maintained – that prison life does not degrade, that it does not warp the character and prevent a man rising on stepping-stones of his dead self to higher things.'

I recognised the gag – one of Jeeves's – and wondered where he could have heard it.

'Look at this chap. I gave him three months not long ago for snatching bags at railways stations, and it is quite evident that his term in jail has had the most excellent effect on him. He has reformed.'

'Oh, yes?' said the Dictator.

Granted that it wasn't quite 'Oh, yeah?' I still didn't like the way he spoke. He was looking at me with a nasty sort of supercilious expression. I remember thinking that he would have been the ideal man to sneer at a cow-creamer.

'What makes you think he has reformed?'

'Of course he has reformed. Look at him. Well groomed, well dressed, a decent member of Society. What his present walk in life is, I do not know, but it is perfectly obvious that he is no longer stealing bags. What are you doing now, young man?'

'Stealing umbrellas, apparently,' said the Dictator. 'I notice he's got yours.'

And I was on the point of denying the accusation hotly – I had, indeed, already opened my lips to do so – when there suddenly struck me like a blow on the upper maxillary from a sock stuffed with wet sand the realisation that there was a lot in it.

I mean to say, I remembered now that I had come out without my umbrella, and yet here I was, beyond any question of doubt, umbrellaed to the gills. What had caused me to take up the one that had been leaning against a seventeenth-century chair, I cannot say, unless it was the primeval instinct which makes a man without an umbrella reach out for the nearest one in sight, like a flower groping toward the sun.

A manly apology seemed in order. I made it as the blunt instrument changed hands.

'I say, I'm most frightfully sorry.'

Old Bassett said he was, too – sorry and disappointed. He said it was this sort of thing that made a man sick at heart.

The Dictator had to shove his oar in. He asked if he should call a policeman, and old Bassett's eyes gleamed for a moment. Being a magistrate makes you love the idea of calling policemen. It's like a tiger tasting blood. But he shook his head.

'No, Roderick. I couldn't. Not today – the happiest day of my life.'

The Dictator pursed his lips, as if feeling that the better the day, the better the deed.

'But listen' I bleated, 'it was a mistake.'

'Ha!' said the Dictator.

'I thought that umbrella was mine.'

'That,' said old Bassett, 'is the fundamental trouble with you, my man. You are totally unable to distinguish between *meum* and *tuum*. Well, I am not going to have you arrested this time, but I advise you to be very careful. Come, Roderick.'

They biffed out, the Dictator pausing at the door to give me another look and say 'Ha!' again.

A most unnerving experience all this had been for a man of sensibility, as you may imagine, and my immediate reaction was a disposition to give Aunt Dahlia's commission the miss-in-balk and return to the flat and get outside another of Jeeves's pick-me-ups. You know how harts pant for cooling streams when heated in the chase. Very much that sort of thing. I realised now what madness it had been to go into

442

the streets of London with only one of them under my belt, and I was on the point of melting away and going back to the fountain head, when the proprietor of the shop emerged from the inner room, accompanied by a rich smell of stew and a sandy cat, and enquired what he could do for me. And so, the subject having come up, I said that I understood that he had an eighteenth-century cow-creamer for sale.

He shook his head. He was a rather mildewed bird of gloomy aspect, almost entirely concealed behind a cascade of white whiskers.

'You're too late. It's promised to a customer.'

'Name of Travers?'

'Ah.'

'Then that's all right. Learn, O thou of unshuffled features and agreeable disposition,' I said, for one likes to be civil, 'that the above Travers is my uncle. He sent me here to have a look at the thing. So dig it out, will you? I expect it's rotten.'

'It's a beautiful cow-creamer.'

'Ha!' I said, borrowing a bit of the Dictator's stuff. 'That's what you think. We shall see.'

I don't mind confessing that I'm not much of a lad for old silver, and though I have never pained him by actually telling him so, I have always felt that Uncle Tom's fondness for it is evidence of a goofiness which he would do well to watch and check before it spreads. So I wasn't expecting the heart to leap up to any great extent at the sight of this exhibit. But when the whiskered ancient pottered off into the shadows and came back with the thing, I scarcely knew whether to laugh or weep. The thought of an uncle paying hard cash for such an object got right in amongst me.

443

It was a silver cow. But when I say 'cow', don't go running away with the idea of some decent, self-respecting cudster such as you may observe loading grass into itself in the nearest meadow. This was a sinister, leering, Underworld sort of animal, the kind that would spit out of the side of its mouth for twopence. It was about four inches high and six long. Its back opened on a hinge. Its tail was arched, so that the tip touched the spine – thus, I suppose, affording a handle for the cream-lover to grasp. The sight of it seemed to take me into a different and dreadful world.

It was, consequently, an easy task for me to carry out the programme indicated by Aunt Dahlia. I curled the lip and clicked the tongue, all in one movement. I also drew in the breath sharply. The whole effect was that of a man absolutely out of sympathy with this cow-creamer, and I saw the mildewed cove start, as if he had been wounded in a tender spot.

'Oh, tut, tut, tut!' I said. 'Oh, dear, dear, dear! Oh, no, no, no, no, no! I don't think much of this,' I said, curling and clicking freely. 'All wrong.'

'All wrong?'

'All wrong. Modern Dutch.'

'Modern Dutch?' He may have frothed at the mouth, or he may not. I couldn't be sure. But the agony of spirit was obviously intense. 'What do you mean, Modern Dutch? It's eighteenth-century English. Look at the hallmark.'

'I can't see any hallmark.'

'Are you blind? Here, take it outside in the street. It's lighter there.'

'Right ho,' I said, and started for the door, sauntering at first in a languid sort of way, like a connoisseur a bit bored at having his time wasted.

I say 'at first', because I had only taken a couple of steps when I tripped over the cat, and you can't combine tripping over cats with languid sauntering. Shifting abruptly into high, I shot out of the door like someone wanted by the police making for the car after a smash-and-grab raid. The cow-creamer flew from my hands, and it was a lucky thing that I happened to barge into a fellow citizen outside, or I should have taken a toss in the gutter.

Well, not absolutely lucky, as a matter of fact, for it turned out to be Sir Watkyn Bassett. He stood there goggling at me with horror and indignation behind the pince-nez, and you could almost see him totting up the score on his fingers. First, bag-snatching, I mean to say; then umbrella-pinching; and now this. His whole demeanour was that of a man confronted with the last straw.

'Call a policeman, Roderick!' he cried, skipping like the high hills.

The Dictator sprang to the task.

'Police' he bawled.

'Police!' yipped old Bassett, up in the tenor clef.

'Police!' roared the Dictator, taking the bass.

And a moment later something large loomed up in the fog and said: 'What's all this?'

Well, I dare say I could have explained everything, if I had stuck around and gone into it, but I didn't want to stick around and go into it. Side-stepping nimbly, I picked up the feet and was gone like the wind. A voice shouted 'Stop! but of course I didn't. Stop, I mean to say! Of all the damn silly ideas. I legged it down byways and along side streets, and eventually fetched up somewhere in the neighbourhood of Sloane Square. There I got aboard a cab and started back to civilisation.

My original intention was to drive to the Drones and get a bite of lunch there, but I hadn't gone far when I realised that I wasn't equal to it. I yield to no man in my appreciation of the Drone Club . . . its sparkling conversation, its camaraderie, its atmosphere redolent of all that is best and brightest in the metropolis . . . but there would, I knew, be a goodish bit of bread thrown hither and thither at its luncheon table, and I was in no vein to cope with flying bread. Changing my strategy in a flash, I told the man to take me to the nearest Turkish bath.

It is always my practice to linger over a Turkish b., and it was consequently getting late by the time I returned to the flat. I had managed to put in two or three hours' sleep in my cubicle, and that, taken in conjunction with the healing flow of persp. in the hot room and the plunge into the icy tank, had brought the roses back to my cheeks to no little extent. It was, indeed, practically with a merry tra-la-la on my lips that I latchkeyed my way in and made for the sitting-room.

And the next moment my fizziness was turned off at the main by the sight of a pile of telegrams on the table.

(1938)

Ken Follett has sold more than 155 million books worldwide. His first bestseller was *Eye of the Needle* (1978), a spy story set during the Second World War. In 1989, he published *The Pillars of the Earth*, a novel about building a cathedral in the Middle Ages, which has since sold more than twenty-five million copies in many languages. More recently, the *Century* trilogy of historical novels – *Fall of Giants* (2010), *Winter of the World* (2012) and *Edge of Eternity* (2014) – told the story of the twentieth century through the eyes of five families.

★

The Early Morning
by Hilaire Belloc

The moon on the one hand, the dawn on the other:
The moon is my sister, the dawn is my brother.
The moon on my left and the dawn on my right.
My brother, good morning; my sister, good night.

(1896)

★

The Memorial Gates stand at the top of London's Constitution Hill, between Buckingham Palace's high-walled garden and gridlocked Hyde Park Corner, where pedestrian crossings have not only red and green stickmen but also red and green stick-horses (for The Household Cavalry).

Erected in 2002 – inaugurated by Queen Elizabeth II during her Golden Jubilee – the austere gateposts bear an overdue tribute to the countless servicemen who sacrificed their lives in the name of Empire, lest we forget: 'In memory of the five million volunteers from the Indian sub-continent, Africa and the Caribbean who fought with Britain in the two World Wars.'

Amid this pomp, angled between the shadows of inglorious colonial history, another inscription lurks – Nigerian writer Ben Okri's seven words are stark, yet blossom as brightly as Green Park's daffodils in springtime:

OUR FUTURE IS GREATER THAN OUR PAST

The Message
by Ben Okri

I

You arrive dirty and hungry. You are covered in grime. You have come from beyond the snowline. It has been an epic journey.

You have travelled through forests, through innumerable cities and villages, barely stopping, travelling mostly on foot, with no change of clothes.

You have come through regions where you were unfamiliar with the language and the customs. You have slept at roadsides, in strange inns. You have travelled alone, bearing a message which only you can carry.

How long have you been travelling? You don't know. Maybe your whole life.

You forego pleasures on the way. It's been hard enough just keeping on the journey. You have travelled nights without sleeping, days without eating. Your destination is your rest and your food. Your mission is to arrive at the court, deliver the message, and then to be free.

Many countries you have crossed, wolves you have battled, hard men you have transcended, cunning men you have eluded, seducing women you have slithered away from.

Youth deserted you in the virgin forests; and yet you travelled with youth, and never lost it. Youth remains in you, in your freedom and the simplicity of your spirit. Encased in the dirt of the road is your preserved freshness.

2

The last part of your journey was the worst. Getting closer

was also getting farther. It is easier to get lost within sight of the palace. It is easier to feel one has arrived when one sees the battlements and turrets, the flags and banners of the castle. Then in renewed hope and exultation one hurries. And yet the way is still far. Distances are deceptive. Hope makes all things near, and so can prove treacherous.

You kept your eyes on the road. You nearly got lost in the village. You were tempted to stay the night, to divulge your destination to an old woman, and thus be given conflicting or self-serving advice. But you kept it to yourself. You imagined you were still at the beginning of your journey. You were conscious that it was still full of perils, and that you still had a long way to go.

Your whole life had been the journey. If you stopped to think now, or confess despair, who knows what snares of your own making you would fall into. So you staked your life on the journey. You might have died on it, but you were vigilant. You took each moment as the whole. That's what you did.

3

And then you found you had arrived. You were in the court. You were in the place. In the grime and dirt of the journey the message was divested of you. It was painless. You didn't even know what it was. The message was on you. The message was in your dirt, on your unwashed body, in your weary but alive spirit. The message was in your eyes. It was in your arrival, in your dreams, in your memory. It was in all you had brought, and the nothing that you had brought.

The message was divested of you. It was shorn off you,

449

and you were light. You were cleaned up of your message. You were scrubbed and shaved of it, bathed and washed of it. The filthy clothes were taken off you, and you were given new ones that shone like light.

4

There had been a mysterious ceremony acknowledging the heroic nature of your journey. But the true gift of it was in your spirit, your inner liberation. There was a new eternal light in you.

Fresh, young, and free, you wander the streets of the kingdom. You have the sense of being in a new world, a luminous world. You are living an enchanted life in the kingdom.

You had set out early and had arrived sooner than you thought. You have a whole new life ahead of you. And so here you are, a youth with a spirit of shining gold, rich beyond measure in the lightness of your being. Everything is before you. Your main quest and journey is over, because you had begun early and arrived early. Now you have it all to live, in peerless freedom. What luck! No need to fret, but just to live, now, the life you want.

Like a youth just arrived in a great city, with hope in his heart, looking to make his fortune and find his true love, in the happiest and most innocent days of his life, like such a youth you wander lightly through the streets of the mysterious kingdom. The pastel sky is touched with blue, and there is dawn sunlight.

(2009)

To crown our disparate dreams, Shakespeare must have the last word.

As you may have noticed, *The Tempest* surges through this volume. In his most famous speech, Prospero (and his creator) may ostensibly be shuffling, vexed, back onto the quotidian mortal coil. Yet in this late play, Shakespeare asks consistently of his reader and audience: which, after all, is the true 'primary world' and which the 'secondary'?

Waking or sleeping life?

Life is but a dream – and so perhaps the answer, simply, has to be . . .

. . . both.

From *The Tempest* (Act 4, Scene 1)
by William Shakespeare

Our revels now are ended. These our actors,
As I foretold you, were all spirits, and
Are melted into air, into thin air;
And, like the baseless fabric of this vision,
The cloud-capp'd towers, the gorgeous palaces,
The solemn temples, the great globe itself,
Yea, all which it inherit, shall dissolve,
And, like this insubstantial pageant faded,
Leave not a rack behind. We are such stuff
As dreams are made on, and our little life
Is rounded with a sleep.

(1610–11)

Afterword

by Diana Athill

The Story: words spoken or written by someone else which take you away from yourself. It is something you *need*: everyone, everywhere, always has responded to it. Bedtime: the time for relaxing on soft pillows. Every child recognizes the connection between these two things, given the chance. I only have to put them together to see the Ugly Duckling swimming about the lake so sadly, so sadly – until that amazing moment when he understands that he is a swan: an imagined event quite unconnected with me but which meant, and still means, so much to me. A precious bedtime story. But did it ever relax me into sleep and dreams? Ben Holden, who has given much thought to the subject, thinks so.

It was bold of him to make this collection of bedtime stories for grown-ups and put them together in such an ambitious way – read, or reread, his introduction to see what I mean. What he calls his 'lofty aims' are very interesting and have made me roam back and forth within his book in a way which increased my already lively feelings about it. In no way was I put off it when at times I failed to be persuaded.

I think there are two ways of reading this book: the romantic, and the prosaic. The romantic is in tune with Ben's own approach to it, the spirit in which he writes sentences such as, 'The fireworks within our brains, the light fantastic that is aflame throughout sleep, even while the body is glacial, is as wondrous and mysterious as the galaxy of stars that flares the night sky.' The prosaic, which I have to admit favouring, says, 'I love the book, but steady on, Ben!' This, I suppose, is because I am one of those people who don't dream – or rather, hardly ever remember their dreams (I accept that I must have them, and hope that they are less boring than the few of them which have occasionally surfaced). To me, when I slip away from consciousness, whether via a story or simply weariness, it just seems that I'm having a good night's sleep.

But that does not mean that I have not been charmed by this collection, so unlike any other, swooping as it does from little jewels of poetry to quite long stories and from voices as unlike each other as those of Sylvia Plath and P. G. Wodehouse. It is truly enjoyable. Not only has it crept at once onto my bedside table, but it is also going to solve my Christmas-present problem – and to those readers whose nights are more thrilling than my own, it will be even more precious.

Diana Athill was a founding director of the British publishing firm of André Deutsch, where for fifty years she worked with writers including Jean Rhys, Stevie Smith, Margaret Atwood, Molly Keane, Jack Kerouac, John Updike, Norman Mailer and Philip Roth. She has published a novel, collections of stories and letters, and seven volumes of memoirs, including a study of old age, *Somewhere Towards the End,* which won the 2008 Costa Award, and *Alive, Alive Oh!* (2015).

Notes and Illuminations

Introduction: Seize the Night

The introductory lines by Wallace Stevens are extracted from the poem 'The House Was Quiet and the World Was Calm'.

p. 4: It could be said that whole nations, as well as individuals, effectively have their own 'slumber numbers' and 'chronotypes'. In May 2016, a study published in *Science Advances* revealed global sleeping patterns. Conducted by a team at the University of Michigan, aided by an app called Entrain, the survey claimed its findings could inform measures to tackle the 'global sleep crisis'. The research showed that the Dutch sleep almost an entire hour more than people in Singapore or Japan (8 hours 12 minutes as opposed to 7 hours 24 minutes). Britons average just under 8 hours. The study also showed that women spend about 30 minutes more in bed each night than men.

The 'widely acknowledged' rule that adults need '7–8 hours' is, for one source, borne out in advice issued during 2016 by the Royal Society of Public Health, which recommended 7.7 hours per night (on average) for an adult, or a mean 'slumber number' spread of 7–9 hours; this followed a sleep pattern survey of 2,000 adults in the UK.

Finnish scientists, meanwhile, concluded in October 2014 that women need marginally less sleep on average than men, 7.6 as opposed to 7.8 hours, following a health study of 3,760 people.

p. 4: For a broader analysis of sleep patterns in animals, see Chapter 4 of *Sleep: A Very Short Introduction* by Steven W. Lockley & Russell G. Foster (eds) (Oxford, 2012).

p. 5: That we produce 2.5 trillion bytes of data was detailed in 2016's 'Big Bang Data' exhibition at Somerset House, London.

p. 5: Professor Russell Foster's quote was referenced as part of the BBC's 'Day of the Body Clock', 12 May 2014.

pp. 5–6: For a succinct and accessible guide to the neurology of sleep, see neuroscientist Jeff Iliff's 2014 TED Talk, *One More Reason to Get a Good Night's Sleep.*

In line with the statement about gene expression and the 24-hour pattern of activity here, the BBC's 'Day of the Body Clock' made the claim that 'about 10% of your DNA has a 24-hour pattern of activity that is behind all behavioural and physiological changes'.

The pituary gland is pea-sized but regulates a monumental range of human activity, including: growth, blood pressure, certain functions of the sex organs, and metabolism, as well as some aspects of pregnancy, childbirth, temperature regulation and pain relief.

p. 6: The recent US survey referenced showing average adult sleep has reduced over the past fifty years is corroborated by the findings of Charles Czeiser, the chief of the Division of Sleep and Circadian Disorders at Brigham and Women's Hospital, whose work asserts that 'over the past five decades our average sleep duration on work nights has decreased by an hour and a half, down from eight and a half to just under seven.' ('Why Can't We Fall Asleep?' by Maria Konnikova, *The New Yorker*, 7 July 2015).

A recent Gallup poll also showed that 40% of all American adults are sleep-deprived and get less than 7 hours per night. This is referenced in Arianna Huffington's *The Sleep Revolution* (Penguin Random House, 2016).

p. 7: Prime Ministers who were famously derided the importance of sleep include Margaret Thatcher, who developed Alzheimer's after leaving Downing Street, and Winston Churchill, who suffered from the 'black dog' of depression and also alcoholism while in office. More recently, 2016 US Presidential candidate Donald Trump proclaimed that sleeping more than four hours a night is a waste of time.

For political summits of global import that ended in disarray and proved ineffective in large part due to the participants' sheer exhaustion through a lack of sleep, look no further than climate-change conferences such as in The Hague in 2000 and the Copenhagen Summit, or the United Nations Climate Change Conference of 2009. The inability to reach conclusive and meaningful resolutions at the conferences was, in part, on both occasions, publically attributed to the participants' lack of sleep after protracted negotiations.

p. 8: The research that proposes fairy-tale archetypes date further back than previously imagined, some 'harking as far back as the Bronze Age' – and referenced again in Chapter Two, 'Once Upon A Time' – was published by the Royal Society of Science in January 2016; it was written by Sara Graça da Silva and Jamshid J. Tehrani and is entitled 'Comparative phylogenetic analyses uncover the ancient roots of Indo-European folktales'.

p. 8: As regards the academically beneficial effects of parents reading to children – a June 2015 Ipsos/Mori poll commissioned by the Book Trust showed that UK fathers, particularly, are not reading enough to their children. Book Trust's Chief Executive, Diana Gerald, elaborated thus: 'Reading together increases children's literacy skills, but research also proves that children who love reading do better at school in all subjects . . . If a parent reads to their children every day, they will be almost 12 months ahead of their age group when they start school. Even reading to them three to five times a week gives them a six-month head start over those who are read to less often.'

Another recent survey, by YouGov for the children's publisher Scholastic, in 2015, found that 83% of children enjoyed being read aloud to, with 68% describing it as a special time with their parents, and yet a separate survey by Settle Stories, of more than 2,000 parents with young children (aged 4–10), found that only 4% read a bedtime story to their child each night, with 69% saying that they do not have the time. Another study, in February of 2015 by TomTom, of 1,000 parents of children aged 1–10, found that 34% never read their kids a bedtime story.

p. 8–9: One-minute bedtime stories are explored in Chapter One, 'The Age of Rage' of *In Praise of Slow: How a Worldwide Movement Is Challenging the Cult of Speed* by Carl Honoré (Orion, 2004).

p. 9: Storybook Dads (and Storybook Mums) operates in 100 UK prisons. It was set up by prison visitor Sharon Berry, at Dartmoor Prison in 2002. Over 200,000 children annually experience the trauma of an imprisoned loved one. Research has also shown that offenders who manage to maintain regular family contact during their prison sentence are up to six times less likely to reoffend. Over 5,200 audio CDs and 431 DVDs of storytelling were produced by prisoners for their children in 2013 alone. For more, visit www.storybookdads.org.uk

p. 10: The anthology demonstrates how various works of art or celebrated writing careers were launched by the bedtime-story routine or sleep (notably, entries on Tolkien and Dahl, but also Maxwell and Gaiman) – but the idea, as stated in the Introduction, that the bedtime-story routine is a formative influence for great writers is also indirectly corroborated by Steven Pinker in *The Sense of Style* (Penguin, 2014). In the first page of his first chapter, Pinker writes about 'the elusive "ear" of a skilled writer', observing: 'Biographers of great authors always try to track down the books their subjects read when they were young, because they know these sources hold the key to their development as writers.'

p. 11: Sleep cycles, as touched upon here, were also traditionally grouped into two distinct sleeps per night for humans, as still is the case with almost all other mammals. A period of wakefulness split the two sequences of sleep. 'Segmented sleep' seems to have dwindled in Europe from around the seventeenth century, coinciding with the illumination of cities – yet can still be traced in the sleep patterns we experience at the beginning and end of our lives.

p. 12: Kafka's quote stems from a letter written to Oskar Pollak on 27 January, 1904.

1. Eventide

p. 34: That 'moon' was one of the first words uttered by Frieda
Hughes was revealed by Ted Hughes on Thames Television
in *The English Programme*, in 1989, as noted in *The Poetry of Ted
Hughes: Language, Illusion & Beyond* by Paul Bentley (Longman,
1988).

pp. 35–36: For more on Charles Dickens' early years in the blacking
factory, turn to Claire Tomalin's masterful *Charles Dickens: A Life*
(2011), Chapter 2, 'A London Education'.

There is also a definitive treatise of Dickens' night-walking in
Matthew Beaumont's *Night Walking: A Nocturnal History of London*
(Verso, 2015). The quote about 'wandering back to that time of my
life' appears in Beaumont's Chapter 12, 'The Dead Night', and is
in turn attributed to John Foster's *The Life of Charles Dickens*, Vol. 1,
5th edition (Chapman & Hall, 1872).

p. 37: The quote from J. Allan Hobson, Professor of Psychiatry at
Harvard Medical School, about dreaming resembling delirium
comes from the second chapter of his book *Dreaming: A Very Short
Introduction* (2002, Oxford University Press).

2. Once Upon a Time

p. 52: For more on the harmful blue light in today's modern electronic
devices, please see the online research article 'Bigger, Brighter,
Bluer – Better? Current light-emitting devices – adverse sleep
properties and preventative strategies' by Paul Gringras, Benita
Middleton, Debra J. Skene and Victoria L. Revell, and published in
October 2015 by Frontiers in Public Health.

In 2016, bowing to the scientific evidence and pressure to
make amends, Apple introduced in operating systems a new (and
somewhat unfortunately named) 'Night Shift' mode, affording
their customers a softer, redder light. Similarly, during December
of 2015, Amazon rolled out 'Blue Shade' night mode for their
Kindle Fire tablets.

pp. 52–53: Dame Marina Warner's description of the fairy-tale tradition features in Chapter 3, 'Voices on the Page', of *Once Upon a Time: A Short History of Fairy Tale* (2014, Oxford University Press).

p. 58: Tolkien's lecture 'On Fairytales' was initially written (and entitled simply 'Fairy Stories') for presentation as the Andrew Lang lecture at the University of St Andrews, Scotland, in 1939. It first appeared in print, with some enhancement, in 1947, in a festschrift volume, *Essays Presented to Charles Williams*, compiled by Tolkien's friend, C. S. Lewis.

pp. 71–72: For Angela Carter's notes on the provenance of the Russian fairy tale (as extracted herein) and traditions thereto, see her notes to 'The Wise Little Girl' in Part Two of her *Book of Fairy Tales* (Virago).

pp. 81–91: 'The Tale of King Yunan and the Sage Duban' has been edited for this anthology by Marina Warner. The full version can be found in Husain Haddawy's translation of *The Arabian Nights* (Norton).

p. 103: The tale of 'Ole Lukøje' by Hans Christian Andersen first appeared in *Fairy Tales Told for Children* (New Collection, Third Booklet; 1842).

p. 104: Susan Holton's short poem 'I'm Looking for the Sandman' (1928) first appeared in the Methodist Book Concern and runs as follows:

> I'm looking for the Sandman.
> He's somewhere 'round 'tis said;
> But as I'm rather sleepy,
> I think I'll go to bed.

p. 104: For more on how Roy Orbison came up with the song 'In Dreams', see Chapter 5, 'Distant Drums' of Alan Clayson's biography *Only the Lonely* (1989, Sidgwick & Jackson).

p. 121: A recording of Les Murray explaining the provenance of 'The Sleepout' (as extracted here) and then reciting the poem himself can be found on www.lesmurray.org

p. 122: 'The Idea of Age' was initially called 'Mrs Vivaldi', and then 'I Dropped Off' – before its author settled on its ultimate title. This is detailed in Nicola Beauman's biography, *The Other Elizabeth*

Taylor (2009, Persephone Books). Beauman also rightly observes (in Chapter 9, 'Penn Cottage 1950–53') that the story is 'a forerunner in miniature' of Taylor's celebrated, subsequent novel *Mrs Palfrey at the Claremont*.

3. Hook, Line and Sinker

p. 143: The Italian word for 'sleep-waking' is *dormiveglia*.

p. 143: Edgar Allan Poe's metaphysical aesthetic and awareness of sleep's powers can be seen in this passage from *Eureka*. Monos here equates mortality to sleep. The sense of time that is conjured is cosmic and, I'd argue, downright circadian:

> 'The day waned; and, as its light faded away, I became possessed by a vague uneasiness, an anxiety such as the sleeper feels when sad real sounds fall continuously within his ear – low distant bell-tones, solemn, at long but equal intervals, and commingling with melancholy dreams. Night arrived; and with its shadows a heavy discomfort. It oppressed my limbs with the oppression of some dull weight, and was palpable. There was also a moaning sound, not unlike the distant reverberation of surf, but more continuous, which, beginning with the first twilight, had grown in strength with the darkness. Suddenly lights were brought into the room, and this reverberation became forthwith interrupted into frequent unequal bursts of the same sound, but less dreary and less distinct. The ponderous oppression was in a great measure relieved; and, issuing from the flame of each lamp, for there were many, there flowed unbrokenly into my ears a strain of melodious monotone . . .
>
> And now, from the wreck and chaos of the usual senses, there appeared to have arisen within me a sixth, all perfect. In its exercise I found a wild delight: yet a delight still physical, inasmuch as the understanding had in it no part. Motion in the animal frame had fully ceased. No muscle quivered; no nerve trilled; no artery throbbed. But there

461

seemed to have sprung up, in the brain, that of which no words could convey to the merely human intelligence even an indistinct conception. Let me term it a mental pendulous pulsation. It was the moral embodiment of man's abstract idea of Time.'

p. 144: Coleridge's best-known poems – 'The Rime of the Ancient Mariner', 'Christabel' and 'Kubla Khan' – in bearing the imprint of his opiate addiction also inhabit dream-states and often tip into the nightmarish. The Mariner pleads, 'O let me be awake, my God', while the poem 'Kubla Khan' presented itself to the poet during a particularly vivid dream, as he recounted in the introductory fragment, 'Kubla Khan: Or, A Vision in a Dream' (1816). This accompanied the poem when it was published in 1816 in an octavo pamphlet entitled 'Christabel: Kubla Khan, A Vision; The Pains of Sleep'.

Coleridge, in ill health, had been prescribed 'an anodyne'. He fell asleep in his chair, reading in *Purchas, His Pilgrimage* of Khan Kubla. The fragment recalls: 'The author continued for about three hours in a profound sleep, at least of the external senses, during which time he had the most vivid confidence, that he could not have composed less than two to three hundred lines; if that indeed can be called composition in which all the images rose up before him as things, with a parallel production of the correspondent expressions, without any sensation of consciousness of effort.'

p. 144: William Wordsworth's poem, 'To Sleep' makes it clear that he understood the importance of sleep and was well acquainted with insomnia (the subject of many other books and an area that I have chosen not to explore here, as this collection is for *everyone*, including but absolutely not limited to those poor souls who struggle with sleep). Wordsworth's poem ends with a rather desperate beckoning:

Without Thee what is all the morning's wealth?
Come, blessed barrier between day and day,
Dear mother of fresh thoughts and joyous health!

4. The Dead Spot

p. 188: Sleep paralysis, as referenced in the introduction to this section, has been experienced by approximately one in three young adults.

pp. 188–189: Philip Larkin's poem 'Aubade' was written in 1977; 'Unfinished Poem' in 1951.

p. 189: Such bedboard talismans to ward off evil spirits are, for example, traditional and still deployed by the Shona people of Eastern Zimbabwe.

p. 190: For more on the dead spot and its happy corollary, plus much more on our body clocks and inherent timetable, seek out the BBC *Horizon* documentary, *The Secret Life of Your Body Clock* (2009).

p. 215: Theories on 'sleep-dependent memory processing' vary and the links between sleep and memory is a topic of much debate in the sleep scientific community.

On 13 May 2016, a study conducted by academics from the University of Bern and McGill University, Canada, was published in *Science* journal that dramatically moved forward our understanding of REM sleep. Using optogenetics – a technique that allows scientists to control neurons with coloured light shone directly into the brain, via a tiny optical fibre-implant – the research team inhibited theta oscillations in mice hippocampus during REM sleep. They found that inhibiting such brain activity during REM sleep prevented the animals from remembering things learned during the day (such as a brand-new object in its cage). 'Disrupting the activity only during REM sleep, and not other sleep, basically obliterates consolidation and memory formation,' said Dr Sylvain Williams. The study is titled 'Causal evidence for the role of REM sleep theta rhythm in contextual memory consolidation'.

p. 215: The recent US studies showing links between sleep and amyloid plaques include the study published by researchers at Stanford University in 2001, 'Association between apolipoprotein E epsilon4 and sleep-disordered breathing in adults'.

p. 219: Isaac Bashevis Singer made this statement in an 'Art of Fiction' interview with Harold Flender for the *Paris Review*, Issue 44, in 1968.

p. 226: E. B. White's observation about New York was also made in an interview for the *Paris Review*, with George Plimpton, Issue 48, 1969.

p. 251: Roald Dahl recounting how he came to write *James and the Giant Peach* appeared in the unpublished manuscript of Ophelia Dahl's *Memories of My Father*.

In his biography, *Storyteller: The Life of Roald Dahl* (2010), Donald Sturrock elaborates on the Dahl household's bedtime-story routine. Sturrock relates that for 'much of his adult life he had enjoyed telling stories to children . . . [his wife, Patricia Neal] recalled that they followed him as if he were the Pied Piper, mesmerising the children with his rich voice, his glittering eyes, his sense of fun and his wild subversive imagination. Now [in 1959] Roald was spending a lot of time with his own children – particularly when Pat was away on movie shoots . . . A story was never far away. Roald read them traditional fairy tales from Norway or from the Brothers Grimm, Beatrix Potter stories, and absurdist fables such as Hilaire Belloc's *Cautionary Tales*. He also began concocting narratives of his own.' (Chapter 13, 'The Master of the Macabre').

p. 251: Roald Dahl's 'night owl' motto features in the Puffin Passport at the back of the 50th-anniversary 'golden ticket', 2014 edition of *Charlie and the Chocolate Factory* (1964).

pp. 251–252: Roald Dahl's selling his short story 'Bedtime' is recounted in Sturrock (Chapter 9, 'A Sort of Fairy Story').

p. 252: Roald Dahl's description of his relationship with his mother appears in *Memories with Food at Gipsy House* (1991), co-written with his wife, Felicity.

5. Be Not Afeard

p. 274: For more on the pineal gland seek out Jeff Iliff's 2014 TED Talk, *One More Reason to Get a Good Night's Sleep*.

René Descartes posited that the pineal gland performed the role of internal clock in the seventeenth century, referring to it in his first and last works, *Treatise of Man* (written before 1637) and *The Passions of the Soul* (1649), and calling it 'the principal seat of the soul and the place in which all our thoughts are formed.'

p. 275: Those innovative Dutch retirement homes feature in the BBC *Horizon* documentary, *The Secret Life of Your Body Clock* (2009), which includes an interview with Eus Van Someren, the pioneering Sleep Professor who masterminded this raising of light levels during daytime, and who also set up a national Sleep Registry in Holland.

p. 276: 'Friendly dream-diarists' include, notably, Graham Greene. His final published work, posthumously, was a memoir told via his dreams, called *A World of My Own* (1992, Reinhard Books/Viking). Greene fashioned the book from over 800 pages of dream diaries, kept from 1965 through to 1989, describing it in his introduction as 'in a sense . . . an autobiography'. Its epigraph is taken from the writing of Heraclitus of Ephesus, 500 BC: 'The waking have one world in common, but the sleeping turn aside each into a world of his own.'

p. 281: For more on Katie Paterson's *Future Library* Project, including filmed interviews with Paterson and Margaret Atwood, visit www.futurelibrary.no

6. Tread Softly

p. 315: As regards babies and sleep – melatonin is passed to the foetus through the placenta, and so even when cocooned within a womb, a biochemical light-dark cycle is being established within each of us. Once born, babies receive melatonin through breast milk. At two weeks, half of a baby's sleep episode consists of REM sleep (as opposed to a quarter for a grown-up) and, by two months, a 24-hour cycle is becoming established.

p. 400: William Maxwell's description of his 'improvisations' is taken from his own Preface to his collected short stories, *All the Days and Nights* (1997, Harvill Panther).

7. Ashore

p. 407: The history of alarm clocks is charted more extensively – alongside superstitions regarding headrests and bedstead rituals in animals – by Paul Martin in Chapter 16 ('And So to Bed') of his indispensable *Counting Sheep: The Science and Pleasures of Sleep and Dreams* (2003, Flamingo).

p. 410: The full text of Seamus Heaney's 'Crediting Poetry' address can be found in *Nobel Lectures: 20 Years of the Nobel Prize for Literature Lectures* (2007, Icon).

p. 419: Richard Ford's observation about 'bad events' is made in his novel *Canada* (2012, Bloomsbury).

Author Biographies

NB: The biographies of those authors – such as Billy Collins and Robert Macfarlane – whose work appears in this volume, but who have themselves also contributed a choice of bedtime story, can be found alongside their choices.

A. Alvarez (1929–) is a British poet, novelist, literary critic, anthologist and author of non-fiction books on diverse topics ranging from suicide, divorce and dreams – *The Savage God* (1972), *Life After Marriage* (1982), *Night* (1995, from which this anthology's extract is taken) – to poker and mountaineering – *The Biggest Game in Town* (1983) and *Feeding the Rat* (1989). His most recent book is *Pondlife: A Swimmer's Journal* (2013).

Margaret Atwood (1939–) is a Canadian novelist, poet and activist. Her novels include *The Handmaid's Tale* (1985), *Cat's Eye* (1988), *Alias Grace* (1996), *The Blind Assassin*, which won the 2000 Booker Prize, and *Oryx and Crake* (2003). Her short-story collections include *Good Bones*, which features 'Adventure Story', and she has also published seven books for children.

Nicholson Baker (1957–) is the American author of *The Mezzanine* (1988), *Vox* (1992), *The Fermata* (1994) and two books narrated by a poet, *The Anthologist* (2009) and *Traveling Sprinkler* (2013). Among his non-fiction works are *U and I* (1991), *Double Fold* (2001) and *Human Smoke* (2008).

J. G. Ballard (1930–2009) was born in Shanghai, interned in a Japanese prison camp from 1943 to 1945 and arrived in England in 1946. He published his first novel, *The Drowned World*, in 1962, and his last, *Kingdom Come*, in 2006. Alongside his short story collections – such as *The Disaster Area* (1967), which features this anthology's story, 'Now Wakes the Sea' – his many novels include *Crash* (1973), *High Rise* (1975), *Empire of the Sun* (1984) and *Cocaine Nights* (1996). His autobiography, *Miracles of Life*, was published in 2008.

Nicola Barker (1966–) was born in Ely, Cambridgeshire. Her eight novels include *Wide Open* (1998), *Darkmans* (2007) and *The Yips* (2012). Her award-winning short-story collections include *Love Your Enemies* (1993), in which 'Dual Balls' appears, and *Heading Inland* (1996).

J. M. Barrie (1860–1937), born in Kirriemuir, Scotland, was inspired to write the story of Peter Pan by his relationship with the sons of Arthur and Sylvia Llewelyn Davies, friends of his while living beside Kensington Gardens in London. The idea of Pan first emerged in the novel *The Little White Bird* (1902), the Peter Pan episode which was reprinted as *Peter Pan in Kensington Gardens* (1906), later adapted for the stage in 1904 to great success, and expanded into the novel *Peter and Wendy* in 1911. His other notable works include the plays *Quality Street* (1901), *The Admirable Crichton* (1902) and *Dear Brutus* (1917).

Hilaire Belloc (1870–1953) was a British writer and poet, born in St Cloud, near Paris. He is today best known for his nonsensical verse for children, *The Bad Child's Book of Beasts* (1896) and the

Cautionary Tales for Children (1907), but also wrote numerous travel books, historical studies and religious books, as well as serving as an MP for the Liberal Party between 1906 and 1910.

Wendell Berry (1934–) was born in Kentucky, where he still lives and tends a hillside farm in his native Henry County. He is the author of over 40 books, including the novel *Hannah Coulter* (2004), the essay collections *Citizenship Papers* (2003) and *The Way of Ignorance* (2005), and *Given: Poems* (2005).

William Blake (1757–1827) was an English poet, painter and engraver. Blake did not go to school in London, where he grew up, but was apprenticed to an engraver. He went on to study at the Royal Academy and published his first collection of poems in 1783, *Political Sketches*. His 'illuminated books' interwove text with his own imaginative engravings: such works include *Songs of Innocence* (1789) and *Songs of Experience* (1794). Other writings include *The Marriage of Heaven and Hell* (1793) and *Jerusalem* (1804–1820). His notable other designs include the 537 coloured illustrations to Edward Young's *Night Thoughts* (1797).

Jorge Luis Borges (1899–1986) considered *Dreamtigers*, the collection eponymous with the poem included herein, to be his most personal work. Published in 1960, it is also known as *The Maker*. The Argentine's seminal works are *Fictions* and *The Aleph*, both published in the 1940s and then in English translation during the 1960s, compilations of short stories interconnected by common themes, notably dreams. Borges' first publication was aged nine: a Spanish translation of Oscar Wilde's story 'The Happy Prince', for a Buenos Aires newspaper.

Humphrey Carpenter (1946–2005) was a writer and journalist. He wrote many books, including *Secret Gardens* (1991) about the golden age of children's literature, and biographies of Tolkien (1977, as extracted in this collection), *The Inklings, W. H. Auden, Ezra Pound, Benjamin Britten,* and *Spike Milligan.* His *Mr Majeika* series of books for young children still enjoys considerable popularity. He wrote, with his wife Mari Prichard, the first edition of *The Oxford Companion to Children's Literature* (1984), later comprehensively revised and updated by Daniel Hahn.

Angela Carter (1940–1992) was a British writer whose novels included *The Magic Toyshop* (1967), *Several Perceptions* (1968), *Nights at the Circus* (1984) and *Wise Children* (1991). Her collection of short stories *The Bloody Chamber* (1979) is a series of retellings of classic fairy tales in her own words, designed to 'extract the latent content from the traditional stories'. She also published a translation of Charles Perrault's fairy tales in 1974. The collection *Angela Carter's Book of Fairy Tales* was originally published as *The Virago Book of Fairy Tales* and today bills itself as 'Angela Carter's pick of Mother Goose's feathers'.

Jimmy Carter (1924–) is the 39th President of the United States. After serving in the US Navy, he took over the family business of peanut farming in Georgia. He became Governor of Georgia (1970–74) and was elected President in 1977, serving until 1981. A prolific human-rights campaigner, Carter received the Nobel Peace Prize in 2002. His books include the memoirs, *Keeping Faith* (1982) and *A Full Life: Reflections at Ninety* (2015). The statement included in this anthology, and carried aboard the *Voyager* spacecraft, was delivered in electronic impulses that could subsequently be transcribed into words.

Charles Causley (1917–2003) was a Cornish poet whose work was not only rooted in Cornwall's landscape and tradition but also informed by his long experience as a primary-school teacher (he taught until 1976), a pursuit that led to much of his writing being for or about children. He is famed for his ballads and much of his work concerns innocence, as a theme. Causley's collections include *Farewell, Aggie Weston* (1951), *Survivor's Leave* (1953), *Johnny Alleluia* (1961) and *A Field of Vision* (1988).

Anton Chekhov (1860–1904) studied medicine at Moscow University and qualified as a doctor in 1884, but wrote stories and sketches throughout his studies. His first book, *Motley Stories*, was published in 1886. His first full-length play, *Ivanov*, was written in 1887, while still a practising doctor. It failed, however, as did *The Seagull* (1896). Chekhov concentrated on short stories instead thereafter but was persuaded to return to drama, with success, by Stanislavsky. He went on to write *Uncle Vanya* (1897), *Three Sisters* (1901), and *The Cherry Orchard* (1904) for the Moscow Art Theatre. The bulk of his many short stories were first translated into English in thirteen volumes, *The Tales of Tchehov*, between 1916 and 1922.

Leonard Cohen (1934–) is a novelist, poet, painter and musician. He was born in Montreal. His artistic career began in 1956 with the publication of his first book of poetry, *Let Us Compare Mythologies*. Since then he has published fifteen books, including two novels, *The Favourite Game* (1963) and *Beautiful Losers* (1966), and volumes of poetry, such as *Stranger Music: Selected Poems and Songs* (1993) and *The Book of Longing* (2006). He has made thirteen studio albums, ranging from 1967's *Songs of Leonard Cohen* to *Popular Problems* in 2014. He lived on the Greek island of Hydra during much of the 1960s, providing the inspiration for 'Dusko's Taverna, 1967'.

Wendy Cope (1945–) is a British poet who has published four collections of adult poetry – *Making Cocoa for Kingsley Amis* (1986),

Serious Concerns (1992), *If I Don't Know* (2001) and *Family Values* (2011) – as well as two books of poetry for children and several anthologies. Her prose publications include *Life, Love and The Archers* (2014), in which the piece 'By Chance', first published in the *Daily Telegraph*, appears.

Michael Cunningham (1952–) is the author of seven novels, including *A Home at the End of the World* (1990), *Flesh and Blood* (1995), *The Hours* (1998, winner of the Pulitzer Prize and PEN/ Faulkner Award), *Specimen Days* (2005), *By Nightfall* (2010) and *The Snow Queen* (2014). His story 'Jacked' is taken from the collection *A Wild Swan and Other Tales* (2015), a series of 'fairy tales for our times'. He has also published *Land's End: A Walk in Provincetown* and is a senior lecturer at Yale University.

Roald Dahl (1916–1994) was born in Cardiff to Norwegian parents. His stories are currently available in 59 languages. UK sales alone of his works are over 50 million and rising, with global sales estimated to be more than 200 million copies sold. As well as his classic children's books – such as *Charlie and the Chocolate Factory* (1964), *Fantastic Mr Fox* (1970), *The BFG* (1982), *The Witches* (1983) and *Matilda* (1988) – Dahl wrote many short stories for adult readers, in collections such as *Someone Like You* (1953), *Kiss Kiss* (1960), *Switch Bitch* (1974) and *Tales of the Unexpected* (1979). His story 'Only This', which features here, appeared in his first collection of stories, *Over to You: Ten Stories of Flyers and Flying* (1946).

Lydia Davis (1947–) is the author of, among other titles, *The Collected Stories of Lydia Davis*, a translation of Flaubert's *Madame Bovary* and a chapbook entitled *The Cows*. In 2013, she was awarded the Man Booker International Prize for Fiction. Her most recent collection of stories is *Can't and Won't*. 'Happiest Moment' first appeared in her collection, *Samuel Johnson Is Indignant* (2001).

Thomas Dekker (1572–1632) wrote extensively about London, where he mainly lived. He collaborated with many contemporaries on various plays, such as *The Honest Whore* and *The Roaring Girl* (with Thomas Middleton, 1604 and 1605), *Westward Ho* (with John Webster, 1604) and *The Witch of Edmonton* (with John Ford and William Rowley, 1621). He was imprisoned several times for debt and Dekker's experiences in prison are evoked in the prose works *Lanthorn and Candle-Light* (1608) and *Dekker His Dream* (1620). The poem 'Golden Slumbers', which inspired the Beatles song of the same title, appeared in his 1603 comedy, *Patient Grissel*.

Charles Dickens (1812–1870) worked as a reporter of debates at the House of Commons, before publishing his collected *Sketches by Boz* (Boz being his younger brother's nickname) in 1836. He would write prolifically from then until the end of his life, from *The Pickwick Papers* (1836) to *The Mystery of Edwin Drood* (1870), which he was writing the day he died suddenly at his home Gads Hill, near Rochester, a property he had coveted as young boy.

Nora Ephron (1941–2012) was an American journalist, author, screenwriter and director. She was nominated for an Academy Award three times, for her original screenplays *Silkwood* (1984), *When Harry Met Sally* (1990) and *Sleepless in Seattle* (1994). Her other writing includes the novel *Heartburn* (1984) and non-fiction collections *Wallflower at the Orgy* (1970), *I Feel Bad About My Neck* (2006) and *I Remember Nothing: And Other Reflections* (2010), in which 'Who Are You' was published.

James Fenton (1949–) is an English poet, journalist and literary critic. He was Oxford Professor of Poetry 1994–99. His collections include *Terminal Moraine* (1972), *Manila Envelope* (1989) and *Out of Danger* (1994), in which 'Fireflies of the Sea' was first published. His collected poems, *Yellow Tulips*, was published in 2015. Fenton's awards include the Queen's Gold Medal for Poetry (2007) and the PEN Pinter Prize (2015).

Robert Frost (1874–1963) was born in San Francisco. He failed to graduate from Harvard University and took up work instead as a teacher, cobbler and New England farmer, all the while writing poetry that was rejected for publication. In 1912, he came to England, where he befriended poet Edward Thomas, whom he would later describe as 'the only brother I ever had'. Encouraged in his writings while in England by poets such as Rupert Brooke, Frost soon published *A Boy's Will* (1913), to immediate acclaim. Subsequent volumes of poetry include *West-Running Brook* (1928), *A Witness Tree* (1942) and *In the Clearing* (1962). 'After Apple Picking' was published in *North of Boston* (1914). Frost won four Pulitzer Prizes and eventually returned to Harvard, 1939–43, as Professor of Poetry.

Neil Gaiman (1960–) is an English-born, now US-resident author of over thirty acclaimed novels and graphic novels. His first novel was *Good Omens* (1990), a collaboration with Terry Pratchett. Notable subsequent novels include *Neverwhere* (1996), *Stardust* (1999), *American Gods* (2001), *Coraline* (2003), *The Graveyard Book* (2008, inspired by Rudyard Kipling's *Jungle Book*, and the first work to be awarded both the Newbery and Carnegie Medals for Children's Literature) and *The Ocean at the End of the Lane* (2013). 'Diamonds and Pearls: A Fairy Tale' was first published in *Who Killed Amanda Palmer: A Collection of Photographic Evidence* (2008), a collaboration with Gaiman's future wife, and reprinted in his short-story collection *Trigger Warning* (2015).

Louise Glück (1943–) has published sixteen collections of poetry, including *The Triumph of Achilles* (1985), *The Wild Iris* (1992) and *Faithful and Virtuous Night* (2014). Her collections' numerous awards include multiple National Book Awards for Poetry and also the Pulitzer Prize. She teaches at Yale University and was appointed the US Poet Laureate from 2003–2004, succeeding Billy Collins. Her poem 'Evening Star' first appeared in *Averno* (2006).

The Brothers Grimm were **Jacob** (1785–1863) and **Wilhelm Grimm** (1786–1859). They were born in Hanau, Germany, and developed a love of folklore while studying together at the University of Marburg. Their first collection of folk tales, *Nursery and Household Tales*, was published in 1812. The Brothers revised and republished the collection many times, 86 stories swelling to more than 200. Those stories included 'Cinderella', 'Snow White', 'Sleeping Beauty', 'Rapunzel', 'Rumpelstiltskin' and 'Hansel and Gretel'.

Thom Gunn (1929–2004) was born in England but emigrated to the United States in 1954. His many collections of poetry include *Touch* (1967), *Jack Straw's Castle* (1976), *The Passages of Joy* (1982), *The Man with Night Sweats* (1992, a series of elegies related to the AIDS crisis, which includes 'The Hug') and his final collection, *Boss Cupid* (2000).

Ivor Gurney (1890–1937) was born in Gloucester, the son of a tailor. He wrote two volumes of verse, *Severn and Somme* (1917) and *War's Embers* (1919). He composed two A. E. Housman song cycles and also set six Edward Thomas poems to music, including the poem in this anthology, 'Lights Out' (1918–25). Gurney was very unsettled after the war and would sleep rough frequently, as well as take night walks back to Gloucestershire from London, as recalled in this anthology's extract from Robert Macfarlane's *The Wild Places*. By the time of his death, he had composed nearly 300 songs and 1,700 poems.

Nathaniel Hawthorne (1804–1864) was born in Salem, Massachusetts. Hawthorne was descended directly from John Hathorne, the only judge of the Salem witch trials not to repent subsequently his verdict. The author added a 'w' to his surname, Hathorne, to distance himself from this relative. His first book was a collection of stories, *Twice-Told Tales*. His novel, *The Scarlet Letter* (1850), was one of the first mass-produced books in the United States, and was followed by, among other works, *The House of the Seven Gables* (1851) and *A Wonder-Book for Boys and Girls* (1851), a book of retold myths.

Seamus Heaney (1939–2013) published twelve volumes of original poems, including *Seeing Things* (1991), in which 'The Rescue' featured. His other works include several books of critical essays, drama and translations, including 2016's posthumous *The Aeneid: Book IV* (2016). He was awarded the 1995 Nobel Prize for Literature.

Ted Hughes (1930–1998) was born in Yorkshire. His first collection of poetry, *The Hawk in the Rain*, was published in 1957. He went on to publish many volumes of both poetry and prose. His works for children include *The Iron Man* (1968). Later works include *Tales from Ovid* (1997) and *Birthday Letters* (1998), the cover for which was designed by his daughter, Frieda. The poem in this collection, 'Full Moon and Little Frieda', was first published in *Wodwo* (1967). Hughes was Poet Laureate from 1984 until his death.

Washington Irving (1783–1859), born in New York, trained as a lawyer before turning to writing. He visited Britain in 1815, where Walter Scott encouraged Irving to publish *The Sketch Book* in 1819–20, which featured picturesque sketches of English life and American adaptations of German folk tales, such as 'Rip Van

Winkle' and 'The Legend of Sleepy Hollow'. The book made Irving a celebrity, and he returned to America in 1832 as the first American author to have achieved international fame. From 1842 to 1846, he was American Ambassador to Spain, and his later works include a five-volume life of George Washington (1855–9).

Shirley Jackson (1916–1965) was an American author who found fame after the publication in *The New Yorker* of her macabre short story 'The Lottery', in 1948. Her subsequent novels include *The Haunting of Hill House* (1959), extracted here and twice filmed for cinema, and *We Have Always Lived in the Castle* (1962). Jackson also wrote a children's novel, *Nine Magic Wishes* (1963), available in an edition illustrated by her grandson, Miles Hyman, as well as a children's play based on 'Hansel and Gretel', entitled *The Bad Children* (1959).

Tove Jansson (1914–2001) was a Finnish writer and artist. Best known as the creator of the *Moomin* stories, she also wrote ten novels for adults, including *The Summer Book* (1972). Her story 'Flying' appeared in the semi-autobiographical collection of short stories, *Sculptor's Daughter* (1968). She was awarded the Hans Christian Andersen Medal for her children's writing in 1966.

Myesha Jenkins (1948–) is an American writer and performer of poetry. Her two collections are *Breaking the Surface* (2005) and *Dreams of Flight* (2011). In 2013, she was awarded a Mbokodo Award for Women in the Arts.

Elizabeth Jennings (1926–2001) was an English poet and critic who published her first collection, *Poems*, in 1953. Over 30 collections followed, among them *Song for a Birth or a Death* (1961), *Growing Points* (1975) and *Praises* (1998). She also wrote two volumes of prose and several collections of poetry for children.

Brian Keenan (1950–) was born in Belfast. He left his hometown in 1985 to take up a teaching position in the American University in Beirut, Lebanon. In April 1986, he was abducted by an Islamic fundamentalist jihad organization, which held him captive until August 1990. He recounted the years in captivity in *An Evil Cradling* (1992). Keenan later wrote *Between Extremes* with his former cellmate, John McCarthy, a chronicle of their journey to Chile, a trip that they had planned while hostages. Keenan's other books include a novel, *Turlough* (2000).

Jane Kenyon (1947–1995) was an American poet and translator. Four collections of Kenyon's poems were published during her lifetime: *From Room to Room* (1978), *The Boat of Quiet Hours* (1986), *Let Evening Come* (1990) and *Constance* (1993).

Rudyard Kipling (1865–1936) was born in Bombay, India, but spent most of his life in England. He was awarded the Nobel Prize for Literature in 1907 for his poetry and prose – works that continue to enthral readers of all ages, from poetry collections such as *Barrack Room Ballads* (1892) to the two *Jungle Books* (1894–5), *Kim* (1901), *Just So Stories* (1902), *Rewards and Fairies* (1910) and the autobiographical *Something of Myself* (1937). The character of Hobden, who appears in his verse story 'The Land', first showed up as a hedger in *Puck of Pook's Hill* (1907), and the poem itself appears at the end of a short story in his collection *A Diversity of Creatures* (1917).

Charles Lamb (1775–1834) was an author, poet and critic, who worked for most of his life as a clerk at East India House in London. In 1796, his sister Mary stabbed their mother to death during an episode of mania. Charles's guardianship of his sister was accepted by the authorities. Together, they went on to write *Tales from Shakespeare* (1807), for younger readers, which found success, as well as a number of children's books, including *Mrs Leicester's School* (1809). Charles Lamb published his collected verse and prose in two volumes, *The Work of Charles Lamb* (1820).

Edward Lear (1812–1888) was born in London, the youngest of 20 children, but spent his later life in Italy. He travelled widely under the 13th Earl of Derby's patronage, publishing *Sketches of Rome* (1842) and *Illustrated Excursions in Italy* (1846). He became a close friend to his patron's grandchildren, for whom he wrote and illustrated *A Book of Nonsense* (1845, published anonymously). Other such works followed: *Nonsense Songs, Stories, Botany and Alphabets* (1871), which contains 'The Owl and The Pussycat', *More Nonsense Rhymes* (1871) and *Laughable Lyrics* (1877).

Colum McCann (1965–) was born in Dublin. His novels include *Dancer* (2003), *Let the Great World Spin*, winner of the 2009 National Book Award, and *Transatlantic* (2013). He has also written two collections of stories. He is the co-founder of the non-profit global story-exchange organization, Narrative 4, and is Professor of Creative Writing at Hunter College, New York. 'The Word Shed' was first published in *The New Yorker* in 2014.

Stéphane Mallarmé (1842–1898) taught English in schools in Paris, before his poetry made him a leading figure for both the Structuralist and Symbolist literary movements. He translated Edgar Allan Poe's *The Raven* before writing 'A Faun's Afternoon' (1876), later set to music by Claude Debussy. His influential works include *Poésies* (1887) and *Vers et Prose* (1893).

Katherine Mansfield (1888–1923) was born and raised in Wellington but left to study in London during 1903. Bar one spell studying music back home, Mansfield never revisited New Zealand. Her first collection of stories, *In a German Pension* (1911), was inspired by her own experiences of giving birth to a stillborn child conceived by a man other than her husband (whom she had left immediately after their wedding ceremony). She published two other collections of short stories before her untimely death due to tuberculosis: *Bliss, and Other Stories* (1920) and *The Garden Party, and Other Stories* (1922). Posthumous collections include *Something Childish, and Other Stories* (1924).

Walter de la Mare (1873–1956) was an English poet, short-story writer and novelist. His first written work, published after years of working for an oil company, appeared to little fanfare in 1902: *Songs of Childhood* (under the name Walter Ramal). He is perhaps best remembered for his works for children, such as the anthology *Come Hither* (1923), and for supernatural short stories, among them 'Seaton's Aunt' and 'All Hallows'. His 1921 novel *Memoirs of a Midget* won the James Tait Black Memorial Prize for fiction and his *Collected Stories for Children* won the 1947 Carnegie Medal for Children's Literature.

Guy de Maupassant (1850–1893) was born in the Norman château of Miromesnil, near Dieppe. He worked as a government clerk before taking to writing at the encouragement of Gustave Flaubert, who was a friend of his mother's. Maupassant earned a reputation in the English-speaking world as the 'French Chekhov' with his nearly 300 short stories, translations of which appeared from 1887. His novels include *Une Vie* or *A Woman's Life* (1883) and *Bel-Ami* (1885).

William Maxwell (1908–2000) was born in Illinois. He was the author of six novels, three short-story collections, an autobiographical memoir and a collection of literary essays and reviews. He also wrote two books for children, including *The Heavenly Tenants* (1946), in which the constellations of the zodiac spring to life. A *New Yorker* editor for 40 years, he became a mentor to many of the most prominent authors of his day (such as John Updike, Vladimir Nabokov and John O'Hara). His novel, *So Long, See You Tomorrow*, won the American Book Award and in 1995, he received the PEN/Malamud Award. The story included in this anthology, 'All the days and all the nights', was first published on the occasion of his 80th birthday.

Czełsaw Miłosz (1911–2004) was born on the Polish–Lithuanian border of Vilnius and fought for the Resistance in Warsaw during the Second World War. He eventually settled, after the war, in California, where he taught at Berkeley, and became a US citizen in 1970. His works include the poetry collections *Poem on Time Frozen* (1933) and *Three Winters* (1936), as well as various novels, many essays and *The Captive Mind* (1953), an apologia for his withdrawal from Poland. He was awarded the Nobel Prize in 1980 and eventually moved back to Europe, living in Cracow. 'Ars Poetica?' first appeared in *City Without a Name* (1969).

William Morris (1834–1896) was an English craftsman, poet and socialist. A professional painter from 1857–1862, Morris was part of the Pre-Raphaelite Brotherhood. He went on to design furniture and revolutionized design and the art of decoration in England. His best-known literary works include *The Earthly Paradise* (1868–1870) and a four-volume epic saga, *The Story of Sigurd the Volsung and the Fall of the Nibelungs* (1876), as well poetic works such as *Love is Enough* (1972) and translations of both Virgil's Aenied (1875) and Homer's *Odyssey* (1887).

Haruki Murakami (1949–) was born in Kyoto, Japan, the only child of Japanese literature teachers. His notable works include *A Wild Sheep Chase* (1982), *Norwegian Wood* (1987), *The Wind-Up Bird Chronicle* (1995), *Kafka on the Shore* (2002) and *1Q84* (2009).

He has also translated English works into Japanese, ranging from Raymond Chandler to J. D. Salinger. His short-story collections include *The Elephant Vanishes* (1993) and *Blind Willow, Sleeping Woman* (2006). 'Scheherazade' was first published in English in the 13 October 2014, issue of *The New Yorker*.

Les Murray (1938–) grew up on a dairy farm at Bunyah on the north coast of New South Wales, Australia. He made literature his full-time career from 1971, having worked as a translator and as a civil servant. Since then, he has published two verse novels, collections of prose writings, and over 30 collections of poetry. He has won prizes including the T. S. Eliot Prize, the Petrarch Prize and The Queen's Gold Medal for Poetry.

Vladimir Nabokov (1899–1977) was born in St Petersburg. He was trilingual from a young age, speaking Russian, English and French fluently; the first book he recalled his mother reading to him was in English, *Misunderstood* (1869) by Florence Montgomery. A prolific writer of novels, short stories, plays and poems in the Russian language, he emigrated to the United States in 1940, after which he wrote in English. His Russian novels include *The Luzhin Defense* (1930) and *The Gift* (1938); his English fiction includes *Lolita* (1955), *Pale Fire* (1962) and *Ada* (1969). His translations include *Eugene Onegin* into English and *Alice in Wonderland* into Russian. His memoir *Speak, Memory* was published in 1951.

Dorthe Nors (1970–) is the Danish author of a celebrated short-story collection, *Karate Chop* (2008), as well as one novella and five novels, including *Mirror, Shoulder, Signal* (2016).

B. J. Novak (1979–) is an American actor, stand-up comedian and writer. He is perhaps best known for his work on the Emmy Award-winning comedy series *The Office*. His books include 2014's

The Book with No Pictures and *One More Thing: Stories and Other Stories,* in which 'The Rematch' appears.

Bernard O'Donoghue (1945–) is an Irish poet and academic, who is an Emeritus fellow at Wadham College, Oxford. His poetry collections include *Gunpowder* (1995, which won the Whitbread Prize for Poetry and in which his poem 'Stealing Away' first appeared), *Here Nor There* (1999), *Outliving* (2003), *Farmers Cross* (2011) and *The Seasons of Cullen Church* (2016). His verse translation of *Sir Gawain and the Green Knight* was published in 2006.

John O'Hara (1905–1970) was born in Pottsville, Pennsylvania, which in his fiction becomes 'Gibbsville', the setting for his first novel, among others, *Appointment in Samarra* (1934). His second novel, *Butterfield 8* (1935), was set in New York, and much of his work would shuttle between the two locales. He published 15 more novels, as well as 247 stories in *The New Yorker*, a tally that still remains a record.

Ben Okri (1959–) is a Nigerian-born, UK-resident novelist and poet. He won the 1991 Booker Prize for his third novel, *The Famished Road*, the first volume of an African trilogy continued in *Songs of Enchantment* (1993) and *Infinite Riches* (1998). His other novels include *Starbook* (2007) and *The Age of Magic* (2014). He has also published poetry, essays and short-story collections, including *Tales of Freedom* (2009), in which 'The Message' appears.

Sharon Olds (1942–) is an American poet whose twelve collections include *Satan Says* (1980), *The Dead and the Living* (1984), *The Wellspring* (1996) and *Stag's Leap* (2012), which won both the Pulitzer and T. S. Eliot Prizes. Olds was New York State Poet Laureate 1998–2000 and is currently a professor at New York University.

Michael Ondaatje (1943–) is a Sri-Lankan-born, Canadian novelist and poet. His six novels include *The English Patient*, which won the 1992 Booker Prize, *Anil's Ghost* (2000) and *Cat's Table* (2011). He has also published numerous poetry collections and edited various anthologies. His memoir, *Running in the Family*, in which 'Harbour' appears, was published in 1982.

Joseph O'Neill (1964–) is an Irish-born, New York-resident novelist. *Netherland*, from which the excerpt in this anthology is taken, was published in 2008. His other novels include *The Dog* (2014). He has also written a work of non-fiction, *Blood-Dark Track: A Family History* (2001), and teaches at Bard College in New York.

Sylvia Plath (1932–1963) was born in Boston, Massachusetts. She moved to Cambridge after winning a Fulbright Fellowship at Newnham College, where she met and married fellow poet, Ted Hughes, in 1956. Plath wrote poetry from a young age and published her first volume, *A Winter Ship*, anonymously in 1960. She put her name to her second collection, *The Colossus and Other Poems* (1960), but her only novel, *The Bell Jar* (1963), was published under the pseudonym Victoria Lucas. Plath committed suicide less than a month after the book's publication. Her posthumous publications include *Ariel* (1965), *Crossing the Water* (1971), *Winter Trees* (1972) and *Johnny Panic and the Bible of Dreams* (1977).

Terry Pratchett (1948–2015) was born in Beaconsfield and was an only child, a status he celebrated in many of his stories, once observing, 'in fiction, only-children are the interesting ones'. His first novel was for children, *The Carpet People* in 1971. *The Colour of Magic* (1983) was the first book in his landmark *Discworld* Series. The series would comprise 41 novels by 2015, the year of his death. Other novels include *Good Omens* (1990), a collaboration with Neil Gaiman, and *Nation* (2008). He was appointed KBE in 2009.

Philip Pullman (1946–) is the British author of the fantasist *His Dark Materials* trilogy and winner of the Carnegie Medal, the Whitbread Prize and the Astrid Lindgren Memorial Award. *Northern Lights* (1995, titled *The Golden Compass* in the US) was voted winner of the 'Carnegie of Carnegies', to commemorate the medal's 70th anniversary. He is also the author of the *Sally Lockhart* series of children's books (1985–1994), and *The Firework-Maker's Daughter* (1995), *The Good Man Jesus and the Scoundrel Christ* (2010) and *Grimm Tales for Young and Old* (2012).

Jean Rhys (1890–1979) was born and raised in Dominica but was resident in England from the age of sixteen; yet it was in Paris, under the encouragement of Ford Madox Ford, that she published her first writings, the collection of stories called *The Left Bank and Other Stories* (1927). Her subsequent novels include *Voyage in the Dark* (1934) and *Good Morning, Midnight* (1939). None was successful and, after the Second World War, Rhys dropped out of sight and was widely thought to have died. Yet, in 1966, she published *Wide Sargasso Sea*, which won several awards. Her final collection of stories, *Sleep It Off, Lady*, which includes 'On Not Shooting Sitting Birds', was published in 1976.

Adrienne Rich (1929–2012) was born in Baltimore. Her father, a renowned pathologist, encouraged her to write poetry at a young age and she learned a love of literature from the shelves of his library, which included volumes of Blake, Keats, Rossetti and Tennyson. Her 25 award-winning poetry collections include *Diving into the Wreck* (1972), for which she won the National Book Award. A prominent feminist, Rich's various non-fiction works include 1976's *Of Woman Born: Motherhood as Experience* *and Institution.* Her poem, 'Dreamwood', first appeared in *Time's Power: Poems 1985–1988*, and will be appearing in the forthcoming *Collected Poems 1950–2012*.

Tim Robinson (1935–) was born in Yorkshire, studied mathematics at Cambridge and taught it in Istanbul, then pursued a career as an avant-garde artist in Vienna and London. In 1972, he removed to the Aran Islands off the west coast of Ireland. He has published books on the largest of the islands, and also subsequent works on Connemara and a translation (in collaboration with Liam Mac Con Iomaire) of the Irish-language modernist novel *Cré na Cille*, published as *Graveyard Clay*. His maps of the Aran Islands, the Burren and Connemara are published by Folding Landscapes, Roundstone, Co. Galway, a small press founded by Robinson and his partner, M.

Theodore Roethke (1908–1963) was an American poet and translator, born in Michigan. His first collection of poems, *Open House* (1941), was rooted in childhood memories of the greenhouses of his father, a florist. Subsequent publications include *The Lost Son and Other Poems* (1948), *Praise to the End!* (1951) and *The Waking* (1953), which won the Pulitzer Prize and brought his poetry wider renown. A book of light verse and nonsense poetry followed: *I Am! Says The Lamb* (1961).

Dante Gabriel Rossetti (1828–1882) was an English poet, painter and translator who formed the Pre-Raphaelite Brotherhood, with William Holman Hunt and John Everett Millais. His verse translations include *The Early Italian Poets* (1861). Several of his poems appeared in the 1850 collection *The Germ*, including the work 'My Sister's Sleep', and later works include *Ballads and Sonnets* (1881). 'Nuptial Sleep' appeared in his sonnet cycle *The House of Life* (1870), its eroticism causing controversy among critics. His artwork can be viewed in galleries and museums such as Tate Britain and the Victoria and Albert Museum, which houses his famous painting, 'The Day Dream'.

Antoine de Saint-Exupéry (1900–1944) was born in Lyon. He learnt to fly in 1921 and soon thereafter joined the French Air Force. In 1931, he published *Night Flight* (*Vol de Nuit*), which established his literary reputation. In 1935, while trying to break the speed record from Paris to Saigon, he crashed in the African desert and almost died of thirst. This was recounted in *Wind, Sand and Stars* (*Terre des Hommes*, 1939). Saint-Exupéry wrote and illustrated *The Little Prince* while living in New York during 1942. Since translated into more than 250 languages, it has become one of the best-selling books ever published. Saint-Exupéry frequently read and wrote while flying, sometimes delaying landing to finish a book. He flew reconnaissance during the Second World War and it was on one such mission during July 1944 that he disappeared, presumed dead.

William Shakespeare (1564–1616) employed imagery of sleep perhaps most prevalently, of all his works, in *Macbeth* (as my dad observed in his 1999 biography). The unmanning of Macbeth during the course of the play, to the point where he receives the news of his wife's death with fatalistic resignation, is measured in terms of increasingly guilty fear – itself in turn charted by his lack of that 'season of all natures', sleep:

> Methought I heard a voice cry, 'Sleep no more!
> Macbeth does murder sleep' – the innocent sleep,
> Sleep that knits up the travell'd sleeve of care,
> The death of each day's life, sore labour's bath,
> Balm of hurt minds, great nature's second course,
> Chief nourisher in life's feast . . .

Charles Simic (1938–) is a Serbian-American poet, translator, essayist and philosopher who has served both as poetry editor of the *Paris Review* and as United States Poet Laureate (appointed 2007). He won the Pulitzer Prize for his collection of prose poems, *The World Doesn't End* (1989). He has published many poetry collections, from 1967's *What the Grass Says* to 2015's *The Lunatic*.

Isaac Bashevis Singer (1904–1991) was brought up in Radzymin, Poland, the son and grandson of rabbis, and much of his novels and short stories are set among the Jewish communities of Poland, Germany and the USA, to where he emigrated in 1935. His novels include *The Family Moskat* (1950), *The Magician of Lublin* (1960) and *Enemies: a Love Story* (1972). He also wrote a play, *Schlemiel the First* (1974), and many stories for children. 'The Re-Encounter' first appeared in the *Atlantic*. Singer was awarded the Nobel Prize for literature in 1978.

Muriel Spark (1918–2006), novelist and poet, was born and educated in Edinburgh, where she attended James Gillespie's High School for Girls, immortalized in her best-known novel, *The Prime of Miss Jean Brodie* (1961). Her other novels include *The Comforters* (1957), *Memento Mori* (1959), *The Girls of Slender Means* (1963), *Loitering with Intent* (1981) and *Aiding and Abetting* (2000). She published a memoir, *Curriculum Vitae,* in 1992 and was appointed DBE the following year.

A. E. Stallings (1968–) is an American-born, Athens-resident poet and translator. She has published three books of poetry: *Archaic Smile* (1999), *Hapax* (2006) and *Olives* (2012).

Robert Louis Stevenson (1850–1895) was a Scottish writer who studied engineering (his father and grandfather both being lighthouse engineers), qualified as a lawyer, yet found fame as a writer – with the adventure story *Treasure Island* (1883). *Kidnapped* (1886) and *The Strange Case of Dr Jekyll and Mr Hyde* (1886), among other novels, followed; the latter having been inspired by a dream ('it practically came to me as a gift'). He published his verse recollections of childhood, *A Child's Garden of Verse*, in 1885, from which 'Escape at Bedtime' is taken. Stevenson spent the last five years of his life in Samoa, where he co-wrote his final works with his stepson, Lloyd Osbourne, such as *The Ebb-Tide* (1894).

Rabindranath Tagore (1861–1941) was a Bengali writer and artist. He began writing poetry at the age of eight, and such was the power of his first collection of poems, at aged 16, published under the pseudonym *Bhānusiṃaha* ('Sun Lion'), that the poems were seized upon by academics as long-lost literary classics. Although known mainly for his poetry, Tagore also wrote eight novels, four novellas, eighty-four short stories, essays, travelogues, drama and 2,230 songs. His nationalist political views were expressed in *Manast* and led to a bungled assassination attempt in 1916.

Elizabeth Taylor (1912–1975) was a librarian as well as the author of twelve novels, including *A Game of Hide and Seek* (1951) and *Mrs Palfrey at the Claremont* (1971), five volumes of short stories and one children's book, *Mossy Trotter*. Her story, 'The Idea of Age', first appeared in *The New Yorker* in 1952. Her husband, John Taylor, was the director of a sweet factory.

Alfred, Lord Tennyson (1809–1892) was Poet Laureate during much of Queen Victoria's reign. He first published poetry at the age of 17, with his brothers, in a local magazine. His volumes of verse include *Poems, Chiefly Lyrical* (1830), which included 'Mariana', the two-volume *Poems*, which included works such as

'Locksley Hall' and 'Ulysses', and *The Princess: A Medley* (1847), as featured in this collection. Subsequent works include *In Memoriam A. H. H.* (1850) and *Maud: A Monodrama* (1855/56), which included the poem 'The Charge of the Light Brigade'.

Edward Thomas (1878–1917) was an English poet and nature writer who was killed in the First World War at Arras in 1917. A prolific writer of reviews, critical studies and biographies, he only wrote poetry from 1914, after encouragement from Robert Frost. He wrote most of his poems while on active service and lived only to see the publication of *Six Poems* (1916), not the later collection *Poems* (1917), published posthumously. He also wrote a novel, *The Happy-Go Lucky Morgans* (1913) and several influential books about the English countryside.

James Thurber (1894–1961), born in Columbus, Ohio, joined the editorial staff of *The New Yorker* magazine in 1927, at the suggestion of his friend, E. B. White, a contributor. Thurber went on to feature some of his pieces published in *The New Yorker* within the collection, *Fables for Our Time and Famous Poems Illustrated* (1940), and a later volume, *Further Fables for our Time* (1956). Failing eyesight – the result of a boyhood accident – forced him to curtail his drawing during his forties, however, and, by 1952, he had given it up altogether. Thurber continued to write until his death and his work, which includes several book-length fairy tales, has been collected in over thirty volumes. The Thurber Prize has been awarded since 1997 for outstanding American humour, to recipients such as Jon Stewart and Ian Frazier. It is administered by Thurber House, a non-profit literary centre and Thurber museum, housed in one of his boyhood homes.

John Updike (1932–2009) was an American novelist, poet and critic. His twenty-one novels include *The Centaur* (1963), the

Rabbit Series (1960–2001), *Couples* (1968), *The Coup* (1978) and *The Witches of Eastwick* (1984). His *Collected Poems 1953–1993* was published in 1993 and, in 2003, he was awarded the National Medal for the Humanities.

Jess Walter (1965–) is an American author of six novels, including *The Financial Lives of the Poets* (2009) and *Beautiful Ruins* (2012). He has also written a collection of short stories, *We Live in Water* (2013), in which 'Can a Corn' appears, and a non-fiction book. He is the recipient of the Edgar Allan Poe Award, among other prizes.

E. B. White (1899–1985) was an American essayist, novelist, children's writer and parodist, who wrote for *The New Yorker* for eleven years, joining the magazine in 1925. As well as *Stuart Little* (1945) and *Charlotte's Web* (1952), his work included a bestselling revision of William Stunk Jr's *Elements of Style* (popularly known as *Stunk and White*, 1959). 'The Second Tree from the Corner' first appeared in *The New Yorker*.

Walt Whitman (1819–1892), born on Long Island, produced the first, self-published edition of *Leaves of Grass* in 1855. Eight further editions were published during the poet's lifetime, Whitman constantly revising and expanding the work until his death, 95 pages growing to nearly 440. Whitman served as a volunteer hospital visitor during the Civil War, experiences that infused the sequence published in *Leaves of Grass* as 'Drum-Taps' (1865). 'On The Beach at Night' appears in 'Sea Drift', a cycle within the third edition of *Leaves of Grass*.

Richard Wilbur (1921–) was born in New York and has published several collections of poetry, from *The Beautiful Changes, and Other Poems* (1947) and *Ceremony, and Other Poems* (1950) through to

New and Collected Poems, which won Wilbur his second Pulitzer Prize, in 1989. He has also translated plays by Molière and Racine, and contributed songs to Leonard Bernstein's operetta *Candide.* Wilbur served as United States poet laureate 1987–1988.

Oscar Wilde (1854–1900) was born in Dublin. His father, Sir William, as well as being Ireland's leading ear and eye surgeon, wrote books in his spare time about Irish folklore and archaeology. Lady Jane Wilde, under the pseudonym 'Speranza', wrote poetry for the revolutionary nationalists, a group known as the 'Young Irelanders'. She would read this poetry to Oscar when still a young child. After studying at Oxford and moving to London, Wilde published *The Happy Prince and Other Tales* in 1888, having already written various fairy stories for magazines. The novel *The Picture of Dorian Gray* (1891) followed, then his plays *Salomé* (1892) and *The Importance of Being Earnest* and *An Ideal Husband* in 1895, before his imprisonment for gross indecency (1895–1897). Over a hundred years later, the first public monument to Wilde was unveiled in central London. The steering committee behind the statue included the poet Seamus Heaney, and it is inscribed with a line from *Lady Windermere's Fan* (1892): 'We are all in the gutter but some of us are looking at the stars'.

Hugo Williams (1942–) is a British poet and travel writer. His first volume of poetry, *Symptoms of Loss*, was published in 1965. Subsequent collections include *Sugar Daddy* (1970), *Dock Leaves* (1994), *Billy's Rain* (1999, winner of the T. S. Eliot Prize), *Dear Room* (2006) and *I Knew the Bride* (2014). He was awarded The Queen's Gold Medal for Poetry in 1994.

P. G. Wodehouse (1881–1975) was born in Guildford, Surrey, but became a US citizen in 1955. He made the US his home after being branded a traitor in Britain during the Second World War:

captured at Le Touquet, he had agreed to make broadcasts for the Germans. His name was subsequently cleared of any wrongdoing but the scandal led to his emigrating. *Piccadilly Jim* (1917) established Wodehouse as a writer and he went on to write over 100 books. He is best known as the creator of Bertie Wooster and his valet, Jeeves.

Tobias Wolff (1945–) is an American author whose works include the memoirs *This Boy's Life* (1989) and *In Pharaoh's Army* (1994); the novel *Old School* (2003); and four collections of short stories, including *The Night in Question* (1997), in which this anthology's story 'Powder' first appeared. Wolff has also edited several anthologies, among them *The Vintage Book of Contemporary American Short Stories* (1994). He is the Ward W. and Priscilla B. Woods Professor of the Humanities at Stanford University.

Virginia Woolf (1882–1941) was born in London, the daughter of Sir Leslie Stephen, the first editor of *The National Dictionary of Biography*. She is the author of *Mrs Dalloway* (1925), *To The Lighthouse* (1927) and *A Room of One's Own* (1929). 'A Haunted House' appeared in *Monday or Tuesday* (1921), the only collection of short stories published during her lifetime, which was cut short when she committed suicide in 1941, Woolf having suffered from a series of mental breakdowns throughout her life.

James Wright (1927–1980), born in Ohio, wrote ten collections of poetry during his lifetime, including *The Branch Will Not Break* (1963), *Shall We Gather at the River* (1967) and *This Journey* (1982). Seven collections of poems and letters have been published posthumously and in tribute to Wright, including *Above the River: the Complete Poems* (1992), in which 'Old Bud' first appeared. His son, Franz Wright, was also an acclaimed poet: they are the only father and son to have won separate Pulitzer Prizes in the same category.

Richard Yates (1926–1992) was born in Yonkers, New York. His novels include *Revolutionary Road* (1961), *The Easter Parade* (1976), *Good School* (1978) and *Cold Spring Harbor* (1986). He was not commercially successful as a writer (in comparison with the influence that it is now acknowledged his work has exerted on notable American writers, from Raymond Carver to Richard Ford) and in the years immediately after his death of emphysema all of his novels were out of print. During his lifetime, just one of his short stories appeared in *The New Yorker*, after repeated rejections. 'Bells in the Morning', which is reproduced in this anthology, first appeared in *The Collected Stories of Richard Yates*, published posthumously in 2001.

Further Reading

In different ways, the below works – among others – have proven invaluable, inspirational or simply of interest during the curation of this book. I recommend them all.

The Complete Insomniac by Hilary Rubinstein (Jonathan Cape, 1974)

Counting Sheep by Paul Martin (HarperCollins, 2002)

Dreaming: A Very Short Introduction by J. Allan Hobson (OUP, 2005)

The End of Night: Searching for Natural Darkness in an age of Artificial Light by Paul Bogard (4th Estate, 2013)

In Praise of Slow: How a Worldwide Movement Is Challenging the Cult of Speed by Carl Honoré (Orion, 2004)

The Last of the Light: About Twilight by Peter Davidson (Reaktion Books, 2015)

Night by A. Alvarez (Norton, 1995)

Night Walking: A Nocturnal History of London by Matthew Beaumont (Verso, 2015)

Nightwalk: A Journey to the Heart of Nature by Chris Yates (William Collins Books)

Once Upon A Time: A Short History of Fairy Tale by Marina Warner (OUP, 2014)

Sleep: A Very Short Introduction by Steven W. Lockley & Russell G. Foster (OUP, 2012)

The Sleep Revolution and *Thrive* by Arianna Huffington (Penguin Random House, 2016 & 2014)

Sleepfaring by Jim Horne (OUP, 2006)

Worlds of Sleep by Lodewijk Brunt and Brigitte Steger [eds] (Frank & Timme, 2008)

About Readathon

Books and Bedtime

Do you remember the book under the bedclothes? If you're the rebellious one who smuggled a torch beneath the covers after lights-out – to discover what happened in the next chapter of your Roald Dahl, Enid Blyton or C. S. Lewis – then you might just agree that hiding under a tent of blankets or duvet was one of childhood's most magical experiences.

What was going on?

Well, at Readathon – the charity that champions children's reading – we contend that reading for children and reading for adults are subtly but significantly different activities. For adults reading a book has connotations that are literary, virtuous, educational and cultural as well as just enjoyable. We grown-ups often regard reading as a means to self-improvement: we call intelligent people 'well-read'; we class difficult or revered books as 'literature'; we might sometimes feel a slight guilty pang that we don't read as much as we'd like to; and if we read just for the fun of it, we may call it 'holiday reading' ('Don't judge me, it's just a book for the beach!').

Yet, for children, reading is a wholly different proposition.

497

Kids don't pick up a book because they think they ought to or because it's been shortlisted for a prize. They don't struggle on to the end of a book from a sense of duty, even though they're not enjoying it. That book under the bedclothes is read for sheer pleasure. All children's reading is 'holiday reading'!

And what a pleasure it is. Go into any playground and you'll see children riding horses, flying planes and scoring imaginary goals at Wembley. Their ability to pretend is better than ours: it's natural for them to imagine that they are playing Quidditch with Harry Potter, outwitting Miss Trunchbull with Matilda or mastering the art of training a dragon with Hiccup.

Readathon's core objective is to encourage children to discover that magic – to read. We provide free resource kits for thousands of teachers in schools throughout the UK to run Readathon's sponsored read. We aim to make reading fun – because we know, first-hand, how vital it is to a child's development. Books incubate the imagination, propelling creative and analytical processes in the brain. This may be why, statistically, children who read for fun are more likely to become adults who succeed in all areas of life than those who don't. Quite simply, without children who develop an imagination, we would not have adults who envisage how to change the world.

Of course, reading gives lease to the imaginations of grown-ups too, which is why Ben's book is such an inspired concept. It gives us grown-ups the longed-for permission to leap with abandon back into the deep end (to use a swimming analogy, in keeping with his watery themes), like we used to when children – limbs akimbo – splashing and bobbing about (or reading) purely for pleasure; as opposed to the dutiful lengths traversed in later life by the lane-swimmer, hoping to beat their best (intellectual) time. *Bedtime Stories for Grown-Ups* leads us by the hand back into the realm of the imagination, as Peter Pan might. The anthology invites, compels us even, to escape, not just because we want to, but because we must: in order to forge new paths of discovery, to help us to understand the world we live in.

For the children who take part in Readathon's sponsored read, there is yet another wonderful dimension to their reading; the funds they raise support our work in all the UK's 30+ children's hospitals. It is this crucial part of our work that first inspired Ben to partner so generously on this project with Readathon.

Our specially designed mobile bookcases go right up to a child's hospital bedside. They are stashed with a regular supply of brand-new books, from which children can choose a book to keep forever. Our professional storytellers also make regular visits to all the wards. They weave precious tales, each one tailored to the age, circumstances and dreams of the specific young patients they encounter.

Before Readathon's programme in hospitals began six years ago, children in hospital were often denied the comfort of bedtime stories. Second-hand books simply pose too much risk of infection, particularly to the immunocompromised on cancer wards and in isolation units.

Today, Readathon provides 27,000 brand-new books and 224 storytelling days to more than 100,000 children – in over 30 hospitals – every year.

It's hard to quantify the value or importance of this work. Suffice to say that, for these children and their families, our stories are a lifeline. A book (or a well-spun tale) offers not only an escape to worlds far away from the hospital, but also an anchor to normal life. It imbues an ill child with renewed confidence while linking back to familiar routines. It provides a welcome distraction from the alien and sometimes scary sounds and sensations of the ward.

As one of Ben's selections — Richard Wilbur's 'A Barred Owl' — tells us:

> Words which can make our terrors bravely clear,
> Can also thus domesticate a fear . . .

For children in hospital, and, moreover, for their exhausted and anxious parents, Ben's beautiful book will do just this. Like the father in Walt Whitman's 'On the Beach at Night', this anthology reveals the hidden stars.

Thank you, Ben.

Brough Girling, Founder of Readathon

To donate, or to order a Readathon kit for your school, please visit Readathon.org

Acknowledgements

Once upon a time, I had an idea for an anthology.

The idea quickly took root and then kept sprouting, day and night, much like a beanstalk. A dreamer, I was excited by its potential – I even started keeping a dream diary – and yet soon realized that it required approbation. To my joy, this was provided by various kind and brilliant souls.

John Carey, Dame Margaret Drabble, Anne and Al Alvarez, and Heather Glen were all generous not only with their time but also their encouragement of the concept's literary or intellectual merit.

Colin Espie, Professor of Sleep Medicine at Oxford University, spoke at length with me at the outset of the process, and Professor Alice M. Gregory, of Goldsmiths, University of London, later went above-and-beyond with her feedback to the manuscript. I am indebted to them both for ensuring this layman's science of sleep makes some sense. Any residual errors are all mine.

Suzanne Baboneau and Ian Chapman championed this project from the off, sending me into dreamland. Their continual support and, later, Suzanne's adroit editorial comments, propelled the book forward. Simon & Schuster, as a whole, but notably Gill Richardson, Toby Jones, Jessica Barratt, Suzanne King, Sophie Orme, Pip Watkins, and Jo Dickinson, have once again proven paragons among publishers. I am so grateful.

I am greatly appreciative also of my agent, Anna Webber, for her warm and wise counsel.

Jessi Gray helped make this project possible – through her expert navigation of the countless permissions and, moreover, with her good-humoured comradeship.

Readathon's work continues to inspire. Brough Girling, Justine Daniels, Cherry Land, Vicki Pember and Heidi Perry have proven wonderful partners. Thank you also to the teams at the Children's Hospital of the John Radcliffe, Oxford, and Evelina Children's Hospital at St Thomas's in London, and to storytellers Adele Moss and Jennifer Lunn – for letting Suzanne and me join them on the wards and witness for ourselves the transformative effect a well-spun story can have on a sick child.

Respect also to all the parents in children's hospitals throughout the UK (and anywhere else). Some might have seen this collection on the Readathon trolleys by now and maybe even perused it. If so, I hope these pages might have offered some solace or respite.

Mates and kindred spirits, including Laura Barber, Lucy Bright, Rebecca Carter, Rowan Cope, Tom Drewett, David Flusfeder, Natalie Galustian, Samar Hammam, Josh Hyams, Cara Jones, Caradoc King, Charlie King and Sam Eades, Joe Shrapnel and Anna Waterhouse, are all due my thanks. Many other friends, agents and publishers have gone to considerable trouble to help along the way. Apologies that I can't acknowledge you all individually here.

Thanks to my family: Mum and Dad, for all the stories; Joe,

Sam, Ursula and Rosemary Holden; Cindy Blake (compiling this book has been just like making a mix CD); Ben and Marce Colegrave (and Bump); Chris, Siena and Violet Feige (and Bump); the Leventis clan; my godchildren, Jack Holden, Ava Thomas and Harlan Shrapnel; and, of course, Salome, George and Ione – sweet dreams are made of you . . .

Finally, I pay tribute to the contributors who so graciously took part in this somewhat unconventional enterprise, taking the trouble not only to choose a bedtime story but also explain why; to Diana Athill for her wonderful Afterword; and to the authors (living or not) of the myriad pieces included herein. I'll live happily, ever after, in the knowledge that I got to share and exalt in your majestic stories.

INDEX

(the articles 'a' and 'the' are ignored for the purposes of alphabetical sorting)

Copyrights and Credits

Introduction

Lines from 'The House was Quiet and the World was Calm' from *The Collected Poems of Wallace Stevens* by Wallace Stevens, copyright © 1954 by Wallace Stevens and copyright renewed 1982 by Holly Stevens. Used by permission of Faber and Faber Ltd and Alfred A Knopf, an imprint of the Knopf Doubleday Publishing Group, a division of Penguin Random House LLC. All rights reserved.

Eventide

'In The Evening' by Billy Collins from *The Trouble with Poetry: and Other Poems*, copyright © 2005 by Billy Collins. Used by permission of Random House, an imprint and division of Penguin Random House LLC. All rights reserved.

'Let Evening Come' by Jane Kenyon from *Collected Poems*, copyright © 2005 by The Estate of Jane Kenyon. Reprinted with the permission of The Permissions Company, Inc. on behalf of Graywolf Press, Minneapolis, Minnesota, www.graywolfpress. org

'Evening Walk' by Charles Simic from *Hotel Insomnia*, copyright © 1992 Charles Simic. Reprinted by permission of Houghton Mifflin & Harcourt Publishing Company. All rights reserved.

Once Upon a Time

The Dead Spot

Be Not Afeard

Tread Softly

Ashore